STEVE DITKO
SPACE WARS

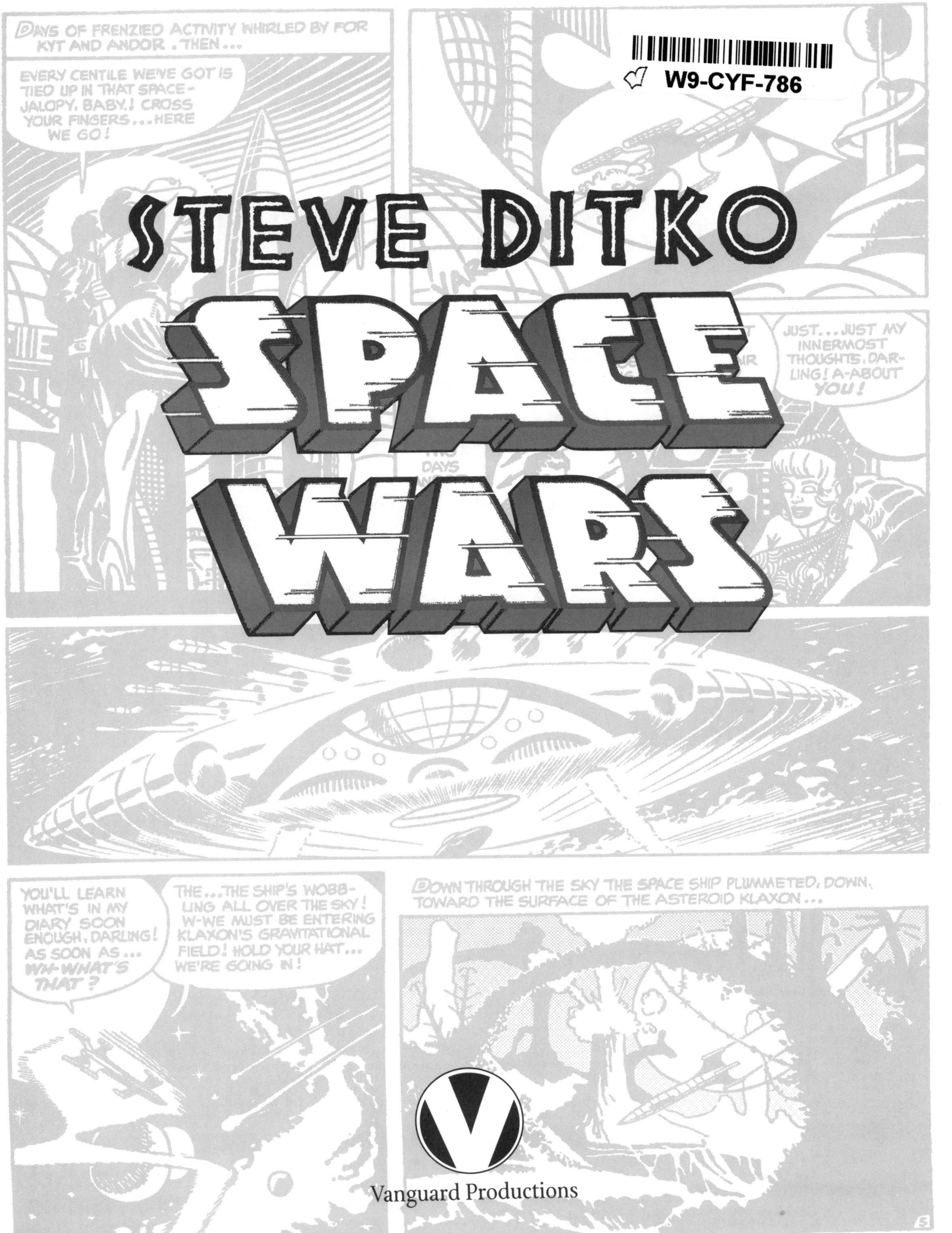

DAYS OF FRENZIED ACTIVITY WHIRLED BY FOR KYT AND ANDOR. THEN...
EVERY CENTILE WE'VE GOT IS TIED UP IN THAT SPACE-JALOPY, BABY.! CROSS YOUR FINGERS...HERE WE GO!
JUST...JUST MY INNERMOST THOUGHTS, DARLING! A-ABOUT YOU!
YOU'LL LEARN WHAT'S IN MY DIARY SOON ENOUGH, DARLING! AS SOON AS... WH-WHAT'S THAT?
THE...THE SHIP'S WOBBLING ALL OVER THE SKY! W-WE MUST BE ENTERING KLAXON'S GRAVITATIONAL FIELD! HOLD YOUR HAT... WE'RE GOING IN!
DOWN THROUGH THE SKY THE SPACE SHIP PLUMMETED, DOWN, TOWARD THE SURFACE OF THE ASTEROID KLAXON...
5

Vanguard Productions

Compiled, Edited and Designed by
J. David Spurlock

Dedicated to
Steve Ditko

For their help and support, special thanks to

Jim Amish,

Blake Bell,

Andrew Gaska,

Arlen Schumer,

and

Jim Vadeboncoeur, Jr.

Hardcover Edition ISBN 1-887591-68-0 $34.95
Trade Paperback Edition ISBN 1-887591-67-2 $16.95

Steve Ditko: Space Wars Published by Vanguard Productions. Office of publication, 390 Campus Drive, Somerset, New Jersey 08873.
Original works © Charlton Comics / ACG. Collective work and art modifications Copyright 2004 Vanguard Productions.

For other Vanguard items go to www.creativemix.com/vanguard

First Printing, February, 2005
Printed in Canada

CONTENTS

STEVE DITKO's BRAVE NEW WORLD

by J. David Spurlock

Forbidden Planet, **The Twilight Zone**, **The Blob**, **The Day the Earth Stood Still**: The 1950s spawned the greatest sci-fi stories ever! Bug-eyed monsters from other worlds invaded our movies, literature, television, and comic books. The young cartoonist, Steve Ditko, honed his storytelling skills throughout the '50s on mystery, horror, and some of the farthest-out sci-fi comics of all time. **Steve Ditko: Space Wars** collects a wealth of the artist's finest work prior to his world-shaking creation with Stan Lee, **Spider-Man**!

The record-breaking box office hit **Spider-Man** began with the credit, "Based on the comic-book by Stan Lee and Steve Ditko." Ditko is the most mysterious man in comic-book history; he refuses to make personal appearances, refuses to be photographed, and refuses to be interviewed. He chooses to speak only through his artistic milieu, which champions, as Arlen Schumer said, "the struggle between good and evil, ugliness and beauty, and the weak versus the strong. His groundbreaking depiction of Spider-Man went against type by portraying him as an everyman loner, underdog -- i.e.., the teenager -- as a super-antihero."

Ditko's next creation, the occultist Dr. Strange, provided a surrealistic journey through alternate dimensions and realities, which served as precursors to the psychedelia of the later '60s. After leaving Marvel in 1966, Ditko created The Creeper for DC Comics and his own Mr. A and The Question, which integrate the Objectivist philosophy of Ayn Rand with his own, and remain as controversial today as ever.

In **Steve Ditko: Space Wars** Ditko's eclectic, sometimes surrealistic work proves both futuristic and retro as he takes us into the cosmos to find star-crossed lovers in the backstabbing debacle, Dead Reckoning. Then, the deadliest space ship in the galaxy hovers menacingly over us while the invader demands complete surrender and our military warns it's useless to resist in The Conquered Earth!; these plus The Creature from Corpus III, The King of Planetoid X, and The Juggernauts of Jupiter are just a sampling of the pulse-pounding tales featured in **Steve Ditko: Space Wars**.

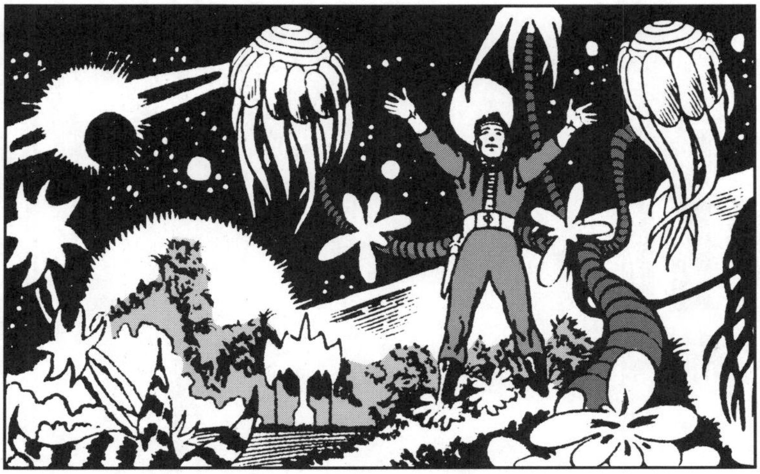

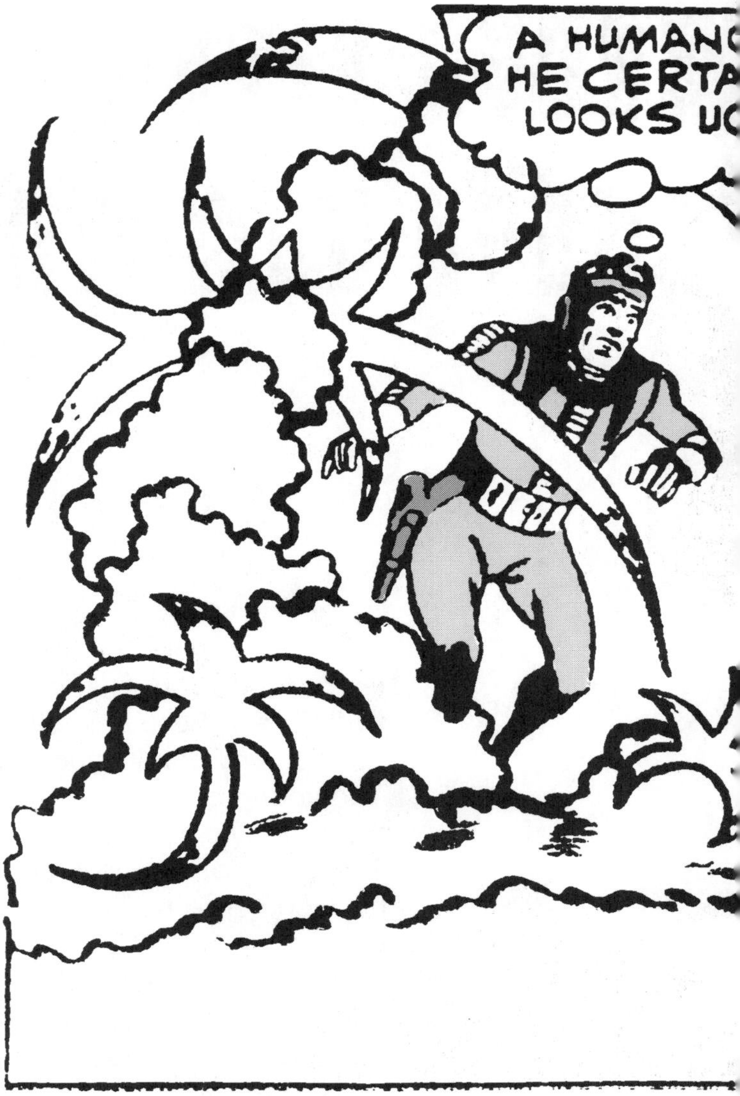
A
HE
LOOKS

Ditko's unique vision is compounded by the artist's mysterious nature. This leads many to see little, if any, connections to the work of other artists. But, while the esthetic of this collection is presented for mass appeal, it's easy to see the developing artist experiment with style in a way that reveals some interest and familiarity with the work of others. It is known that Ditko studied under noted Batman and Black Terror artist Jerry Robinson at the School for Cartoonists and Illustrators, now known as the School of Visual Arts, in New York. It is also known that Ditko was an admirer of the work of Robinson's associate, Mort Meskin. Though Meskin had also taught at CI/SVA, all indications are that he gave up teaching prior to Ditko's enrollment. It is possible that the two might have met later as both contributed to the Simon & Kirby Studio-packaged Harvey publication, **Captain 3-D**. There are also similarities between Ditko's work and that of early Joe Kubert. These similarities could be coincidental or Ditko might have admired Kubert early on and Kubert did do some work with Meskin so, there could be a common influence there. But a discerning eye can see when studying this sci-fi collection that Ditko was also paying attention to the groundbreaking sci-fi work produced at E.C. comics by the likes of Wally Wood, Al Williamson, Roy Krenkel and Frank Frazetta. Though he's not known for likenesses, some faces and mannerisms in the stories here might indicate that Ditko enjoyed movies as well as comics. Also of note is Ditko's occasional, but grand, humor as seen in *The Gloomy One* and *Way Out, Man*. It's little known but, many years later Ditko produced straight-out humour for **Cracked** magazine.

For the most academically minded Ditko aficionado we present here, the list of contents in chronological order citing original publication and date. Note that the often used Charlton publication inventory numbers sometimes reveal a chronology different from that of the publication dates.

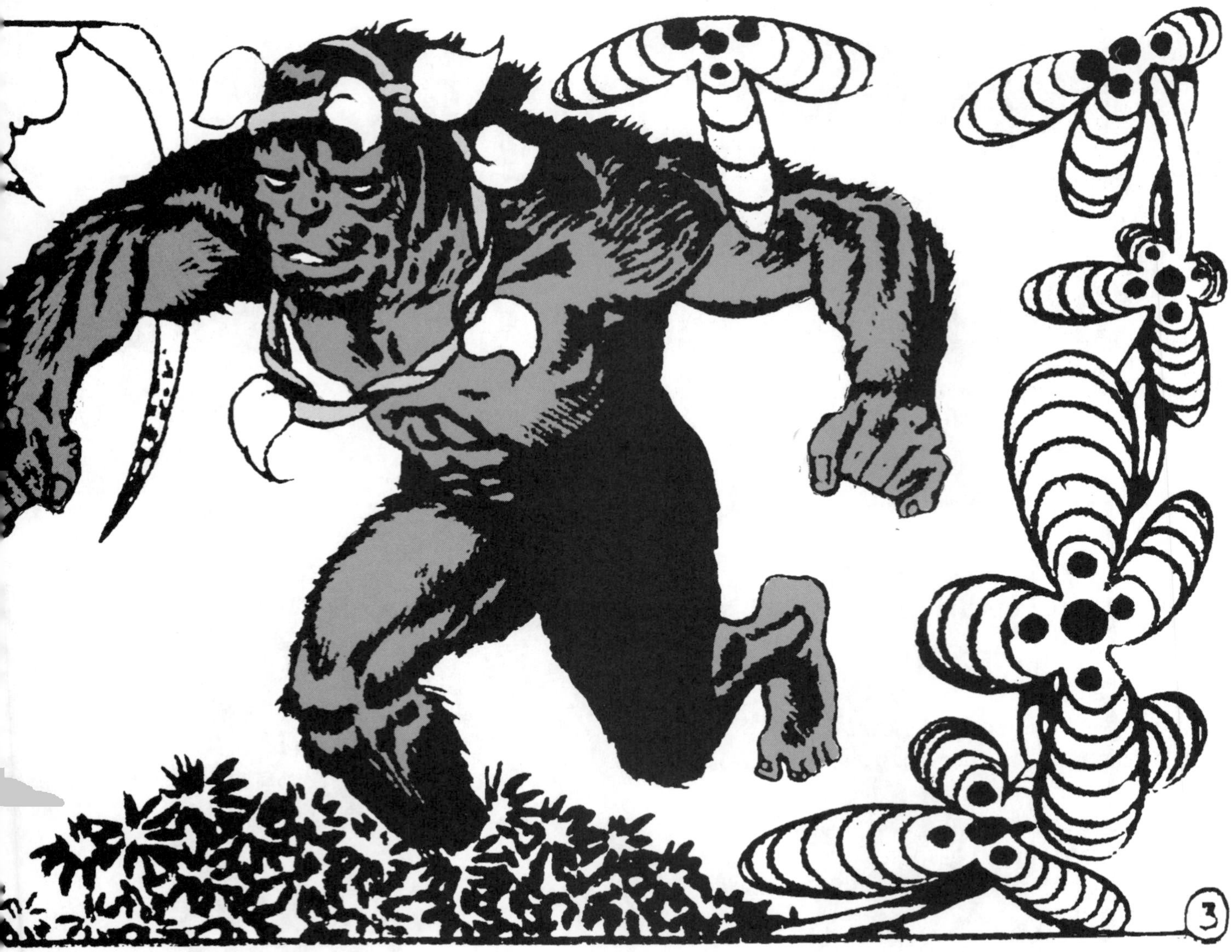

Dead Reckoning - **Space Adventures** #11: May '54
King Of Planetoid X - **Mysteries Of Unexplored Worlds** #7: Feb '58 (s1282)
The Gloomy One - **Strange Suspense Stories** #31: Feb '57 (s1283)
Mystery Planet - **Strange Suspense Stories** #36: Mar '58 (s1490)
The Conquered Earth - **Out Of This World** #4: Jun '57 (s1495)
The Secret Of Capt. X - **Out Of This World** #8: May '58 - (s1500)
Strange Guests of Tsarus - **Mysteries Of Unexplored Worlds** #3: Apr '57 (s1509)
The Decision - **Unusual Tales** #8: Aug '57 (3 pages)
Plague - **Out Of This World** #6: Nov '57 (s2208)
There It Is Again - **Strange Suspense Stories** #35: Dec '57 (s2414)
Journey's End **Out of this World** #9: Aug '58 (2814)
The Greater Jovians - **Outer Space** #20: Dec '58 (s4440)
The Hostile Planet - **Space Adventures** #27: Feb '59 (s4580)
They Must Be Like Us - **Unusual Tales** #15: Feb '59 (4582)
The Moon Snatchers - **Space Adventures** #27: Feb '59 (s4697)
The Juggernauts Of Jupiter - **Unusual Tales** #15: Feb '59 (s4714)
The Enchanted Planet - **Space Adventures** #31: Nov '59 (5767)
The Amazing Guest Of Planet 23 - **Unusual Tales** #23: Aug '60 (5939)
The Deadly Cargo Of Spaceship 90 - **Space Adventures** #32: Jan '60 (6030)
The Blue Men Of Bantro - **Space War** #6: Aug '60
Way Out Man - **Unusual Tales** #29: Aug '61 (A-393)

STEVE DITKO SPACE WARS

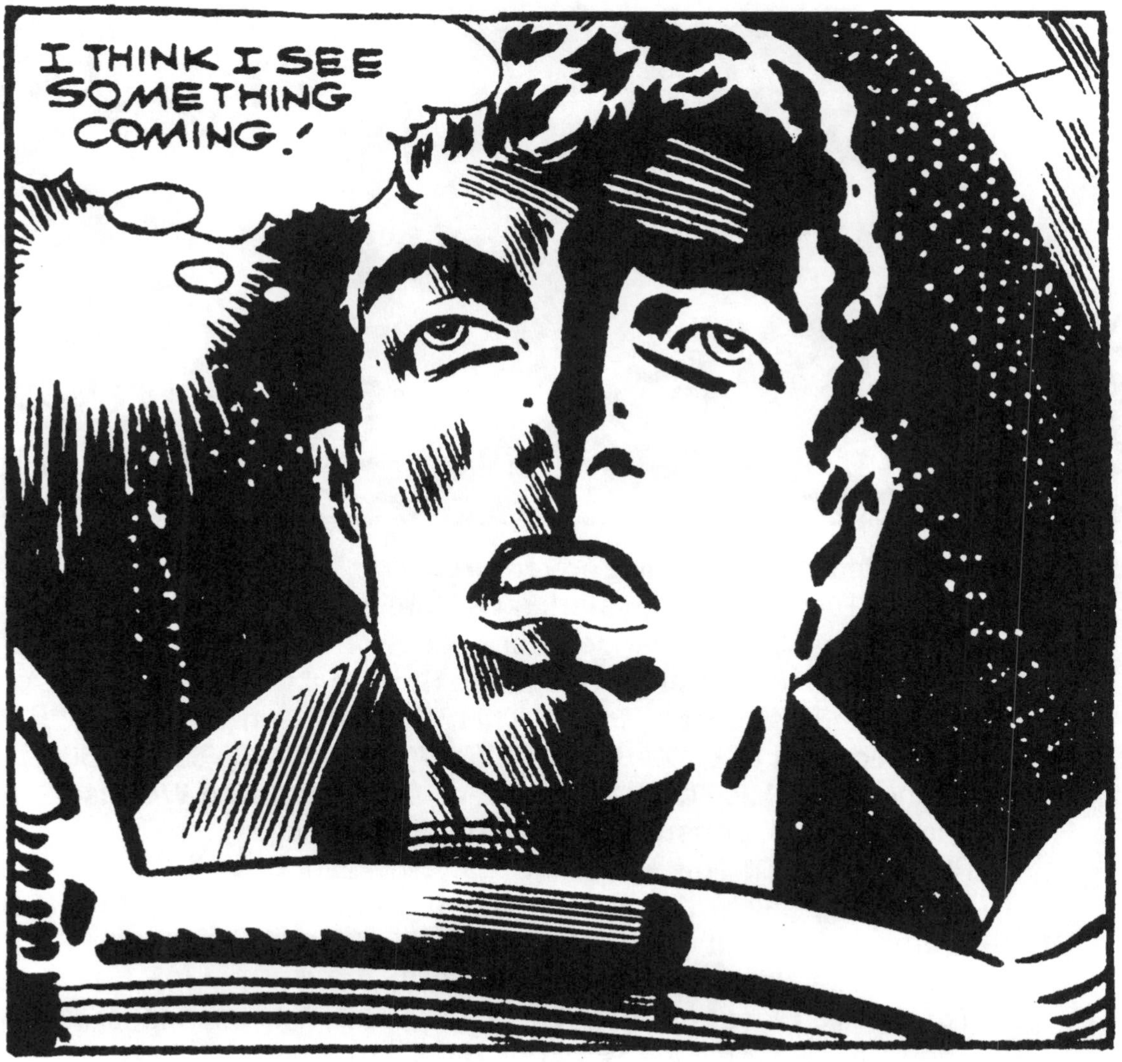
I THINK I SEE SOMETHING COMING!

Mystery PLANET

IN COUNTLESS OBSERVATORIES ALL OVER THE PLANET EARTH, MEN SCANNED THE SKIES, PROBING THE MYSTERIES OF UNKNOWN WORLDS, WATCHING THE GALAXIES ALREADY CHARTED AND EXPLORED BY OUR SPACE SERVICE! ONLY ONE MAN, DR. ANTON WRADEK, RECEIVED ALL THE ASTRONOMERS' REPORTS ... AND IT WAS HE WHO FIRST WITNESSED THE MYSTERIOUS PLANET IN ACTION -- BUT LATER, COMMANDER BRYAN BODINE SAW IT REPEATED ... AND THEN FELT THE GIGANTIC MAW ENGULF HIS SPACE SHIP TOO ...

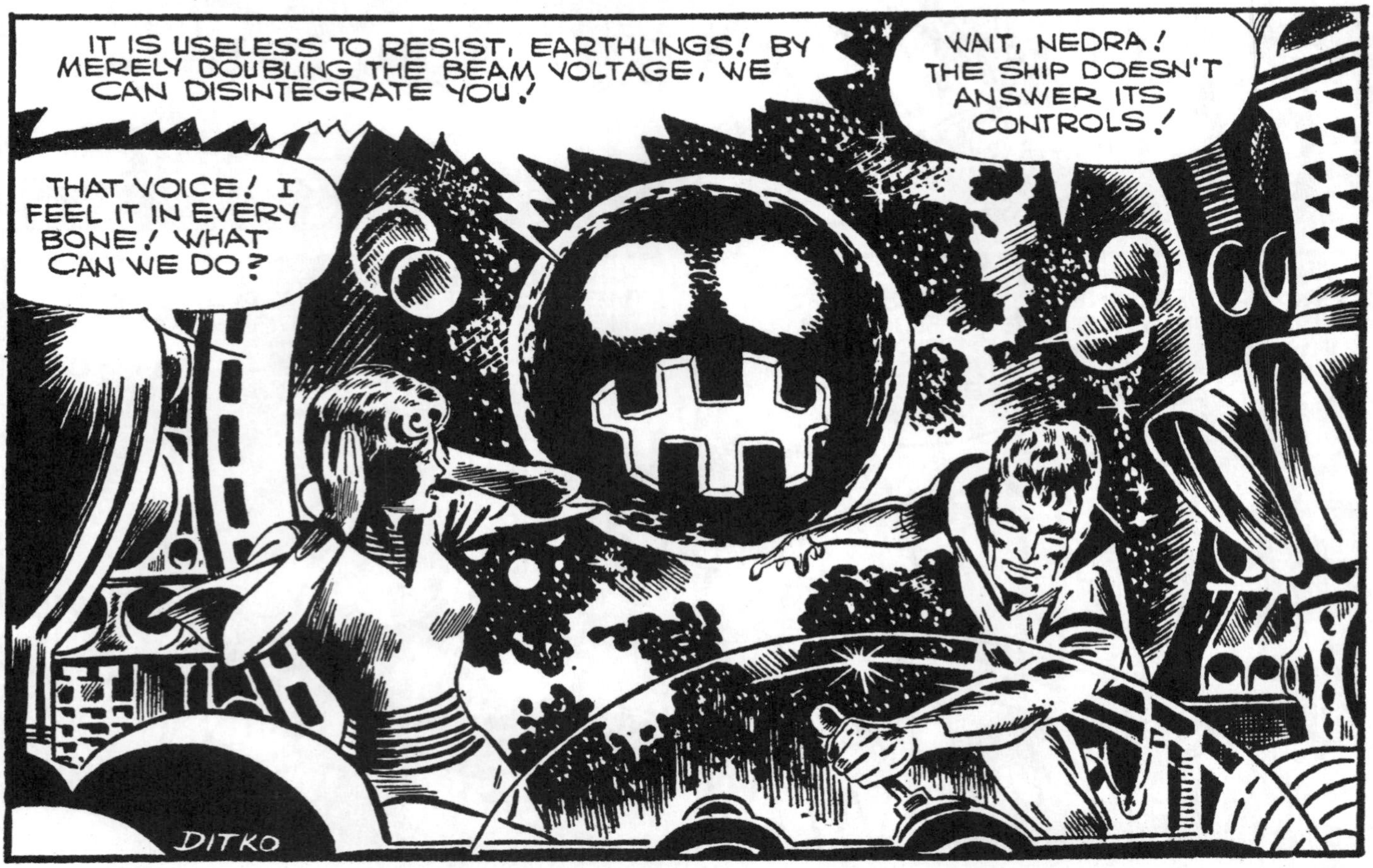
IT IS USELESS TO RESIST, EARTHLINGS! BY MERELY DOUBLING THE BEAM VOLTAGE, WE CAN DISINTEGRATE YOU!
WAIT, NEDRA! THE SHIP DOESN'T ANSWER ITS CONTROLS!
THAT VOICE! I FEEL IT IN EVERY BONE! WHAT CAN WE DO?
DITKO

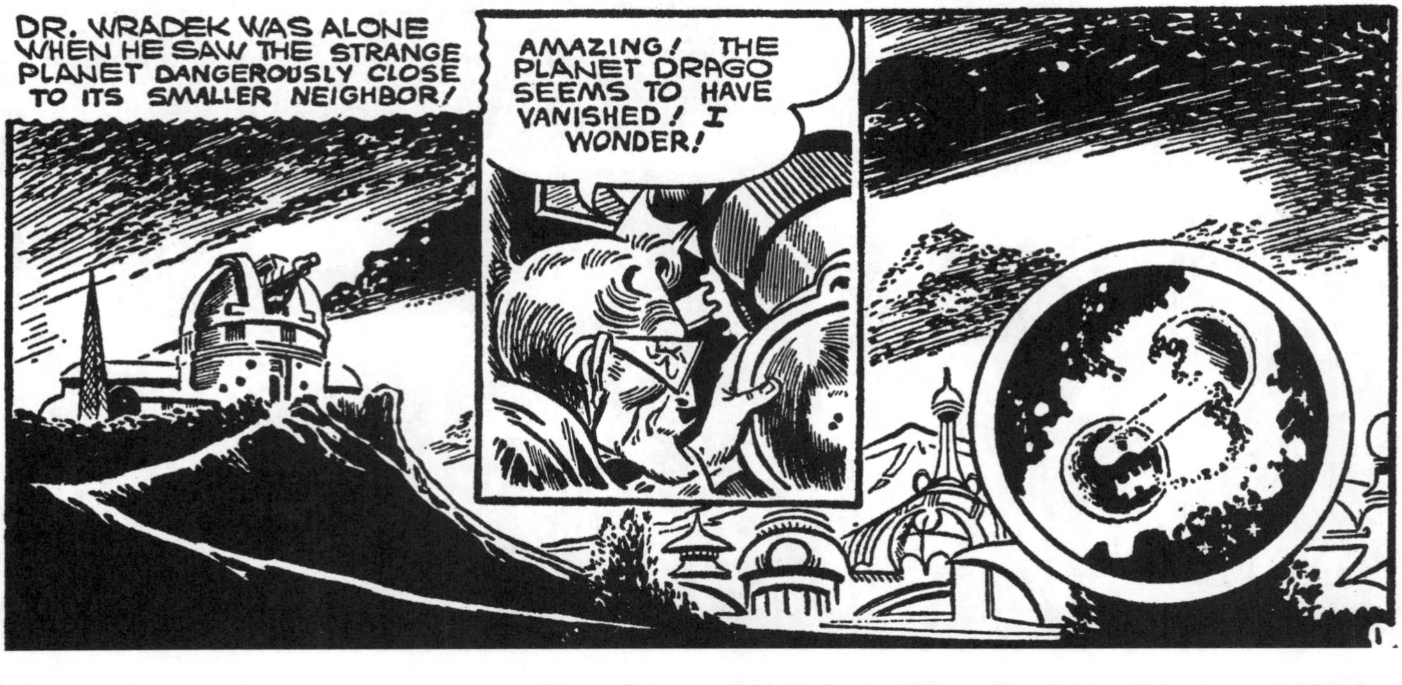
DR. WRADEK WAS ALONE WHEN HE SAW THE STRANGE PLANET DANGEROUSLY CLOSE TO ITS SMALLER NEIGHBOR!
AMAZING! THE PLANET DRAGO SEEMS TO HAVE VANISHED! I WONDER!
1

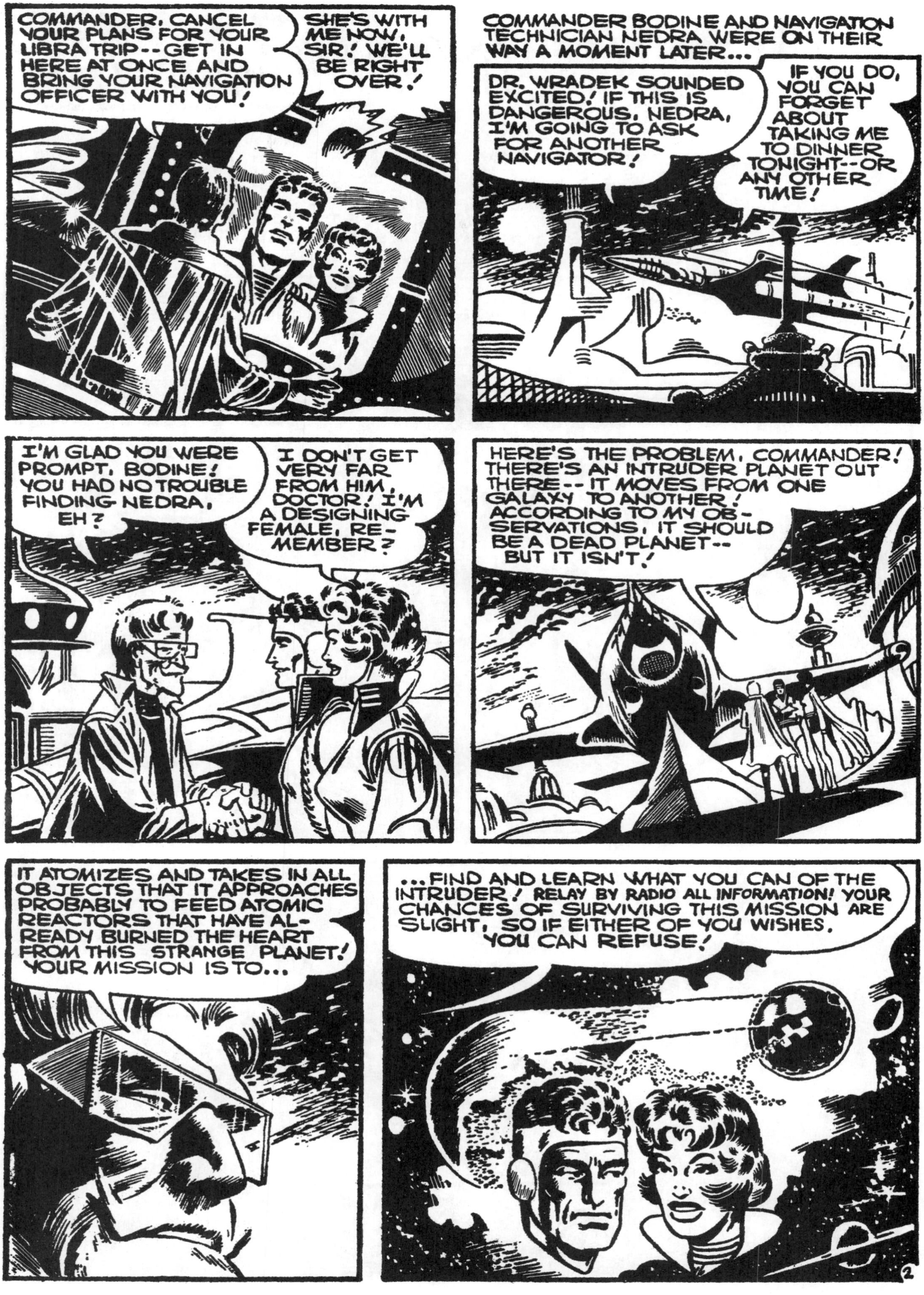
COMMANDER, CANCEL YOUR PLANS FOR YOUR LIBRA TRIP--GET IN HERE AT ONCE AND BRING YOUR NAVIGATION OFFICER WITH YOU!
SHE'S WITH ME NOW, SIR! WE'LL BE RIGHT OVER!
COMMANDER BODINE AND NAVIGATION TECHNICIAN NEDRA WERE ON THEIR WAY A MOMENT LATER...
DR. WRADEK SOUNDED EXCITED! IF THIS IS DANGEROUS, NEDRA, I'M GOING TO ASK FOR ANOTHER NAVIGATOR!
IF YOU DO, YOU CAN FORGET ABOUT TAKING ME TO DINNER TONIGHT--OR ANY OTHER TIME!
I'M GLAD YOU WERE PROMPT, BODINE! YOU HAD NO TROUBLE FINDING NEDRA, EH?
I DON'T GET VERY FAR FROM HIM, DOCTOR! I'M A DESIGNING FEMALE, REMEMBER?
HERE'S THE PROBLEM, COMMANDER! THERE'S AN INTRUDER PLANET OUT THERE-- IT MOVES FROM ONE GALAXY TO ANOTHER! ACCORDING TO MY OBSERVATIONS, IT SHOULD BE A DEAD PLANET-- BUT IT ISN'T!
IT ATOMIZES AND TAKES IN ALL OBJECTS THAT IT APPROACHES PROBABLY TO FEED ATOMIC REACTORS THAT HAVE ALREADY BURNED THE HEART FROM THIS STRANGE PLANET! YOUR MISSION IS TO...
...FIND AND LEARN WHAT YOU CAN OF THE INTRUDER! RELAY BY RADIO ALL INFORMATION! YOUR CHANCES OF SURVIVING THIS MISSION ARE SLIGHT, SO IF EITHER OF YOU WISHES, YOU CAN REFUSE!
2

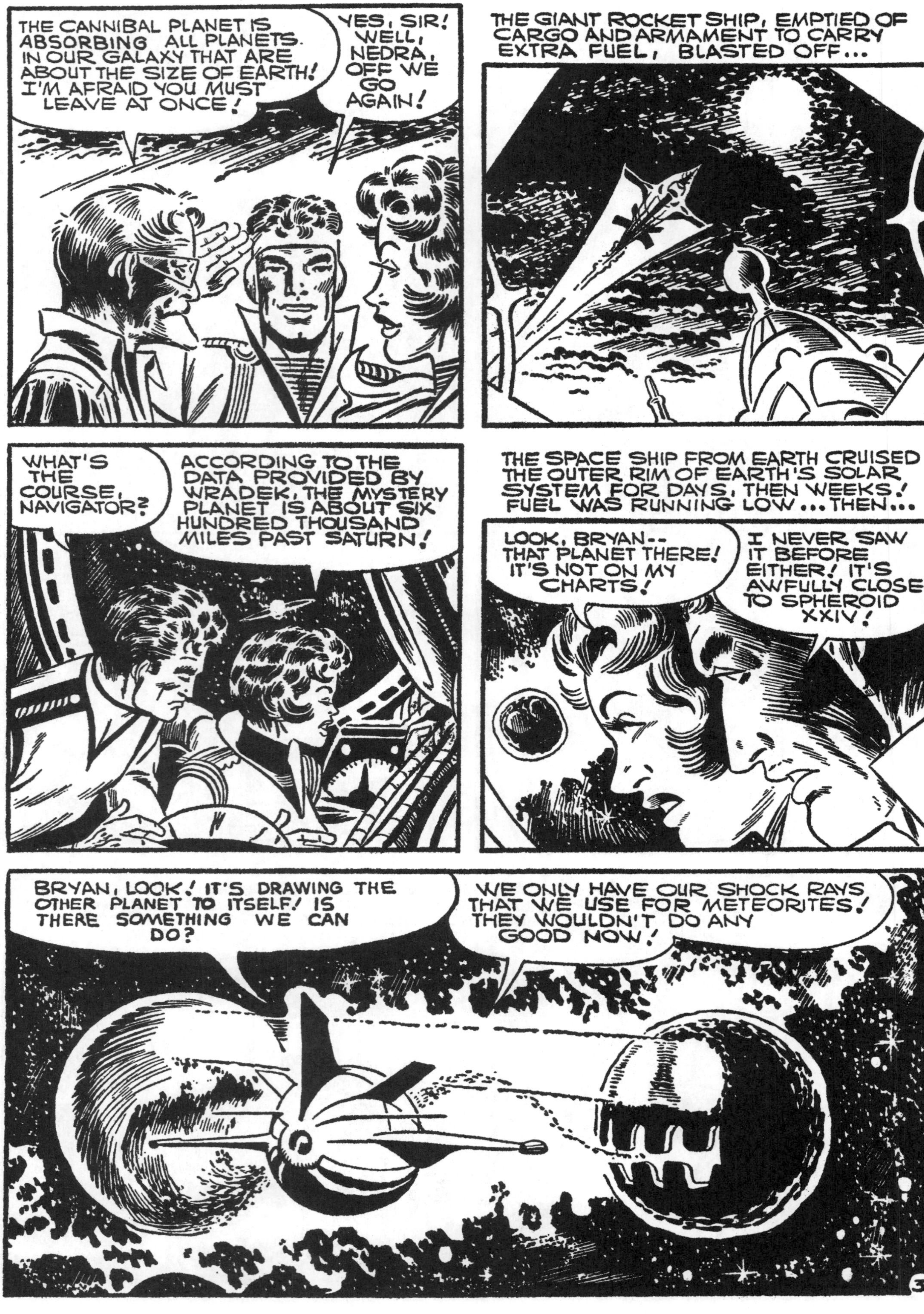
THE CANNIBAL PLANET IS ABSORBING ALL PLANETS IN OUR GALAXY THAT ARE ABOUT THE SIZE OF EARTH! I'M AFRAID YOU MUST LEAVE AT ONCE!
YES, SIR! WELL, NEDRA, OFF WE GO AGAIN!
THE GIANT ROCKET SHIP, EMPTIED OF CARGO AND ARMAMENT TO CARRY EXTRA FUEL, BLASTED OFF...
WHAT'S THE COURSE, NAVIGATOR?
ACCORDING TO THE DATA PROVIDED BY WRADEK, THE MYSTERY PLANET IS ABOUT SIX HUNDRED THOUSAND MILES PAST SATURN!
THE SPACE SHIP FROM EARTH CRUISED THE OUTER RIM OF EARTH'S SOLAR SYSTEM FOR DAYS, THEN WEEKS! FUEL WAS RUNNING LOW... THEN...
LOOK, BRYAN-- THAT PLANET THERE! IT'S NOT ON MY CHARTS!
I NEVER SAW IT BEFORE EITHER! IT'S AWFULLY CLOSE TO SPHEROID XXIV!
BRYAN, LOOK! IT'S DRAWING THE OTHER PLANET TO ITSELF! IS THERE SOMETHING WE CAN DO?
WE ONLY HAVE OUR SHOCK RAYS THAT WE USE FOR METEORITES! THEY WOULDN'T DO ANY GOOD NOW!
3

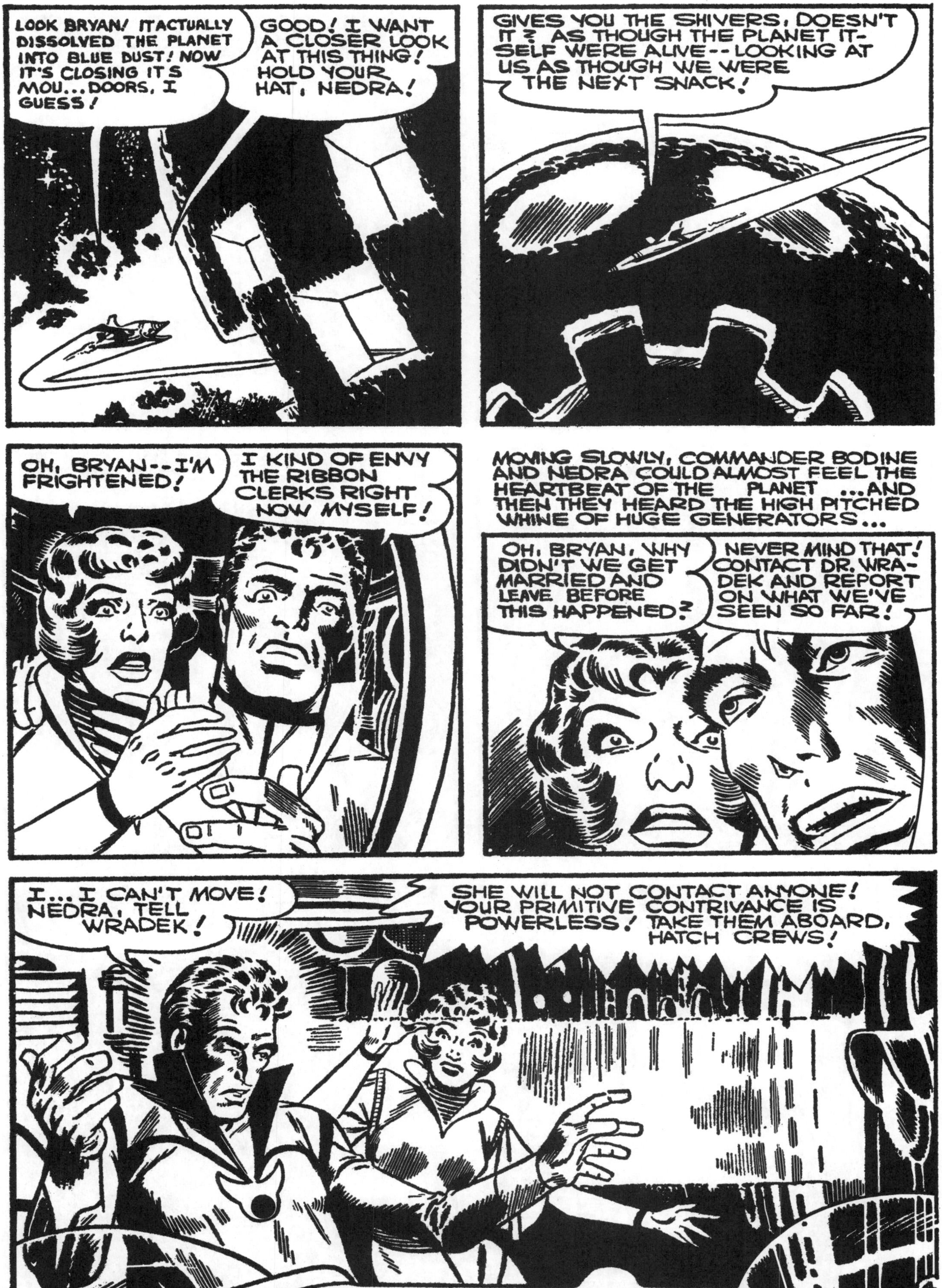
LOOK BRYAN! IT ACTUALLY DISSOLVED THE PLANET INTO BLUE DUST! NOW IT'S CLOSING ITS MOU... DOORS, I GUESS!
GOOD! I WANT A CLOSER LOOK AT THIS THING! HOLD YOUR HAT, NEDRA!
GIVES YOU THE SHIVERS, DOESN'T IT? AS THOUGH THE PLANET IT-SELF WERE ALIVE--LOOKING AT US AS THOUGH WE WERE THE NEXT SNACK!
OH, BRYAN--I'M FRIGHTENED!
I KIND OF ENVY THE RIBBON CLERKS RIGHT NOW MYSELF!
MOVING SLOWLY, COMMANDER BODINE AND NEDRA COULD ALMOST FEEL THE HEARTBEAT OF THE PLANET ...AND THEN THEY HEARD THE HIGH PITCHED WHINE OF HUGE GENERATORS...
OH, BRYAN, WHY DIDN'T WE GET MARRIED AND LEAVE BEFORE THIS HAPPENED?
NEVER MIND THAT! CONTACT DR. WRA-DEK AND REPORT ON WHAT WE'VE SEEN SO FAR!
I... I CAN'T MOVE! NEDRA, TELL WRADEK!
SHE WILL NOT CONTACT ANYONE! YOUR PRIMITIVE CONTRIVANCE IS POWERLESS! TAKE THEM ABOARD, HATCH CREWS!
4

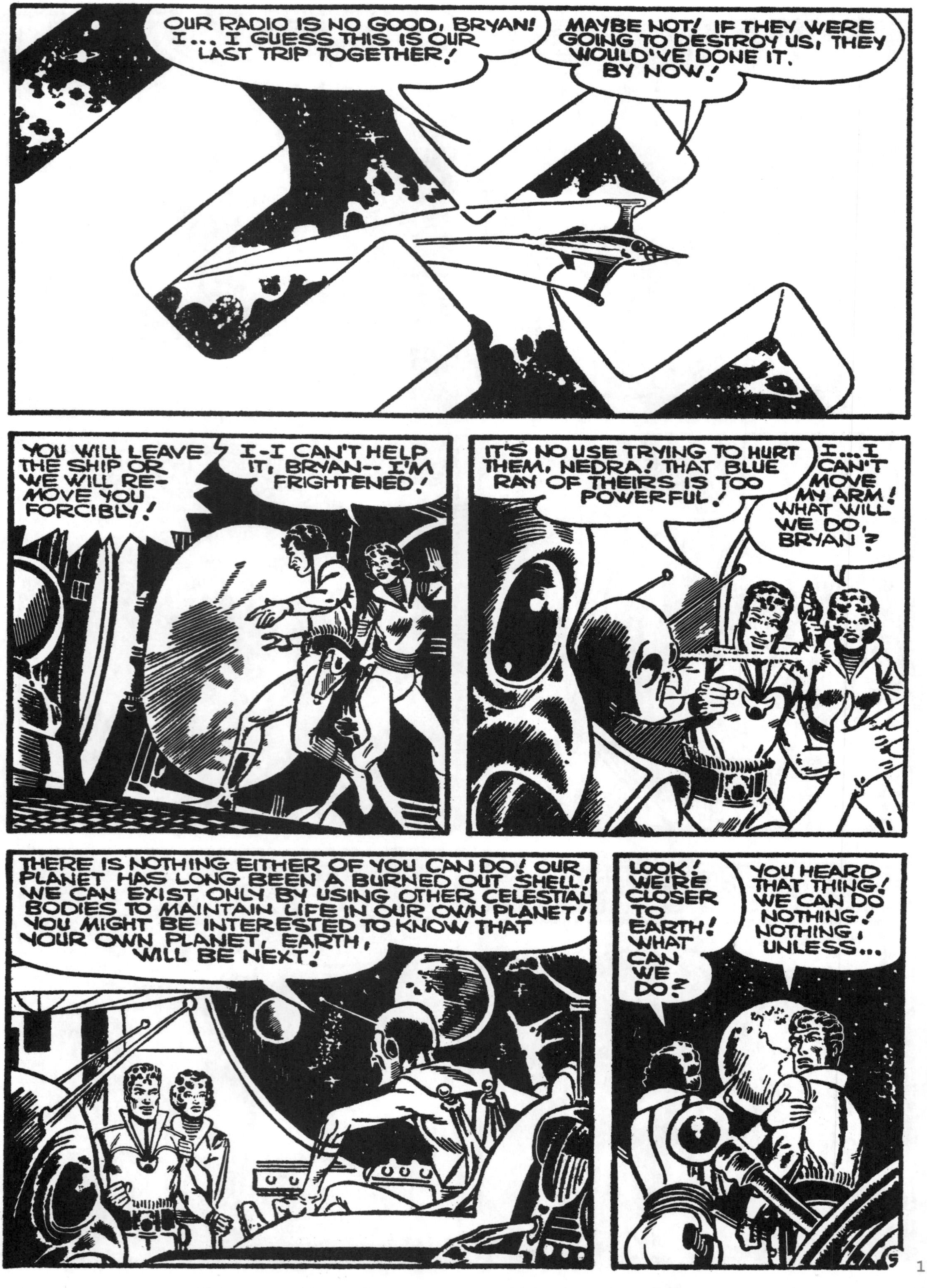
OUR RADIO IS NO GOOD, BRYAN! I... I GUESS THIS IS OUR LAST TRIP TOGETHER!
MAYBE NOT! IF THEY WERE GOING TO DESTROY US, THEY WOULD'VE DONE IT BY NOW!
YOU WILL LEAVE THE SHIP OR WE WILL RE-MOVE YOU FORCIBLY!
I-I CAN'T HELP IT, BRYAN-- I'M FRIGHTENED!
IT'S NO USE TRYING TO HURT THEM, NEDRA! THAT BLUE RAY OF THEIRS IS TOO POWERFUL!
I...I CAN'T MOVE MY ARM! WHAT WILL WE DO, BRYAN?
THERE IS NOTHING EITHER OF YOU CAN DO! OUR PLANET HAS LONG BEEN A BURNED OUT SHELL! WE CAN EXIST ONLY BY USING OTHER CELESTIAL BODIES TO MAINTAIN LIFE IN OUR OWN PLANET! YOU MIGHT BE INTERESTED TO KNOW THAT YOUR OWN PLANET, EARTH, WILL BE NEXT!
LOOK! WE'RE CLOSER TO EARTH! WHAT CAN WE DO?
YOU HEARD THAT THING! WE CAN DO NOTHING! NOTHING, UNLESS...

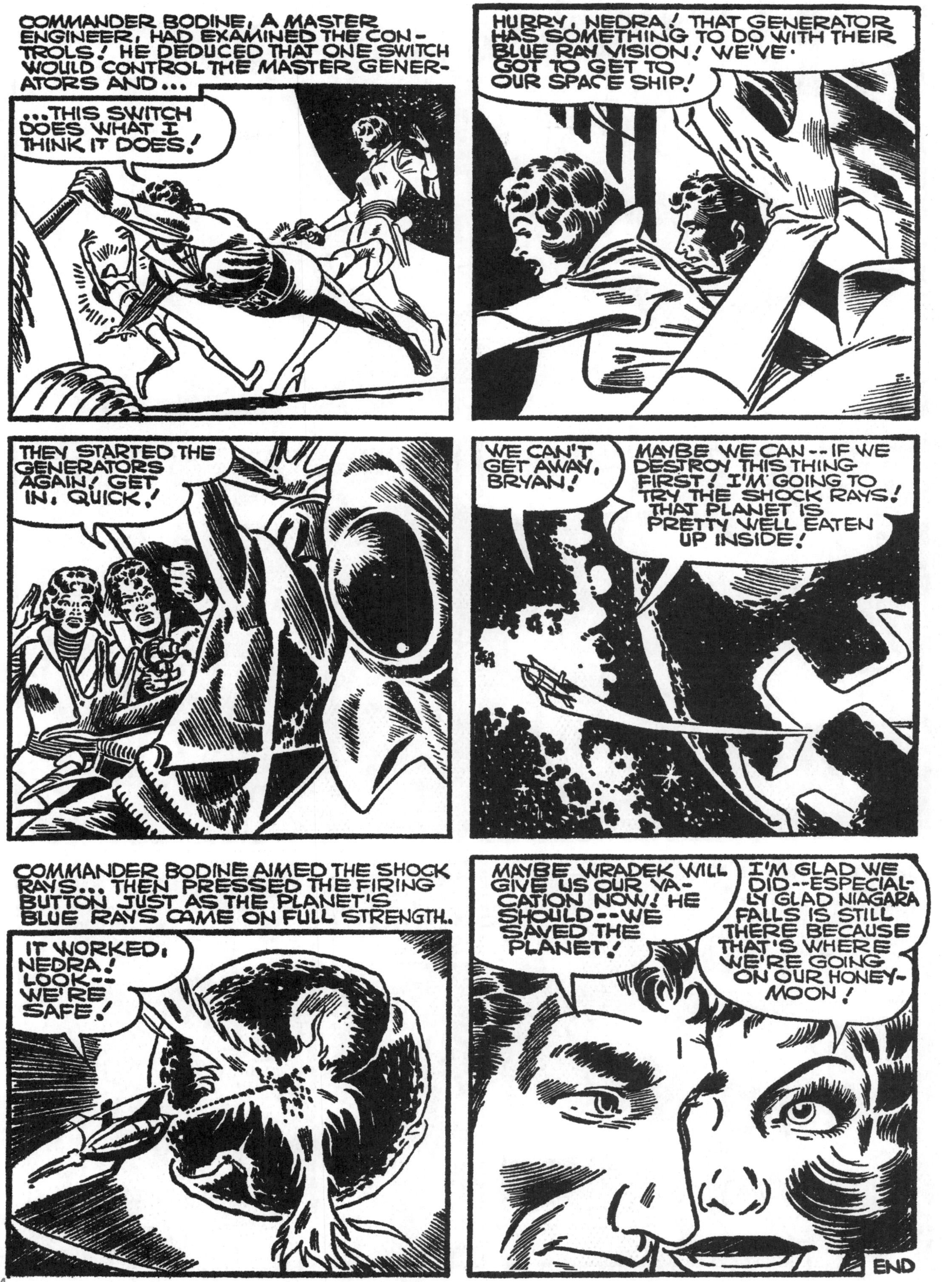
COMMANDER BODINE, A MASTER ENGINEER, HAD EXAMINED THE CONTROLS! HE DEDUCED THAT ONE SWITCH WOULD CONTROL THE MASTER GENERATORS AND...
...THIS SWITCH DOES WHAT I THINK IT DOES!
HURRY, NEDRA! THAT GENERATOR HAS SOMETHING TO DO WITH THEIR BLUE RAY VISION! WE'VE GOT TO GET TO OUR SPACE SHIP!
THEY STARTED THE GENERATORS AGAIN! GET IN, QUICK!
WE CAN'T GET AWAY, BRYAN!
MAYBE WE CAN--IF WE DESTROY THIS THING FIRST! I'M GOING TO TRY THE SHOCK RAYS! THAT PLANET IS PRETTY WELL EATEN UP INSIDE!
COMMANDER BODINE AIMED THE SHOCK RAYS... THEN PRESSED THE FIRING BUTTON JUST AS THE PLANET'S BLUE RAYS CAME ON FULL STRENGTH.
IT WORKED, NEDRA! LOOK--WE'RE SAFE!
MAYBE WRADEK WILL GIVE US OUR VACATION NOW! HE SHOULD--WE SAVED THE PLANET!
I'M GLAD WE DID--ESPECIALLY GLAD NIAGARA FALLS IS STILL THERE BECAUSE THAT'S WHERE WE'RE GOING ON OUR HONEYMOON!
END

THE DEADLY CARGO OF SPACESHIP 90

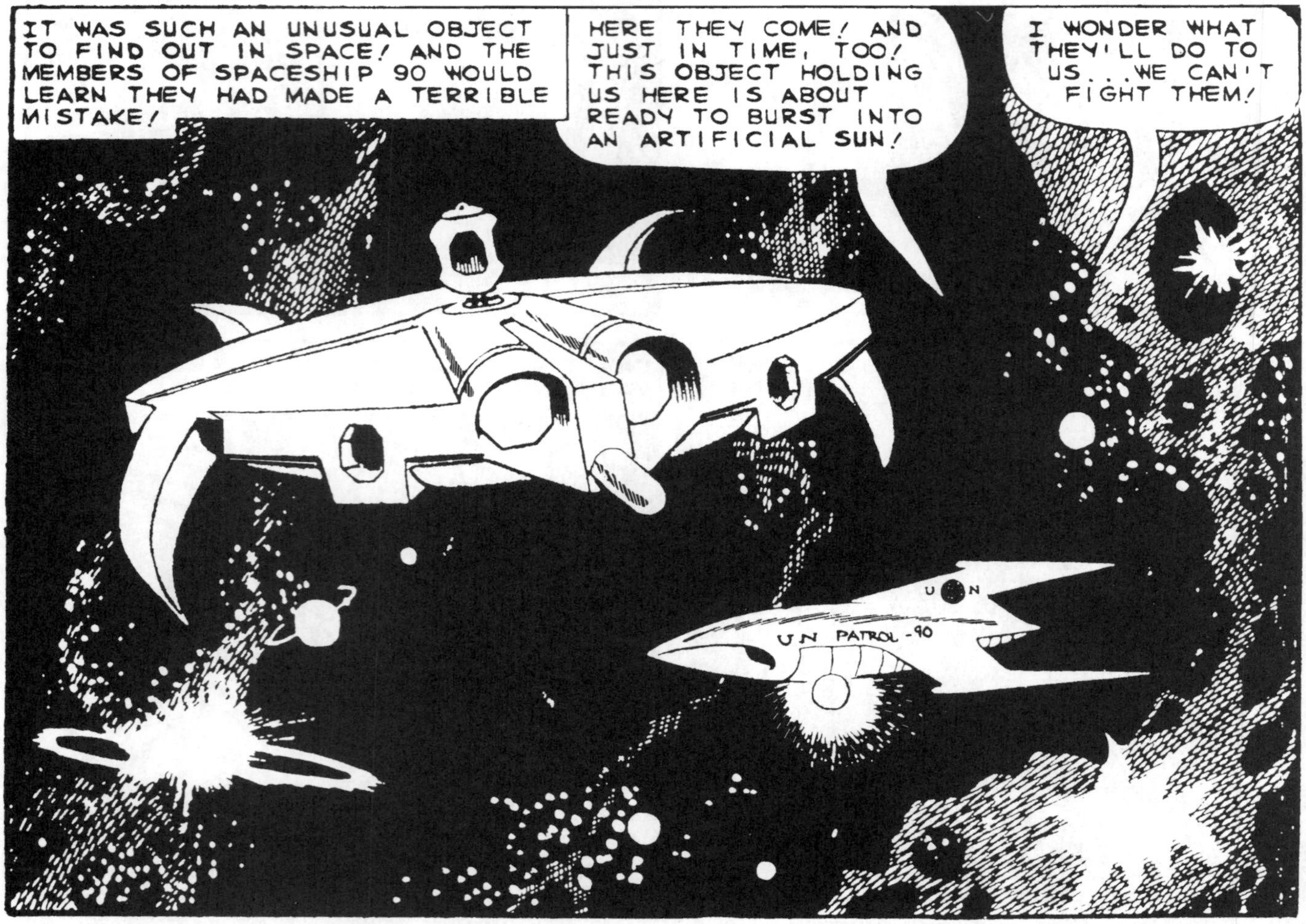
IT WAS SUCH AN UNUSUAL OBJECT TO FIND OUT IN SPACE! AND THE MEMBERS OF SPACESHIP 90 WOULD LEARN THEY HAD MADE A TERRIBLE MISTAKE!
HERE THEY COME! AND JUST IN TIME, TOO! THIS OBJECT HOLDING US HERE IS ABOUT READY TO BURST INTO AN ARTIFICIAL SUN!
I WONDER WHAT THEY'LL DO TO US...WE CAN'T FIGHT THEM!
U N
U.N PATROL-90

ON ONE OF ITS LONG SWEEPS AROUND THE SOLAR SYSTEM, FAR BEYOND PLUTO, THE CREW OF U.N. PATROL SHIP 90 WERE EAGER TO RETURN TO EARTH FOR A LEAVE.

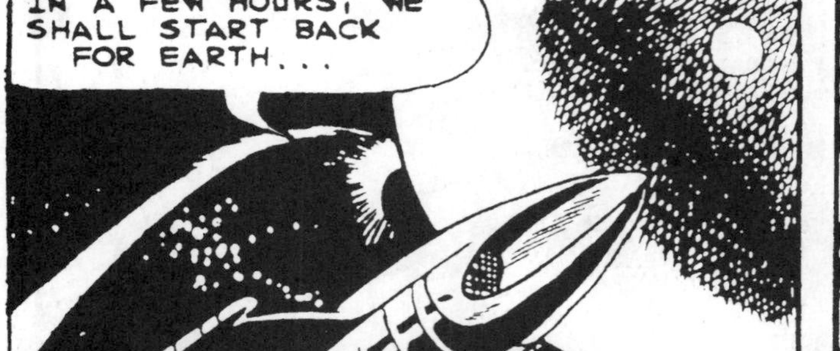
IN A FEW HOURS, WE SHALL START BACK FOR EARTH...

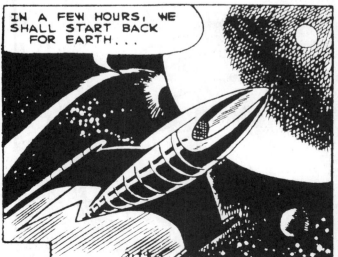

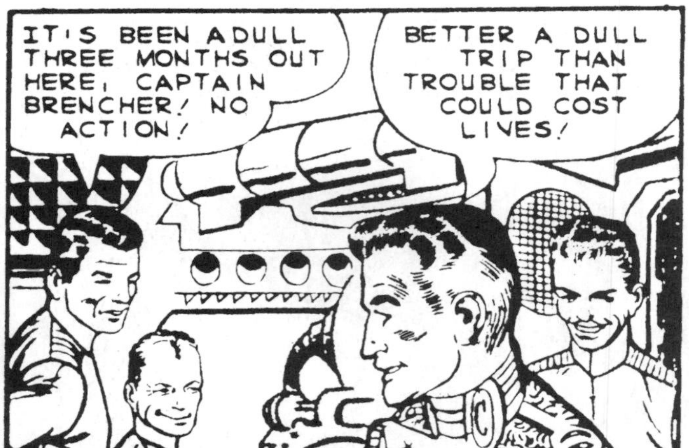
IT'S BEEN A DULL THREE MONTHS OUT HERE, CAPTAIN BRENCHER! NO ACTION!
BETTER A DULL TRIP THAN TROUBLE THAT COULD COST LIVES!
UN
UN

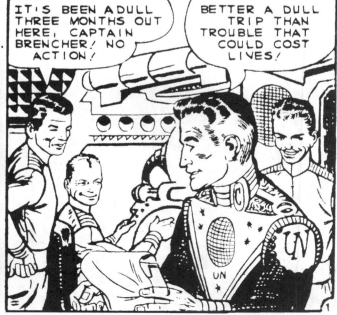

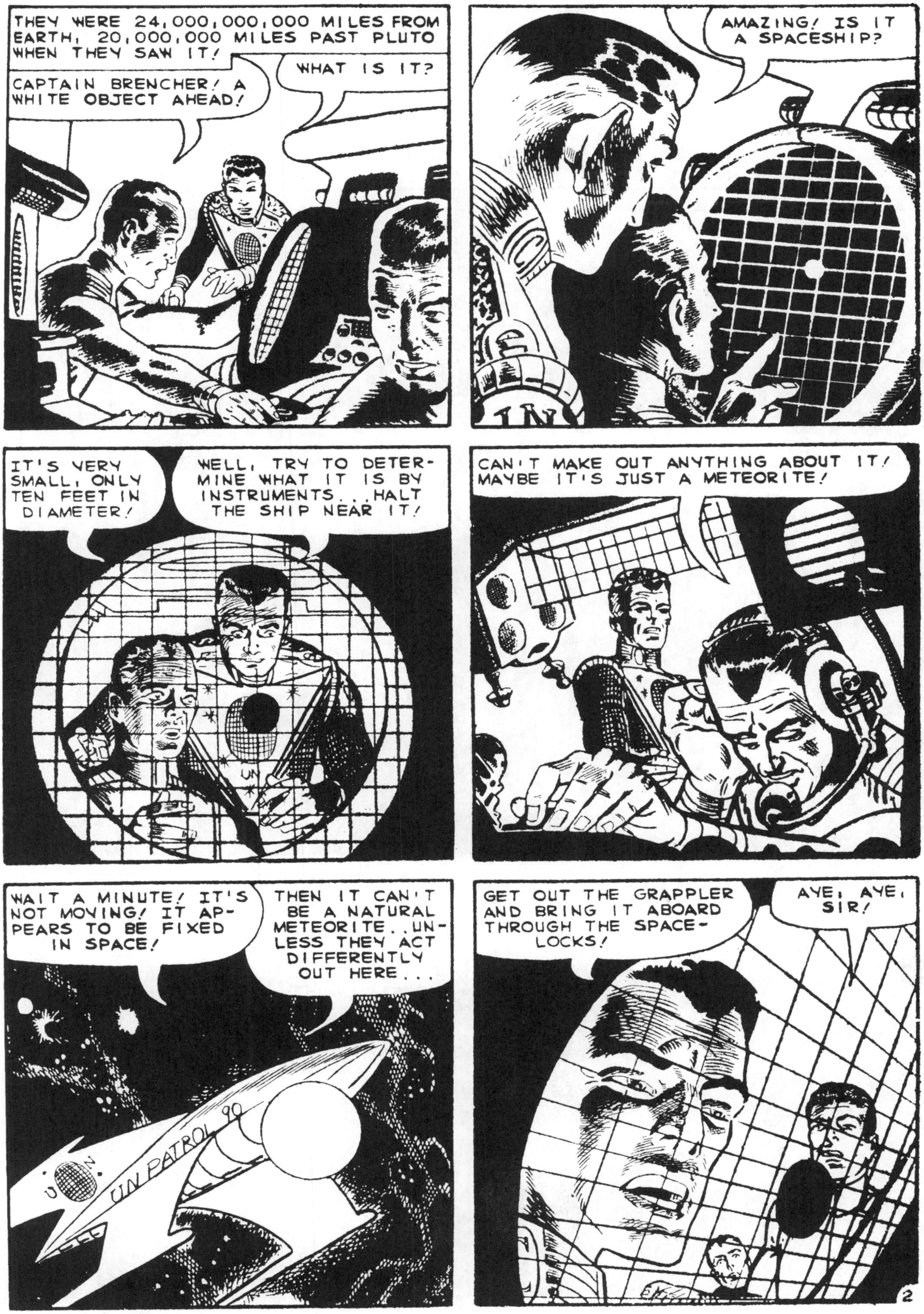
THEY WERE 24,000,000,000 MILES FROM EARTH, 20,000,000 MILES PAST PLUTO WHEN THEY SAW IT!
CAPTAIN BRENCHER! A WHITE OBJECT AHEAD!
WHAT IS IT?
AMAZING! IS IT A SPACESHIP?
IT'S VERY SMALL, ONLY TEN FEET IN DIAMETER!
WELL, TRY TO DETERMINE WHAT IT IS BY INSTRUMENTS. . HALT THE SHIP NEAR IT!
CAN'T MAKE OUT ANYTHING ABOUT IT! MAYBE IT'S JUST A METEORITE!
WAIT A MINUTE! IT'S NOT MOVING! IT APPEARS TO BE FIXED IN SPACE!
THEN IT CAN'T BE A NATURAL METEORITE. . UNLESS THEY ACT DIFFERENTLY OUT HERE . . .
UN PATROL 90
GET OUT THE GRAPPLER AND BRING IT ABOARD THROUGH THE SPACE-LOCKS!
AYE, AYE, SIR!
2

THE OBJECT WAS BROUGHT INTO THE PATROL SHIP WHERE IT CONTINUED TO PUZZLE THE SCIENTIST-PATROL OFFICERS...
IT'S VERY HARD, LIKE QUARTZ IN APPEARANCE...ANYWAY, WE HAVE A GIFT FOR THE MUSEUM OF PLANETARY HISTORY IN NEW YORK!
BACK TOWARD EARTH THE SHIP STARTED WITH ITS MYSTERIOUS FIND...
I CAN'T GET HOME TOO SOON FOR ME!
HEY! THERE'S A MESSAGE COMING IN...BUT IT'S FROM BEYOND WHERE WE WERE!
CAN YOU MAKE IT OUT? I DIDN'T KNOW ANY EARTH SHIPS WERE IN THAT REGION!
U.N.
WARNING TO EARTHMEN! WARNING TO EARTHMEN! RETURN THE SPHERE YOU HAVE TAKEN! RETURN IT TO THE POINT WHERE YOU FOUND IT!
IT--IT MUST BE-LONG TO SOME BEINGS!
WE ARE OF THE PLANET ORCAN, 30 BIL-LION MILES FROM YOUR SUN! RETURN THE SPHERE OR YOUR PLANET WILL BE DESTROYED!
IT IS AN ARTIFICIAL SUN WHICH IS SET TO EXPLODE INTO BRIL-LIANCE IN ONE DAY, YOUR TIME!
A SUN! THIS IS JUST LIKE A SUPER HY-DROGEN BOMB!
U.N
3

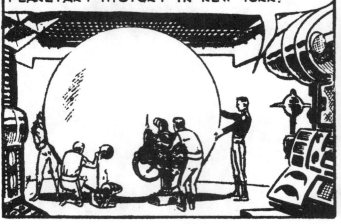

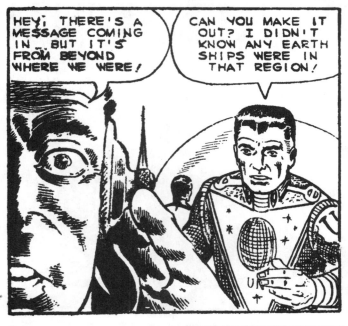

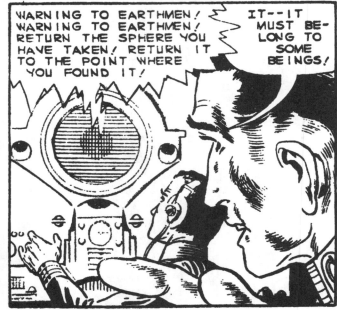

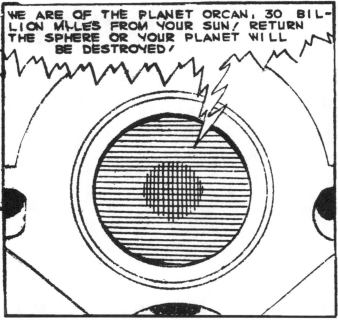

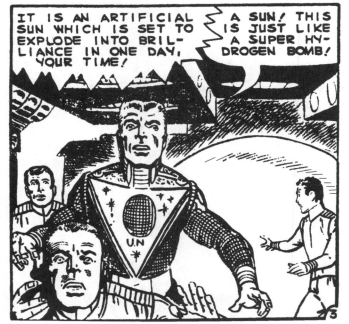

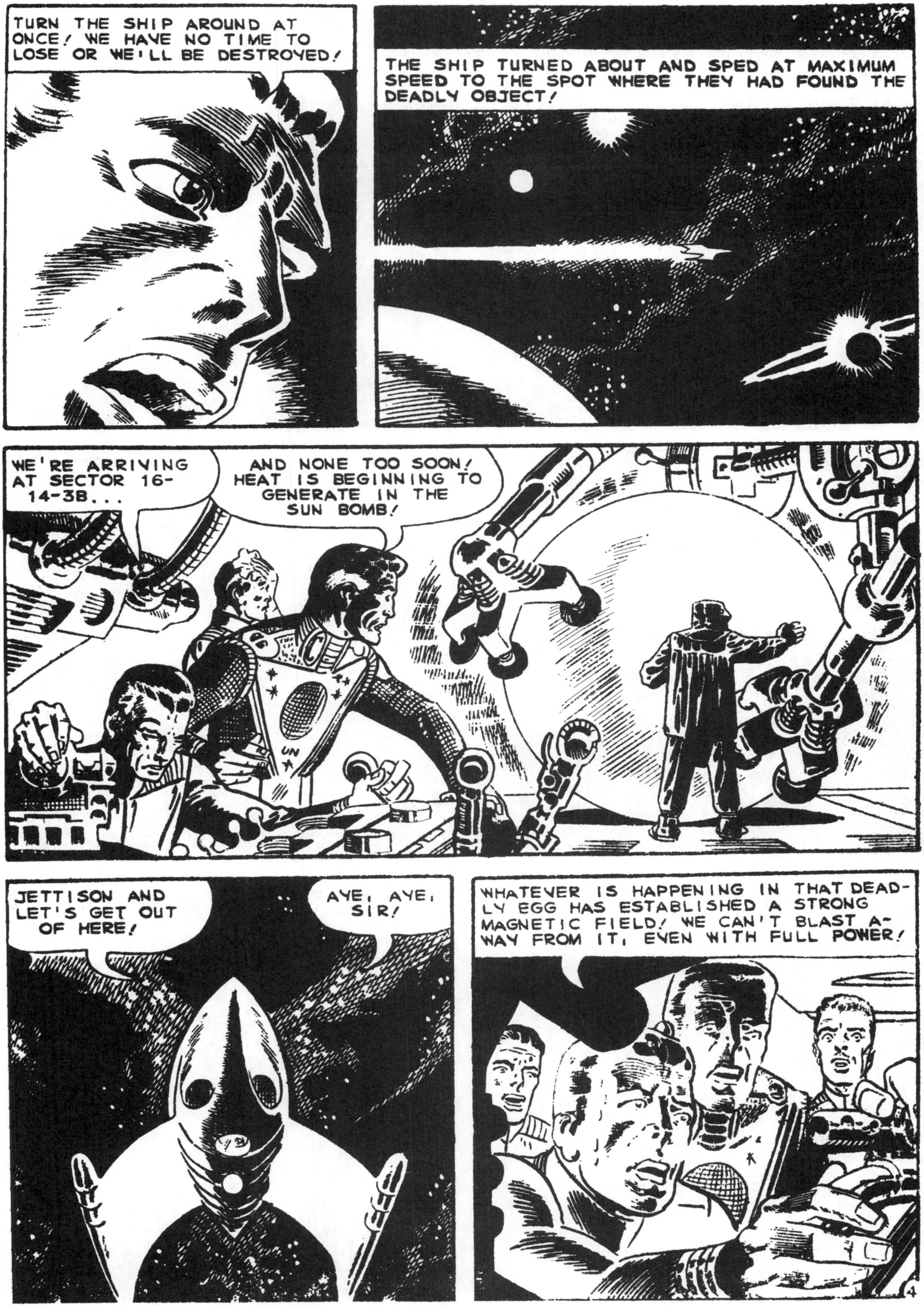
TURN THE SHIP AROUND AT ONCE! WE HAVE NO TIME TO LOSE OR WE'LL BE DESTROYED!
THE SHIP TURNED ABOUT AND SPED AT MAXIMUM SPEED TO THE SPOT WHERE THEY HAD FOUND THE DEADLY OBJECT!
WE'RE ARRIVING AT SECTOR 16-14-3B...
AND NONE TOO SOON! HEAT IS BEGINNING TO GENERATE IN THE SUN BOMB!
UN
JETTISON AND LET'S GET OUT OF HERE!
AYE, AYE, SIR!
WHATEVER IS HAPPENING IN THAT DEADLY EGG HAS ESTABLISHED A STRONG MAGNETIC FIELD! WE CAN'T BLAST AWAY FROM IT, EVEN WITH FULL POWER!
4

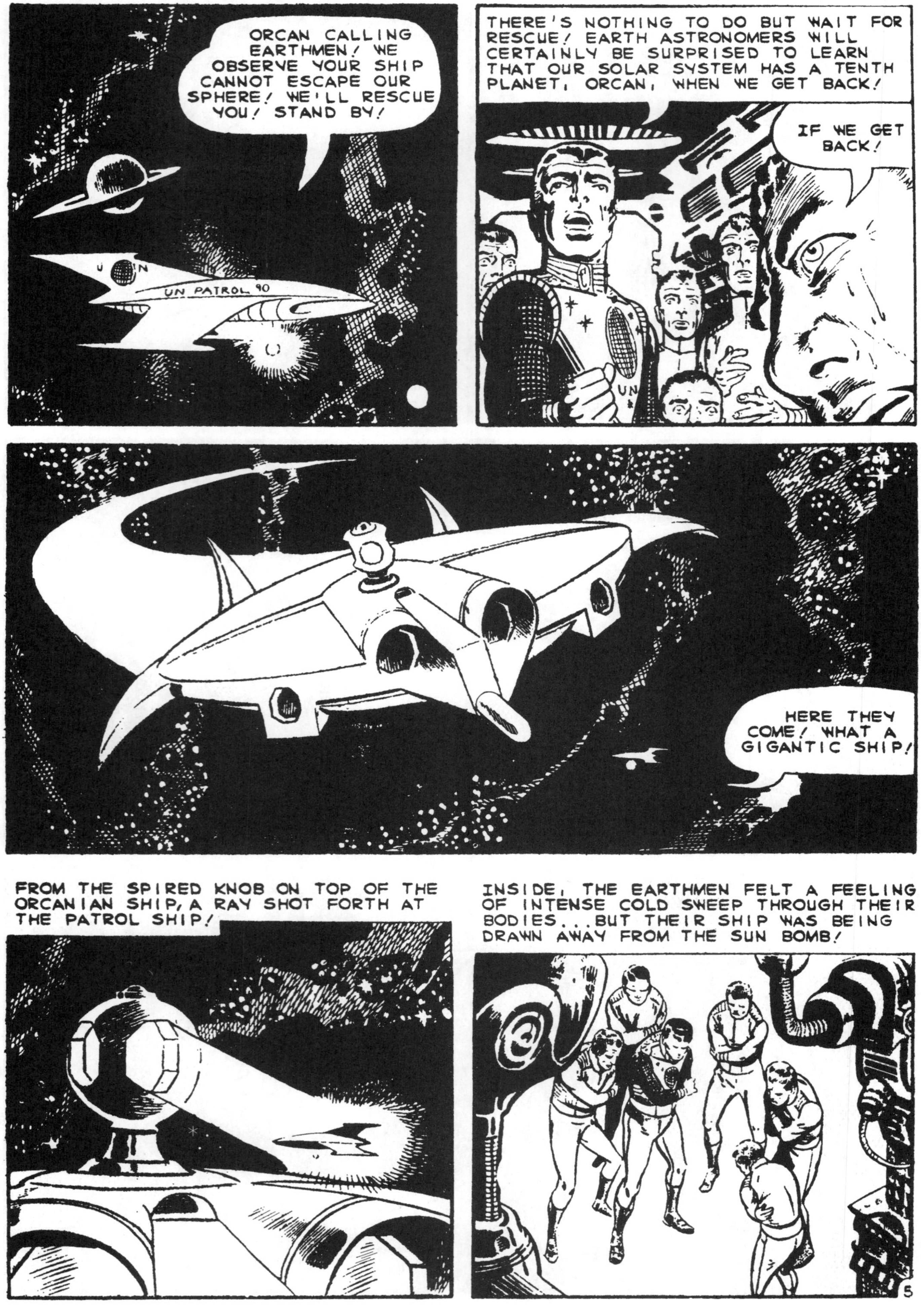
ORCAN CALLING EARTHMEN! WE OBSERVE YOUR SHIP CANNOT ESCAPE OUR SPHERE! WE'LL RESCUE YOU! STAND BY!
U N
UN PATROL 90
THERE'S NOTHING TO DO BUT WAIT FOR RESCUE! EARTH ASTRONOMERS WILL CERTAINLY BE SURPRISED TO LEARN THAT OUR SOLAR SYSTEM HAS A TENTH PLANET, ORCAN, WHEN WE GET BACK!
IF WE GET BACK!
HERE THEY COME! WHAT A GIGANTIC SHIP!
FROM THE SPIRED KNOB ON TOP OF THE ORCANIAN SHIP, A RAY SHOT FORTH AT THE PATROL SHIP!
INSIDE, THE EARTHMEN FELT A FEELING OF INTENSE COLD SWEEP THROUGH THEIR BODIES...BUT THEIR SHIP WAS BEING DRAWN AWAY FROM THE SUN BOMB!
5

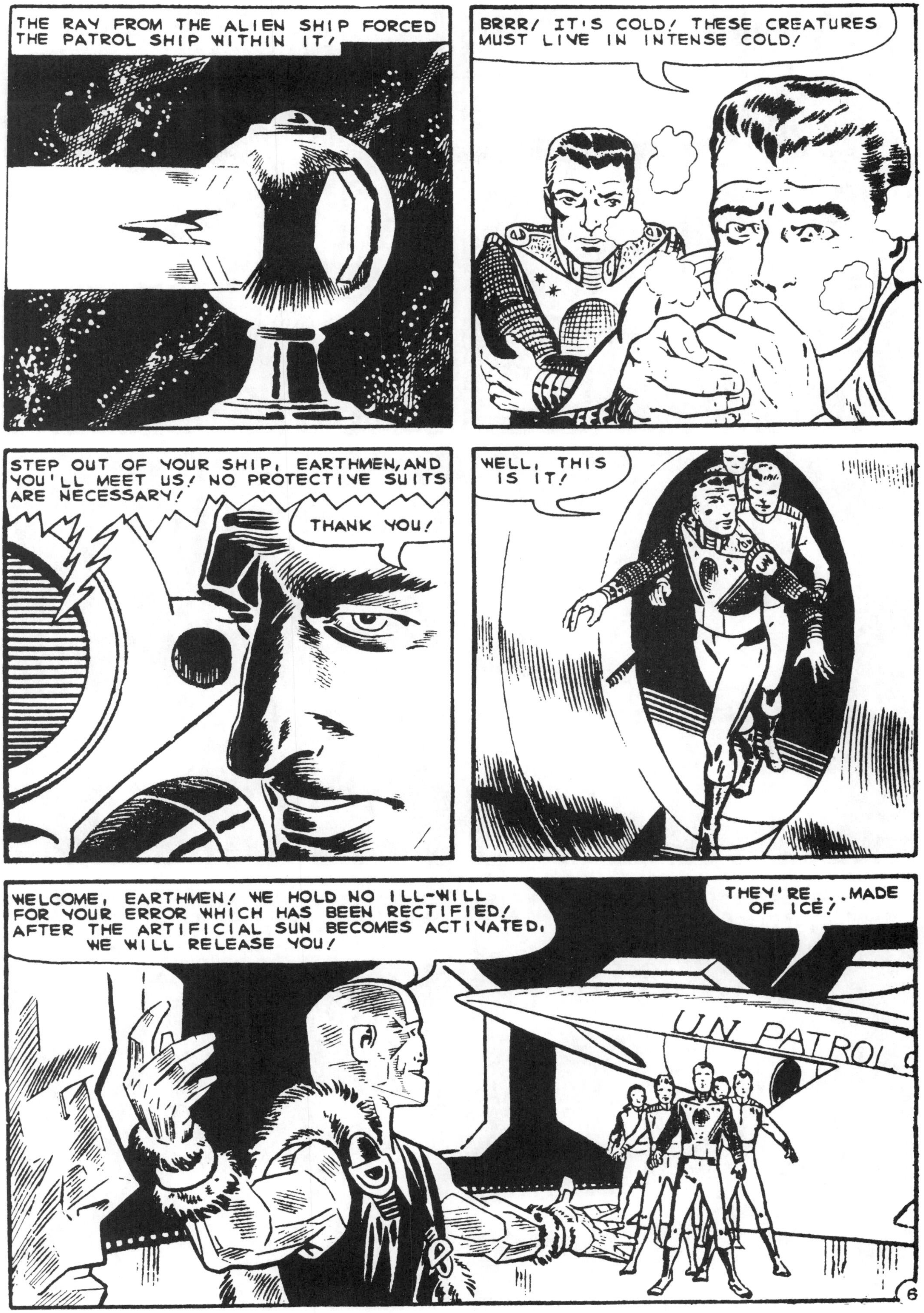
THE RAY FROM THE ALIEN SHIP FORCED THE PATROL SHIP WITHIN IT!
BRRR! IT'S COLD! THESE CREATURES MUST LIVE IN INTENSE COLD!
STEP OUT OF YOUR SHIP, EARTHMEN, AND YOU'LL MEET US! NO PROTECTIVE SUITS ARE NECESSARY!
THANK YOU!
WELL, THIS IS IT!
WELCOME, EARTHMEN! WE HOLD NO ILL-WILL FOR YOUR ERROR WHICH HAS BEEN RECTIFIED! AFTER THE ARTIFICIAL SUN BECOMES ACTIVATED, WE WILL RELEASE YOU!
THEY'RE...MADE OF ICE!
U.N. PATROL
6

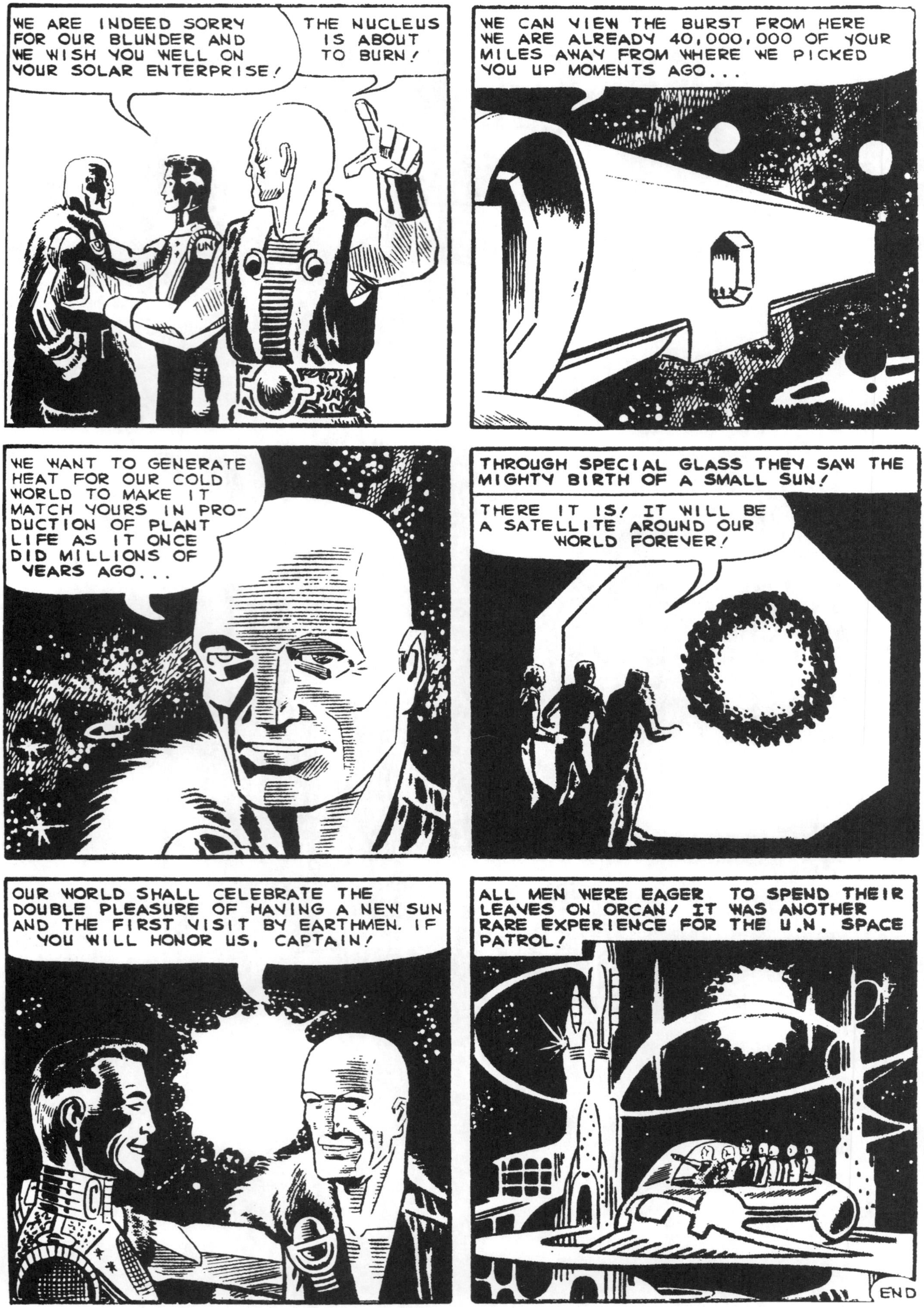
WE ARE INDEED SORRY FOR OUR BLUNDER AND WE WISH YOU WELL ON YOUR SOLAR ENTERPRISE!
THE NUCLEUS IS ABOUT TO BURN!
WE CAN VIEW THE BURST FROM HERE WE ARE ALREADY 40,000,000 OF YOUR MILES AWAY FROM WHERE WE PICKED YOU UP MOMENTS AGO...
WE WANT TO GENERATE HEAT FOR OUR COLD WORLD TO MAKE IT MATCH YOURS IN PRO-DUCTION OF PLANT LIFE AS IT ONCE DID MILLIONS OF YEARS AGO...
THROUGH SPECIAL GLASS THEY SAW THE MIGHTY BIRTH OF A SMALL SUN!
THERE IT IS! IT WILL BE A SATELLITE AROUND OUR WORLD FOREVER!
OUR WORLD SHALL CELEBRATE THE DOUBLE PLEASURE OF HAVING A NEW SUN AND THE FIRST VISIT BY EARTHMEN. IF YOU WILL HONOR US, CAPTAIN!
ALL MEN WERE EAGER TO SPEND THEIR LEAVES ON ORCAN! IT WAS ANOTHER RARE EXPERIENCE FOR THE U.N. SPACE PATROL!
UN
UN
END

STEVE DITKO
SPACE WARS

THE MAS- SIVE DOOR SPLIN- TERED OPEN! THEY MARCHED MENACING- LY FOR- WARD, THEIR EMOTION COILS SEETH- ING WITH MENACE...

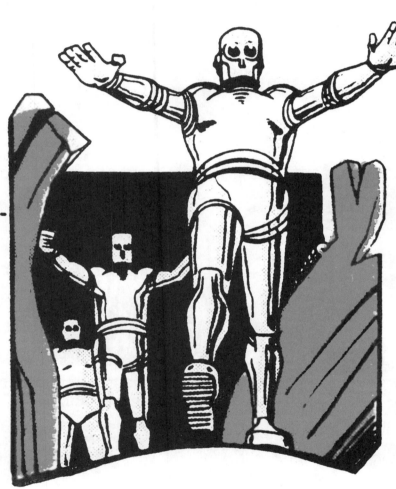

THE DECISION

THEY WERE THE SUPREME COUNCIL OF THE GENERAL ASSEMBLY OF ALL THE NATIONS OF THE WORLD! THEIRS WERE THE KEENEST MINDS OF THE UNIVERSE... THEY REPRESENTED A LIVING COMPENDIUM OF ALL EXTANT KNOWLEDGE AND WISDOM...

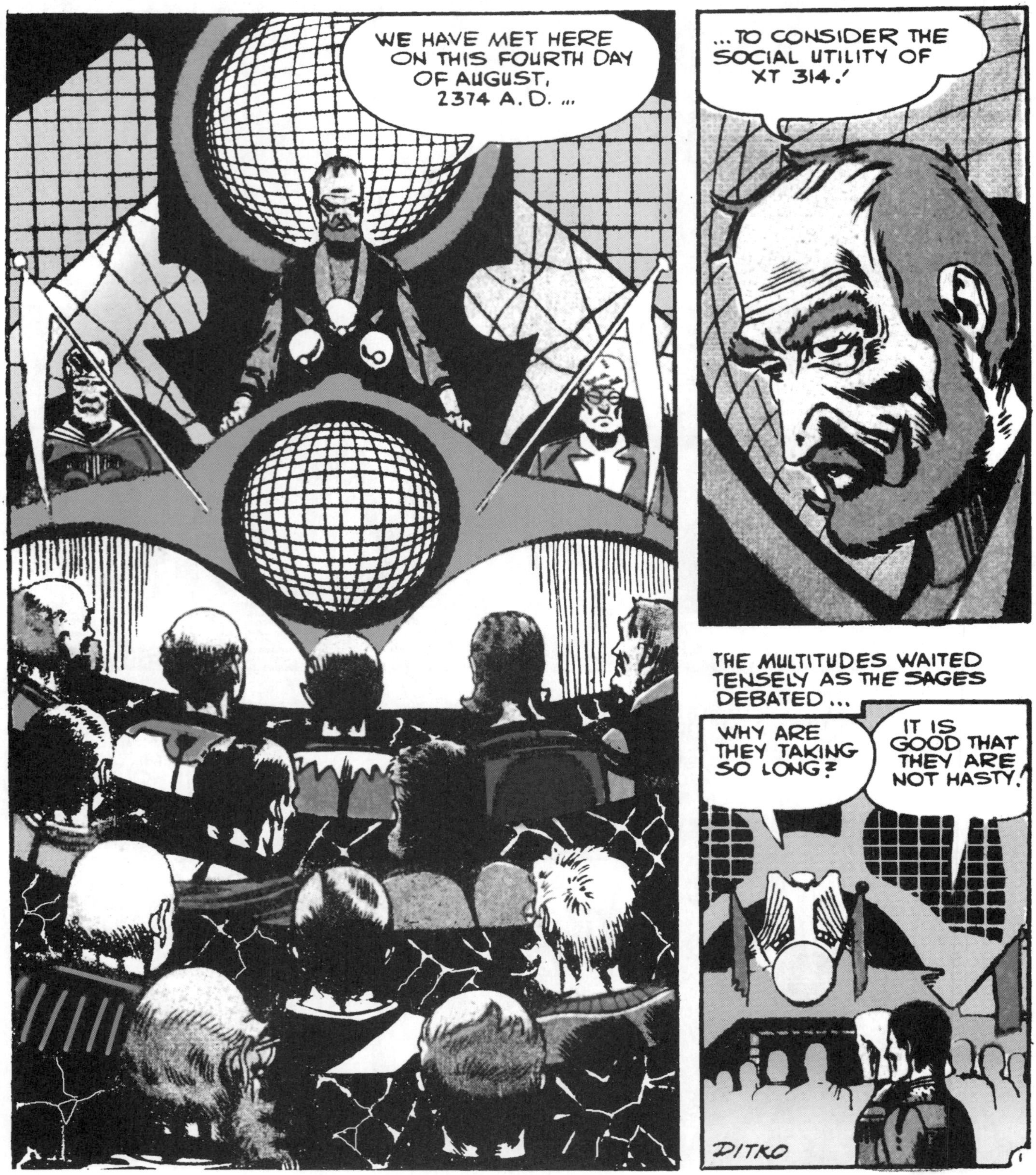
WE HAVE MET HERE ON THIS FOURTH DAY OF AUGUST, 2374 A.D. ...
...TO CONSIDER THE SOCIAL UTILITY OF XT 314.!
THE MULTITUDES WAITED TENSELY AS THE SAGES DEBATED...
WHY ARE THEY TAKING SO LONG?
IT IS GOOD THAT THEY ARE NOT HASTY!
DITKO

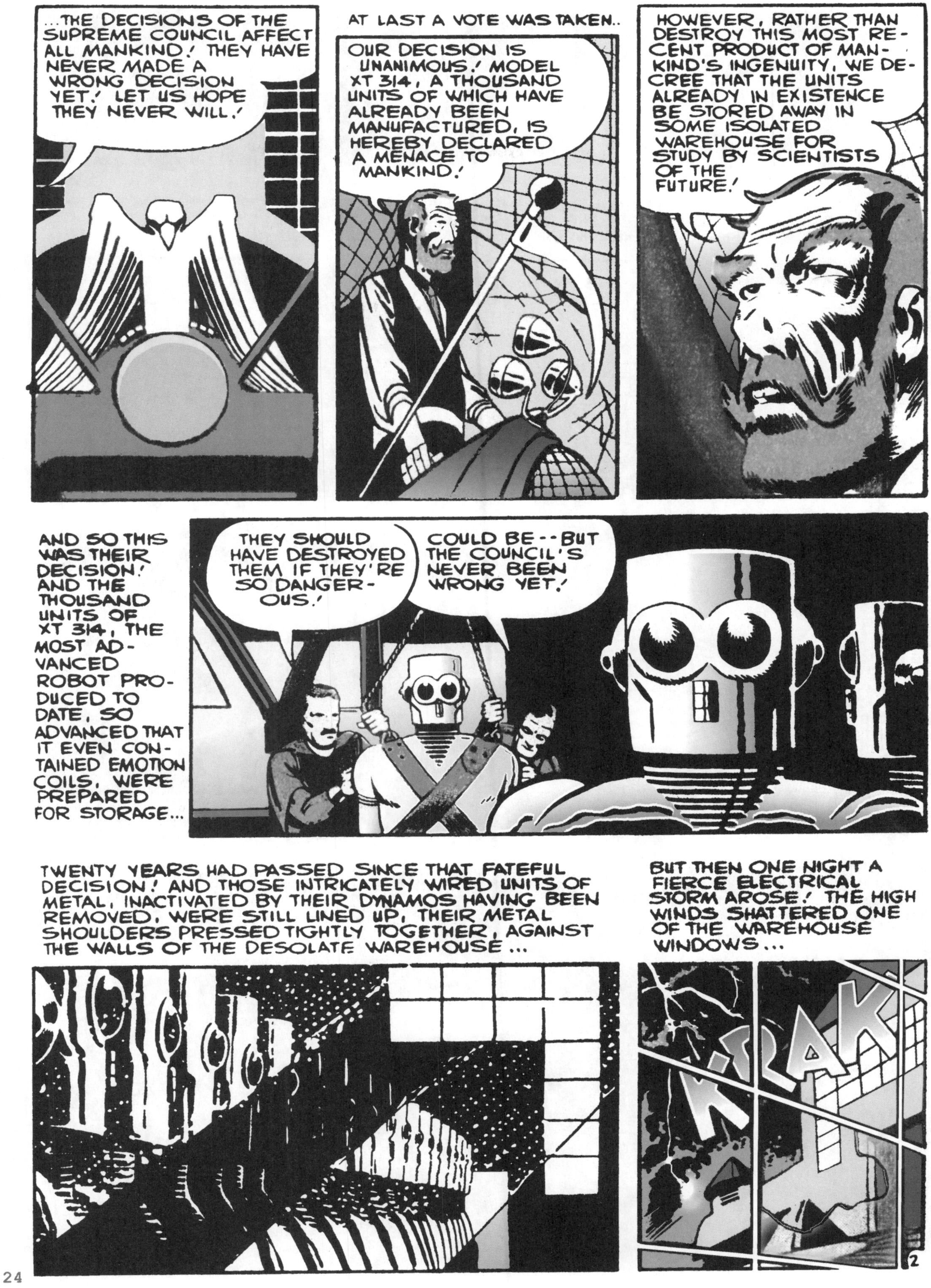
...THE DECISIONS OF THE SUPREME COUNCIL AFFECT ALL MANKIND! THEY HAVE NEVER MADE A WRONG DECISION YET! LET US HOPE THEY NEVER WILL!
AT LAST A VOTE WAS TAKEN..
OUR DECISION IS UNANIMOUS! MODEL XT 314, A THOUSAND UNITS OF WHICH HAVE ALREADY BEEN MANUFACTURED, IS HEREBY DECLARED A MENACE TO MANKIND!
HOWEVER, RATHER THAN DESTROY THIS MOST RECENT PRODUCT OF MANKIND'S INGENUITY, WE DECREE THAT THE UNITS ALREADY IN EXISTENCE BE STORED AWAY IN SOME ISOLATED WAREHOUSE FOR STUDY BY SCIENTISTS OF THE FUTURE!
AND SO THIS WAS THEIR DECISION! AND THE THOUSAND UNITS OF XT 314, THE MOST ADVANCED ROBOT PRODUCED TO DATE, SO ADVANCED THAT IT EVEN CONTAINED EMOTION COILS, WERE PREPARED FOR STORAGE...
THEY SHOULD HAVE DESTROYED THEM IF THEY'RE SO DANGEROUS!
COULD BE--BUT THE COUNCIL'S NEVER BEEN WRONG YET!
TWENTY YEARS HAD PASSED SINCE THAT FATEFUL DECISION! AND THOSE INTRICATELY WIRED UNITS OF METAL, INACTIVATED BY THEIR DYNAMOS HAVING BEEN REMOVED, WERE STILL LINED UP, THEIR METAL SHOULDERS PRESSED TIGHTLY TOGETHER, AGAINST THE WALLS OF THE DESOLATE WAREHOUSE ...
BUT THEN ONE NIGHT A FIERCE ELECTRICAL STORM AROSE! THE HIGH WINDS SHATTERED ONE OF THE WAREHOUSE WINDOWS...
KRAK!
2

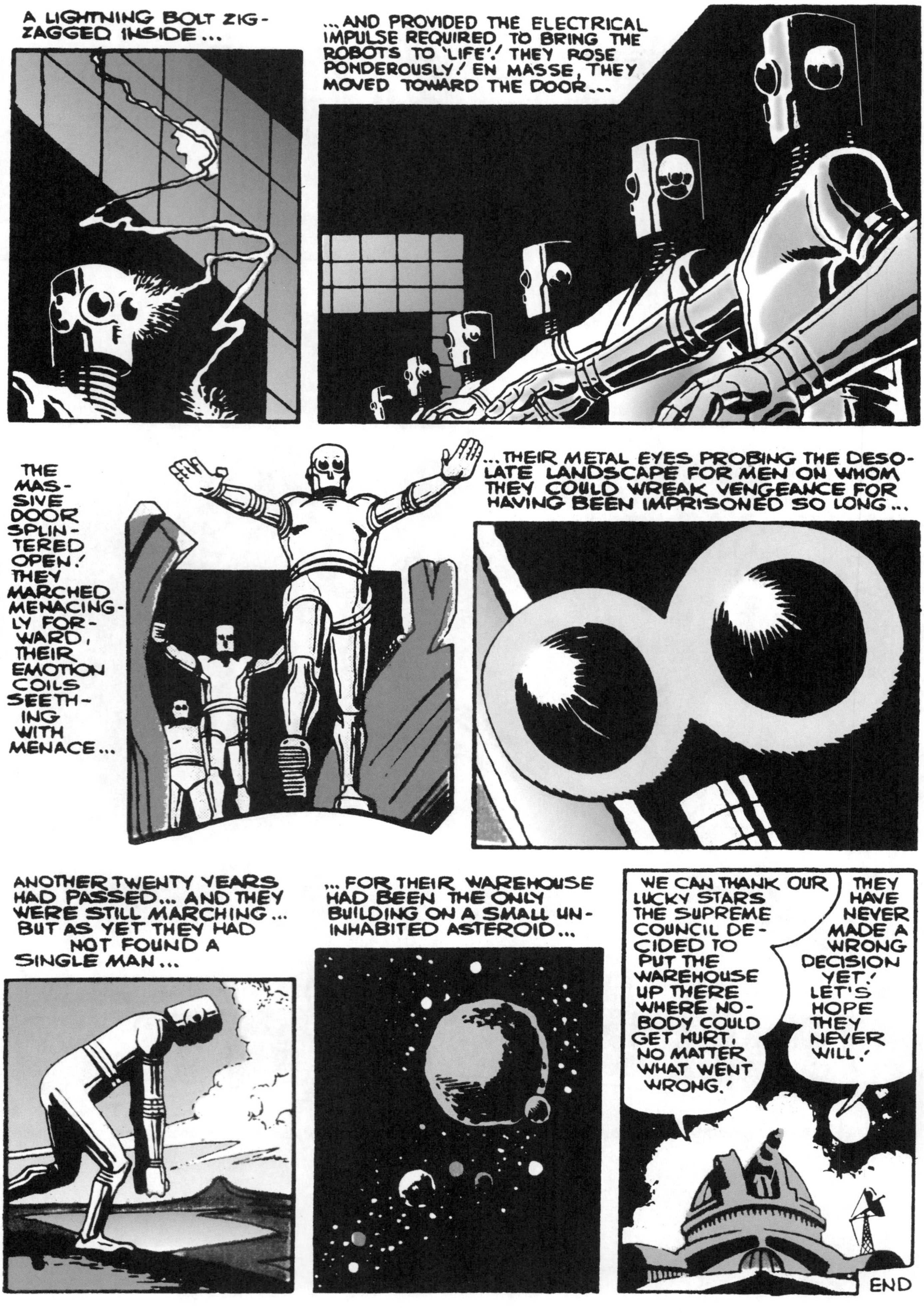
A LIGHTNING BOLT ZIG-ZAGGED INSIDE...
...AND PROVIDED THE ELECTRICAL IMPULSE REQUIRED TO BRING THE ROBOTS TO 'LIFE'! THEY ROSE PONDEROUSLY! EN MASSE, THEY MOVED TOWARD THE DOOR...
THE MASSIVE DOOR SPLINTERED OPEN! THEY MARCHED MENACINGLY FORWARD, THEIR EMOTION COILS SEETHING WITH MENACE...
...THEIR METAL EYES PROBING THE DESOLATE LANDSCAPE FOR MEN ON WHOM THEY COULD WREAK VENGEANCE FOR HAVING BEEN IMPRISONED SO LONG...
ANOTHER TWENTY YEARS HAD PASSED... AND THEY WERE STILL MARCHING... BUT AS YET THEY HAD NOT FOUND A SINGLE MAN...
...FOR THEIR WAREHOUSE HAD BEEN THE ONLY BUILDING ON A SMALL UNINHABITED ASTEROID...
WE CAN THANK OUR LUCKY STARS THE SUPREME COUNCIL DECIDED TO PUT THE WAREHOUSE UP THERE WHERE NOBODY COULD GET HURT, NO MATTER WHAT WENT WRONG!
THEY HAVE NEVER MADE A WRONG DECISION YET! LET'S HOPE THEY NEVER WILL!
END

STEVE DITKO SPACE WARS

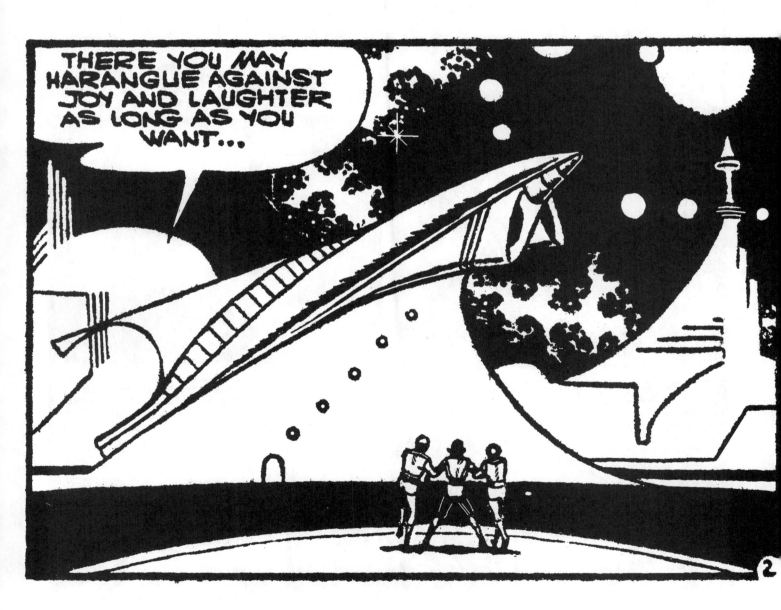

THE GLOOMY ONE

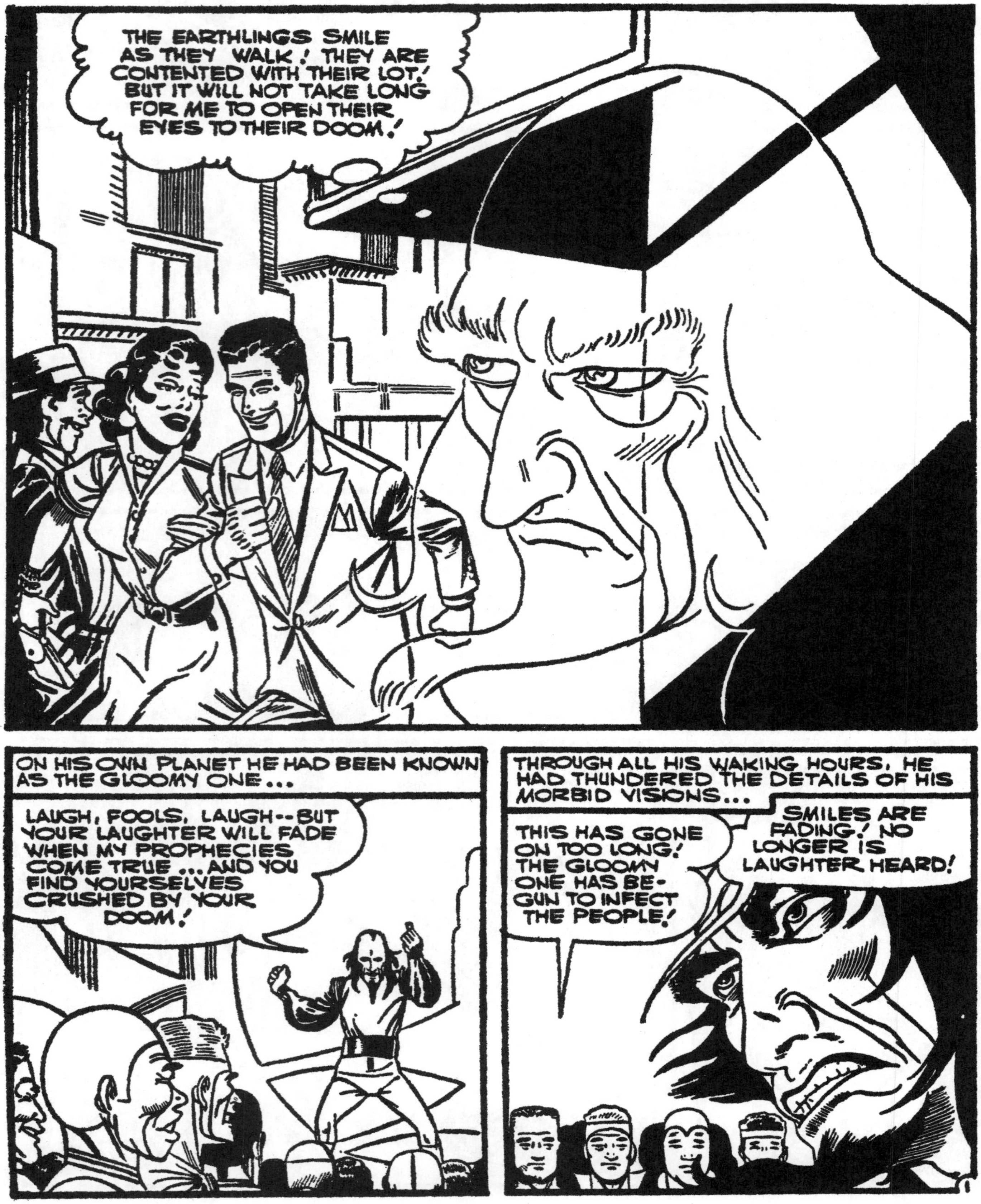

THE EARTHLINGS SMILE AS THEY WALK! THEY ARE CONTENTED WITH THEIR LOT! BUT IT WILL NOT TAKE LONG FOR ME TO OPEN THEIR EYES TO THEIR DOOM!
ON HIS OWN PLANET HE HAD BEEN KNOWN AS THE GLOOMY ONE ...
LAUGH, FOOLS, LAUGH--BUT YOUR LAUGHTER WILL FADE WHEN MY PROPHECIES COME TRUE ... AND YOU FIND YOURSELVES CRUSHED BY YOUR DOOM!
THROUGH ALL HIS WAKING HOURS, HE HAD THUNDERED THE DETAILS OF HIS MORBID VISIONS...
THIS HAS GONE ON TOO LONG! THE GLOOMY ONE HAS BE-GUN TO INFECT THE PEOPLE!
SMILES ARE FADING! NO LONGER IS LAUGHTER HEARD!

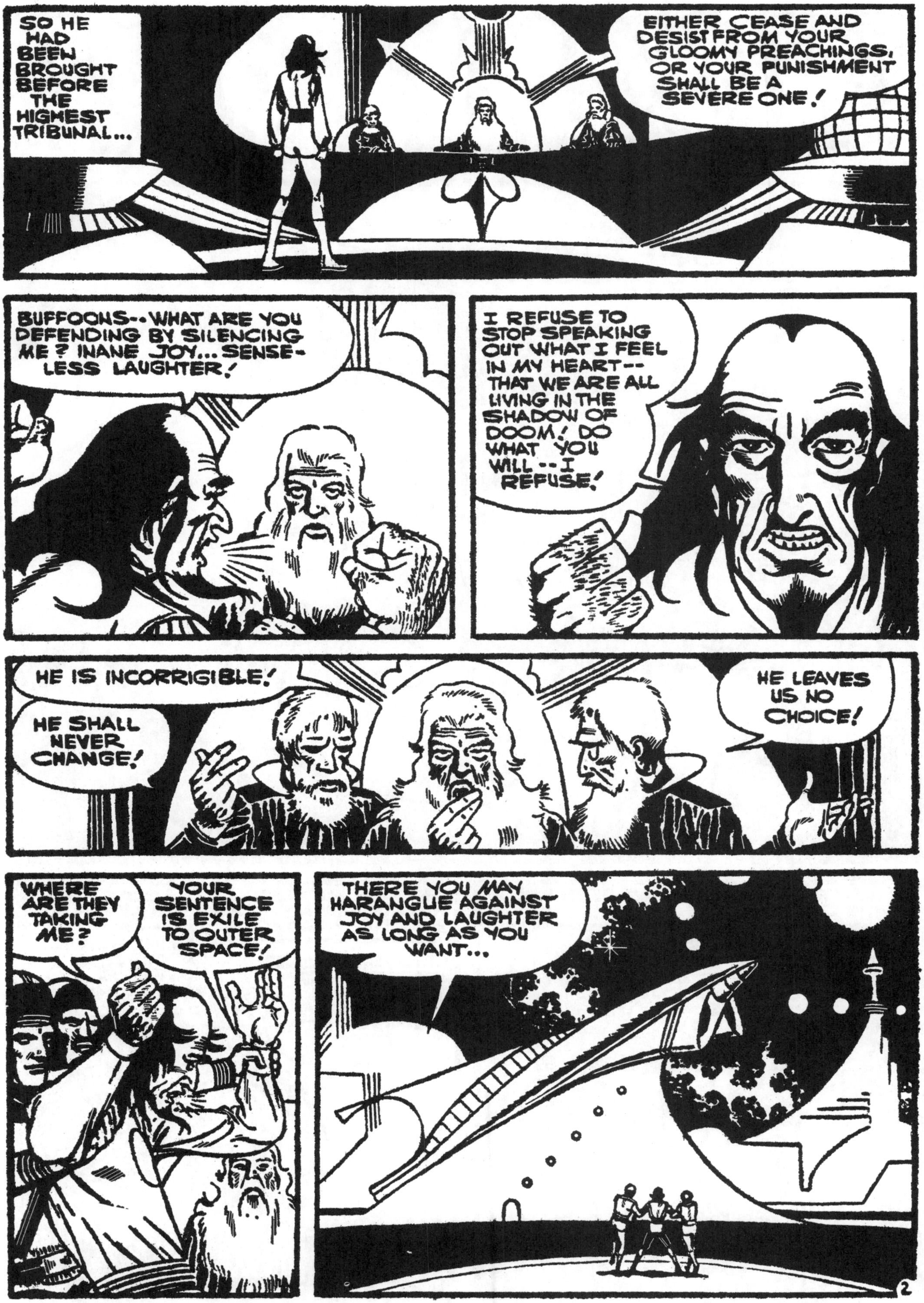
SO HE HAD BEEN BROUGHT BEFORE THE HIGHEST TRIBUNAL...
EITHER CEASE AND DESIST FROM YOUR GLOOMY PREACHINGS, OR YOUR PUNISHMENT SHALL BE A SEVERE ONE!
BUFFOONS--WHAT ARE YOU DEFENDING BY SILENCING ME? INANE JOY... SENSELESS LAUGHTER!
I REFUSE TO STOP SPEAKING OUT WHAT I FEEL IN MY HEART--THAT WE ARE ALL LIVING IN THE SHADOW OF DOOM! DO WHAT YOU WILL--I REFUSE!
HE IS INCORRIGIBLE!
HE SHALL NEVER CHANGE!
HE LEAVES US NO CHOICE!
WHERE ARE THEY TAKING ME?
YOUR SENTENCE IS EXILE TO OUTER SPACE!
THERE YOU MAY HARANGUE AGAINST JOY AND LAUGHTER AS LONG AS YOU WANT...
2

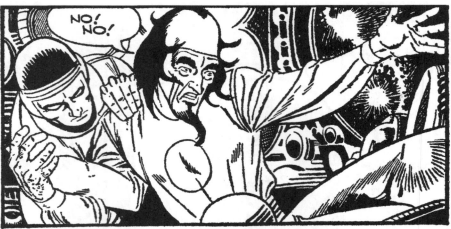

...BUT ONLY THE RUSHING METEORS AND THE LIFELESS PLANETOIDS WILL HEAR YOU!

NO! NO!

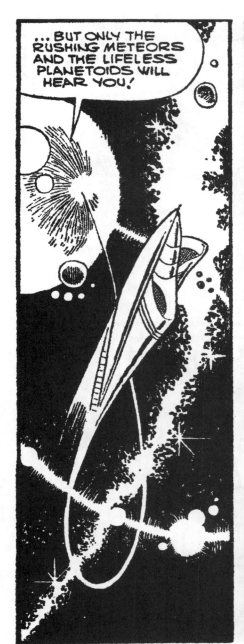

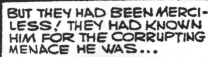

BUT THEY HAD BEEN MERCILESS! THEY HAD KNOWN HIM FOR THE CORRUPTING MENACE HE WAS...

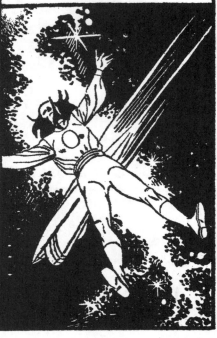

HE HAD FLOATED IN THE DARKNESS, SOBBING AND RANTING, AS THE CENTURIES HAD KEPT INCHING BY WITH INSUFFERABLE SLOWNESS...

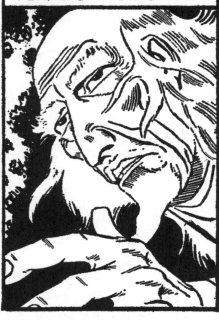

BUT THEN, SUDDENLY...

I'VE ENTERED THE GRAVITATIONAL SPHERE OF A PLANET...I'M BEING PULLED DOWN!

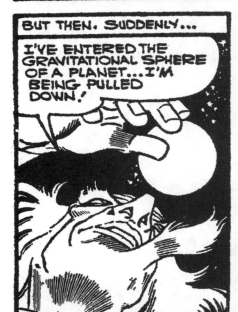

HE HAD LANDED ON EARTH! AFTER USING THE LAST FEW REMAINING OUNCES OF HIS STRENGTH TO RENDER HIMSELF INVISIBLE, HE HAD BEGUN DRAGGING HIMSELF ALONG THE STREETS, AND THEN THE OLD DESIRE TO COMBAT JOY AND LAUGHTER HAD RISEN AGAIN INSIDE OF HIM...

THE EARTHLINGS LAUGH-- BUT NOT FOR LONG!

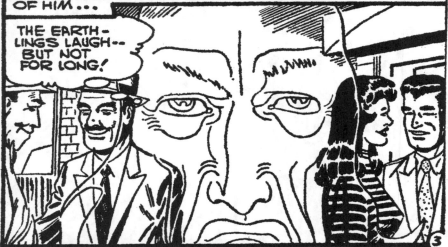

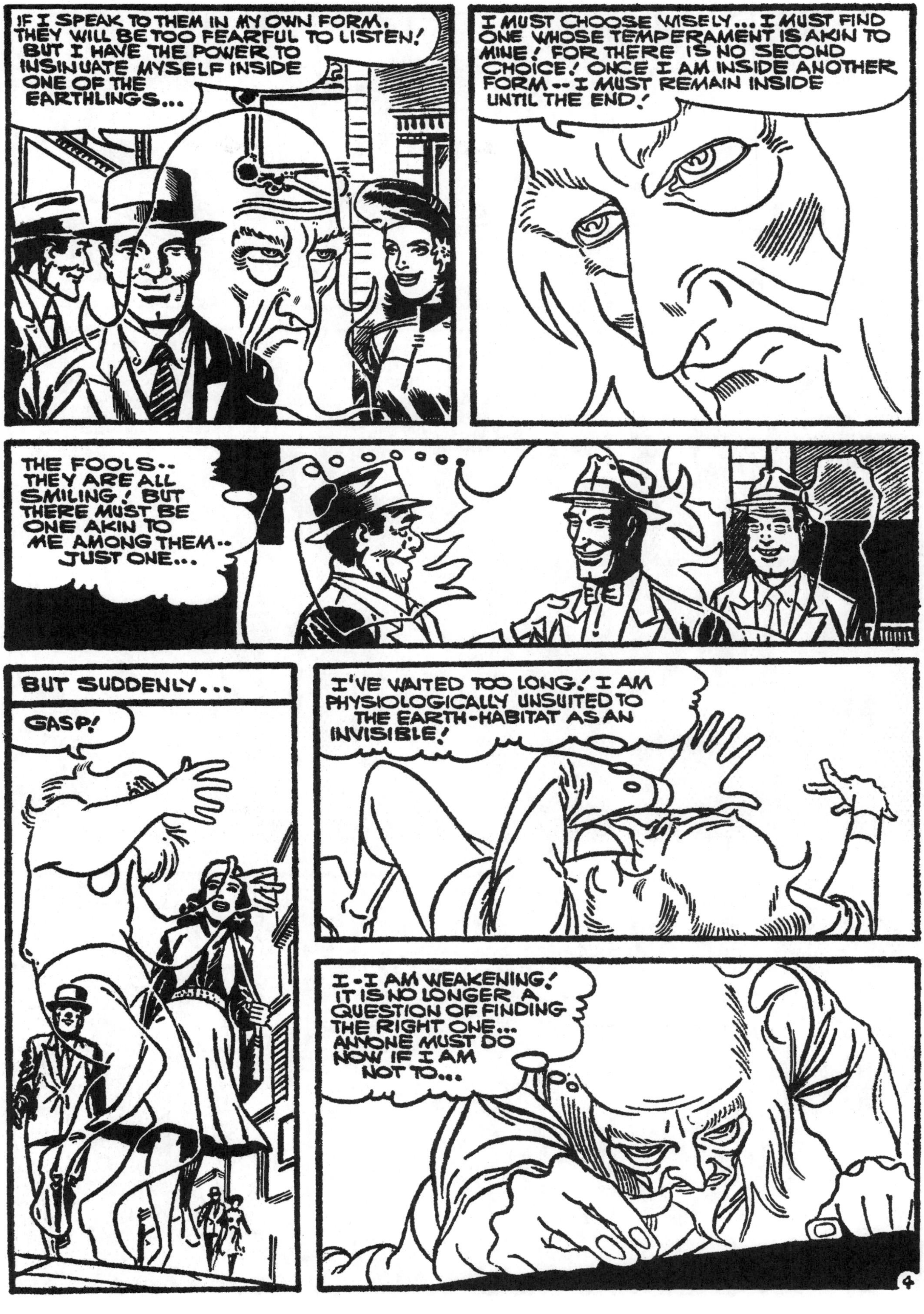
IF I SPEAK TO THEM IN MY OWN FORM, THEY WILL BE TOO FEARFUL TO LISTEN! BUT I HAVE THE POWER TO INSINUATE MYSELF INSIDE ONE OF THE EARTHLINGS...
I MUST CHOOSE WISELY... I MUST FIND ONE WHOSE TEMPERAMENT IS AKIN TO MINE! FOR THERE IS NO SECOND CHOICE! ONCE I AM INSIDE ANOTHER FORM -- I MUST REMAIN INSIDE UNTIL THE END!
THE FOOLS.. THEY ARE ALL SMILING! BUT THERE MUST BE ONE AKIN TO ME AMONG THEM.. JUST ONE...
BUT SUDDENLY...
GASP!
I'VE WAITED TOO LONG! I AM PHYSIOLOGICALLY UNSUITED TO THE EARTH-HABITAT AS AN INVISIBLE!
I-I AM WEAKENING! IT IS NO LONGER A QUESTION OF FINDING THE RIGHT ONE... ANYONE MUST DO NOW IF I AM NOT TO...
4

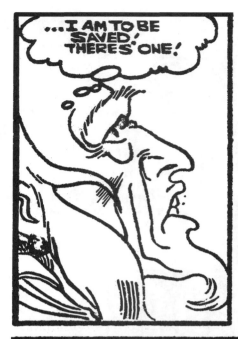

...I AM TO BE SAVED! THERE'S ONE!

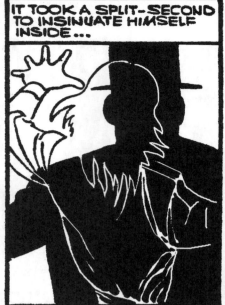

IT TOOK A SPLIT-SECOND TO INSINUATE HIMSELF INSIDE...

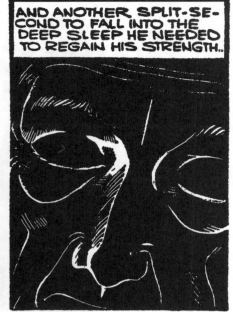

AND ANOTHER SPLIT-SECOND TO FALL INTO THE DEEP SLEEP HE NEEDED TO REGAIN HIS STRENGTH..

AND SO IT WAS NOT UNTIL THE NEXT DAY THAT HE LEARNED WHAT HIS DOOM WAS TO BE INSIDE THE FORM WHERE HE HAD IMPRISONED HIMSELF -- AND WOULD HAVE TO STAY UNTIL THE END...

OH, GROAN... NO!!

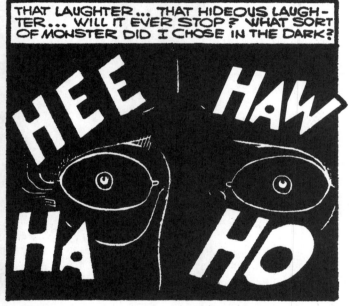

THAT LAUGHTER... THAT HIDEOUS LAUGHTER... WILL IT EVER STOP? WHAT SORT OF MONSTER DID I CHOSE IN THE DARK?

HEE HAW HA HO

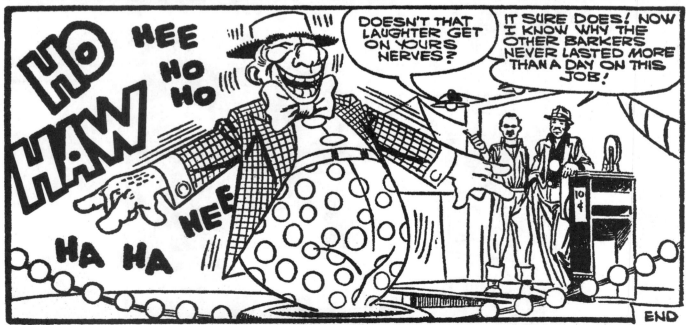

HO HAW HEE HO HO HEE HA HA

DOESN'T THAT LAUGHTER GET ON YOURS NERVES?

IT SURE DOES! NOW I KNOW WHY THE OTHER BARKERS NEVER LASTED MORE THAN A DAY ON THIS JOB!

END

STEVE DITKO
SPACE WARS

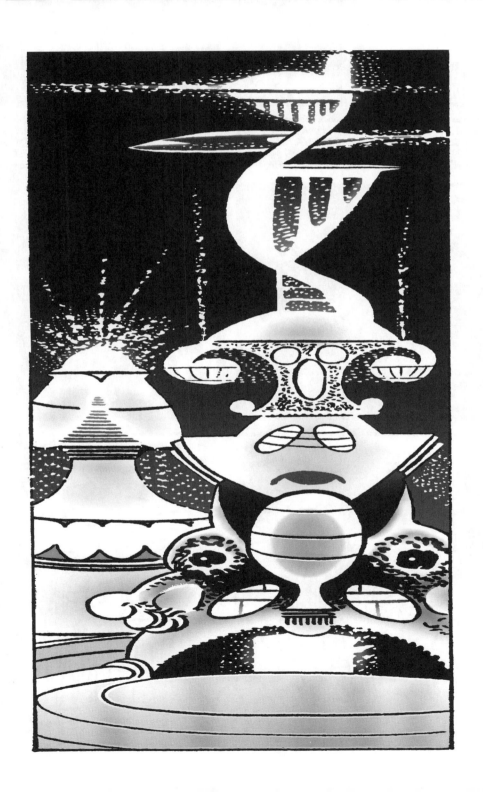

THE JUGGERNAUTS OF JUPITER

THE ALL HIGHEST OF NEPTUNE WAS PLEASED TO LEARN THAT A SUCCESSFUL LANDING HAD BEEN MADE ON JUPITER...

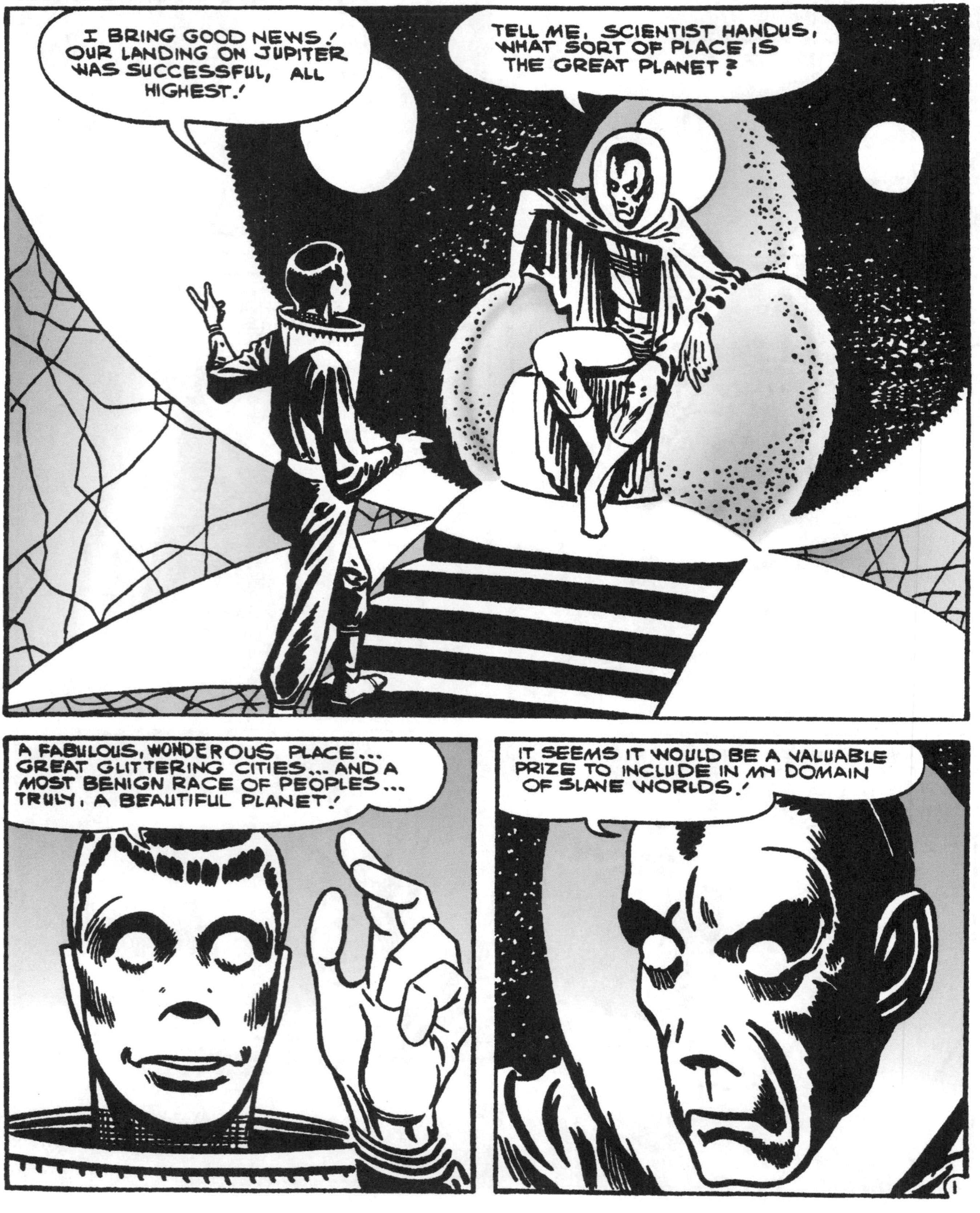
I BRING GOOD NEWS! OUR LANDING ON JUPITER WAS SUCCESSFUL, ALL HIGHEST!
TELL ME, SCIENTIST HANDUS, WHAT SORT OF PLACE IS THE GREAT PLANET?
A FABULOUS, WONDEROUS PLACE... GREAT GLITTERING CITIES... AND A MOST BENIGN RACE OF PEOPLES... TRULY, A BEAUTIFUL PLANET!
IT SEEMS IT WOULD BE A VALUABLE PRIZE TO INCLUDE IN MY DOMAIN OF SLAVE WORLDS!

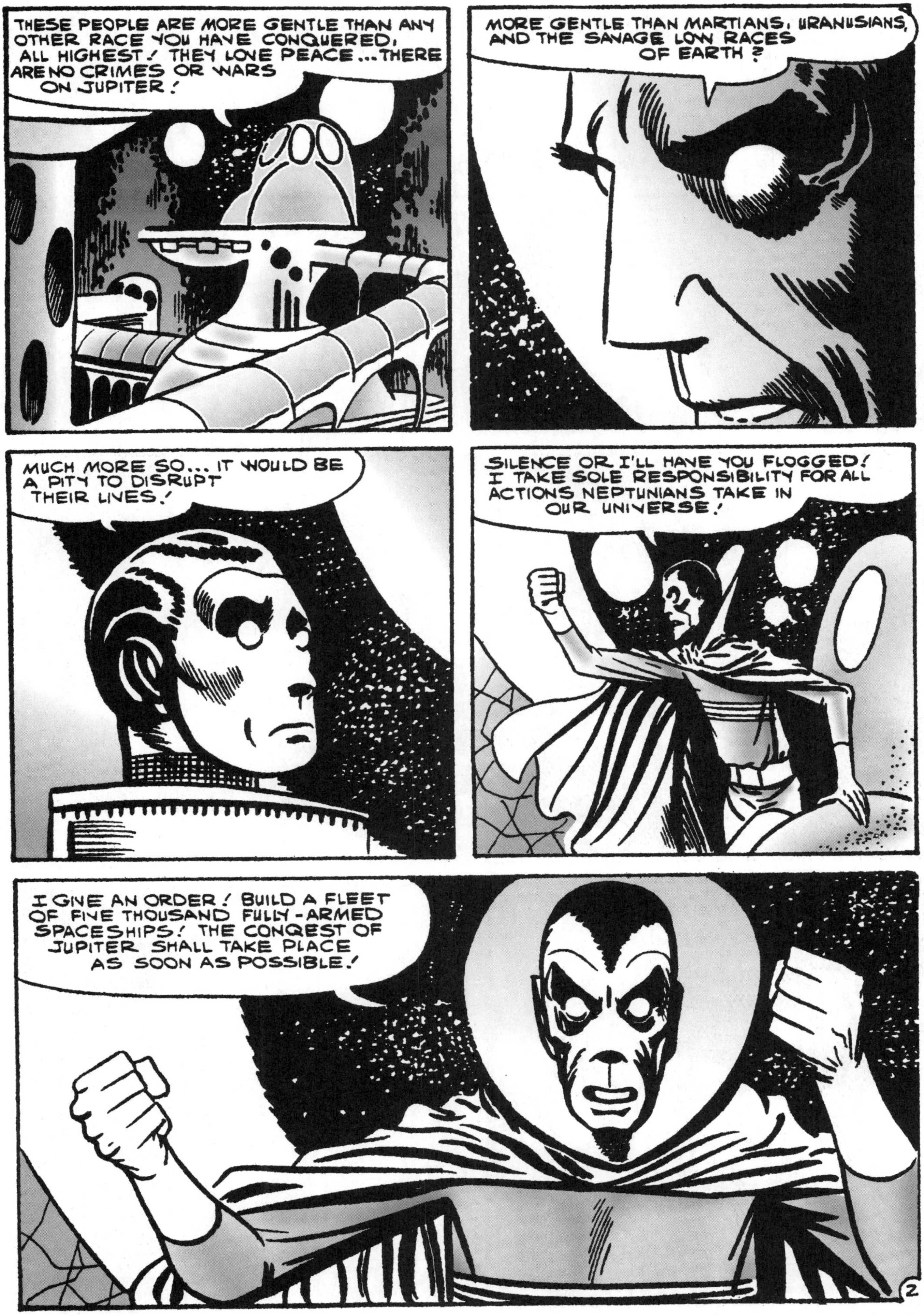
THESE PEOPLE ARE MORE GENTLE THAN ANY OTHER RACE YOU HAVE CONQUERED, ALL HIGHEST! THEY LOVE PEACE... THERE ARE NO CRIMES OR WARS ON JUPITER!
MORE GENTLE THAN MARTIANS, URANUSIANS, AND THE SAVAGE LOW RACES OF EARTH?
MUCH MORE SO... IT WOULD BE A PITY TO DISRUPT THEIR LIVES!
SILENCE OR I'LL HAVE YOU FLOGGED! I TAKE SOLE RESPONSIBILITY FOR ALL ACTIONS NEPTUNIANS TAKE IN OUR UNIVERSE!
I GIVE AN ORDER! BUILD A FLEET OF FIVE THOUSAND FULLY-ARMED SPACESHIPS! THE CONQEST OF JUPITER SHALL TAKE PLACE AS SOON AS POSSIBLE!
2

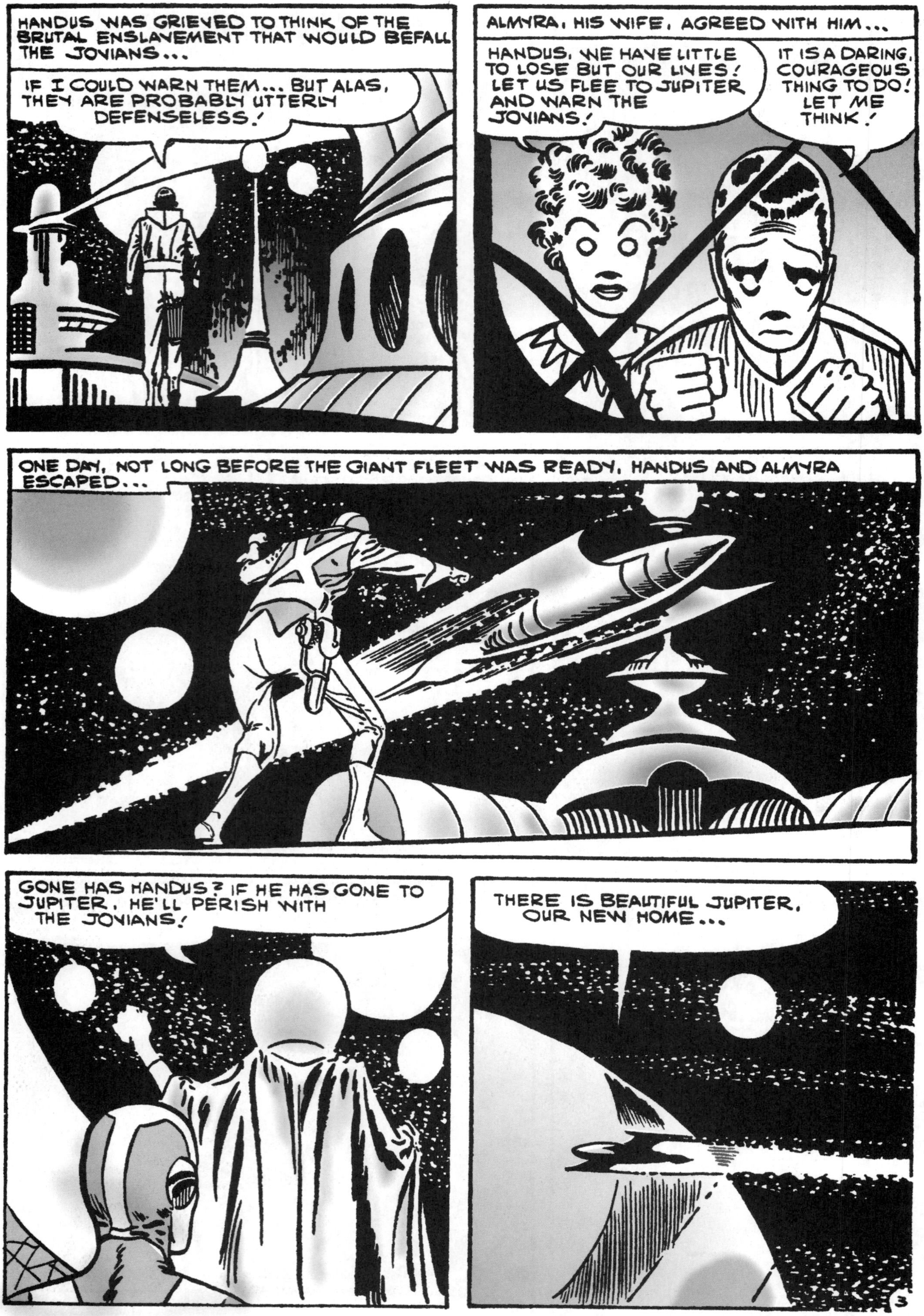
HANDUS WAS GRIEVED TO THINK OF THE BRUTAL ENSLAVEMENT THAT WOULD BEFALL THE JOVIANS...
IF I COULD WARN THEM... BUT ALAS, THEY ARE PROBABLY UTTERLY DEFENSELESS!
ALMYRA, HIS WIFE, AGREED WITH HIM...
HANDUS, WE HAVE LITTLE TO LOSE BUT OUR LIVES! LET US FLEE TO JUPITER AND WARN THE JOVIANS!
IT IS A DARING, COURAGEOUS THING TO DO! LET ME THINK!
ONE DAY, NOT LONG BEFORE THE GIANT FLEET WAS READY, HANDUS AND ALMYRA ESCAPED...
GONE HAS HANDUS? IF HE HAS GONE TO JUPITER, HE'LL PERISH WITH THE JOVIANS!
THERE IS BEAUTIFUL JUPITER, OUR NEW HOME...
3

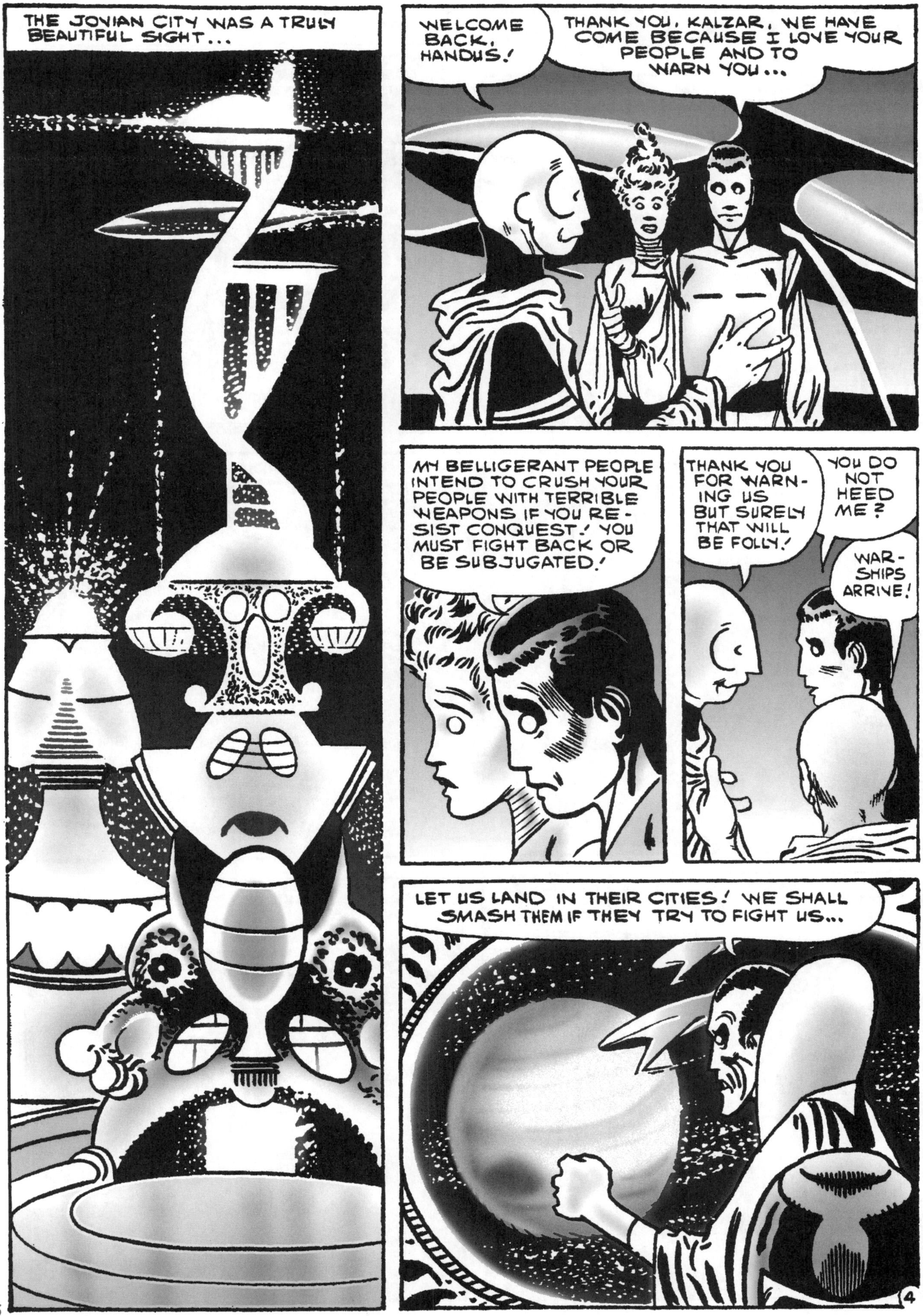
THE JOVIAN CITY WAS A TRULY BEAUTIFUL SIGHT...
WELCOME BACK, HANDUS!
THANK YOU, KALZAR, WE HAVE COME BECAUSE I LOVE YOUR PEOPLE AND TO WARN YOU...
MY BELLIGERANT PEOPLE INTEND TO CRUSH YOUR PEOPLE WITH TERRIBLE WEAPONS IF YOU RE-SIST CONQUEST! YOU MUST FIGHT BACK OR BE SUBJUGATED!
THANK YOU FOR WARN-ING US BUT SURELY THAT WILL BE FOLLY!
YOU DO NOT HEED ME?
WAR-SHIPS ARRIVE!
LET US LAND IN THEIR CITIES! WE SHALL SMASH THEM IF THEY TRY TO FIGHT US...
4

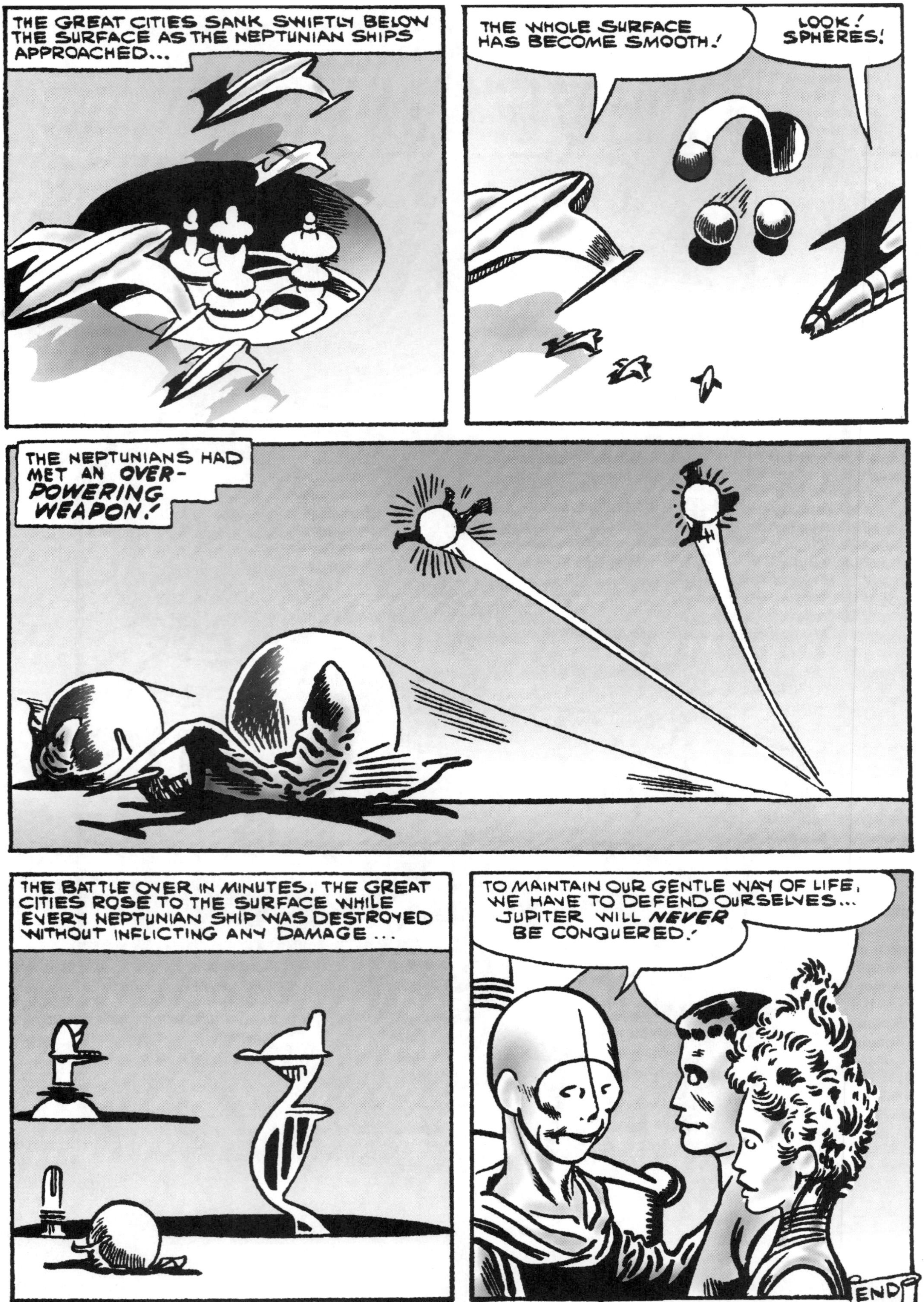
THE GREAT CITIES SANK SWIFTLY BELOW THE SURFACE AS THE NEPTUNIAN SHIPS APPROACHED...
THE WHOLE SURFACE HAS BECOME SMOOTH!
LOOK! SPHERES!
THE NEPTUNIANS HAD MET AN *OVER-POWERING WEAPON!*
THE BATTLE OVER IN *MINUTES*, THE GREAT CITIES ROSE TO THE SURFACE WHILE EVERY NEPTUNIAN SHIP WAS DESTROYED WITHOUT INFLICTING ANY DAMAGE ...
TO MAINTAIN OUR GENTLE WAY OF LIFE, WE HAVE TO DEFEND OURSELVES... JUPITER WILL ***NEVER*** BE CONQUERED!
END

STEVE DITKO SPACE WARS

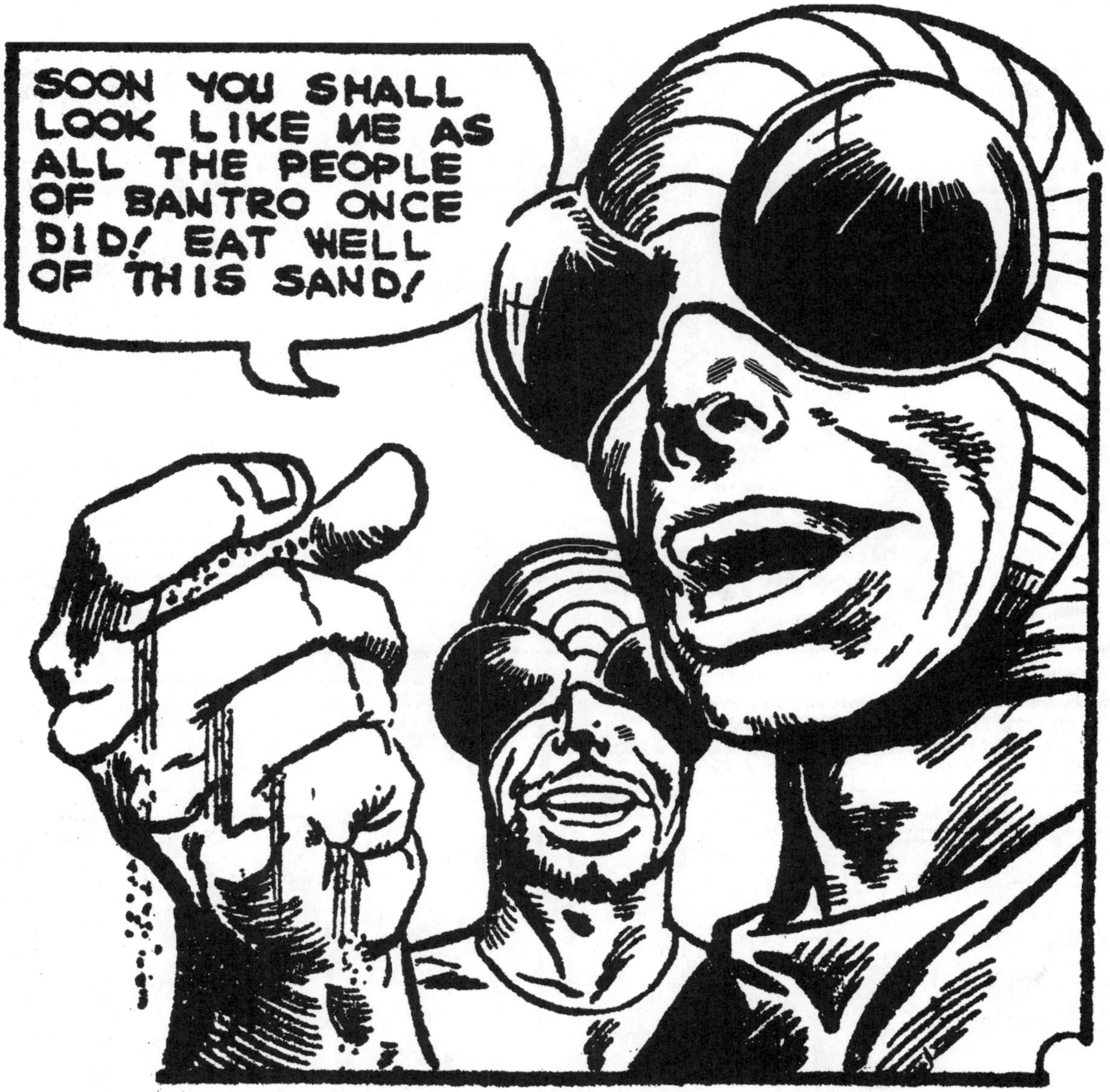
SOON YOU SHALL LOOK LIKE ME AS ALL THE PEOPLE OF BANTRO ONCE DID! EAT WELL OF THIS SAND!

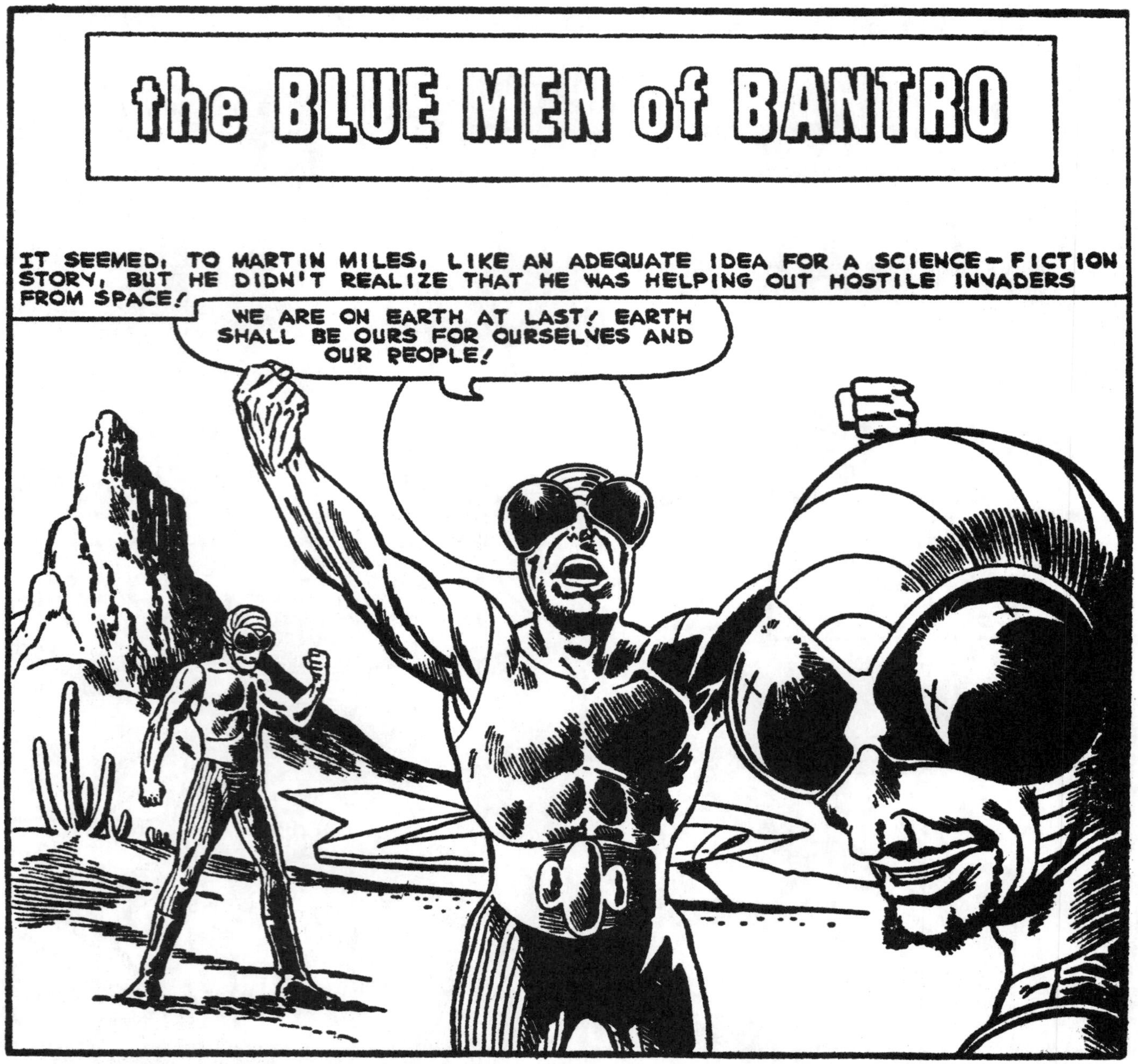
the BLUE MEN of BANTRO
IT SEEMED, TO MARTIN MILES, LIKE AN ADEQUATE IDEA FOR A SCIENCE-FICTION STORY, BUT HE DIDN'T REALIZE THAT HE WAS HELPING OUT HOSTILE INVADERS FROM SPACE!
WE ARE ON EARTH AT LAST! EARTH SHALL BE OURS FOR OURSELVES AND OUR PEOPLE!

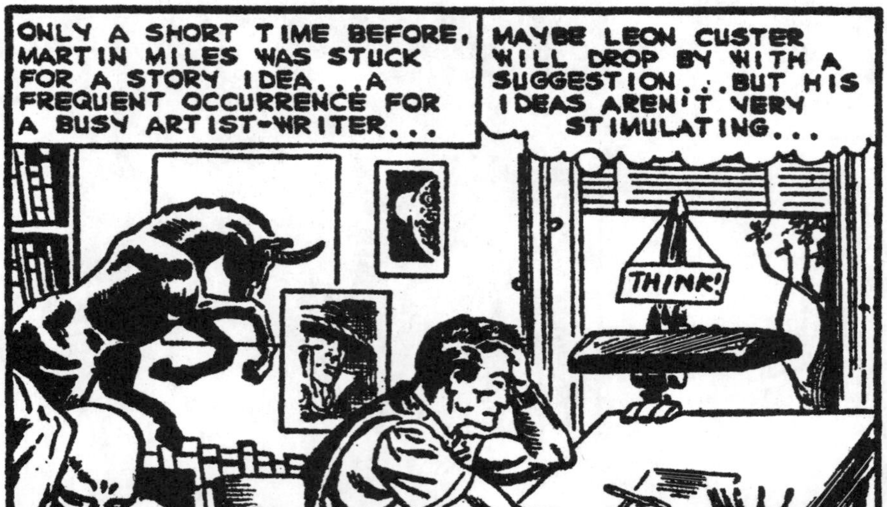
ONLY A SHORT TIME BEFORE, MARTIN MILES WAS STUCK FOR A STORY IDEA...A FREQUENT OCCURRENCE FOR A BUSY ARTIST-WRITER...
MAYBE LEON CUSTER WILL DROP BY WITH A SUGGESTION...BUT HIS IDEAS AREN'T VERY STIMULATING...
THINK!

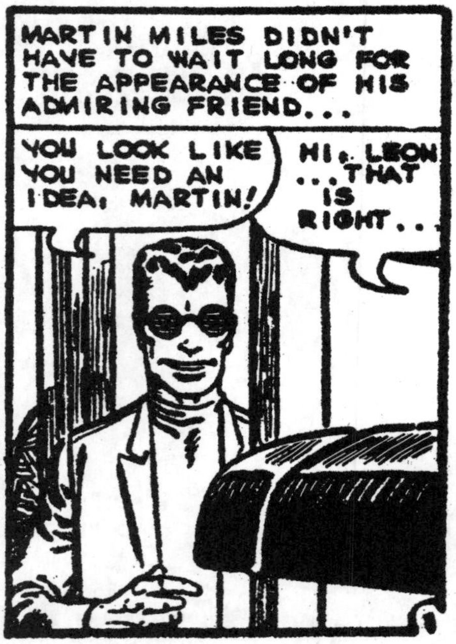
MARTIN MILES DIDN'T HAVE TO WAIT LONG FOR THE APPEARANCE OF HIS ADMIRING FRIEND...
YOU LOOK LIKE YOU NEED AN IDEA, MARTIN!
HI, LEON ...THAT IS RIGHT...

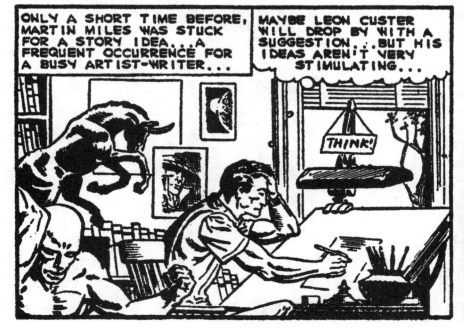

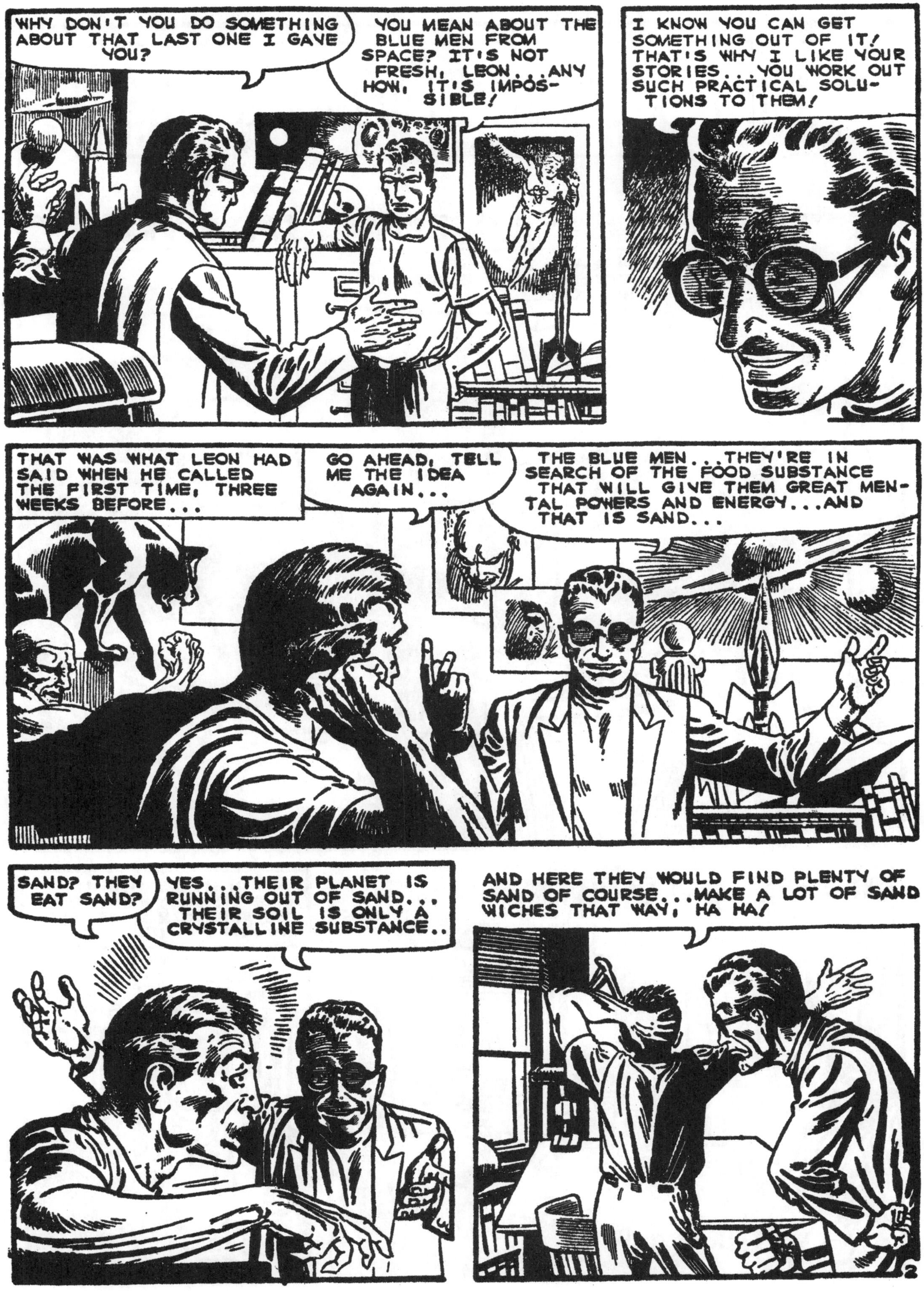
WHY DON'T YOU DO SOMETHING ABOUT THAT LAST ONE I GAVE YOU?
YOU MEAN ABOUT THE BLUE MEN FROM SPACE? IT'S NOT FRESH, LEON... ANY HOW, IT'S IMPOSSIBLE!
I KNOW YOU CAN GET SOMETHING OUT OF IT! THAT'S WHY I LIKE YOUR STORIES... YOU WORK OUT SUCH PRACTICAL SOLUTIONS TO THEM!
THAT WAS WHAT LEON HAD SAID WHEN HE CALLED THE FIRST TIME, THREE WEEKS BEFORE...
GO AHEAD, TELL ME THE IDEA AGAIN...
THE BLUE MEN... THEY'RE IN SEARCH OF THE FOOD SUBSTANCE THAT WILL GIVE THEM GREAT MENTAL POWERS AND ENERGY... AND THAT IS SAND...
SAND? THEY EAT SAND?
YES... THEIR PLANET IS RUNNING OUT OF SAND... THEIR SOIL IS ONLY A CRYSTALLINE SUBSTANCE..
AND HERE THEY WOULD FIND PLENTY OF SAND OF COURSE... MAKE A LOT OF SAND WICHES THAT WAY, HA HA!
2

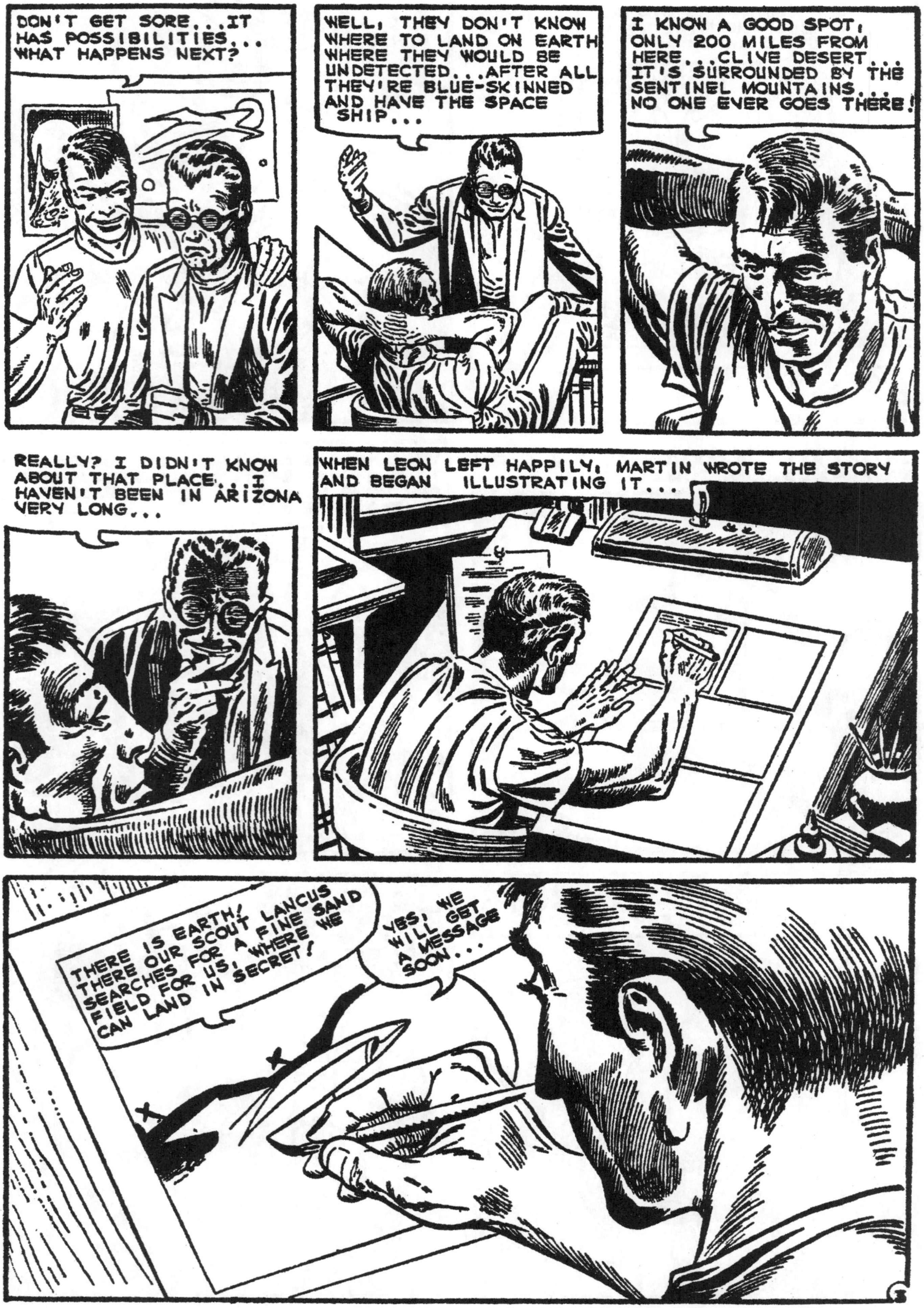
DON'T GET SORE...IT HAS POSSIBILITIES... WHAT HAPPENS NEXT?
WELL, THEY DON'T KNOW WHERE TO LAND ON EARTH WHERE THEY WOULD BE UNDETECTED...AFTER ALL THEY'RE BLUE-SKINNED AND HAVE THE SPACE SHIP...
I KNOW A GOOD SPOT, ONLY 200 MILES FROM HERE...CLIVE DESERT... IT'S SURROUNDED BY THE SENTINEL MOUNTAINS... NO ONE EVER GOES THERE!
REALLY? I DIDN'T KNOW ABOUT THAT PLACE... I HAVEN'T BEEN IN ARIZONA VERY LONG...
WHEN LEON LEFT HAPPILY, MARTIN WROTE THE STORY AND BEGAN ILLUSTRATING IT...
THERE IS EARTH! THERE OUR SCOUT LANCUS SEARCHES FOR A FINE SAND FIELD FOR US, WHERE WE CAN LAND IN SECRET!
YES, WE WILL GET A MESSAGE SOON...

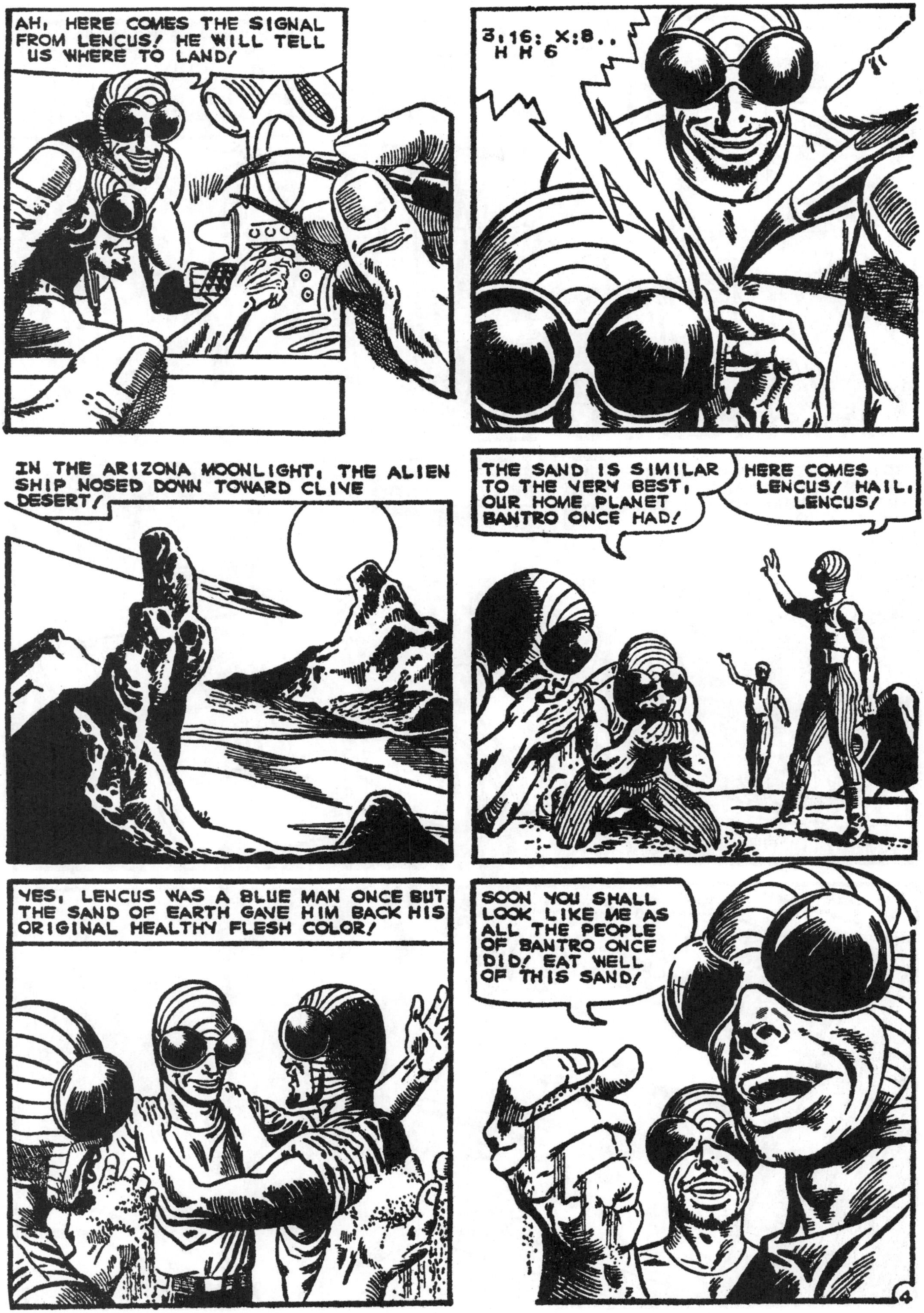
AH, HERE COMES THE SIGNAL FROM LENCUS! HE WILL TELL US WHERE TO LAND!
3,16: X:8.. H H 6
IN THE ARIZONA MOONLIGHT, THE ALIEN SHIP NOSED DOWN TOWARD CLIVE DESERT!
THE SAND IS SIMILAR TO THE VERY BEST, OUR HOME PLANET BANTRO ONCE HAD!
HERE COMES LENCUS! HAIL, LENCUS!
YES, LENCUS WAS A BLUE MAN ONCE BUT THE SAND OF EARTH GAVE HIM BACK HIS ORIGINAL HEALTHY FLESH COLOR!
SOON YOU SHALL LOOK LIKE ME AS ALL THE PEOPLE OF BANTRO ONCE DID! EAT WELL OF THIS SAND!
4

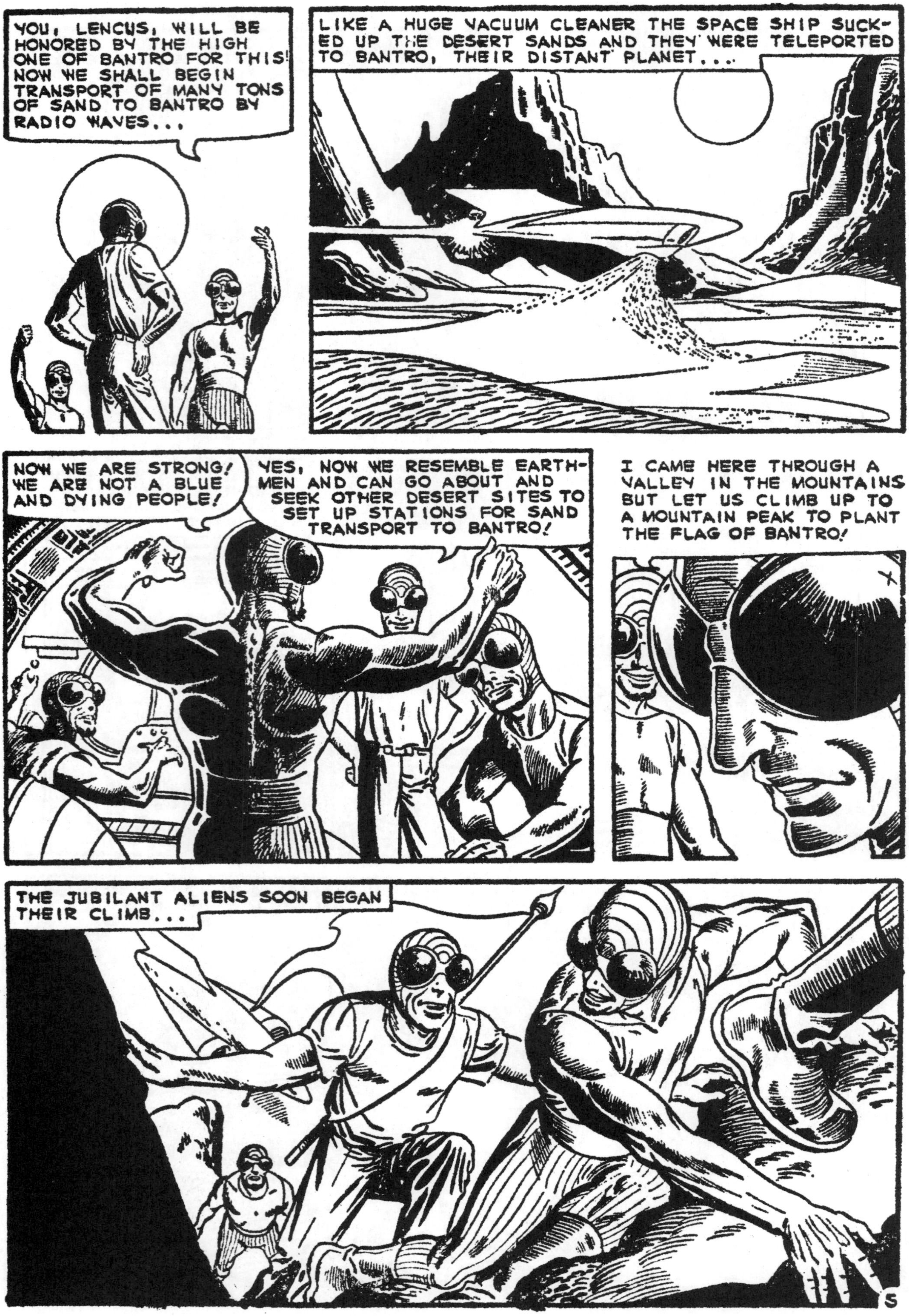
YOU, LENCUS, WILL BE HONORED BY THE HIGH ONE OF BANTRO FOR THIS! NOW WE SHALL BEGIN TRANSPORT OF MANY TONS OF SAND TO BANTRO BY RADIO WAVES...
LIKE A HUGE VACUUM CLEANER THE SPACE SHIP SUCKED UP THE DESERT SANDS AND THEY WERE TELEPORTED TO BANTRO, THEIR DISTANT PLANET...
NOW WE ARE STRONG! WE ARE NOT A BLUE AND DYING PEOPLE!
YES, NOW WE RESEMBLE EARTHMEN AND CAN GO ABOUT AND SEEK OTHER DESERT SITES TO SET UP STATIONS FOR SAND TRANSPORT TO BANTRO!
I CAME HERE THROUGH A VALLEY IN THE MOUNTAINS BUT LET US CLIMB UP TO A MOUNTAIN PEAK TO PLANT THE FLAG OF BANTRO!
THE JUBILANT ALIENS SOON BEGAN THEIR CLIMB...
5

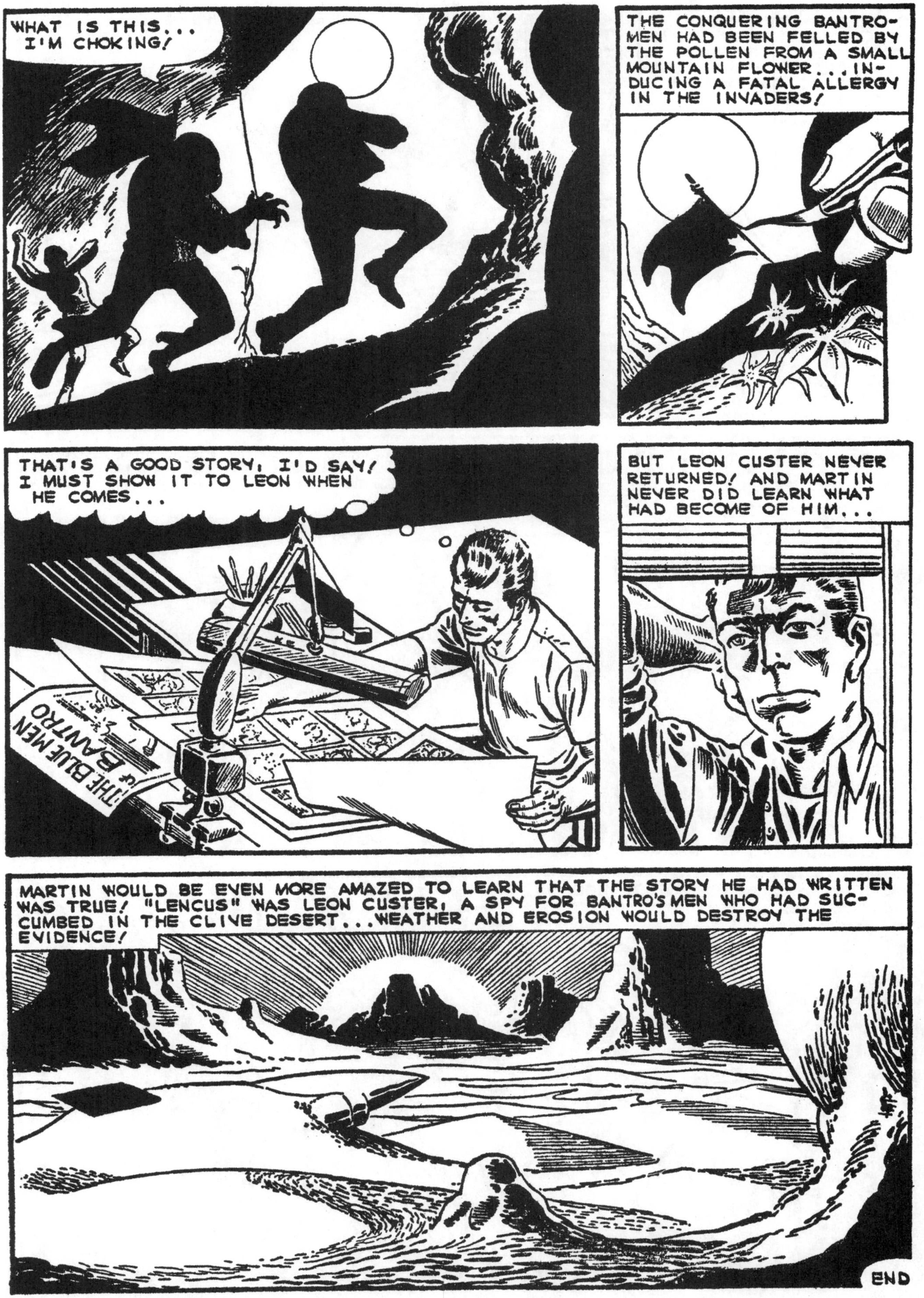
WHAT IS THIS... I'M CHOKING!
THE CONQUERING BANTRO-MEN HAD BEEN FELLED BY THE POLLEN FROM A SMALL MOUNTAIN FLOWER...INDUCING A FATAL ALLERGY IN THE INVADERS!
THAT'S A GOOD STORY, I'D SAY! I MUST SHOW IT TO LEON WHEN HE COMES...
THE BLUE MEN of BANTRO
BUT LEON CUSTER NEVER RETURNED! AND MARTIN NEVER DID LEARN WHAT HAD BECOME OF HIM...
MARTIN WOULD BE EVEN MORE AMAZED TO LEARN THAT THE STORY HE HAD WRITTEN WAS TRUE! "LENCUS" WAS LEON CUSTER, A SPY FOR BANTRO'S MEN WHO HAD SUCCUMBED IN THE CLIVE DESERT...WEATHER AND EROSION WOULD DESTROY THE EVIDENCE!
END

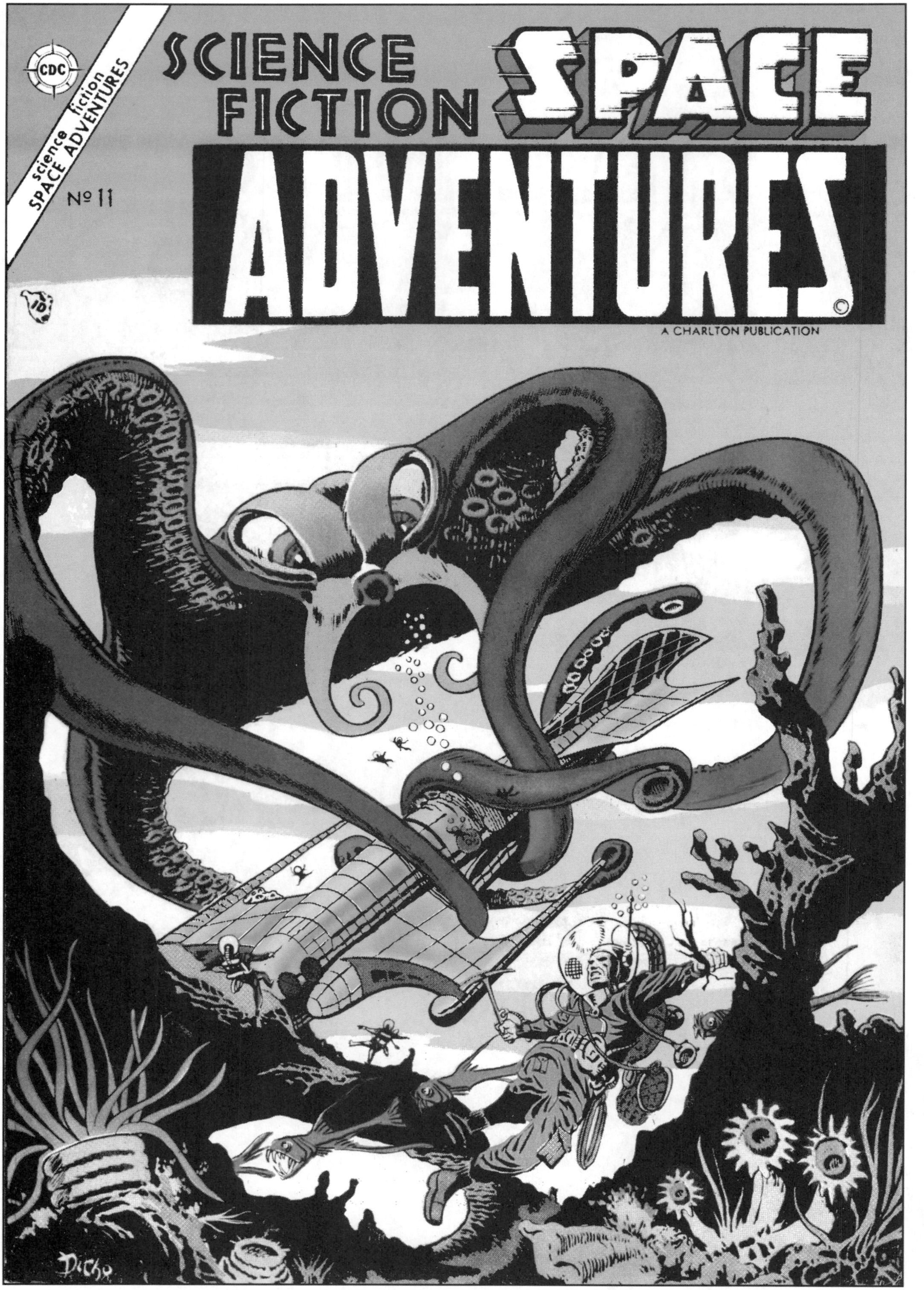
science fiction SPACE ADVENTURES
CDC
Nº 11
SCIENCE FICTION
SPACE
ADVENTURES ©
A CHARLTON PUBLICATION

STEVE DITKO SPACE WARS

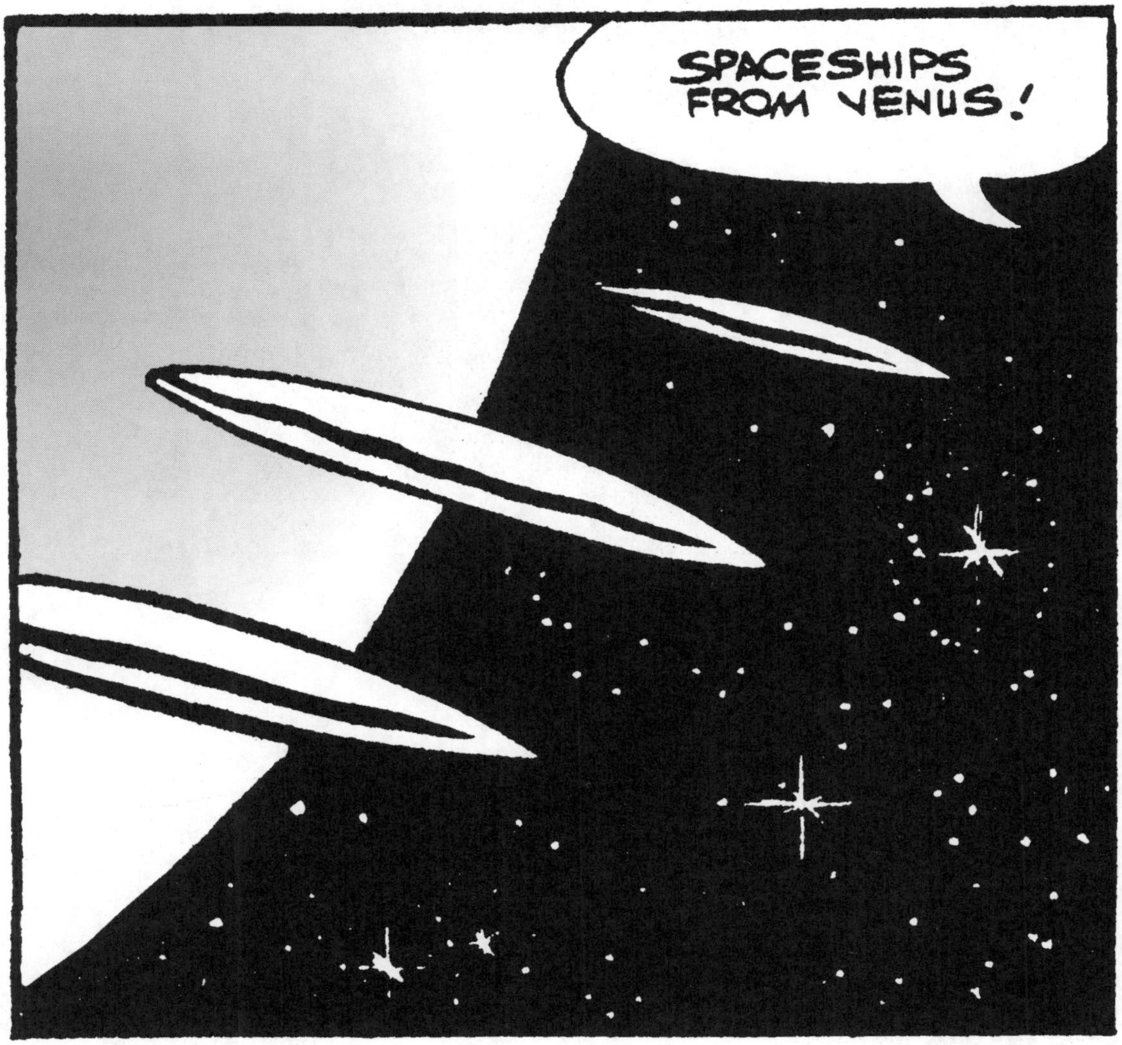
SPACESHIPS FROM VENUS!

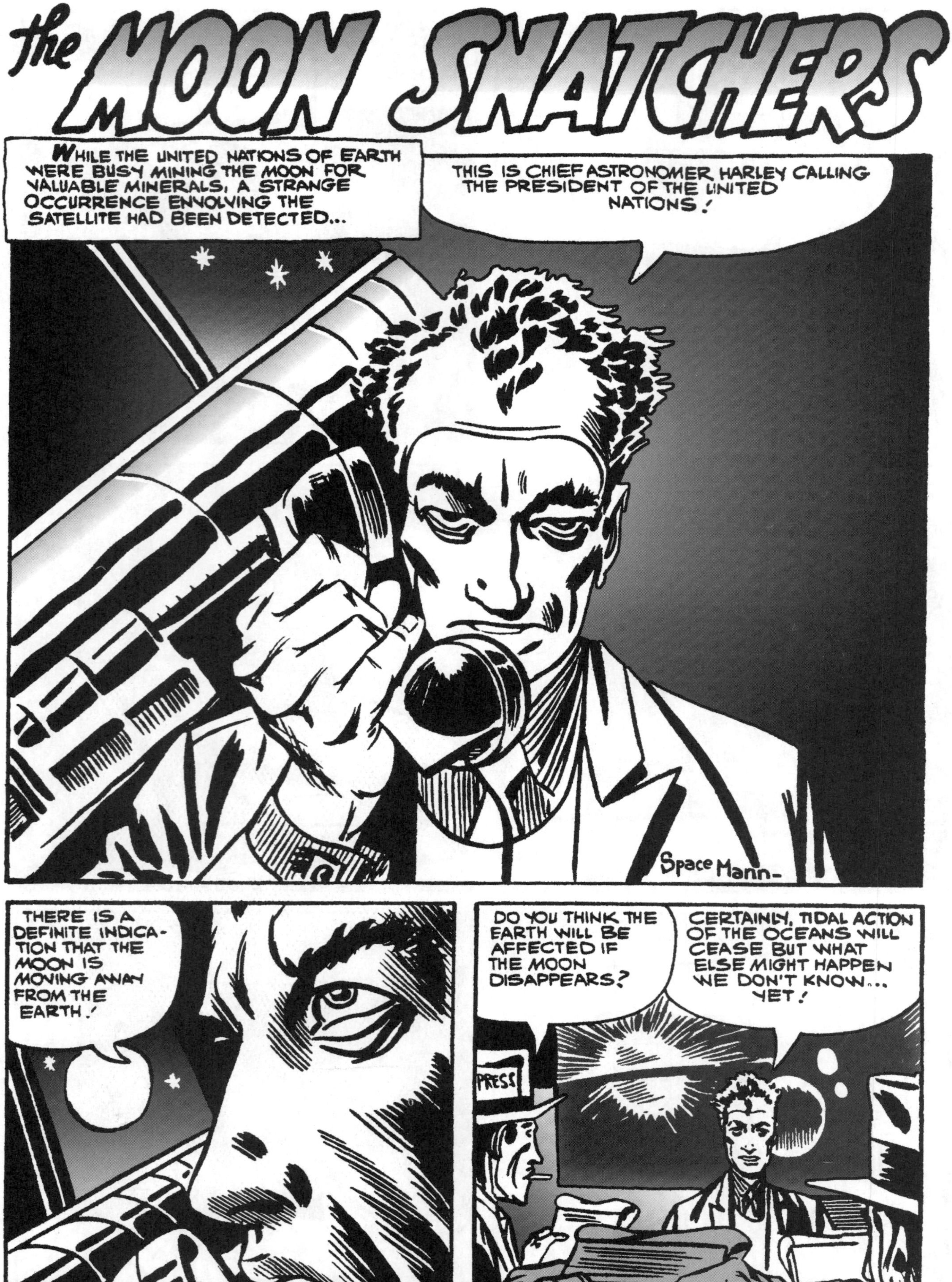
the MOON SNATCHERS
WHILE THE UNITED NATIONS OF EARTH WERE BUSY MINING THE MOON FOR VALUABLE MINERALS, A STRANGE OCCURRENCE ENVOLVING THE SATELLITE HAD BEEN DETECTED...
THIS IS CHIEF ASTRONOMER HARLEY CALLING THE PRESIDENT OF THE UNITED NATIONS!
Space Mann
THERE IS A DEFINITE INDICATION THAT THE MOON IS MOVING AWAY FROM THE EARTH!
DO YOU THINK THE EARTH WILL BE AFFECTED IF THE MOON DISAPPEARS?
CERTAINLY, TIDAL ACTION OF THE OCEANS WILL CEASE BUT WHAT ELSE MIGHT HAPPEN WE DON'T KNOW... YET!
PRESS
1

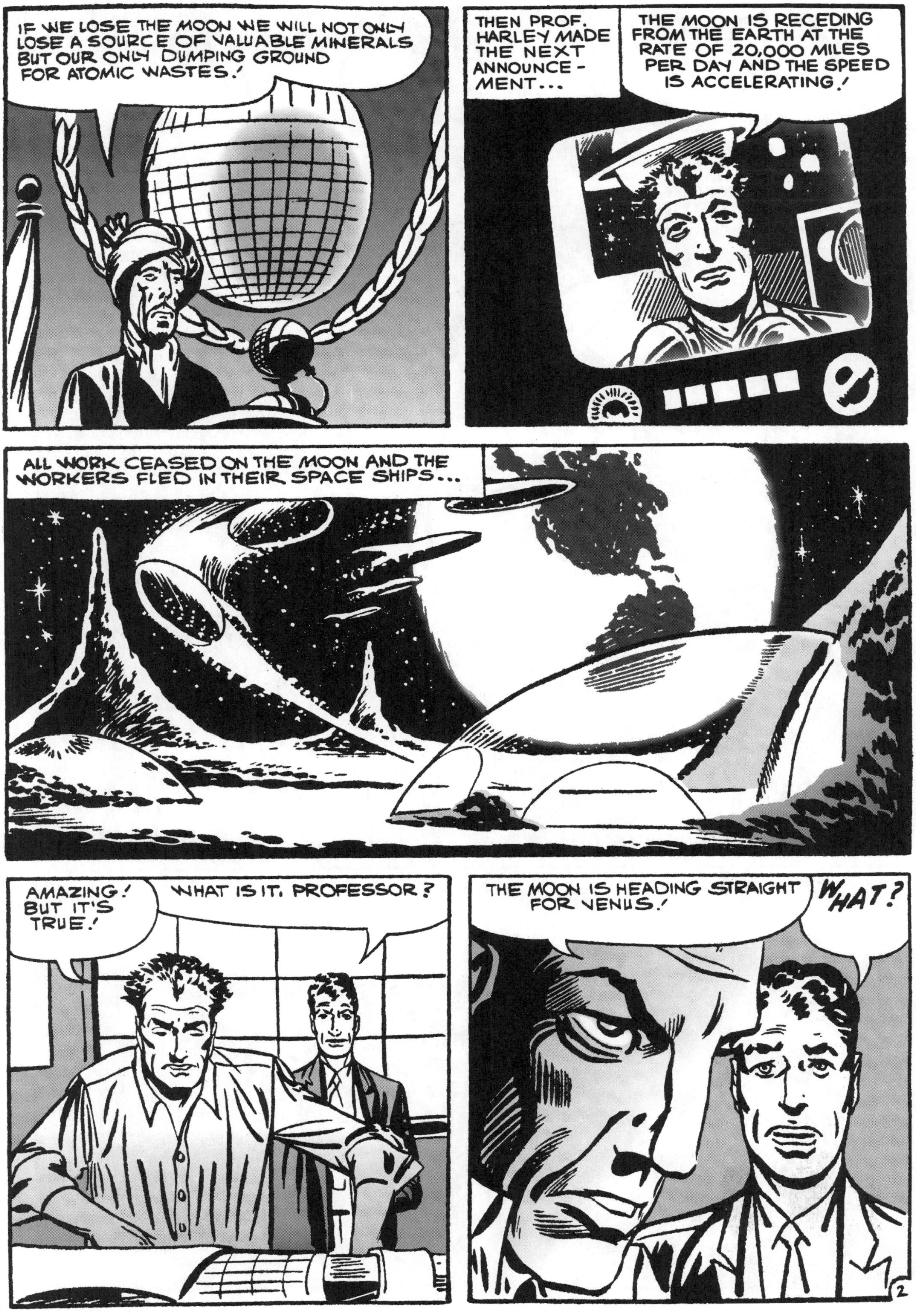
IF WE LOSE THE MOON WE WILL NOT ONLY LOSE A SOURCE OF VALUABLE MINERALS BUT OUR ONLY DUMPING GROUND FOR ATOMIC WASTES!
THEN PROF. HARLEY MADE THE NEXT ANNOUNCE-MENT...
THE MOON IS RECEDING FROM THE EARTH AT THE RATE OF 20,000 MILES PER DAY AND THE SPEED IS ACCELERATING!
ALL WORK CEASED ON THE MOON AND THE WORKERS FLED IN THEIR SPACE SHIPS...
AMAZING! BUT IT'S TRUE!
WHAT IS IT, PROFESSOR?
THE MOON IS HEADING STRAIGHT FOR VENUS!
WHAT?
2

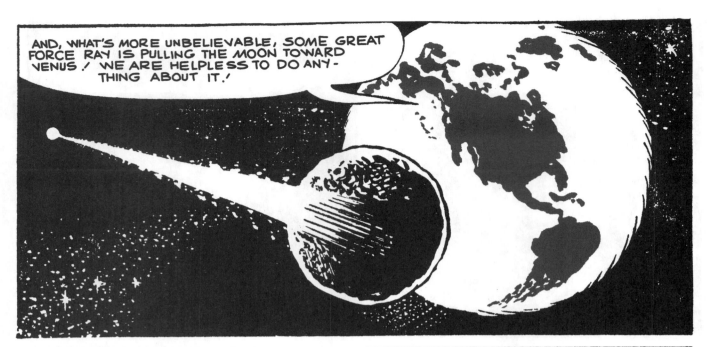

AND, WHAT'S MORE UNBELIEVABLE, SOME GREAT FORCE RAY IS PULLING THE MOON TOWARD VENUS! WE ARE HELPLESS TO DO ANY-THING ABOUT IT!

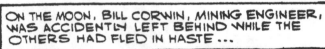

ON THE MOON, BILL CORWIN, MINING ENGINEER, WAS ACCIDENTLY LEFT BEHIND WHILE THE OTHERS HAD FLED IN HASTE...

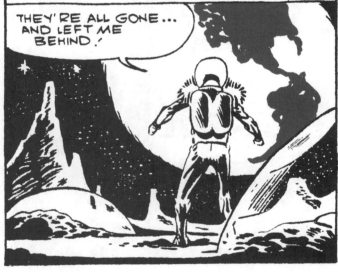

THEY'RE ALL GONE... AND LEFT ME BEHIND!

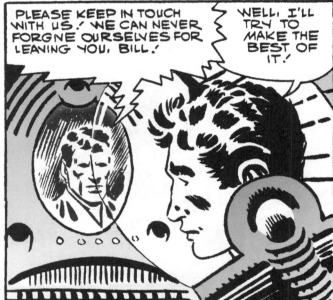

PLEASE KEEP IN TOUCH WITH US! WE CAN NEVER FORGIVE OURSELVES FOR LEAVING YOU, BILL!

WELL, I'LL TRY TO MAKE THE BEST OF IT!

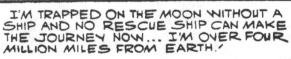

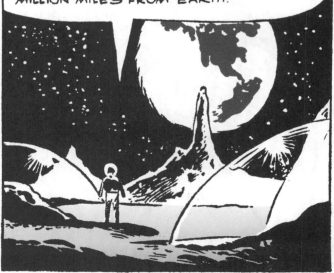

I'M TRAPPED ON THE MOON WITHOUT A SHIP AND NO RESCUE SHIP CAN MAKE THE JOURNEY NOW... I'M OVER FOUR MILLION MILES FROM EARTH!

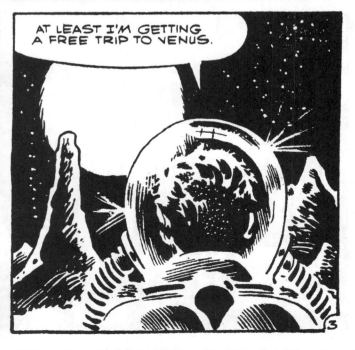

AT LEAST I'M GETTING A FREE TRIP TO VENUS.

3

49

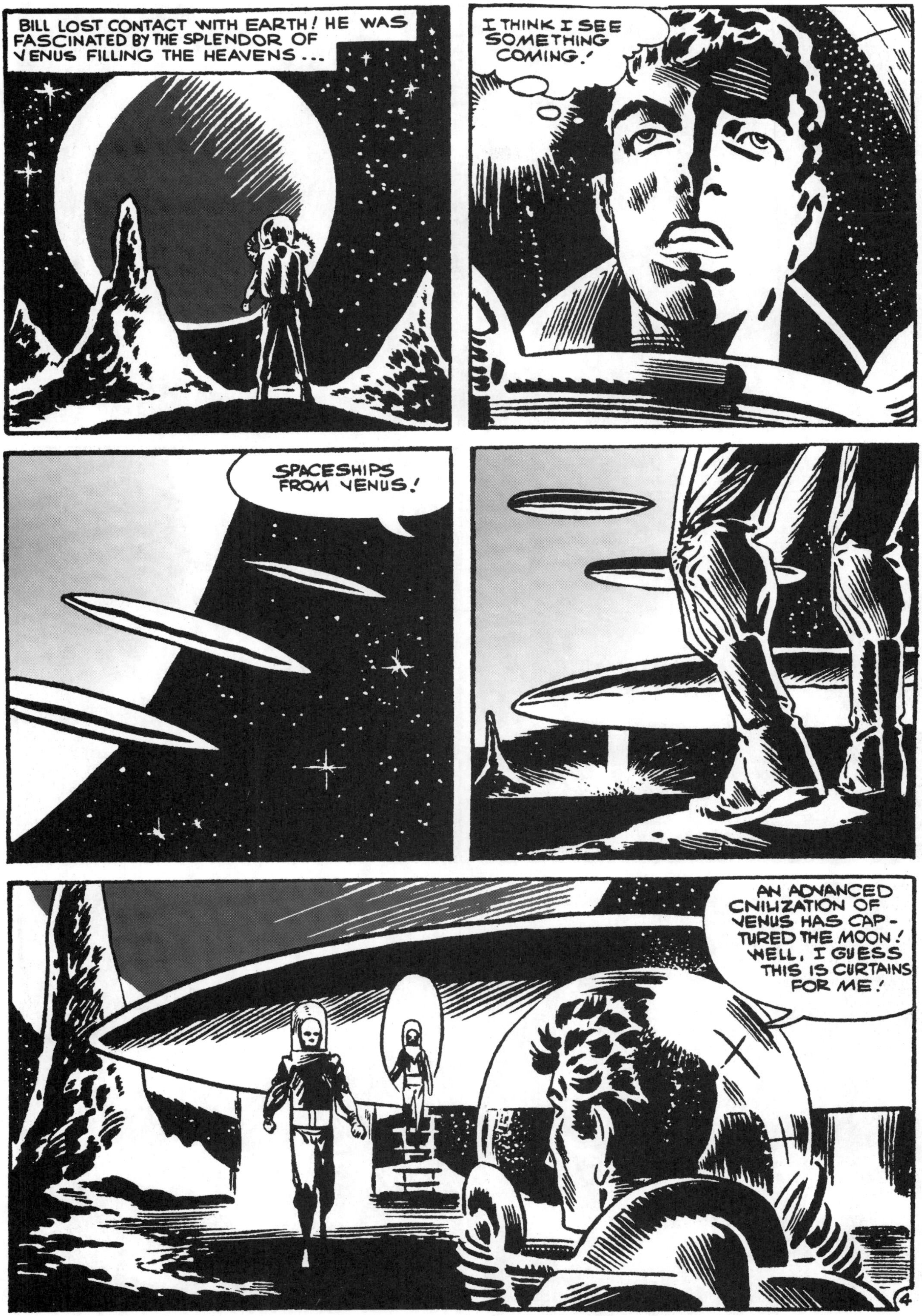
BILL LOST CONTACT WITH EARTH! HE WAS FASCINATED BY THE SPLENDOR OF VENUS FILLING THE HEAVENS...
I THINK I SEE SOMETHING COMING!
SPACESHIPS FROM VENUS!
AN ADVANCED CIVILIZATION OF VENUS HAS CAPTURED THE MOON! WELL, I GUESS THIS IS CURTAINS FOR ME!
4

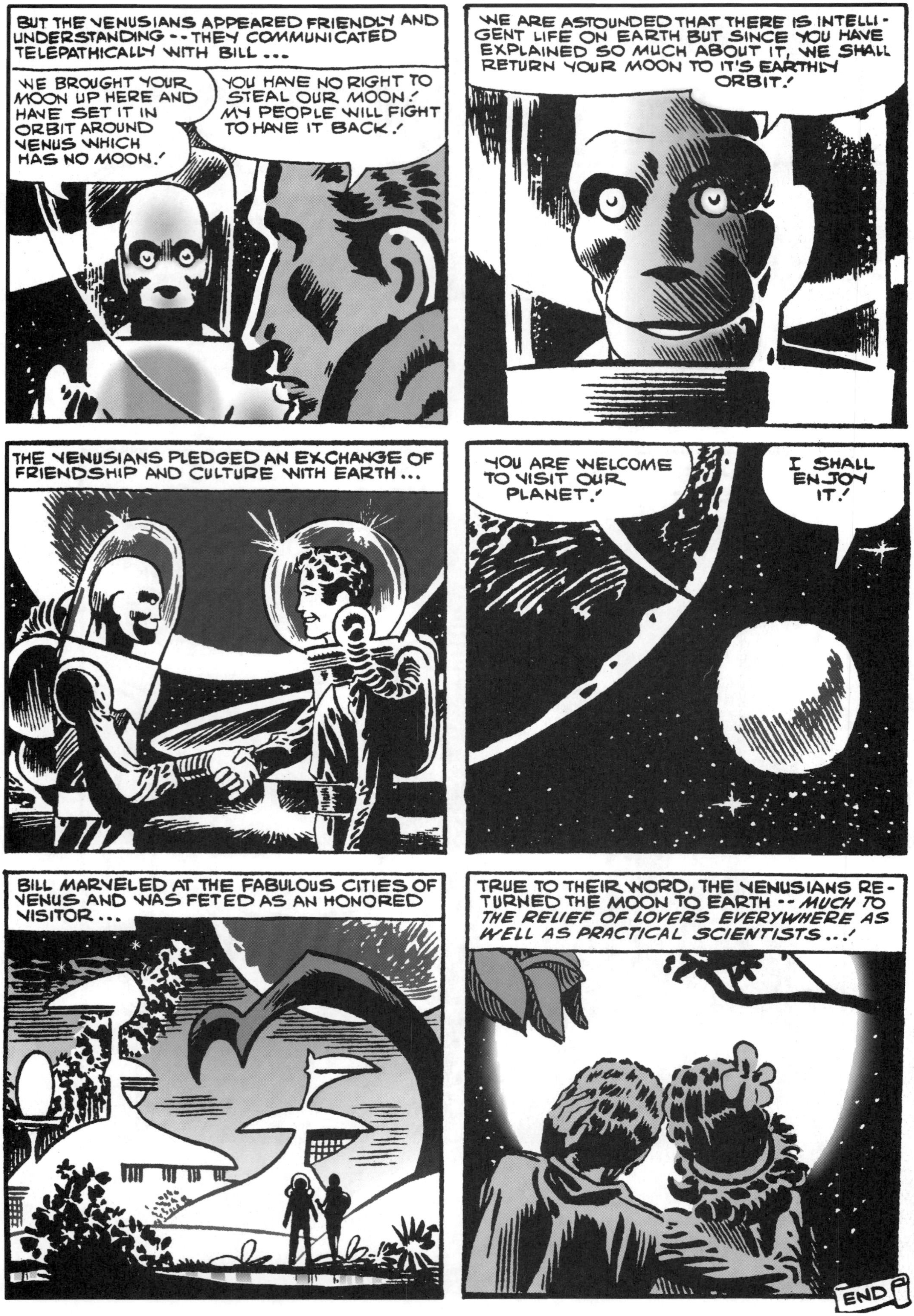
BUT THE VENUSIANS APPEARED FRIENDLY AND UNDERSTANDING -- THEY COMMUNICATED TELEPATHICALLY WITH BILL ...
WE BROUGHT YOUR MOON UP HERE AND HAVE SET IT IN ORBIT AROUND VENUS WHICH HAS NO MOON!
YOU HAVE NO RIGHT TO STEAL OUR MOON! MY PEOPLE WILL FIGHT TO HAVE IT BACK!
WE ARE ASTOUNDED THAT THERE IS INTELLIGENT LIFE ON EARTH BUT SINCE YOU HAVE EXPLAINED SO MUCH ABOUT IT, WE SHALL RETURN YOUR MOON TO IT'S EARTHLY ORBIT!
THE VENUSIANS PLEDGED AN EXCHANGE OF FRIENDSHIP AND CULTURE WITH EARTH ...
YOU ARE WELCOME TO VISIT OUR PLANET!
I SHALL ENJOY IT!
BILL MARVELED AT THE FABULOUS CITIES OF VENUS AND WAS FETED AS AN HONORED VISITOR ...
TRUE TO THEIR WORD, THE VENUSIANS RETURNED THE MOON TO EARTH -- *MUCH TO THE RELIEF OF LOVERS EVERYWHERE AS WELL AS PRACTICAL SCIENTISTS ...!*
END

STEVE DITKO SPACE WARS

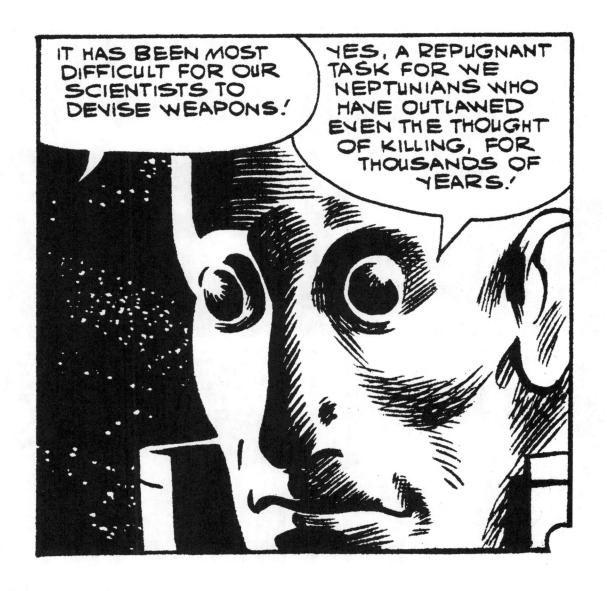

IT HAS BEEN MOST DIFFICULT FOR OUR SCIENTISTS TO DEVISE WEAPONS!

YES, A REPUGNANT TASK FOR WE NEPTUNIANS WHO HAVE OUTLAWED EVEN THE THOUGHT OF KILLING, FOR THOUSANDS OF YEARS!

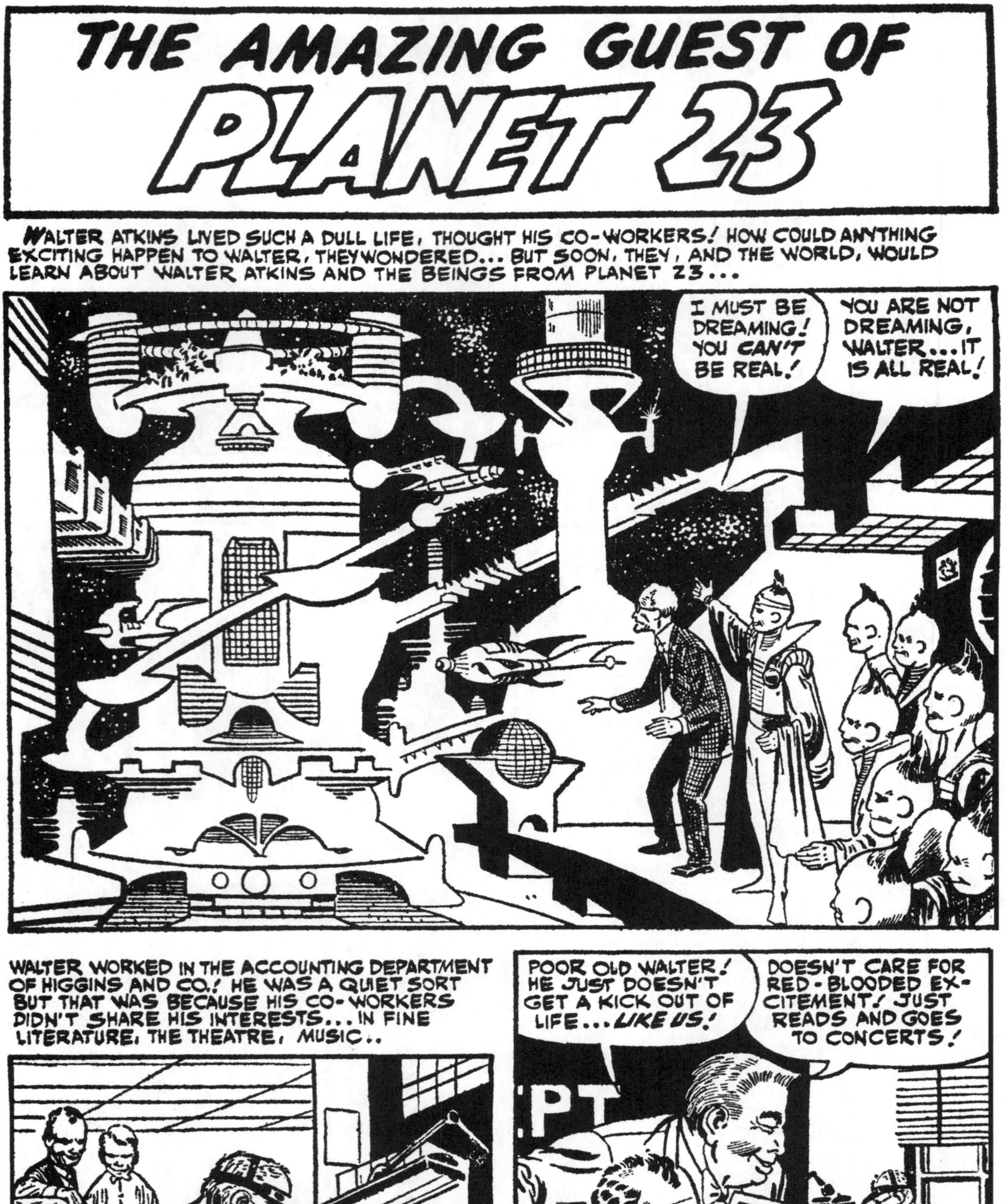
THE AMAZING GUEST OF PLANET 23
WALTER ATKINS LIVED SUCH A DULL LIFE, THOUGHT HIS CO-WORKERS! HOW COULD ANYTHING EXCITING HAPPEN TO WALTER, THEY WONDERED... BUT SOON, THEY, AND THE WORLD, WOULD LEARN ABOUT WALTER ATKINS AND THE BEINGS FROM PLANET 23...
I MUST BE DREAMING! YOU CAN'T BE REAL!
YOU ARE NOT DREAMING, WALTER... IT IS ALL REAL!
WALTER WORKED IN THE ACCOUNTING DEPARTMENT OF HIGGINS AND CO.! HE WAS A QUIET SORT BUT THAT WAS BECAUSE HIS CO-WORKERS DIDN'T SHARE HIS INTERESTS... IN FINE LITERATURE, THE THEATRE, MUSIC..
POOR OLD WALTER! HE JUST DOESN'T GET A KICK OUT OF LIFE... LIKE US!
DOESN'T CARE FOR RED-BLOODED EXCITEMENT! JUST READS AND GOES TO CONCERTS!
PT
RACING
SPORT SECTION

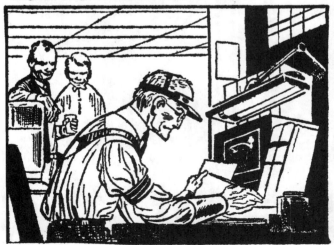

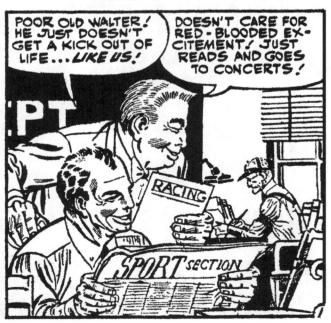

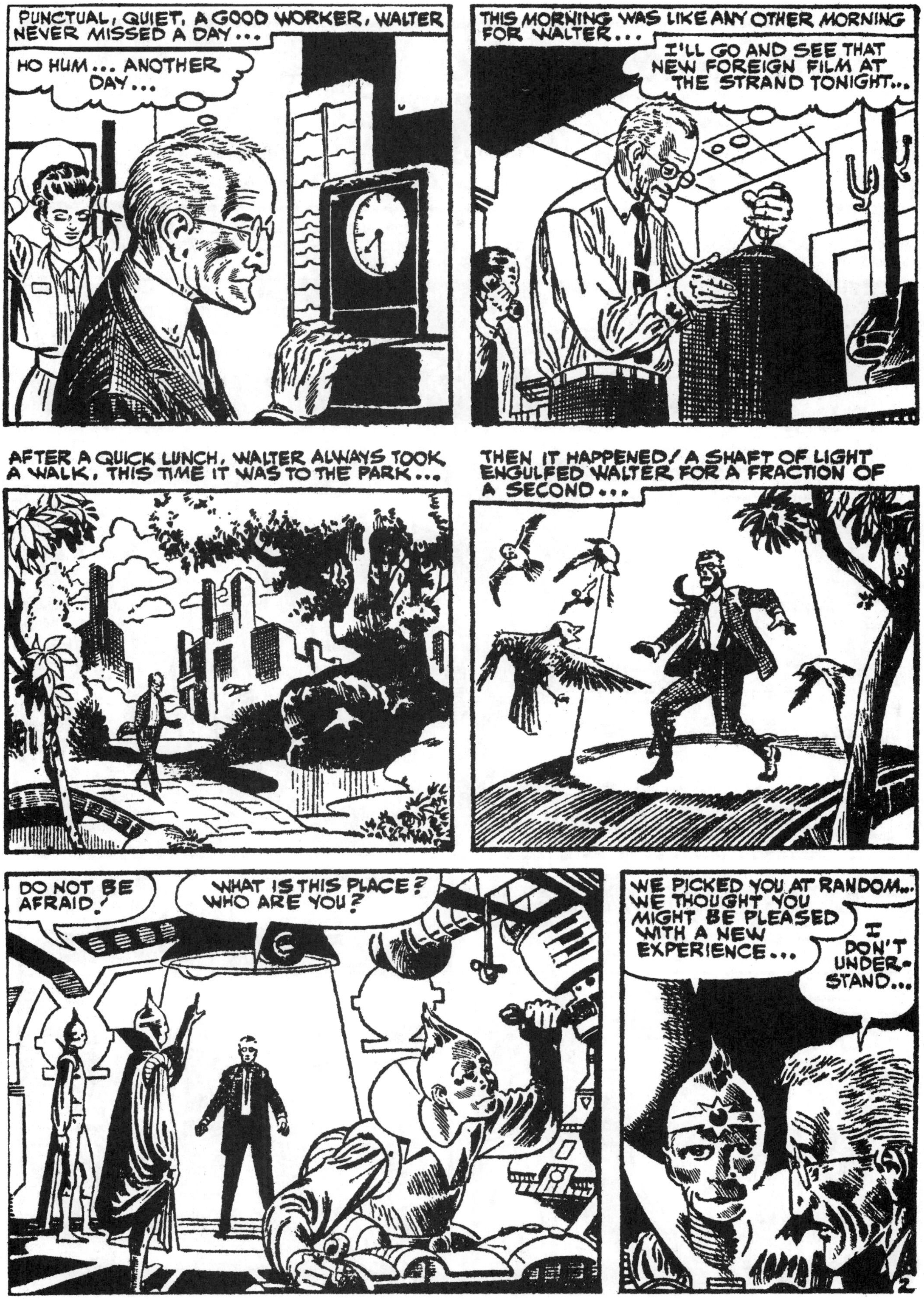
PUNCTUAL, QUIET, A GOOD WORKER, WALTER NEVER MISSED A DAY...
HO HUM... ANOTHER DAY...
THIS MORNING WAS LIKE ANY OTHER MORNING FOR WALTER...
I'LL GO AND SEE THAT NEW FOREIGN FILM AT THE STRAND TONIGHT...
AFTER A QUICK LUNCH, WALTER ALWAYS TOOK A WALK. THIS TIME IT WAS TO THE PARK...
THEN IT HAPPENED! A SHAFT OF LIGHT ENGULFED WALTER FOR A FRACTION OF A SECOND...
DO NOT BE AFRAID!
WHAT IS THIS PLACE? WHO ARE YOU?
WE PICKED YOU AT RANDOM... WE THOUGHT YOU MIGHT BE PLEASED WITH A NEW EXPERIENCE...
I DON'T UNDER-STAND...

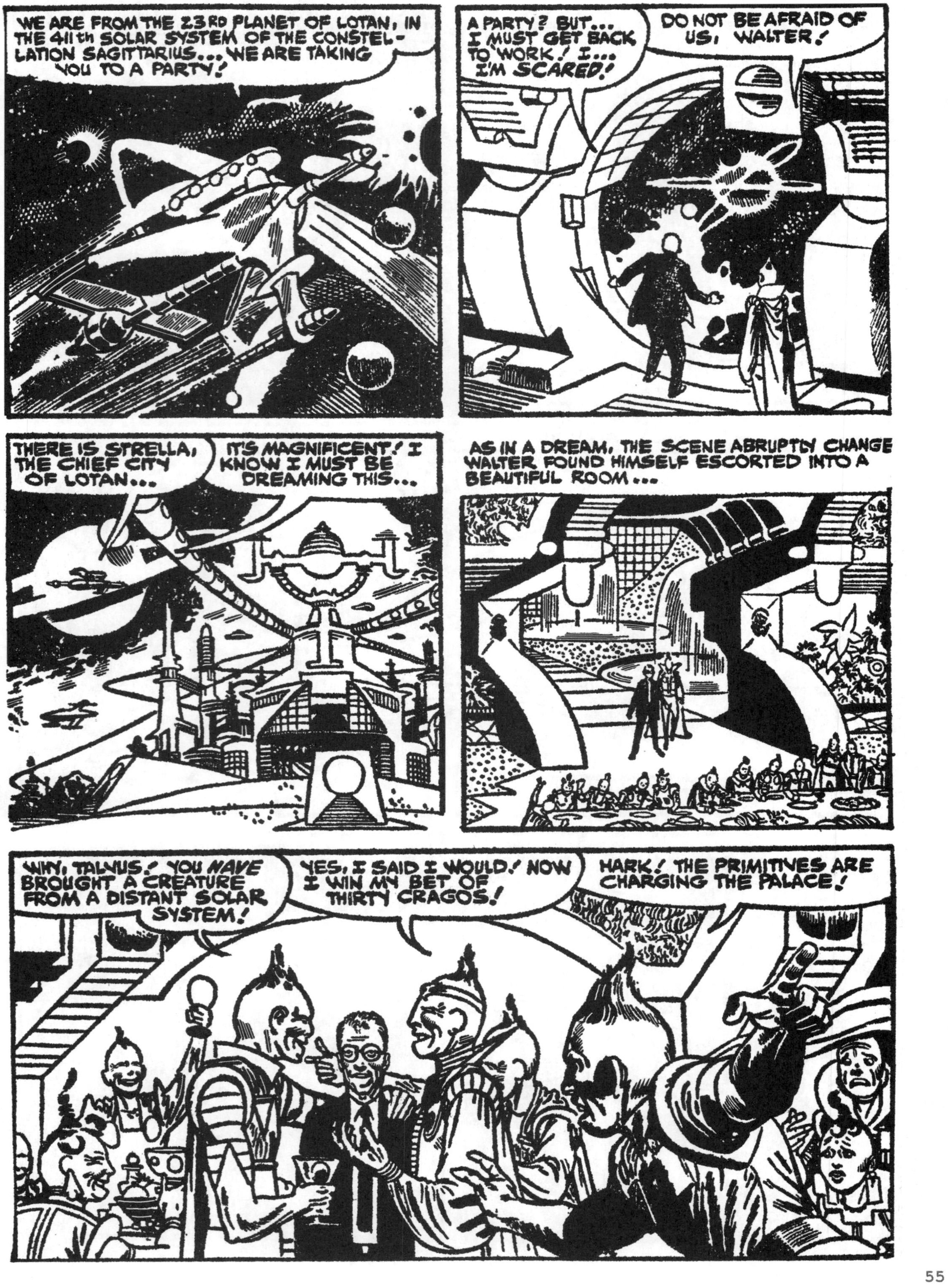
WE ARE FROM THE 23RD PLANET OF LOTAN, IN THE 411th SOLAR SYSTEM OF THE CONSTEL-LATION SAGITTARIUS..., WE ARE TAKING YOU TO A PARTY!
A PARTY? BUT... I MUST GET BACK TO WORK! I... I'M SCARED!
DO NOT BE AFRAID OF US, WALTER!
THERE IS STRELLA, THE CHIEF CITY OF LOTAN...
IT'S MAGNIFICENT! I KNOW I MUST BE DREAMING THIS...
AS IN A DREAM, THE SCENE ABRUPTLY CHANGE WALTER FOUND HIMSELF ESCORTED INTO A BEAUTIFUL ROOM...
WHY, TALNUS! YOU HAVE BROUGHT A CREATURE FROM A DISTANT SOLAR SYSTEM!
YES, I SAID I WOULD! NOW I WIN MY BET OF THIRTY CRAGOS!
HARK! THE PRIMITIVES ARE CHARGING THE PALACE!

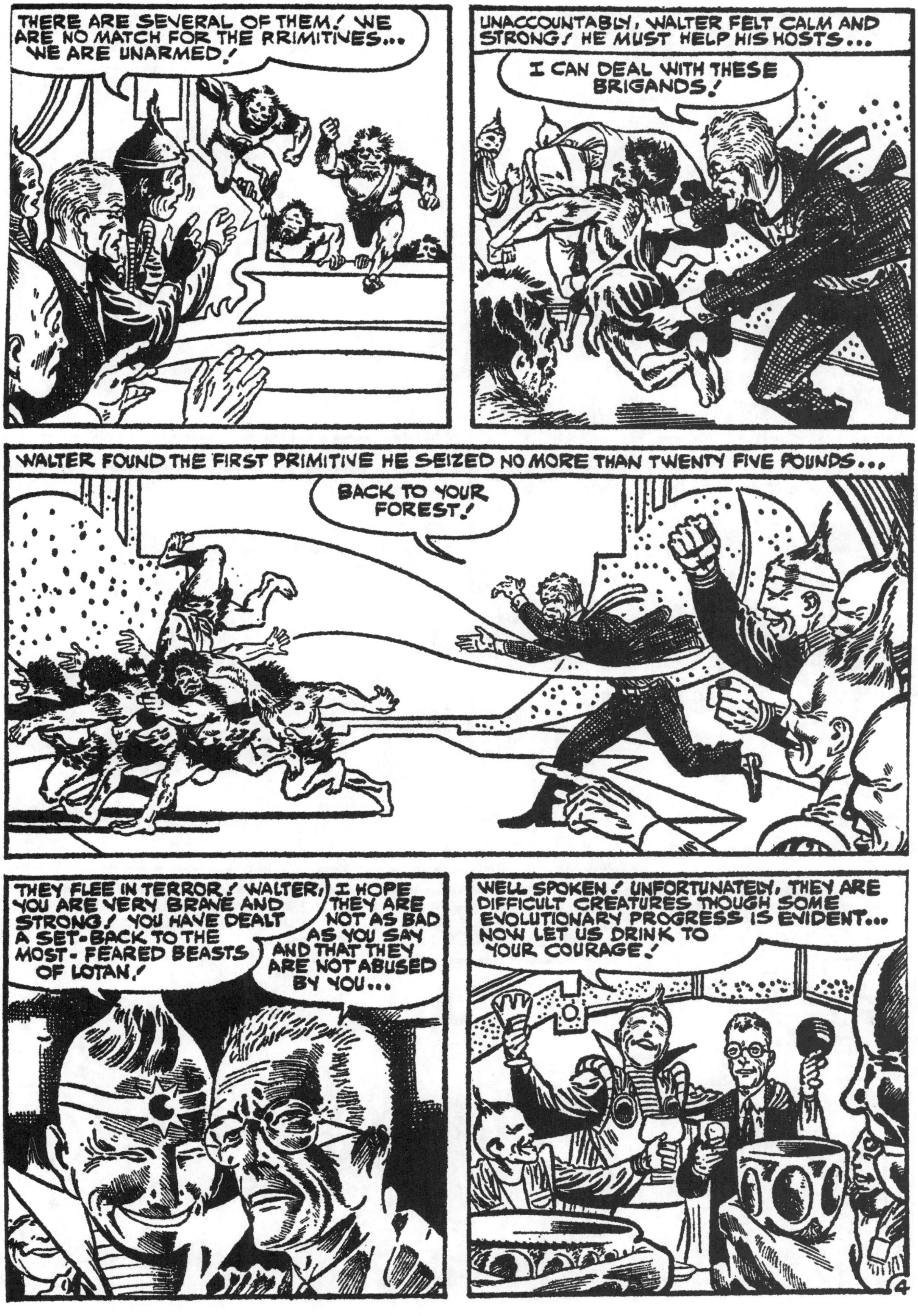
THERE ARE SEVERAL OF THEM! WE ARE NO MATCH FOR THE RRIMITIVES... WE ARE UNARMED!
UNACCOUNTABLY, WALTER FELT CALM AND STRONG! HE MUST HELP HIS HOSTS...
I CAN DEAL WITH THESE BRIGANDS!
WALTER FOUND THE FIRST PRIMITIVE HE SEIZED NO MORE THAN TWENTY FIVE POUNDS...
BACK TO YOUR FOREST!
THEY FLEE IN TERROR! WALTER, YOU ARE VERY BRAVE AND STRONG! YOU HAVE DEALT A SET-BACK TO THE MOST-FEARED BEASTS OF LOTAN!
I HOPE THEY ARE NOT AS BAD AS YOU SAY AND THAT THEY ARE NOT ABUSED BY YOU...
WELL SPOKEN! UNFORTUNATELY, THEY ARE DIFFICULT CREATURES THOUGH SOME EVOLUTIONARY PROGRESS IS EVIDENT... NOW LET US DRINK TO YOUR COURAGE!
4

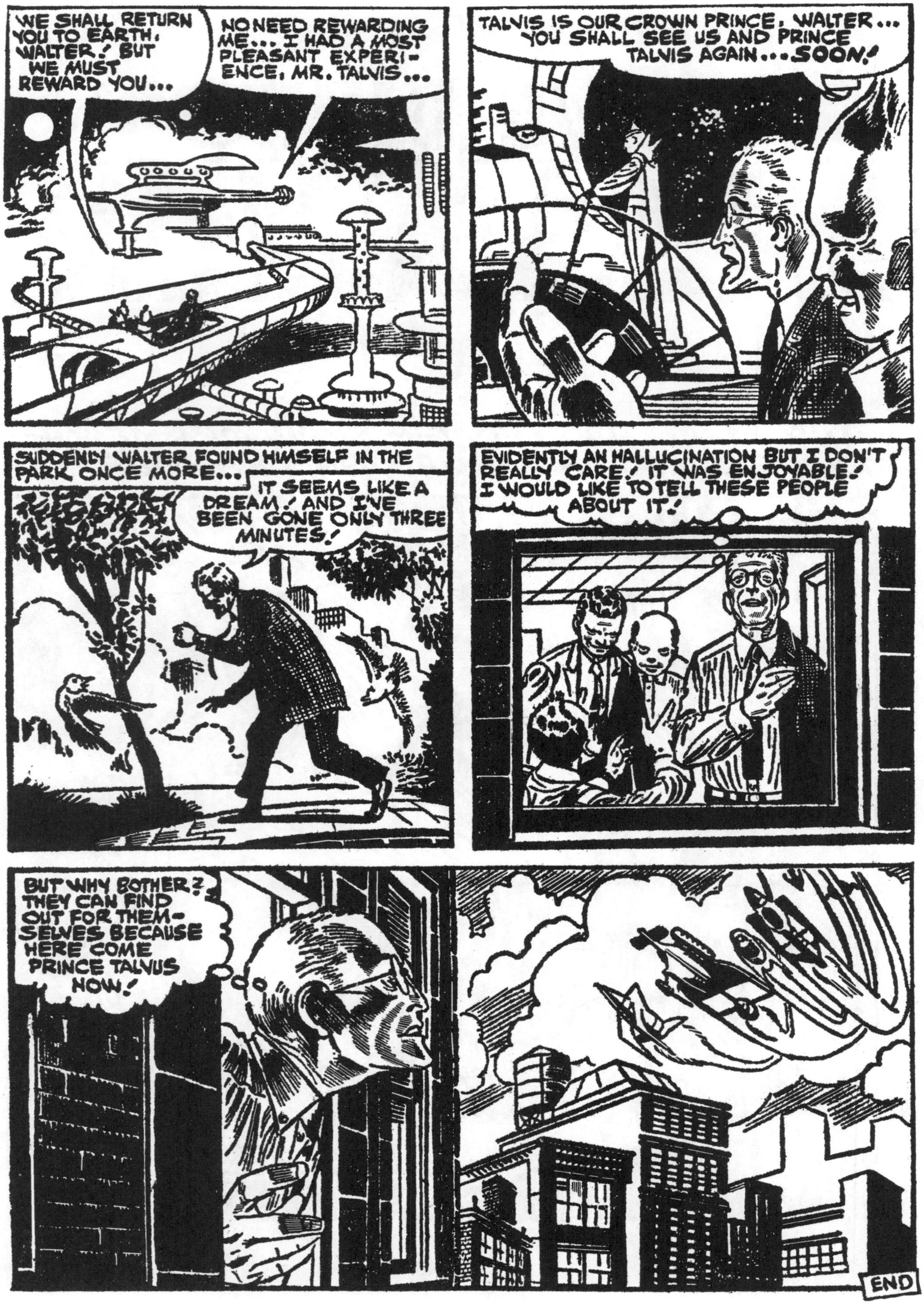
WE SHALL RETURN YOU TO EARTH, WALTER! BUT WE MUST REWARD YOU...
NO NEED REWARDING ME... I HAD A MOST PLEASANT EXPERIENCE, MR. TALVIS...
TALVIS IS OUR CROWN PRINCE, WALTER... YOU SHALL SEE US AND PRINCE TALVIS AGAIN...SOON!
SUDDENLY WALTER FOUND HIMSELF IN THE PARK ONCE MORE...
IT SEEMS LIKE A DREAM! AND I'VE BEEN GONE ONLY THREE MINUTES!
EVIDENTLY AN HALLUCINATION BUT I DON'T REALLY CARE! IT WAS ENJOYABLE! I WOULD LIKE TO TELL THESE PEOPLE ABOUT IT!
BUT WHY BOTHER? THEY CAN FIND OUT FOR THEMSELVES BECAUSE HERE COME PRINCE TALVUS NOW!
END

STEVE DITKO
SPACE WARS

AND EJUAN HAD LED THE SURVIVORS OF THE TOWNS TO HIS UNDERGROUND CHAMBER!

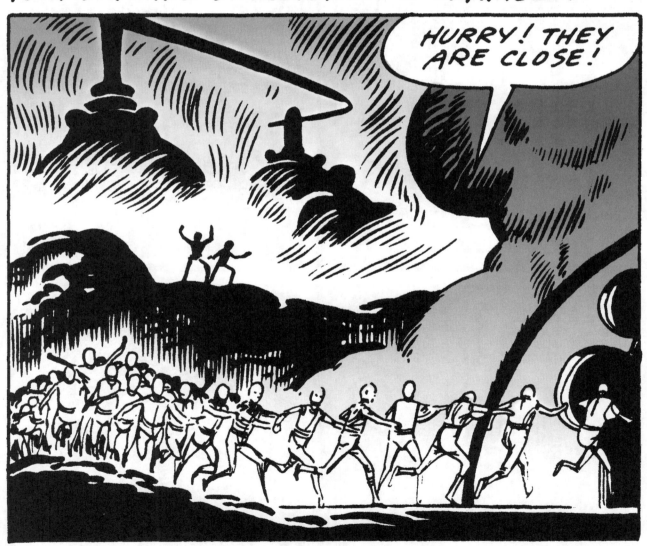

HURRY! THEY ARE CLOSE!

"JOURNEY'S END!"

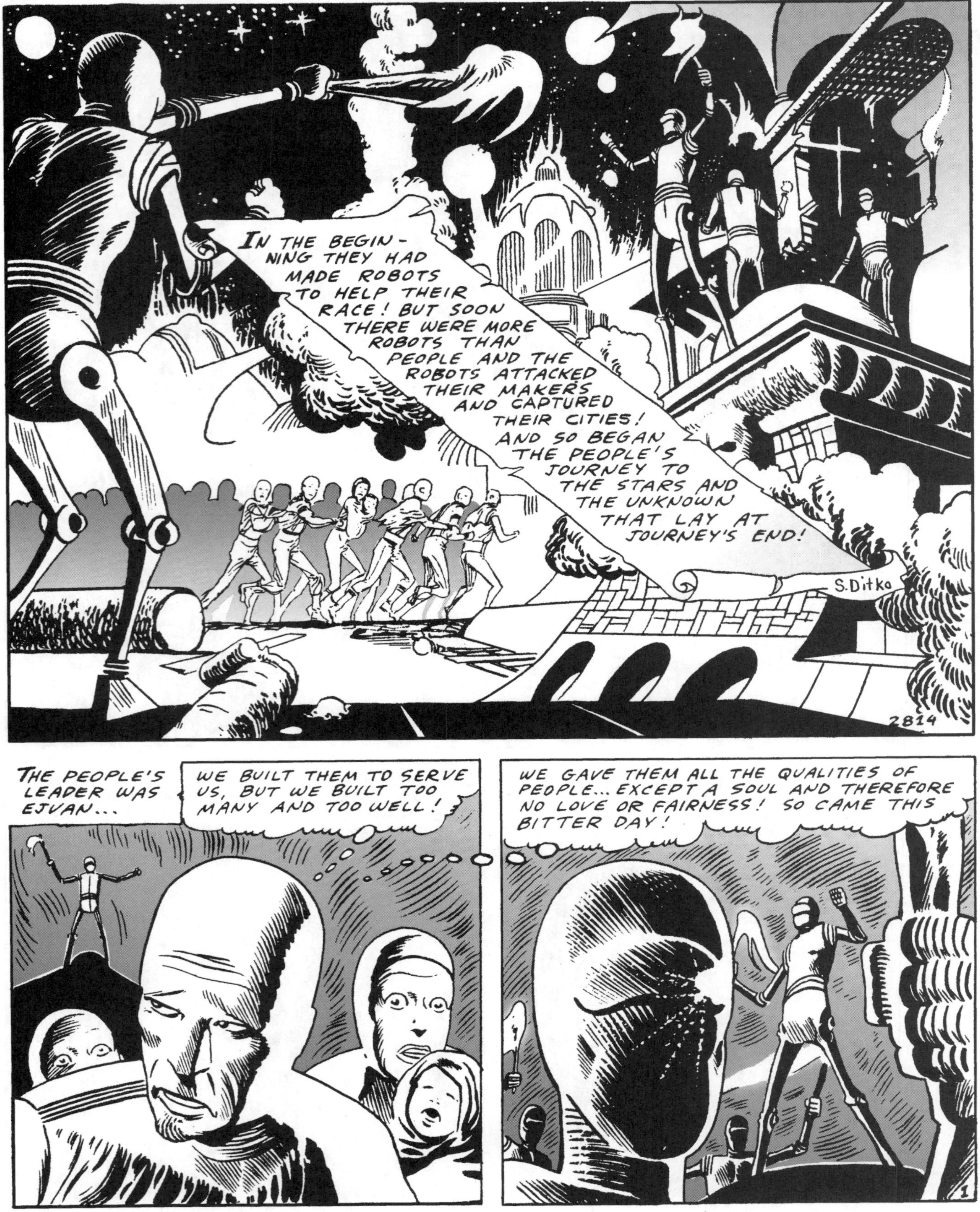
IN THE BEGINNING THEY HAD MADE ROBOTS TO HELP THEIR RACE! BUT SOON THERE WERE MORE ROBOTS THAN PEOPLE AND THE ROBOTS ATTACKED THEIR MAKERS AND CAPTURED THEIR CITIES! AND SO BEGAN THE PEOPLE'S JOURNEY TO THE STARS AND THE UNKNOWN THAT LAY AT JOURNEY'S END!
S. Ditko
2814
THE PEOPLE'S LEADER WAS EJVAN...
WE BUILT THEM TO SERVE US, BUT WE BUILT TOO MANY AND TOO WELL!
WE GAVE THEM ALL THE QUALITIES OF PEOPLE... EXCEPT A SOUL AND THEREFORE NO LOVE OR FAIRNESS! SO CAME THIS BITTER DAY!
1

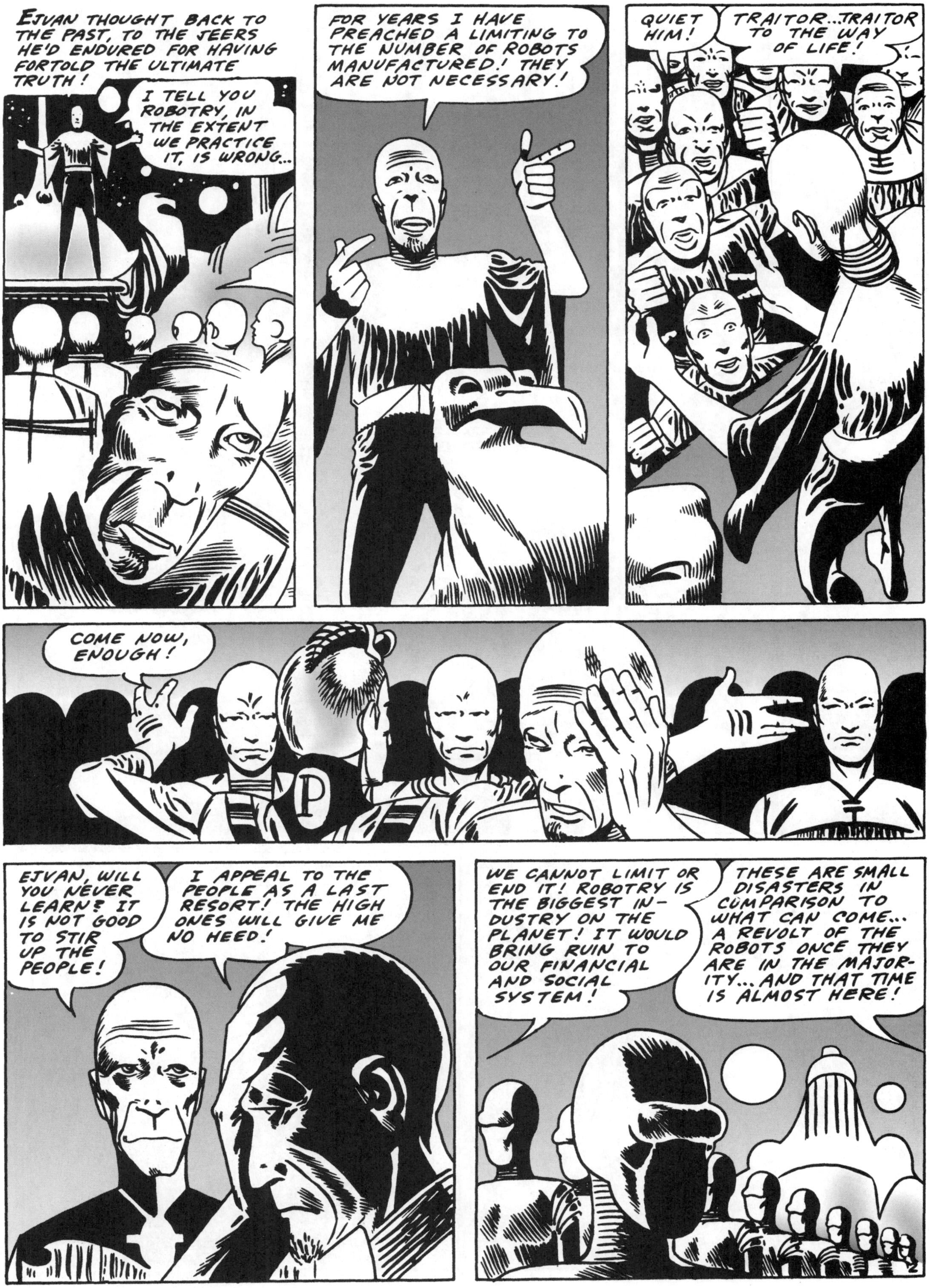
EJVAN THOUGHT BACK TO THE PAST, TO THE JEERS HE'D ENDURED FOR HAVING FORTOLD THE ULTIMATE TRUTH!
I TELL YOU ROBOTRY, IN THE EXTENT WE PRACTICE IT, IS WRONG...
FOR YEARS I HAVE PREACHED A LIMITING TO THE NUMBER OF ROBOTS MANUFACTURED! THEY ARE NOT NECESSARY!
QUIET HIM!
TRAITOR...TRAITOR TO THE WAY OF LIFE!
COME NOW, ENOUGH!
P
EJVAN, WILL YOU NEVER LEARN? IT IS NOT GOOD TO STIR UP THE PEOPLE!
I APPEAL TO THE PEOPLE AS A LAST RESORT! THE HIGH ONES WILL GIVE ME NO HEED!
WE CANNOT LIMIT OR END IT! ROBOTRY IS THE BIGGEST IN-DUSTRY ON THE PLANET! IT WOULD BRING RUIN TO OUR FINANCIAL AND SOCIAL SYSTEM!
THESE ARE SMALL DISASTERS IN COMPARISON TO WHAT CAN COME... A REVOLT OF THE ROBOTS ONCE THEY ARE IN THE MAJOR-ITY... AND THAT TIME IS ALMOST HERE!

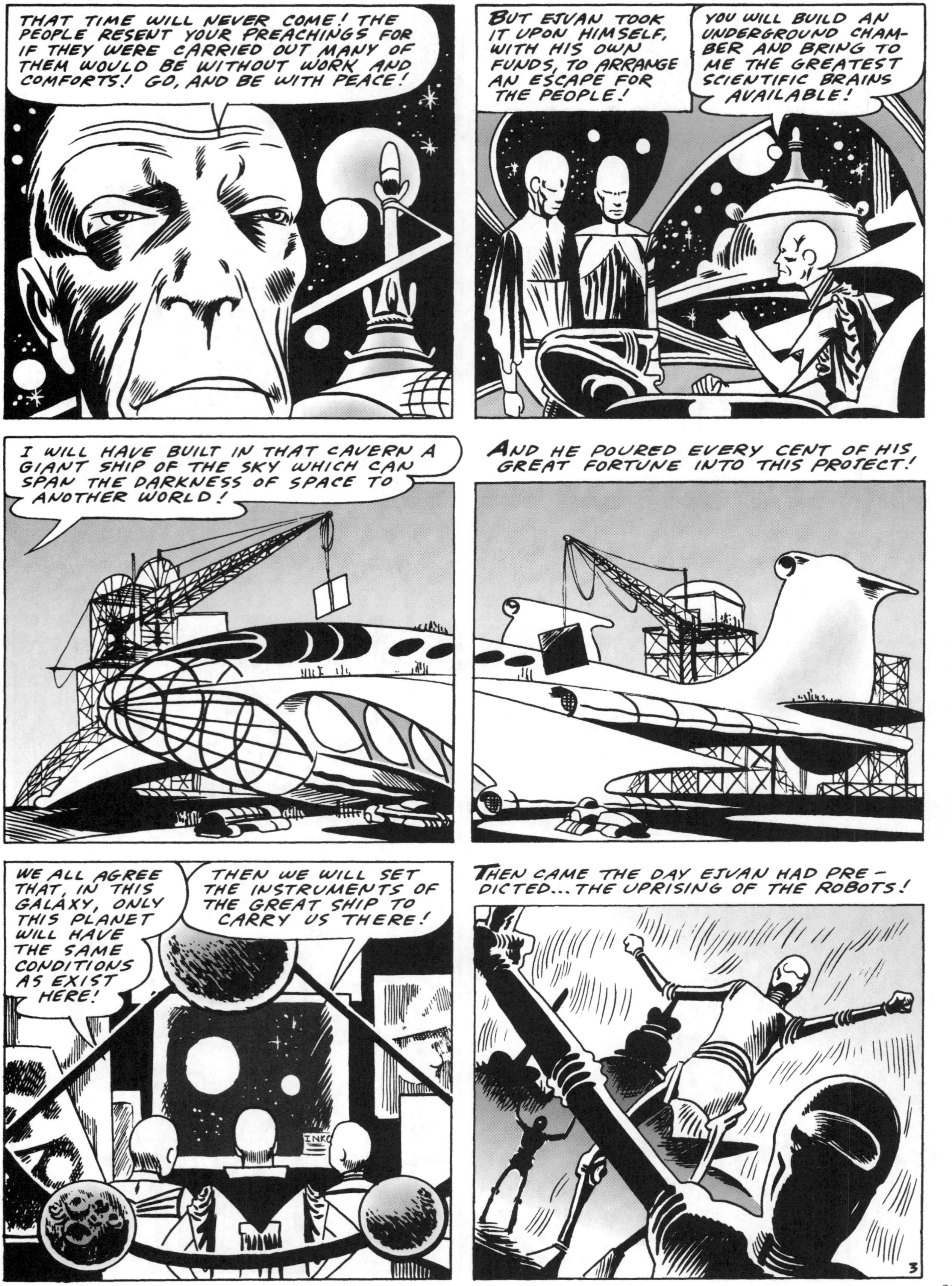
THAT TIME WILL NEVER COME! THE PEOPLE RESENT YOUR PREACHINGS FOR IF THEY WERE CARRIED OUT MANY OF THEM WOULD BE WITHOUT WORK AND COMFORTS! GO, AND BE WITH PEACE!
BUT EJVAN TOOK IT UPON HIMSELF, WITH HIS OWN FUNDS, TO ARRANGE AN ESCAPE FOR THE PEOPLE!
YOU WILL BUILD AN UNDERGROUND CHAMBER AND BRING TO ME THE GREATEST SCIENTIFIC BRAINS AVAILABLE!
I WILL HAVE BUILT IN THAT CAVERN A GIANT SHIP OF THE SKY WHICH CAN SPAN THE DARKNESS OF SPACE TO ANOTHER WORLD!
AND HE POURED EVERY CENT OF HIS GREAT FORTUNE INTO THIS PROJECT!
WE ALL AGREE THAT, IN THIS GALAXY, ONLY THIS PLANET WILL HAVE THE SAME CONDITIONS AS EXIST HERE!
THEN WE WILL SET THE INSTRUMENTS OF THE GREAT SHIP TO CARRY US THERE!
THEN CAME THE DAY EJVAN HAD PREDICTED... THE UPRISING OF THE ROBOTS!
3

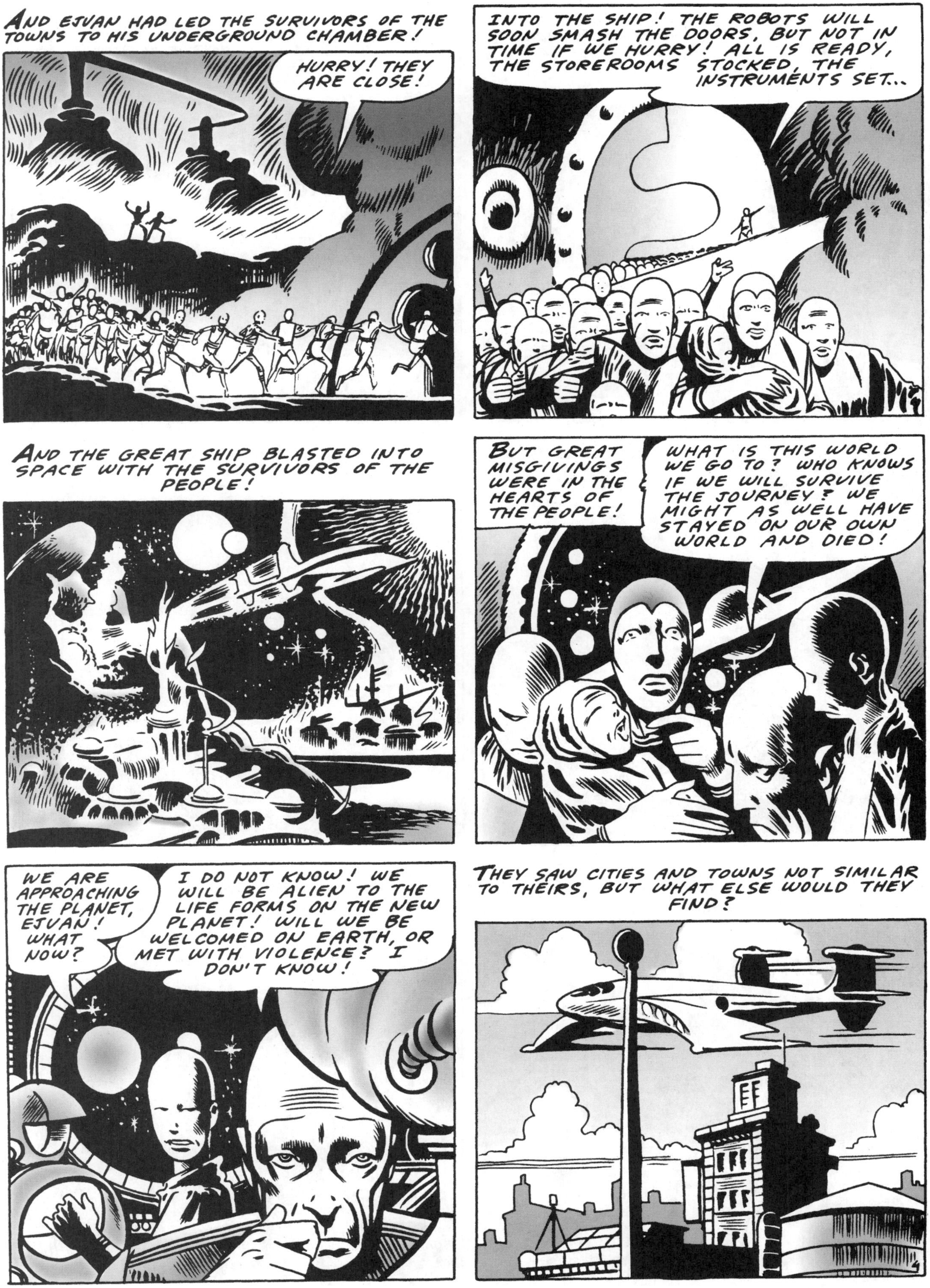

AND EJUAN HAD LED THE SURVIVORS OF THE TOWNS TO HIS UNDERGROUND CHAMBER!
HURRY! THEY ARE CLOSE!
INTO THE SHIP! THE ROBOTS WILL SOON SMASH THE DOORS, BUT NOT IN TIME IF WE HURRY! ALL IS READY, THE STOREROOMS STOCKED, THE INSTRUMENTS SET...
AND THE GREAT SHIP BLASTED INTO SPACE WITH THE SURVIVORS OF THE PEOPLE!
BUT GREAT MISGIVINGS WERE IN THE HEARTS OF THE PEOPLE!
WHAT IS THIS WORLD WE GO TO? WHO KNOWS IF WE WILL SURVIVE THE JOURNEY? WE MIGHT AS WELL HAVE STAYED ON OUR OWN WORLD AND DIED!
WE ARE APPROACHING THE PLANET, EJUAN! WHAT NOW?
I DO NOT KNOW! WE WILL BE ALIEN TO THE LIFE FORMS ON THE NEW PLANET! WILL WE BE WELCOMED ON EARTH, OR MET WITH VIOLENCE? I DON'T KNOW!
THEY SAW CITIES AND TOWNS NOT SIMILAR TO THEIRS, BUT WHAT ELSE WOULD THEY FIND?

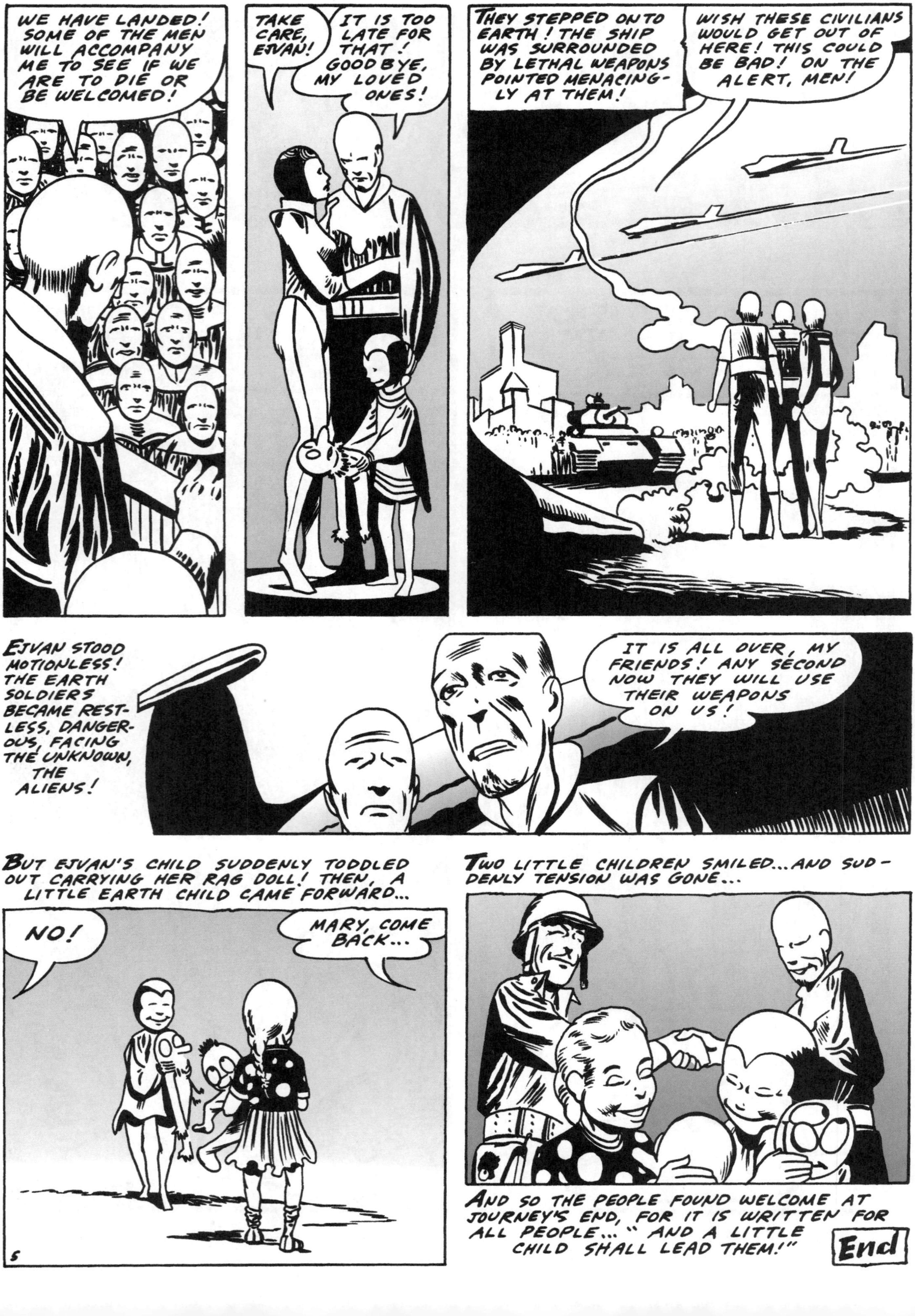
WE HAVE LANDED! SOME OF THE MEN WILL ACCOMPANY ME TO SEE IF WE ARE TO DIE OR BE WELCOMED!
TAKE CARE, EJVAN!
IT IS TOO LATE FOR THAT! GOOD BYE, MY LOVED ONES!
THEY STEPPED ONTO EARTH! THE SHIP WAS SURROUNDED BY LETHAL WEAPONS POINTED MENACINGLY AT THEM!
WISH THESE CIVILIANS WOULD GET OUT OF HERE! THIS COULD BE BAD! ON THE ALERT, MEN!
EJVAN STOOD MOTIONLESS! THE EARTH SOLDIERS BECAME RESTLESS, DANGEROUS, FACING THE UNKNOWN, THE ALIENS!
IT IS ALL OVER, MY FRIENDS! ANY SECOND NOW THEY WILL USE THEIR WEAPONS ON US!
BUT EJVAN'S CHILD SUDDENLY TODDLED OUT CARRYING HER RAG DOLL! THEN, A LITTLE EARTH CHILD CAME FORWARD...
NO!
MARY, COME BACK...
5
TWO LITTLE CHILDREN SMILED... AND SUDDENLY TENSION WAS GONE...
AND SO THE PEOPLE FOUND WELCOME AT JOURNEY'S END, FOR IT IS WRITTEN FOR ALL PEOPLE... "AND A LITTLE CHILD SHALL LEAD THEM!"
End

STEVE DITKO SPACE WARS

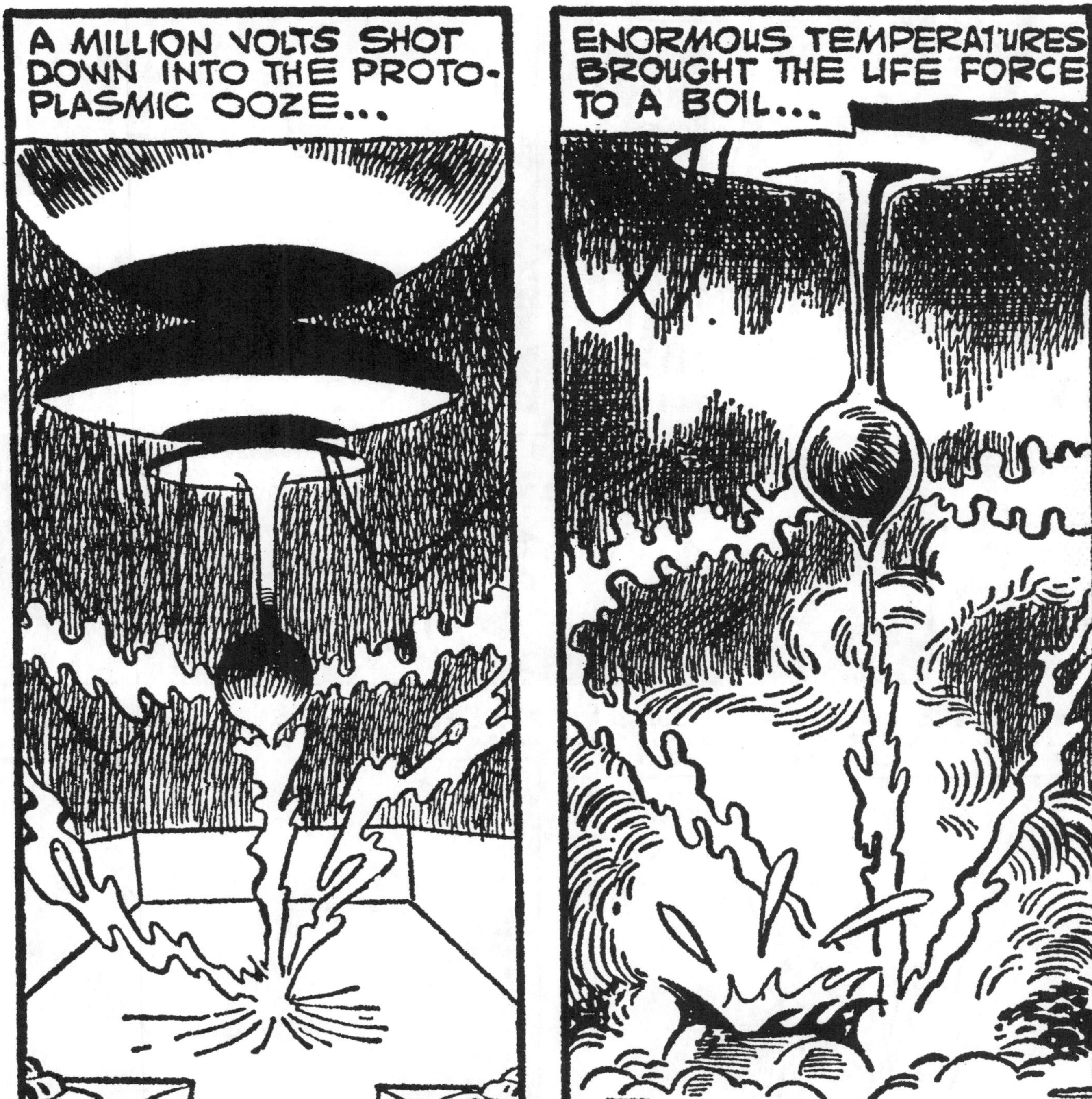
A MILLION VOLTS SHOT DOWN INTO THE PROTO-PLASMIC OOZE...
ENORMOUS TEMPERATURES BROUGHT THE LIFE FORCE TO A BOIL...

There it is Again

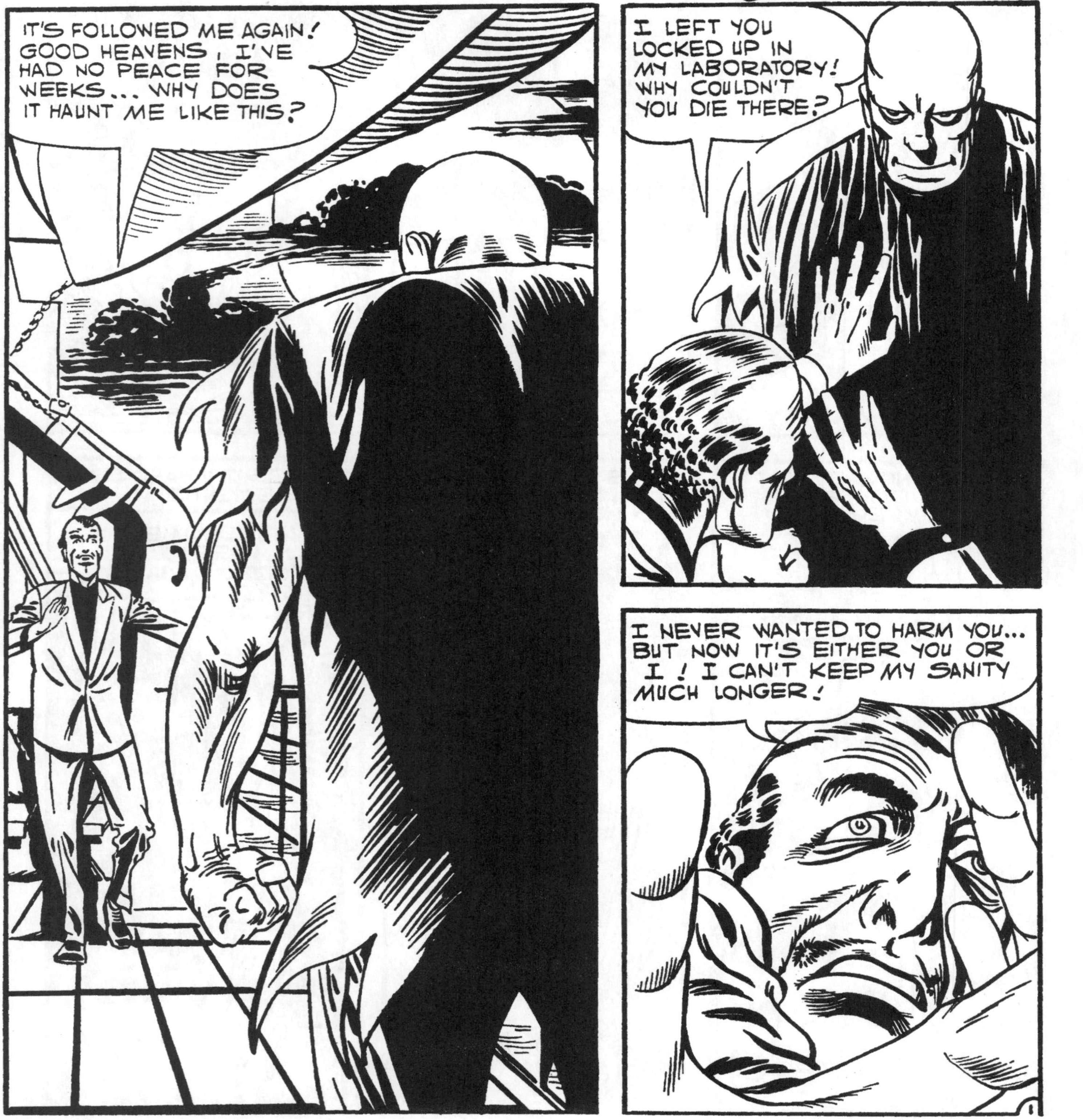
IT'S FOLLOWED ME AGAIN! GOOD HEAVENS, I'VE HAD NO PEACE FOR WEEKS... WHY DOES IT HAUNT ME LIKE THIS?
I LEFT YOU LOCKED UP IN MY LABORATORY! WHY COULDN'T YOU DIE THERE?
I NEVER WANTED TO HARM YOU... BUT NOW IT'S EITHER YOU OR I! I CAN'T KEEP MY SANITY MUCH LONGER!

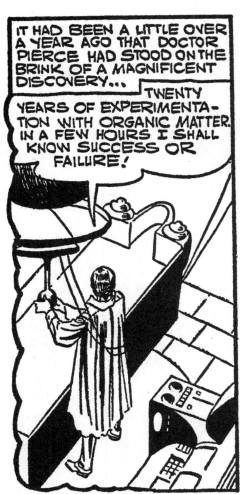

IT HAD BEEN A LITTLE OVER A YEAR AGO THAT DOCTOR PIERCE HAD STOOD ON THE BRINK OF A MAGNIFICENT DISCOVERY...

TWENTY YEARS OF EXPERIMENTATION WITH ORGANIC MATTER. IN A FEW HOURS I SHALL KNOW SUCCESS OR FAILURE!

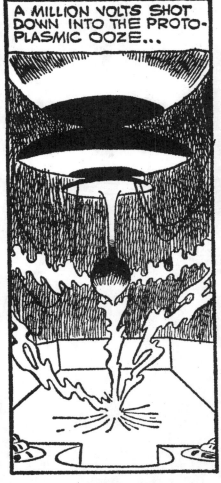

A MILLION VOLTS SHOT DOWN INTO THE PROTOPLASMIC OOZE...

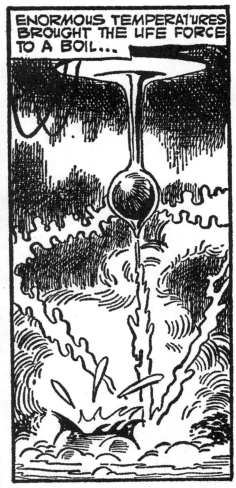

ENORMOUS TEMPERATURES BROUGHT THE LIFE FORCE TO A BOIL...

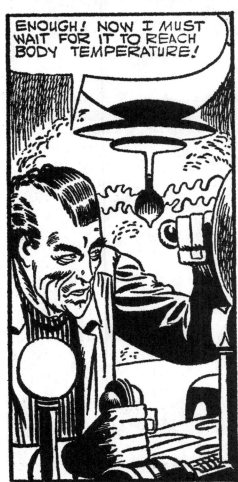

ENOUGH! NOW I MUST WAIT FOR IT TO REACH BODY TEMPERATURE!

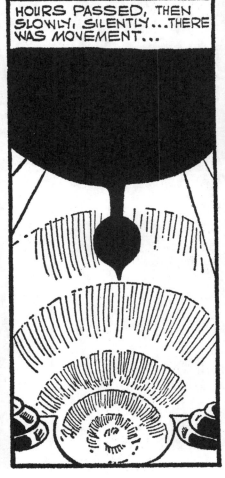

HOURS PASSED, THEN SLOWLY, SILENTLY...THERE WAS MOVEMENT...

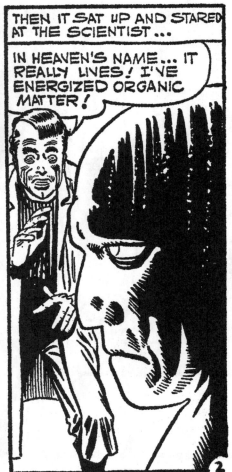

THEN IT SAT UP AND STARED AT THE SCIENTIST...

IN HEAVEN'S NAME... IT REALLY LIVES! I'VE ENERGIZED ORGANIC MATTER!

2

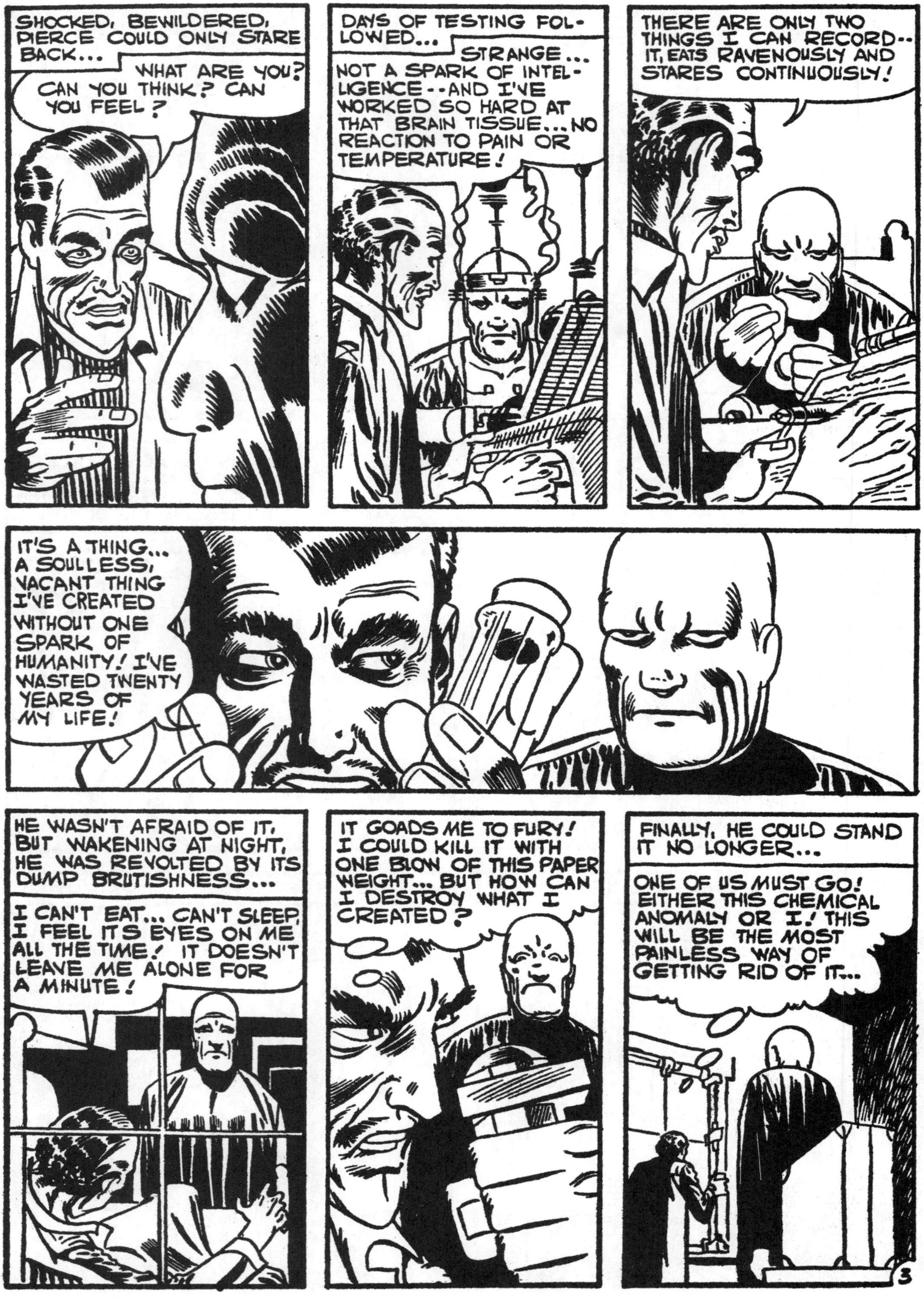
SHOCKED, BEWILDERED, PIERCE COULD ONLY STARE BACK...
WHAT ARE YOU? CAN YOU THINK? CAN YOU FEEL?
DAYS OF TESTING FOLLOWED...
STRANGE... NOT A SPARK OF INTELLIGENCE--AND I'VE WORKED SO HARD AT THAT BRAIN TISSUE... NO REACTION TO PAIN OR TEMPERATURE!
THERE ARE ONLY TWO THINGS I CAN RECORD-- IT EATS RAVENOUSLY AND STARES CONTINUOUSLY!
IT'S A THING... A SOULLESS, VACANT THING I'VE CREATED WITHOUT ONE SPARK OF HUMANITY! I'VE WASTED TWENTY YEARS OF MY LIFE!
HE WASN'T AFRAID OF IT, BUT WAKENING AT NIGHT, HE WAS REVOLTED BY ITS DUMP BRUTISHNESS...
I CAN'T EAT... CAN'T SLEEP, I FEEL IT'S EYES ON ME ALL THE TIME! IT DOESN'T LEAVE ME ALONE FOR A MINUTE!
IT GOADS ME TO FURY! I COULD KILL IT WITH ONE BLOW OF THIS PAPER WEIGHT... BUT HOW CAN I DESTROY WHAT I CREATED?
FINALLY, HE COULD STAND IT NO LONGER...
ONE OF US MUST GO! EITHER THIS CHEMICAL ANOMALY OR I! THIS WILL BE THE MOST PAINLESS WAY OF GETTING RID OF IT...
3

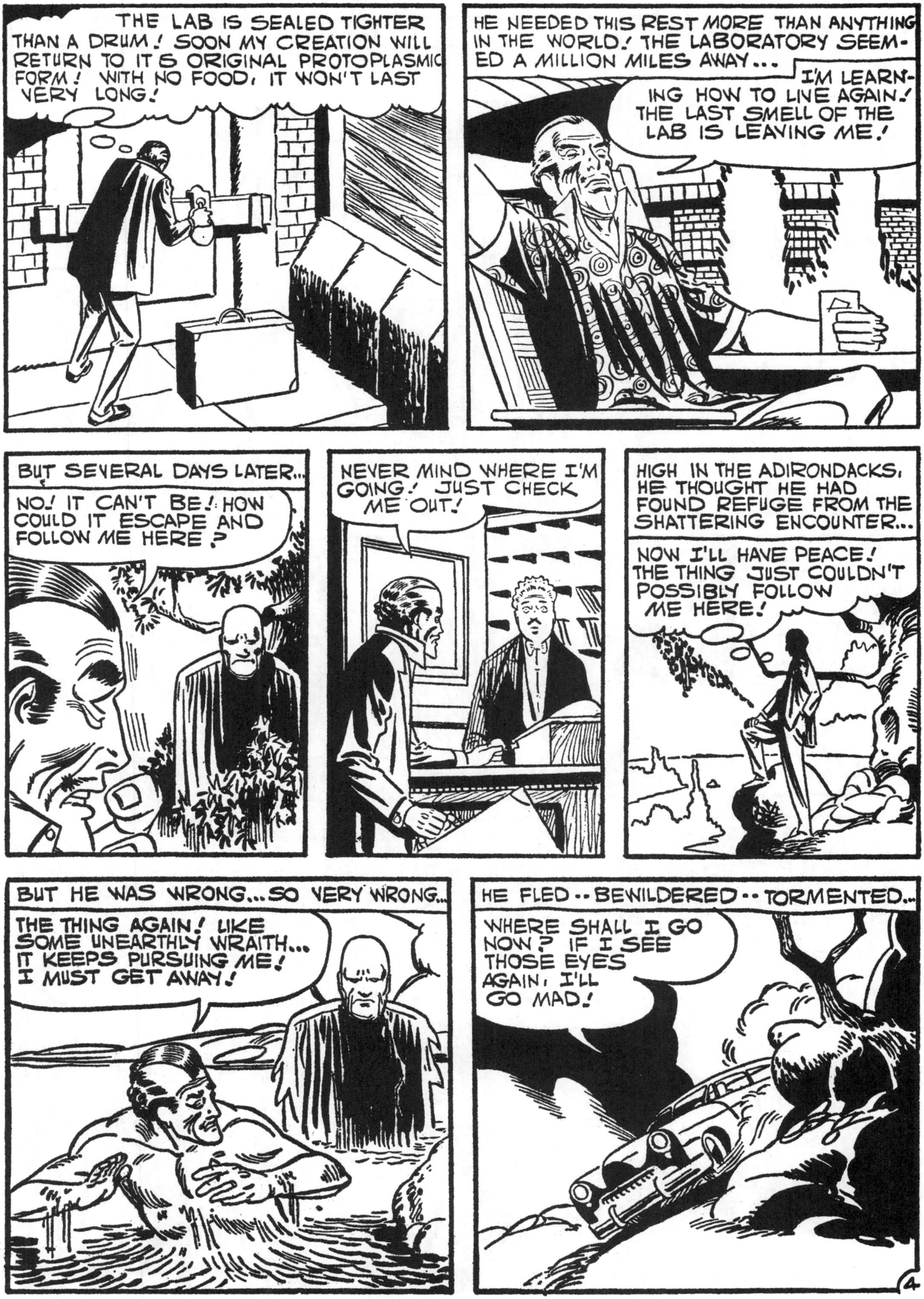
THE LAB IS SEALED TIGHTER THAN A DRUM! SOON MY CREATION WILL RETURN TO ITS ORIGINAL PROTOPLASMIC FORM! WITH NO FOOD, IT WON'T LAST VERY LONG!
HE NEEDED THIS REST MORE THAN ANYTHING IN THE WORLD! THE LABORATORY SEEMED A MILLION MILES AWAY...
I'M LEARNING HOW TO LIVE AGAIN! THE LAST SMELL OF THE LAB IS LEAVING ME!
BUT SEVERAL DAYS LATER...
NO! IT CAN'T BE! HOW COULD IT ESCAPE AND FOLLOW ME HERE?
NEVER MIND WHERE I'M GOING! JUST CHECK ME OUT!
HIGH IN THE ADIRONDACKS, HE THOUGHT HE HAD FOUND REFUGE FROM THE SHATTERING ENCOUNTER...
NOW I'LL HAVE PEACE! THE THING JUST COULDN'T POSSIBLY FOLLOW ME HERE!
BUT HE WAS WRONG...SO VERY WRONG...
THE THING AGAIN! LIKE SOME UNEARTHLY WRAITH... IT KEEPS PURSUING ME! I MUST GET AWAY!
HE FLED--BEWILDERED--TORMENTED...
WHERE SHALL I GO NOW? IF I SEE THOSE EYES AGAIN, I'LL GO MAD!
4

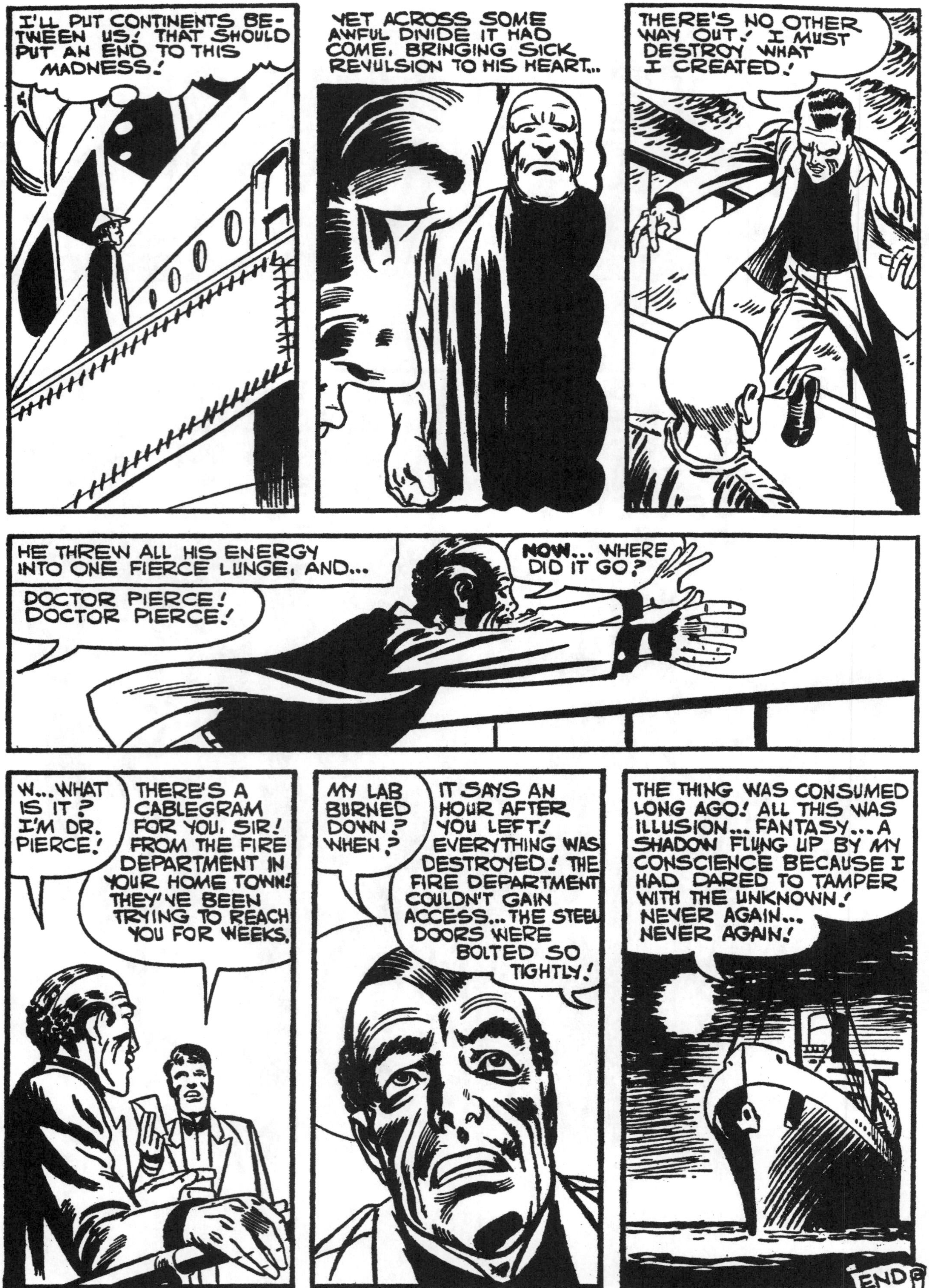

I'LL PUT CONTINENTS BETWEEN US! THAT SHOULD PUT AN END TO THIS MADNESS!
YET ACROSS SOME AWFUL DIVIDE IT HAD COME, BRINGING SICK REVULSION TO HIS HEART...
THERE'S NO OTHER WAY OUT! I MUST DESTROY WHAT I CREATED!
HE THREW ALL HIS ENERGY INTO ONE FIERCE LUNGE, AND...
NOW... WHERE DID IT GO?
DOCTOR PIERCE! DOCTOR PIERCE!
W...WHAT IS IT? I'M DR. PIERCE!
THERE'S A CABLEGRAM FOR YOU, SIR! FROM THE FIRE DEPARTMENT IN YOUR HOME TOWN! THEY'VE BEEN TRYING TO REACH YOU FOR WEEKS.
MY LAB BURNED DOWN? WHEN?
IT SAYS AN HOUR AFTER YOU LEFT! EVERYTHING WAS DESTROYED! THE FIRE DEPARTMENT COULDN'T GAIN ACCESS... THE STEEL DOORS WERE BOLTED SO TIGHTLY!
THE THING WAS CONSUMED LONG AGO! ALL THIS WAS ILLUSION... FANTASY... A SHADOW FLUNG UP BY MY CONSCIENCE BECAUSE I HAD DARED TO TAMPER WITH THE UNKNOWN! NEVER AGAIN... NEVER AGAIN!
END

STEVE DITKO SPACE WARS

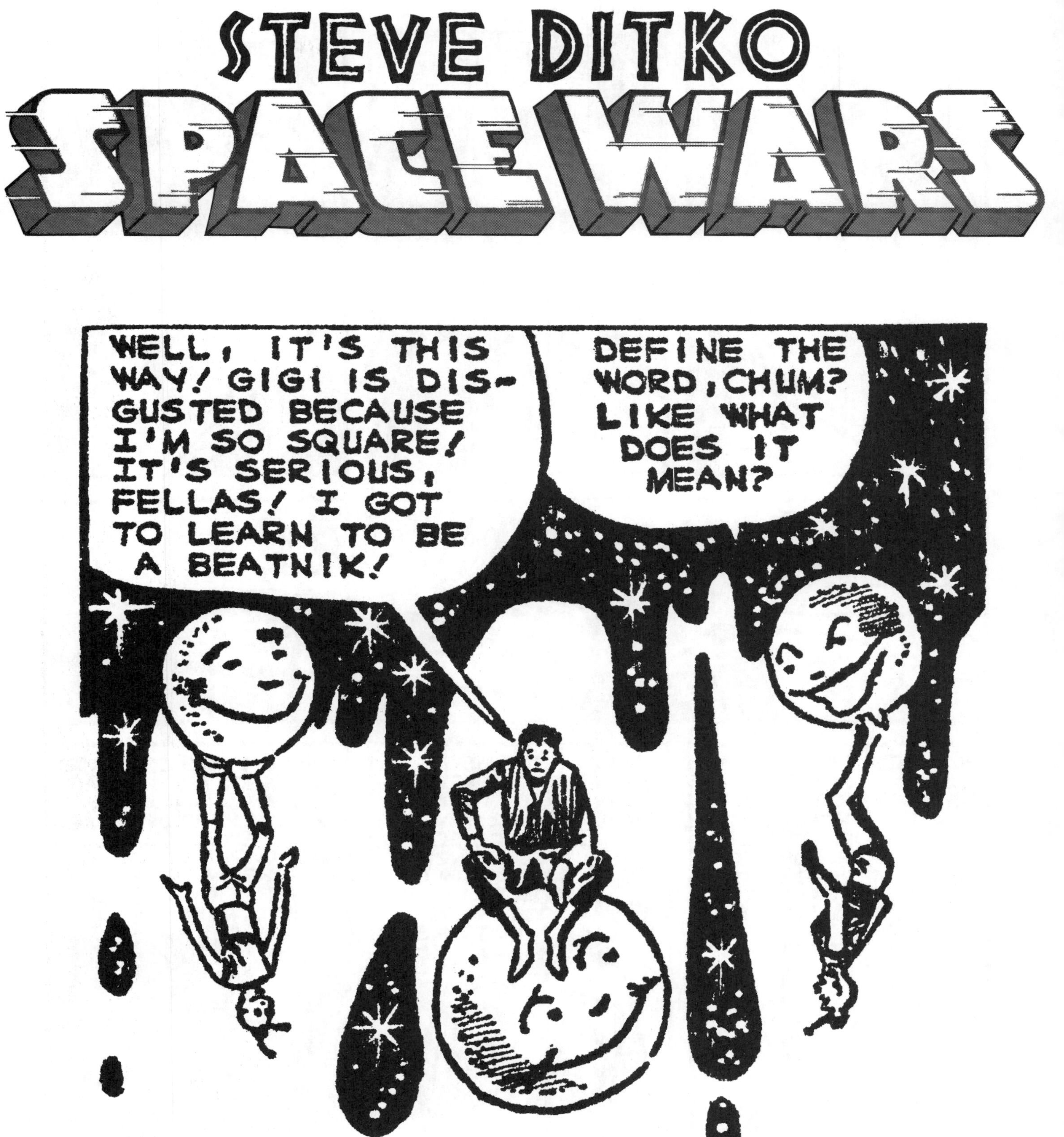
WELL, IT'S THIS WAY! GIGI IS DIS-GUSTED BECAUSE I'M SO SQUARE! IT'S SERIOUS, FELLAS! I GOT TO LEARN TO BE A BEATNIK!
DEFINE THE WORD, CHUM? LIKE WHAT DOES IT MEAN?

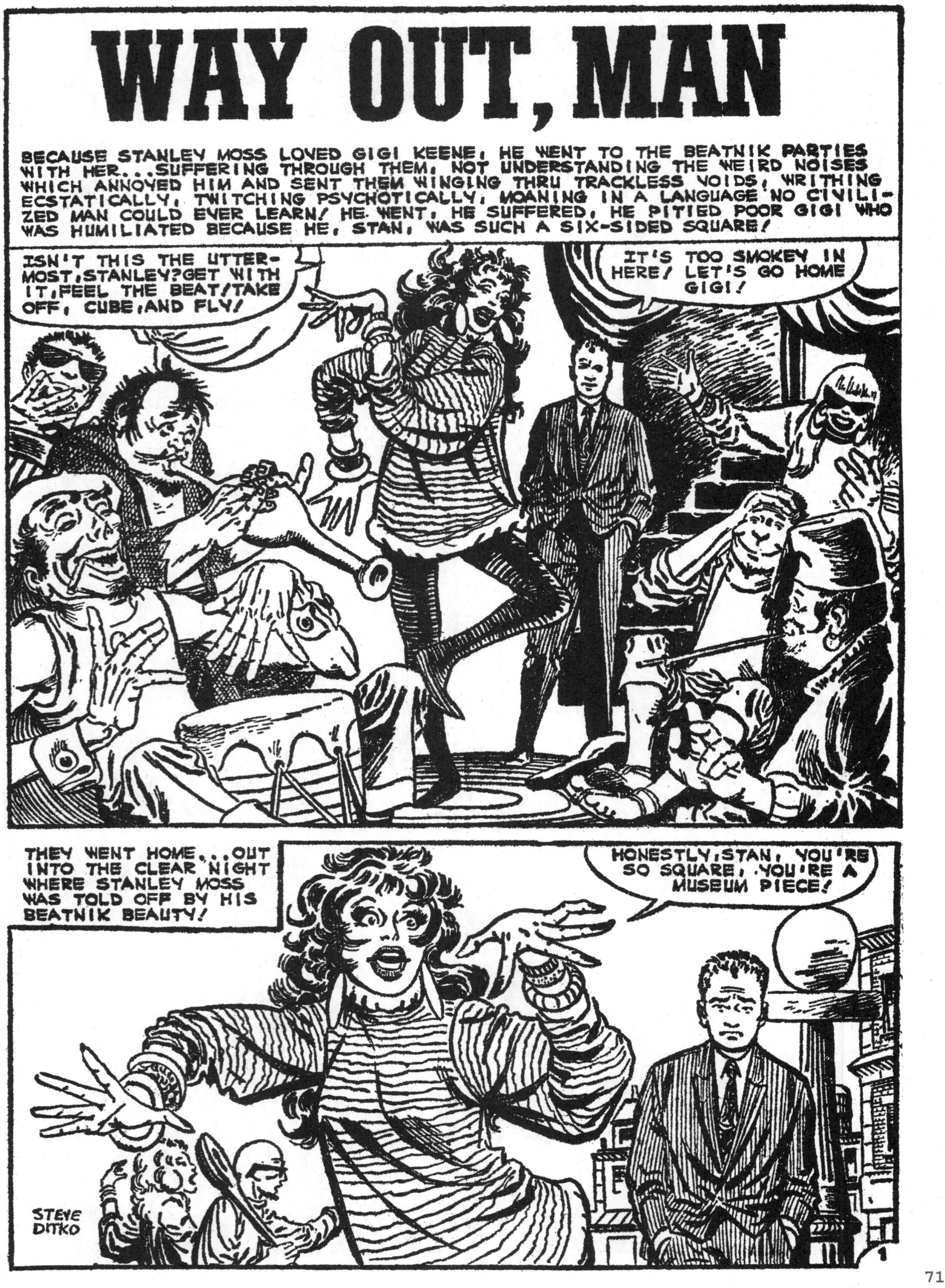

WAY OUT, MAN
BECAUSE STANLEY MOSS LOVED GIGI KEENE, HE WENT TO THE BEATNIK PARTIES WITH HER...SUFFERING THROUGH THEM, NOT UNDERSTANDING THE WEIRD NOISES WHICH ANNOYED HIM AND SENT THEM WINGING THRU TRACKLESS VOIDS, WRITHING ECSTATICALLY, TWITCHING PSYCHOTICALLY, MOANING IN A LANGUAGE NO CIVILIZED MAN COULD EVER LEARN! HE WENT, HE SUFFERED, HE PITIED POOR GIGI WHO WAS HUMILIATED BECAUSE HE, STAN, WAS SUCH A SIX-SIDED SQUARE!
ISN'T THIS THE UTTERMOST, STANLEY? GET WITH IT, FEEL THE BEAT! TAKE OFF, CUBE, AND FLY!
IT'S TOO SMOKEY IN HERE! LET'S GO HOME GIGI!
THEY WENT HOME...OUT INTO THE CLEAR NIGHT WHERE STANLEY MOSS WAS TOLD OFF BY HIS BEATNIK BEAUTY!
HONESTLY, STAN, YOU'RE SO SQUARE, YOU'RE A MUSEUM PIECE!
STEVE DITKO
1

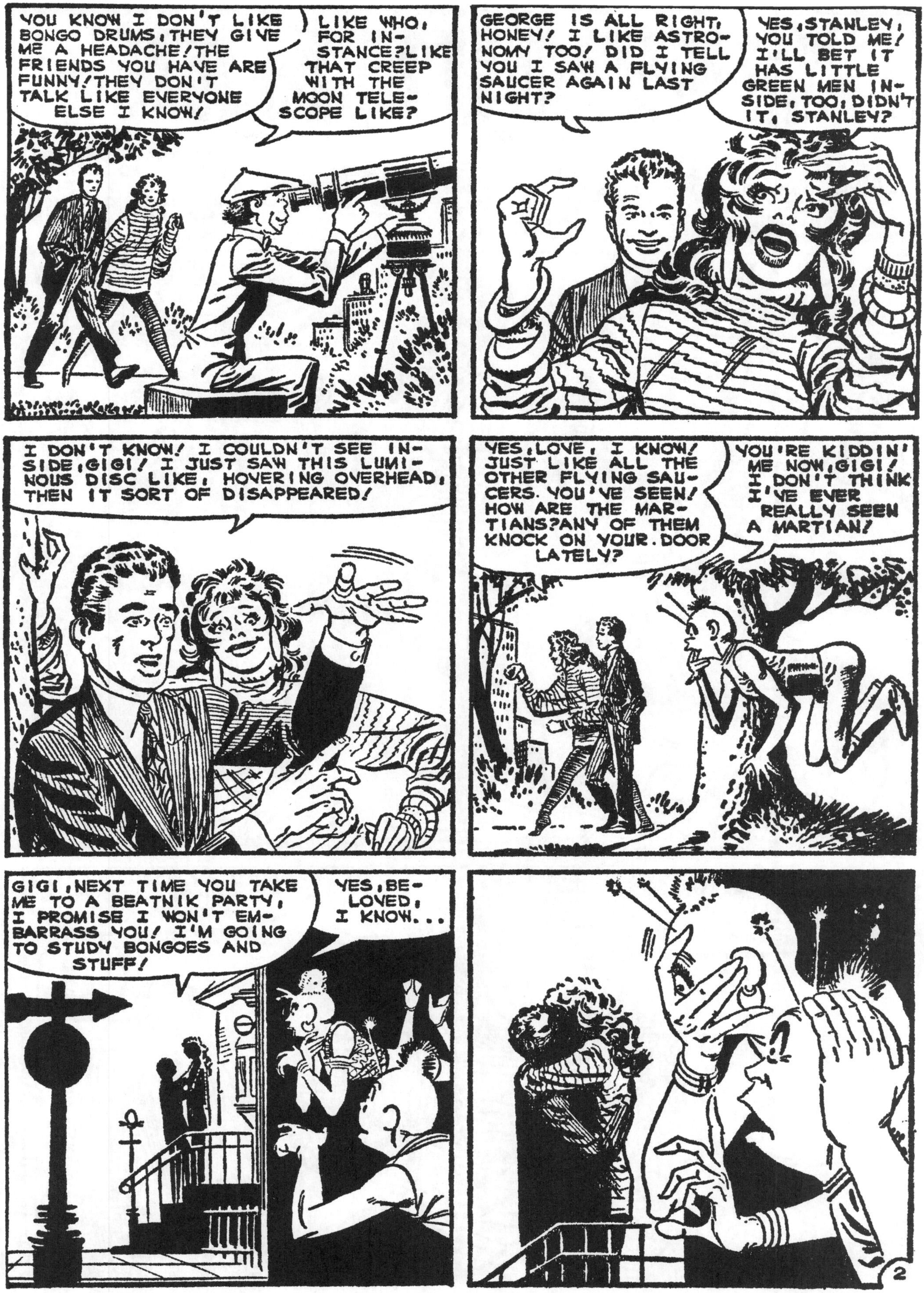
YOU KNOW I DON'T LIKE BONGO DRUMS, THEY GIVE ME A HEADACHE! THE FRIENDS YOU HAVE ARE FUNNY! THEY DON'T TALK LIKE EVERYONE ELSE I KNOW!
LIKE WHO, FOR INSTANCE? LIKE THAT CREEP WITH THE MOON TELESCOPE LIKE?
GEORGE IS ALL RIGHT, HONEY! I LIKE ASTRONOMY TOO! DID I TELL YOU I SAW A FLYING SAUCER AGAIN LAST NIGHT?
YES, STANLEY, YOU TOLD ME! I'LL BET IT HAS LITTLE GREEN MEN INSIDE, TOO, DIDN'T IT, STANLEY?
I DON'T KNOW! I COULDN'T SEE INSIDE, GIGI! I JUST SAW THIS LUMINOUS DISC LIKE, HOVERING OVERHEAD, THEN IT SORT OF DISAPPEARED!
YES, LOVE, I KNOW! JUST LIKE ALL THE OTHER FLYING SAUCERS YOU'VE SEEN! HOW ARE THE MARTIANS? ANY OF THEM KNOCK ON YOUR DOOR LATELY?
YOU'RE KIDDIN' ME NOW, GIGI! I DON'T THINK I'VE EVER REALLY SEEN A MARTIAN!
GIGI, NEXT TIME YOU TAKE ME TO A BEATNIK PARTY, I PROMISE I WON'T EMBARRASS YOU! I'M GOING TO STUDY BONGOES AND STUFF!
YES, BELOVED, I KNOW...
2

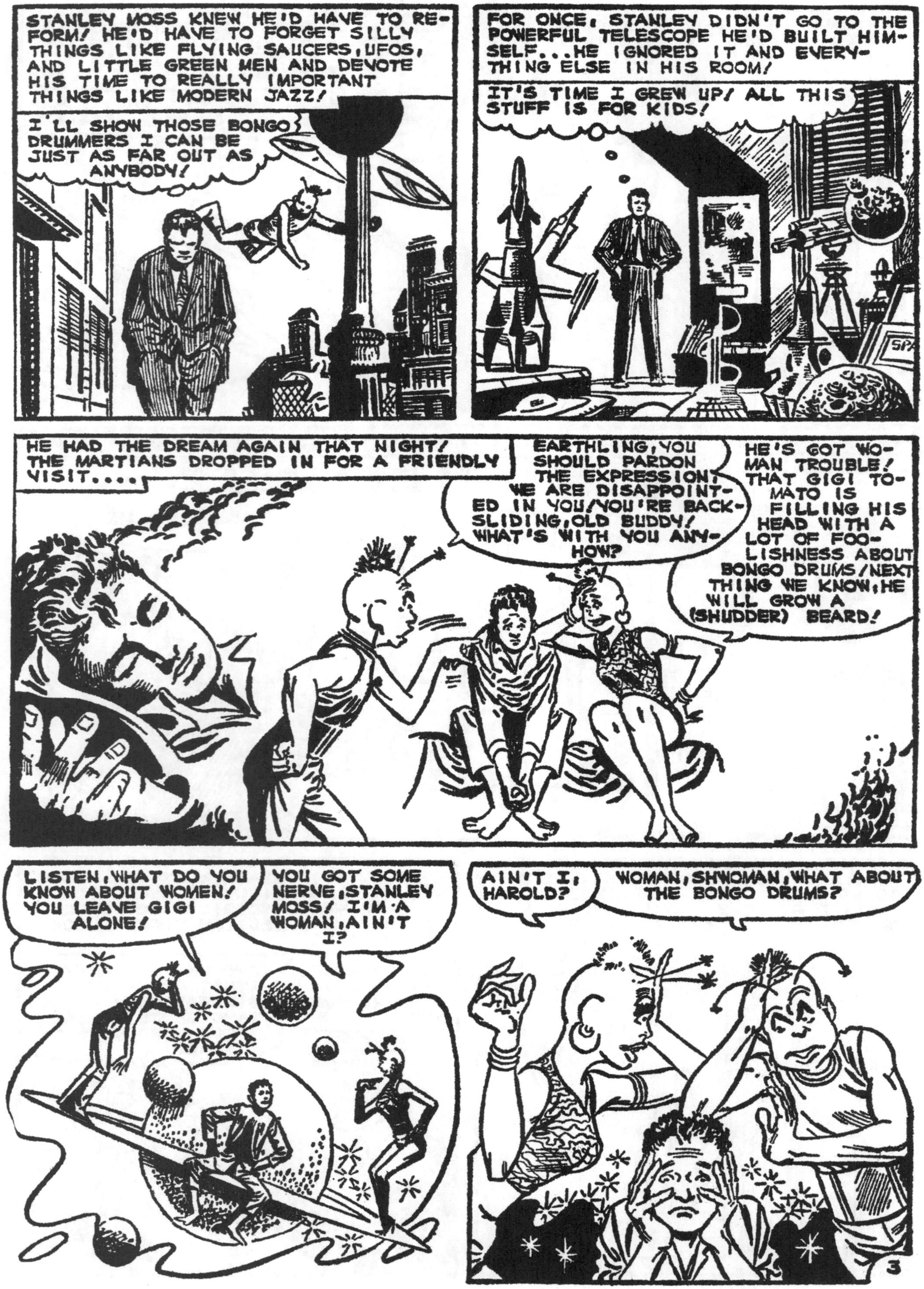

STANLEY MOSS KNEW HE'D HAVE TO REFORM! HE'D HAVE TO FORGET SILLY THINGS LIKE FLYING SAUCERS, UFOS, AND LITTLE GREEN MEN AND DEVOTE HIS TIME TO REALLY IMPORTANT THINGS LIKE MODERN JAZZ!
I'LL SHOW THOSE BONGO DRUMMERS I CAN BE JUST AS FAR OUT AS ANYBODY!
FOR ONCE, STANLEY DIDN'T GO TO THE POWERFUL TELESCOPE HE'D BUILT HIMSELF...HE IGNORED IT AND EVERYTHING ELSE IN HIS ROOM!
IT'S TIME I GREW UP! ALL THIS STUFF IS FOR KIDS!
HE HAD THE DREAM AGAIN THAT NIGHT! THE MARTIANS DROPPED IN FOR A FRIENDLY VISIT....
EARTHLING, YOU SHOULD PARDON THE EXPRESSION! WE ARE DISAPPOINTED IN YOU! YOU'RE BACKSLIDING, OLD BUDDY! WHAT'S WITH YOU ANYHOW?
HE'S GOT WOMAN TROUBLE! THAT GIGI TOMATO IS FILLING HIS HEAD WITH A LOT OF FOOLISHNESS ABOUT BONGO DRUMS! NEXT THING WE KNOW, HE WILL GROW A (SHUDDER) BEARD!
LISTEN, WHAT DO YOU KNOW ABOUT WOMEN! YOU LEAVE GIGI ALONE!
YOU GOT SOME NERVE, STANLEY MOSS! I'M A WOMAN, AIN'T I?
AIN'T I, HAROLD?
WOMAN, SHWOMAN, WHAT ABOUT THE BONGO DRUMS?
3

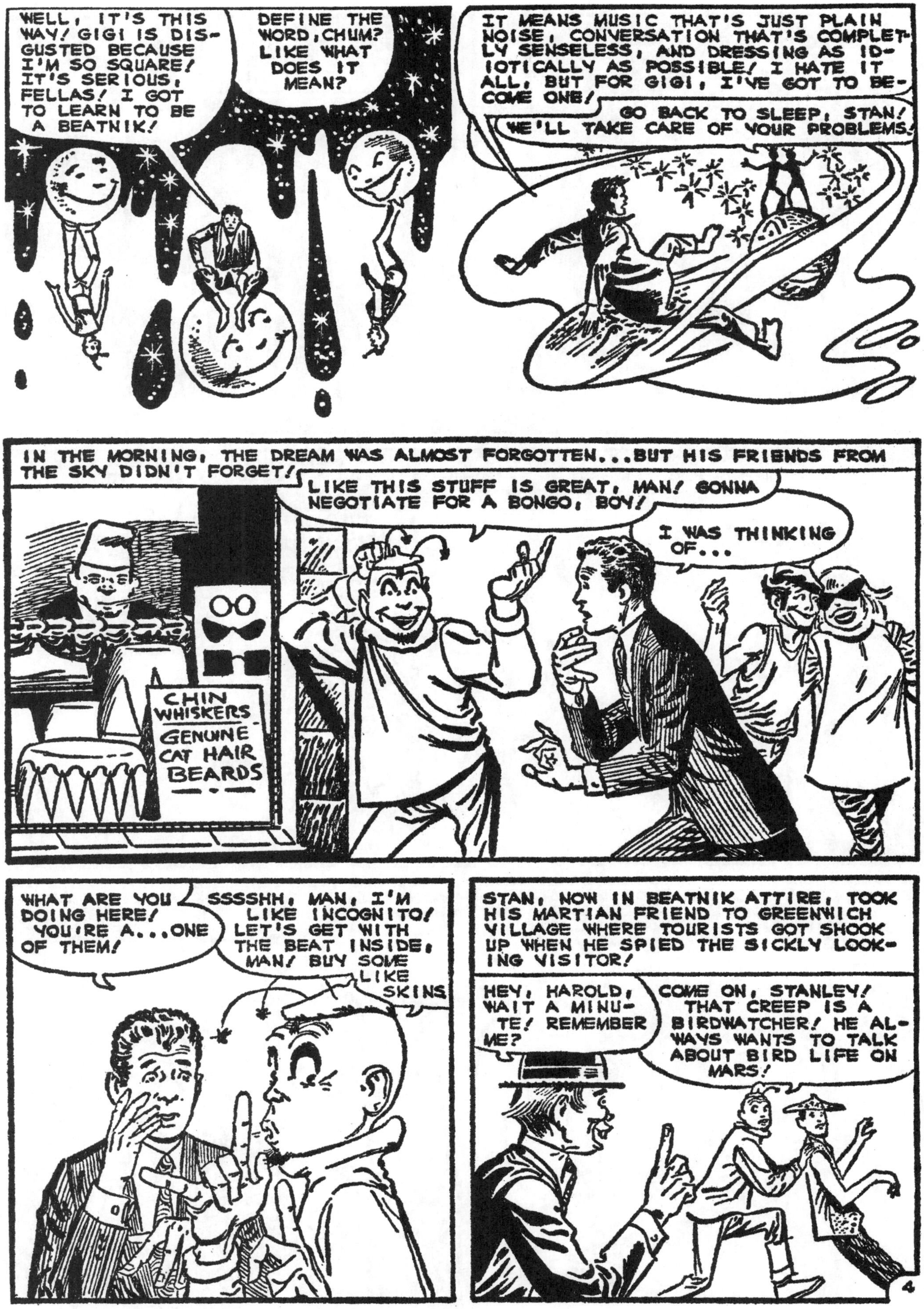
WELL, IT'S THIS WAY! GIGI IS DISGUSTED BECAUSE I'M SO SQUARE! IT'S SERIOUS, FELLAS! I GOT TO LEARN TO BE A BEATNIK!
DEFINE THE WORD, CHUM? LIKE WHAT DOES IT MEAN?
IT MEANS MUSIC THAT'S JUST PLAIN NOISE, CONVERSATION THAT'S COMPLETLY SENSELESS, AND DRESSING AS IDIOTICALLY AS POSSIBLE! I HATE IT ALL, BUT FOR GIGI, I'VE GOT TO BECOME ONE!
GO BACK TO SLEEP, STAN! WE'LL TAKE CARE OF YOUR PROBLEMS!
IN THE MORNING, THE DREAM WAS ALMOST FORGOTTEN...BUT HIS FRIENDS FROM THE SKY DIDN'T FORGET!
LIKE THIS STUFF IS GREAT, MAN! GONNA NEGOTIATE FOR A BONGO, BOY!
I WAS THINKING OF...
CHIN WHISKERS
GENUINE CAT HAIR BEARDS
WHAT ARE YOU DOING HERE! YOU'RE A...ONE OF THEM!
SSSSHH, MAN, I'M LIKE INCOGNITO! LET'S GET WITH THE BEAT INSIDE, MAN! BUY SOME LIKE SKINS
STAN, NOW IN BEATNIK ATTIRE, TOOK HIS MARTIAN FRIEND TO GREENWICH VILLAGE WHERE TOURISTS GOT SHOOK UP WHEN HE SPIED THE SICKLY LOOKING VISITOR!
HEY, HAROLD, WAIT A MINUTE! REMEMBER ME?
COME ON, STANLEY! THAT CREEP IS A BIRDWATCHER! HE ALWAYS WANTS TO TALK ABOUT BIRD LIFE ON MARS!
4

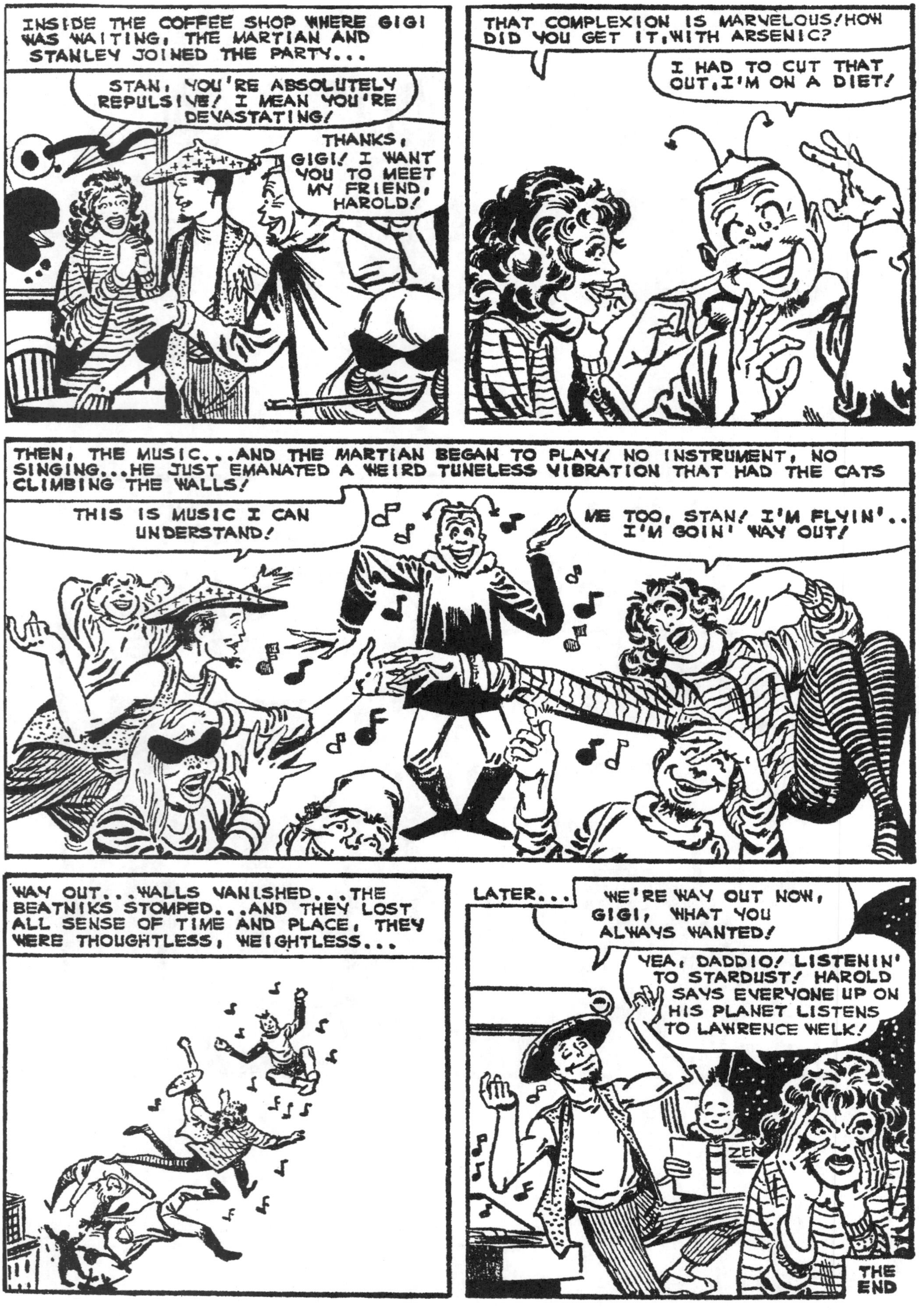
INSIDE THE COFFEE SHOP WHERE GIGI WAS WAITING, THE MARTIAN AND STANLEY JOINED THE PARTY...
STAN, YOU'RE ABSOLUTELY REPULSIVE! I MEAN YOU'RE DEVASTATING!
THANKS, GIGI! I WANT YOU TO MEET MY FRIEND, HAROLD!
THAT COMPLEXION IS MARVELOUS! HOW DID YOU GET IT, WITH ARSENIC?
I HAD TO CUT THAT OUT, I'M ON A DIET!
THEN, THE MUSIC...AND THE MARTIAN BEGAN TO PLAY! NO INSTRUMENT, NO SINGING...HE JUST EMANATED A WEIRD TUNELESS VIBRATION THAT HAD THE CATS CLIMBING THE WALLS!
THIS IS MUSIC I CAN UNDERSTAND!
ME TOO, STAN! I'M FLYIN'.. I'M GOIN' WAY OUT!
WAY OUT...WALLS VANISHED...THE BEATNIKS STOMPED...AND THEY LOST ALL SENSE OF TIME AND PLACE, THEY WERE THOUGHTLESS, WEIGHTLESS...
LATER...
WE'RE WAY OUT NOW, GIGI, WHAT YOU ALWAYS WANTED!
YEA, DADDIO! LISTENIN' TO STARDUST! HAROLD SAYS EVERYONE UP ON HIS PLANET LISTENS TO LAWRENCE WELK!
ZEN
THE END

STEVE DITKO SPACE WARS

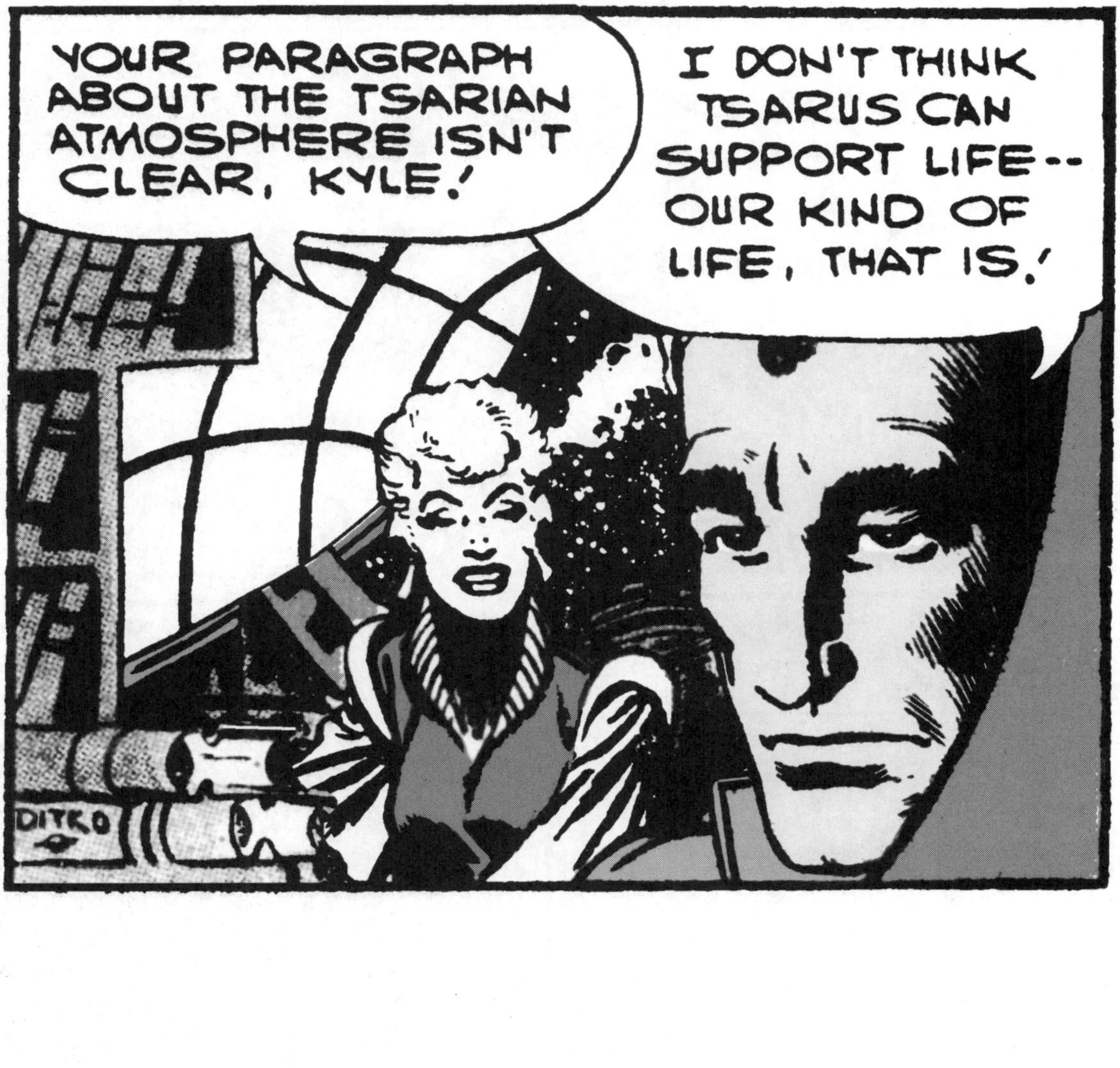

YOUR PARAGRAPH ABOUT THE TSARIAN ATMOSPHERE ISN'T CLEAR, KYLE!
I DON'T THINK TSARUS CAN SUPPORT LIFE-- OUR KIND OF LIFE, THAT IS!
DITKO

The STRANGE GUESTS OF TSARUS

IN THE UNENDING SEARCH FOR KNOWLEDGE OF THE UNIVERSE AROUND US, THE SCIENTISTS OF ALL THE KNOWN WORLDS WERE PUZZLED BY A SMALL PLANET OUT PAST SATURN! INTREPID EXPLORERS WENT THERE... AND REPORTED FINDING CIVILIZATION, FRIENDLY BEINGS! OTHERS WHO FOLLOWED CONFIRMED IT! YET, DR. KYLE DURAN, WRITING A TEXTBOOK ON THE NEW NEIGHBOR FOUND ONE THING PUZZLING...

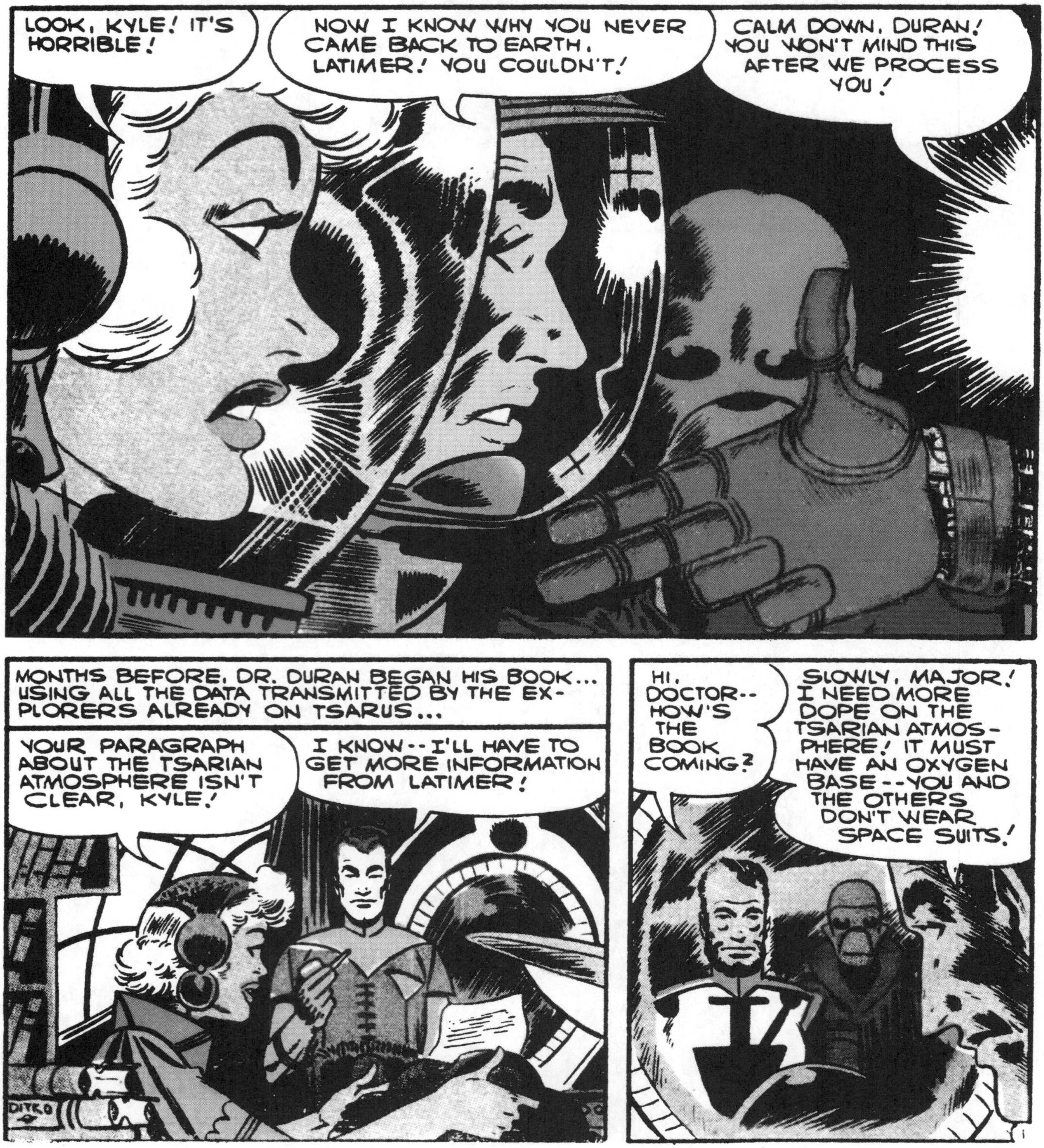

LOOK, KYLE! IT'S HORRIBLE!
NOW I KNOW WHY YOU NEVER CAME BACK TO EARTH, LATIMER! YOU COULDN'T!
CALM DOWN, DURAN! YOU WON'T MIND THIS AFTER WE PROCESS YOU!
MONTHS BEFORE, DR. DURAN BEGAN HIS BOOK... USING ALL THE DATA TRANSMITTED BY THE EXPLORERS ALREADY ON TSARUS...
YOUR PARAGRAPH ABOUT THE TSARIAN ATMOSPHERE ISN'T CLEAR, KYLE!
I KNOW--I'LL HAVE TO GET MORE INFORMATION FROM LATIMER!
DITKO
HI, DOCTOR--HOW'S THE BOOK COMING?
SLOWLY, MAJOR! I NEED MORE DOPE ON THE TSARIAN ATMOSPHERE! IT MUST HAVE AN OXYGEN BASE--YOU AND THE OTHERS DON'T WEAR SPACE SUITS!

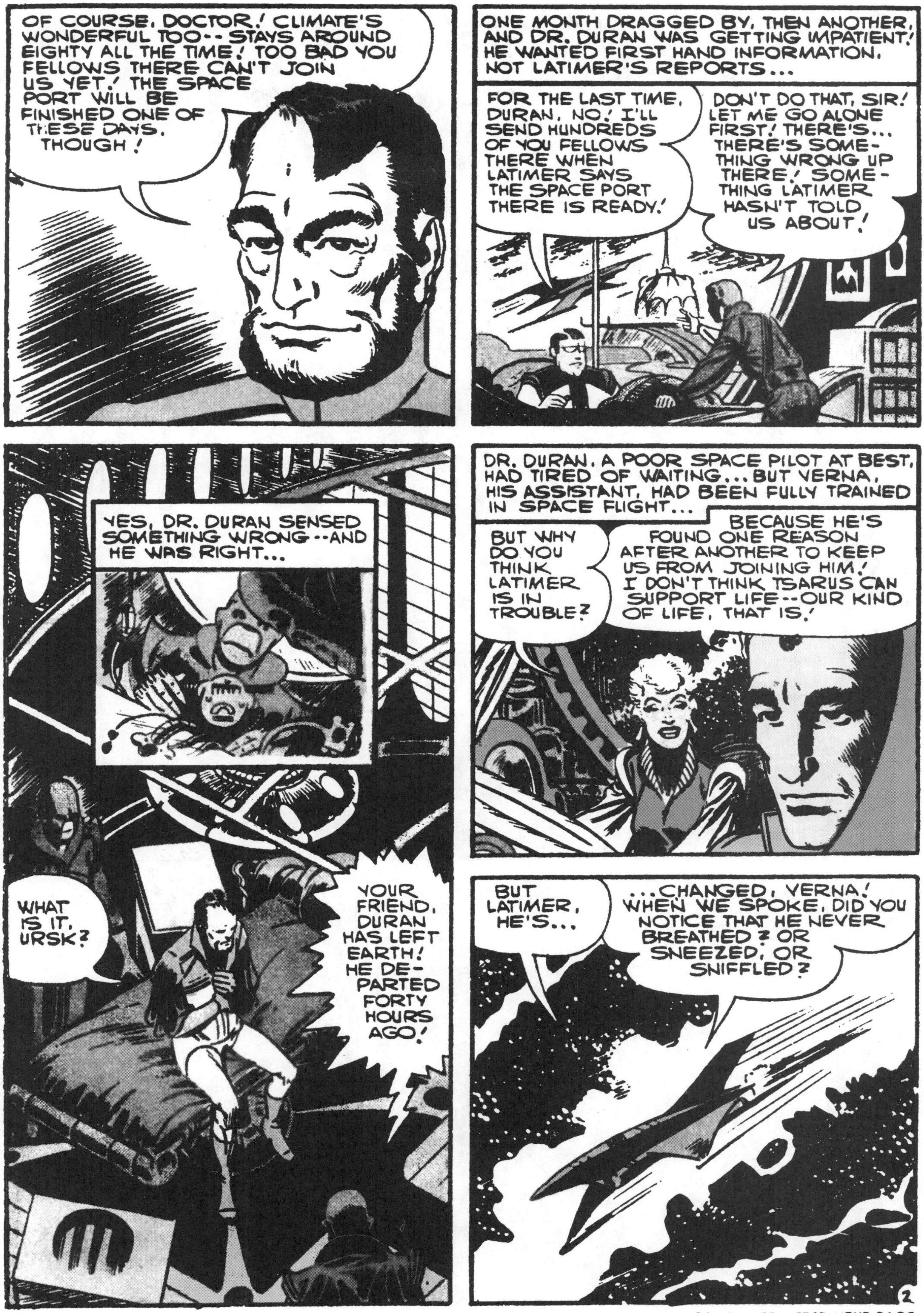
OF COURSE, DOCTOR! CLIMATE'S WONDERFUL TOO-- STAYS AROUND EIGHTY ALL THE TIME! TOO BAD YOU FELLOWS THERE CAN'T JOIN US YET! THE SPACE PORT WILL BE FINISHED ONE OF THESE DAYS, THOUGH!
ONE MONTH DRAGGED BY, THEN ANOTHER, AND DR. DURAN WAS GETTING IMPATIENT! HE WANTED FIRST HAND INFORMATION, NOT LATIMER'S REPORTS...
FOR THE LAST TIME, DURAN, NO! I'LL SEND HUNDREDS OF YOU FELLOWS THERE WHEN LATIMER SAYS THE SPACE PORT THERE IS READY!
DON'T DO THAT, SIR! LET ME GO ALONE FIRST! THERE'S... THERE'S SOME-THING WRONG UP THERE! SOME-THING LATIMER HASN'T TOLD US ABOUT!
YES, DR. DURAN SENSED SOMETHING WRONG--AND HE WAS RIGHT...
WHAT IS IT, URSK?
YOUR FRIEND, DURAN HAS LEFT EARTH! HE DE-PARTED FORTY HOURS AGO!
DR. DURAN, A POOR SPACE PILOT AT BEST, HAD TIRED OF WAITING... BUT VERNA, HIS ASSISTANT, HAD BEEN FULLY TRAINED IN SPACE FLIGHT...
BUT WHY DO YOU THINK LATIMER IS IN TROUBLE?
BECAUSE HE'S FOUND ONE REASON AFTER ANOTHER TO KEEP US FROM JOINING HIM! I DON'T THINK TSARUS CAN SUPPORT LIFE--OUR KIND OF LIFE, THAT IS!
BUT LATIMER, HE'S...
...CHANGED, VERNA! WHEN WE SPOKE, DID YOU NOTICE THAT HE NEVER BREATHED? OR SNEEZED, OR SNIFFLED?
2

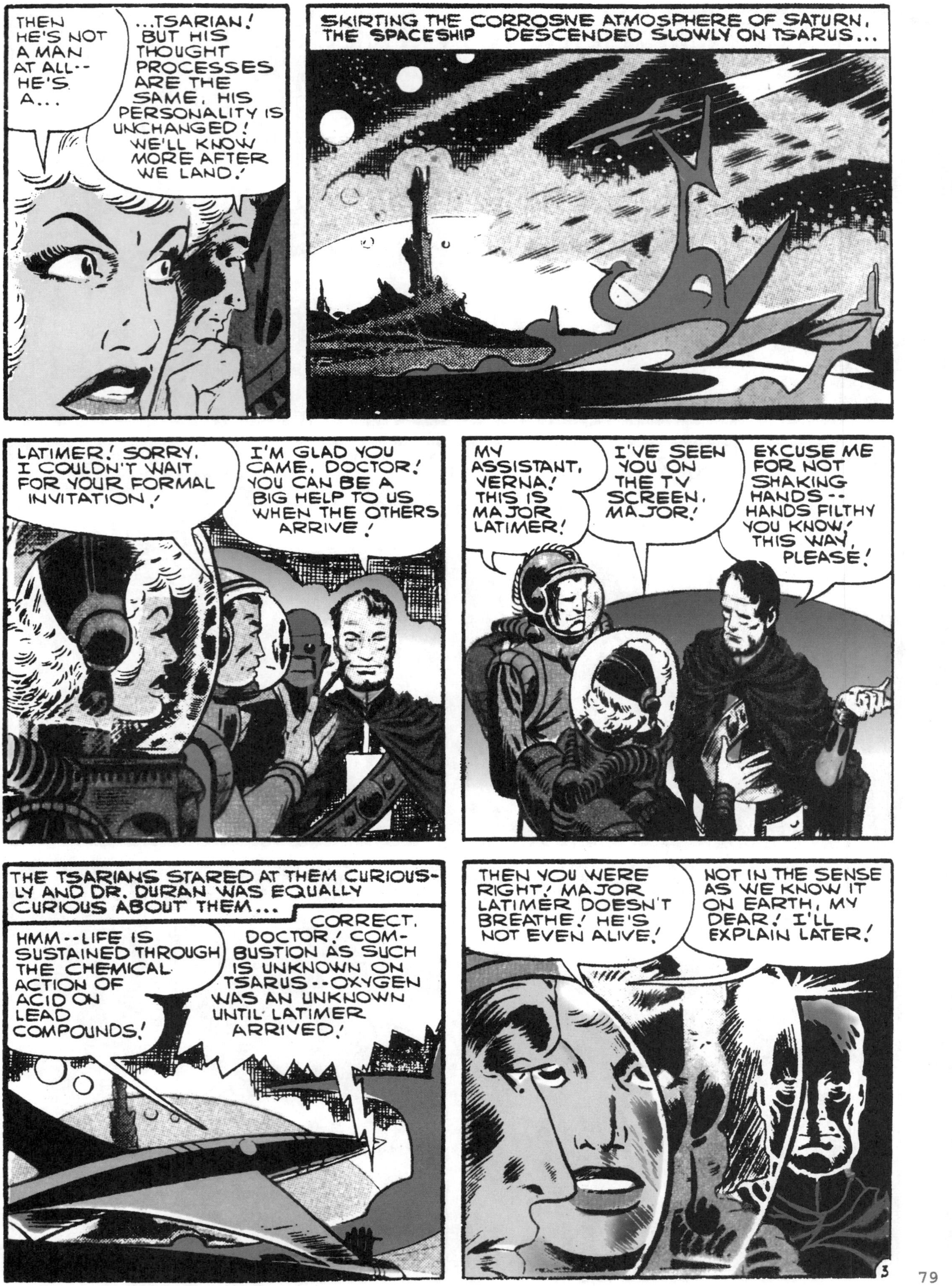
THEN HE'S NOT A MAN AT ALL-- HE'S A...
...TSARIAN! BUT HIS THOUGHT PROCESSES ARE THE SAME, HIS PERSONALITY IS UNCHANGED! WE'LL KNOW MORE AFTER WE LAND!
SKIRTING THE CORROSIVE ATMOSPHERE OF SATURN, THE SPACESHIP DESCENDED SLOWLY ON TSARUS...
LATIMER! SORRY, I COULDN'T WAIT FOR YOUR FORMAL INVITATION!
I'M GLAD YOU CAME, DOCTOR! YOU CAN BE A BIG HELP TO US WHEN THE OTHERS ARRIVE!
MY ASSISTANT, VERNA! THIS IS MAJOR LATIMER!
I'VE SEEN YOU ON THE TV SCREEN, MAJOR!
EXCUSE ME FOR NOT SHAKING HANDS -- HANDS FILTHY YOU KNOW! THIS WAY, PLEASE!
THE TSARIANS STARED AT THEM CURIOUSLY AND DR. DURAN WAS EQUALLY CURIOUS ABOUT THEM...
HMM--LIFE IS SUSTAINED THROUGH THE CHEMICAL ACTION OF ACID ON LEAD COMPOUNDS!
CORRECT, DOCTOR! COMBUSTION AS SUCH IS UNKNOWN ON TSARUS--OXYGEN WAS AN UNKNOWN UNTIL LATIMER ARRIVED!
THEN YOU WERE RIGHT! MAJOR LATIMER DOESN'T BREATHE! HE'S NOT EVEN ALIVE!
NOT IN THE SENSE AS WE KNOW IT ON EARTH, MY DEAR! I'LL EXPLAIN LATER!
3

MAJOR LATIMER HAD ALREADY PRE-PARED A ROOM AND A MEAL FOR THE NEWLY ARRIVED PAIR! HE AND URSK, THE RULING TSARIAN SCIENTIST JOINED THEM...
WHEW! IT'S A PLEASURE TO BREATHE NORMALLY AGAIN! WHY THE HELMET, LATIMER? ALLERGIC TO OXYGEN NOW?
I SEE YOU'VE FIGURED IT OUT, DURAN!
YES, LATIMER--I HAVE! YOU'RE STILL LATIMER MENTALLY--BUT THE REST OF YOU IS METERS, DIALS, WIRE AND MOTORS! WOULDN'T YOU LIKE TO ENJOY A STEAK ONCE MORE--OR HOLD HANDS WITH A PRETTY GIRL LIKE VERNA?
STOP IT, DURAN! I...I'M CONTENT NOW! I'M HAPPY!
WE MADE THAT ADJUSTMENT, TOO, DOCTOR! WHEN YOU AND THE FEMALE ARE PROCESSED, WE WILL ADJUST IT SO YOU WILL BE HAPPY TOO!
I'LL DO MY OWN ADJUSTING--AND YOU CAN FORGET THAT 'PROCESSING' BUSINESS!
THE FOOD, ALL SYNTHETIC, WAS DELICIOUS! AFTER THE MEAL, LATIMER SHOWED THEM AROUND...
WHAT HAPPENED, LATIMER? DID THEY OVER-POWER YOU?
NO, THEY WERE FRIENDLY! I TRUSTED THEM AND THEN THEY SLIPPED ME AN ANESTHETIC INTO MY OXYGEN FLASK!
WE USED THE SAME METHOD ON YOU AND VERNA!
TAKE THEM TO THE PROCESSING ROOM! URSK IS WAITING!
4

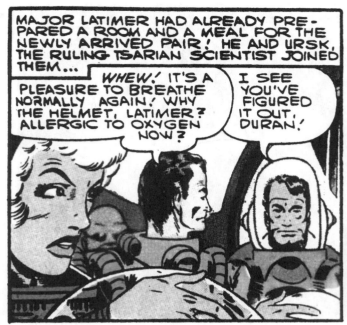

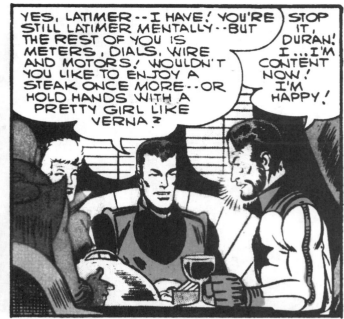

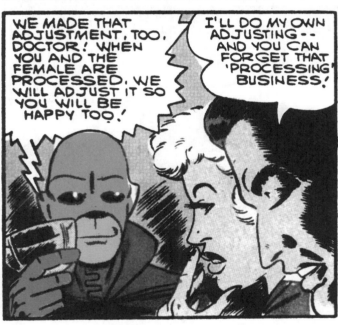

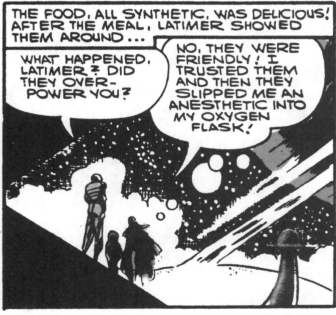

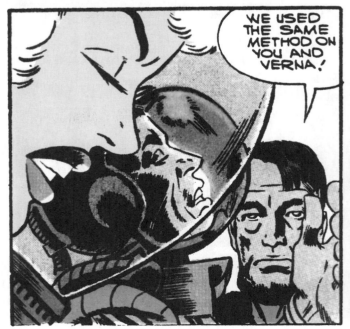

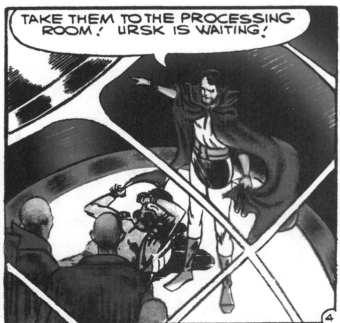

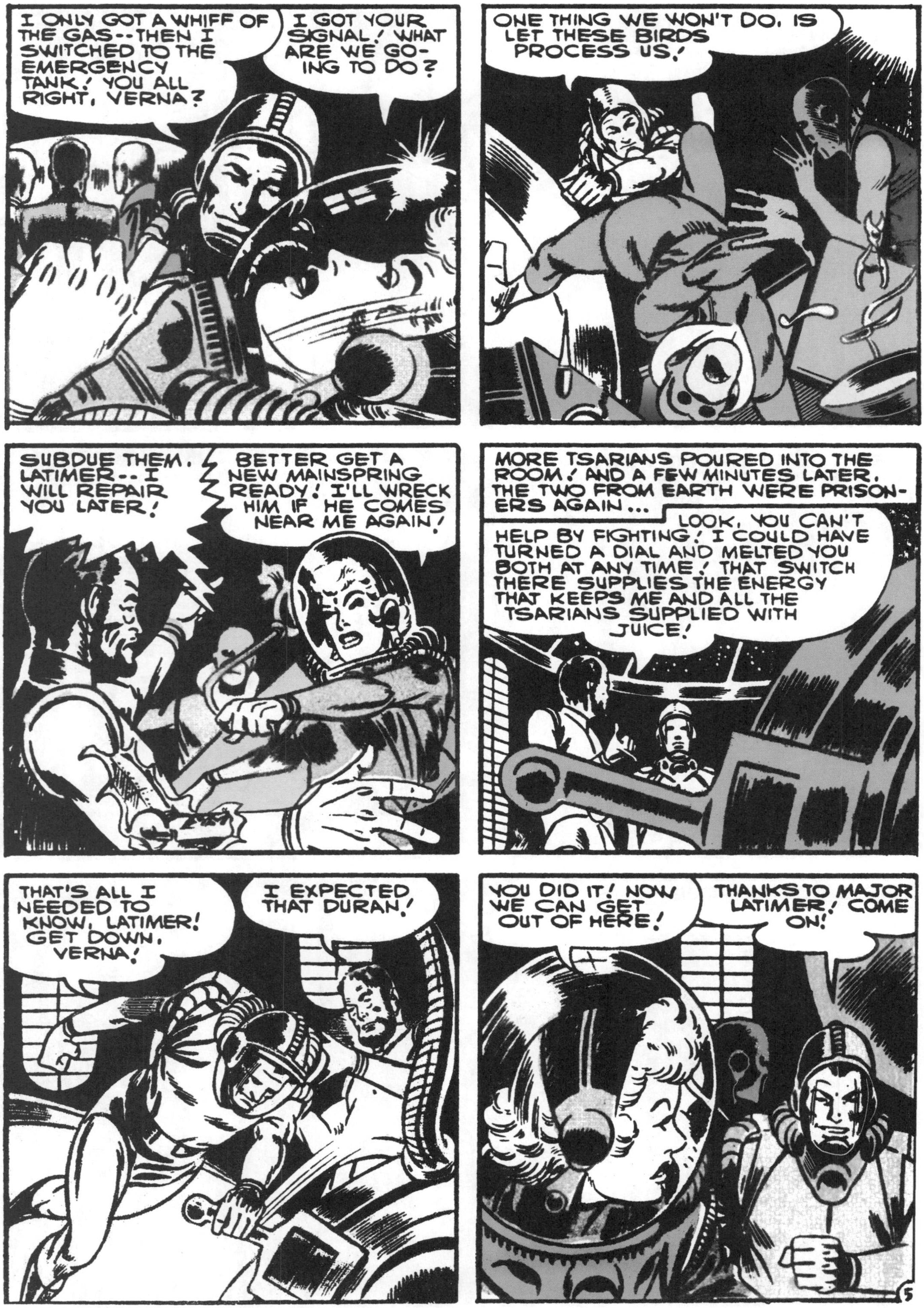
I ONLY GOT A WHIFF OF THE GAS--THEN I SWITCHED TO THE EMERGENCY TANK! YOU ALL RIGHT, VERNA?
I GOT YOUR SIGNAL! WHAT ARE WE GO-ING TO DO?
ONE THING WE WON'T DO, IS LET THESE BIRDS PROCESS US!
SUBDUE THEM, LATIMER--I WILL REPAIR YOU LATER!
BETTER GET A NEW MAINSPRING READY! I'LL WRECK HIM IF HE COMES NEAR ME AGAIN!
MORE TSARIANS POURED INTO THE ROOM! AND A FEW MINUTES LATER, THE TWO FROM EARTH WERE PRISON-ERS AGAIN...
LOOK, YOU CAN'T HELP BY FIGHTING! I COULD HAVE TURNED A DIAL AND MELTED YOU BOTH AT ANY TIME! THAT SWITCH THERE SUPPLIES THE ENERGY THAT KEEPS ME AND ALL THE TSARIANS SUPPLIED WITH JUICE!
THAT'S ALL I NEEDED TO KNOW, LATIMER! GET DOWN, VERNA!
I EXPECTED THAT DURAN!
YOU DID IT! NOW WE CAN GET OUT OF HERE!
THANKS TO MAJOR LATIMER! COME ON!
5

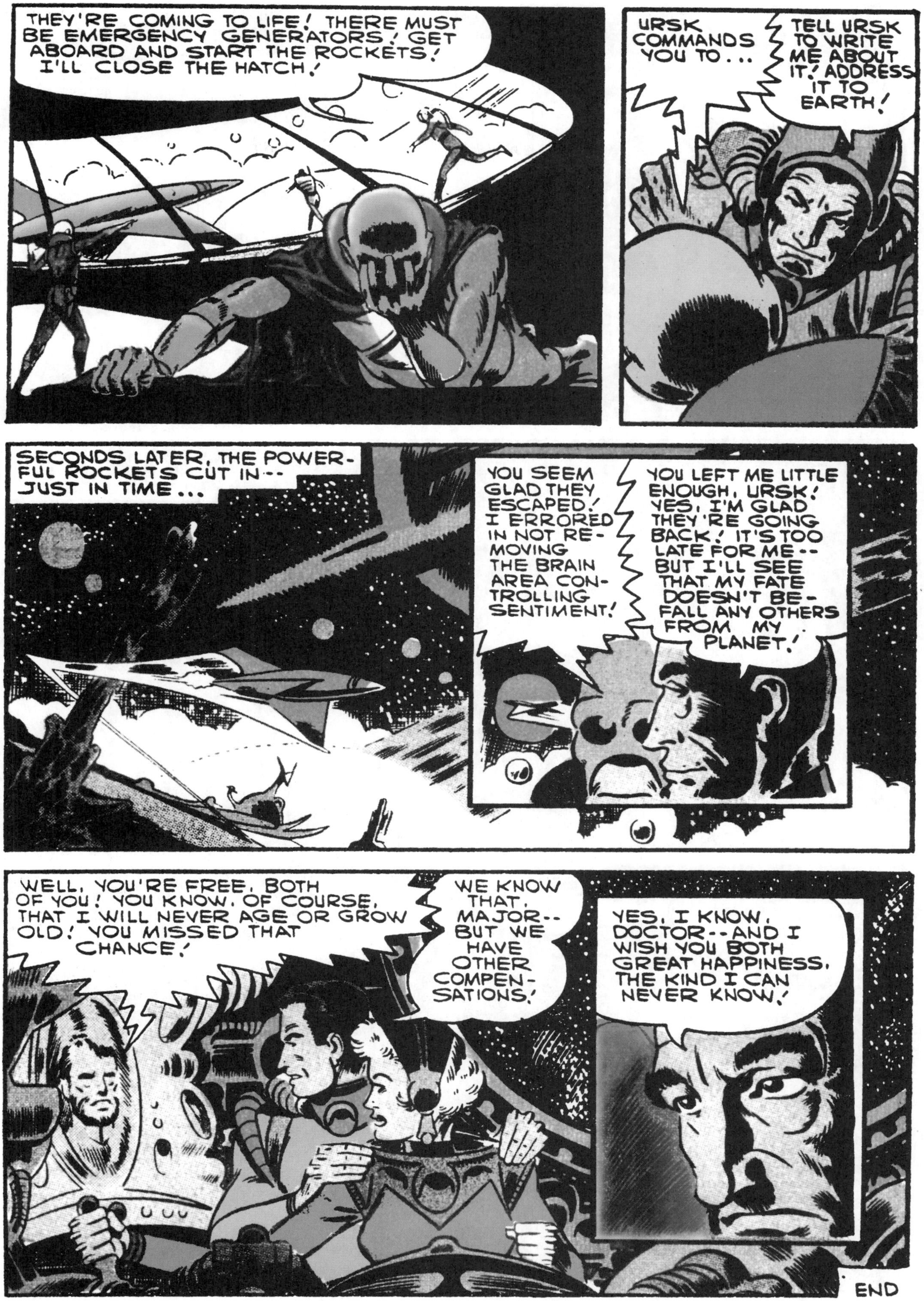
THEY'RE COMING TO LIFE! THERE MUST BE EMERGENCY GENERATORS! GET ABOARD AND START THE ROCKETS! I'LL CLOSE THE HATCH!
URSK COMMANDS YOU TO...
TELL URSK TO WRITE ME ABOUT IT! ADDRESS IT TO EARTH!
SECONDS LATER, THE POWERFUL ROCKETS CUT IN--JUST IN TIME...
YOU SEEM GLAD THEY ESCAPED! I ERRORED IN NOT REMOVING THE BRAIN AREA CONTROLLING SENTIMENT!
YOU LEFT ME LITTLE ENOUGH, URSK! YES, I'M GLAD THEY'RE GOING BACK! IT'S TOO LATE FOR ME--BUT I'LL SEE THAT MY FATE DOESN'T BEFALL ANY OTHERS FROM MY PLANET!
WELL, YOU'RE FREE, BOTH OF YOU! YOU KNOW, OF COURSE, THAT I WILL NEVER AGE OR GROW OLD! YOU MISSED THAT CHANCE!
WE KNOW THAT, MAJOR--BUT WE HAVE OTHER COMPENSATIONS!
YES, I KNOW, DOCTOR--AND I WISH YOU BOTH GREAT HAPPINESS, THE KIND I CAN NEVER KNOW!
END

STEVE DITKO SPACE WARS

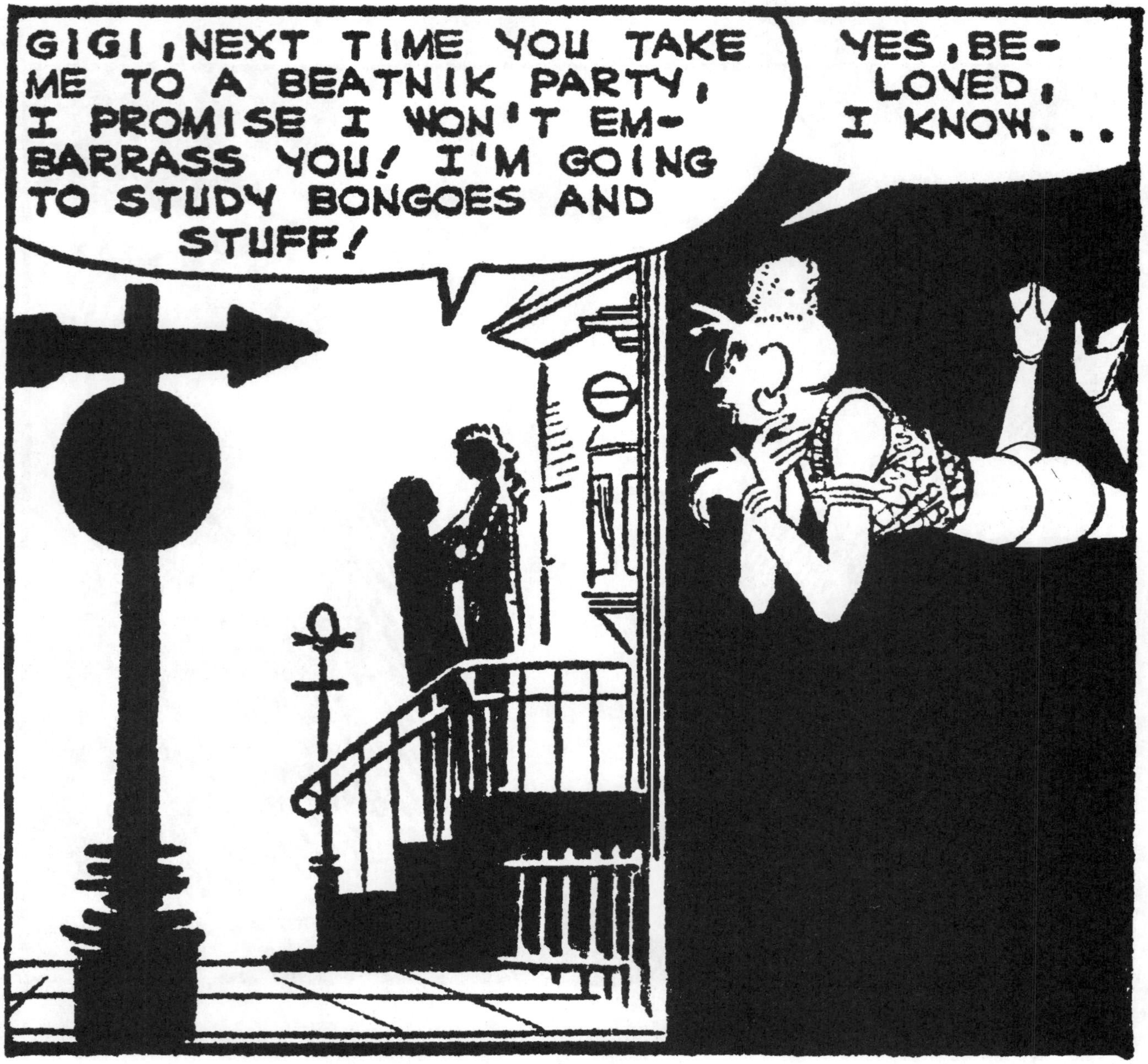
GIGI, NEXT TIME YOU TAKE ME TO A BEATNIK PARTY, I PROMISE I WON'T EMBARRASS YOU! I'M GOING TO STUDY BONGOES AND STUFF!
YES, BELOVED, I KNOW...

STEVE DITKO
SPACE WARS

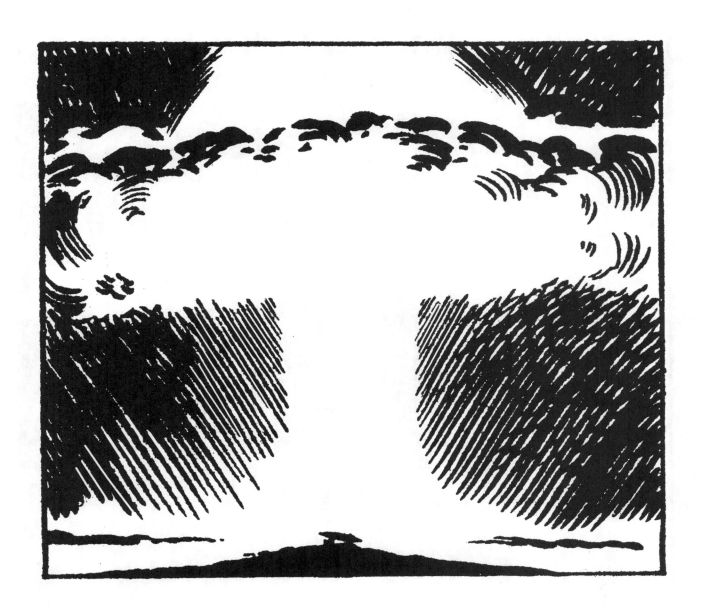

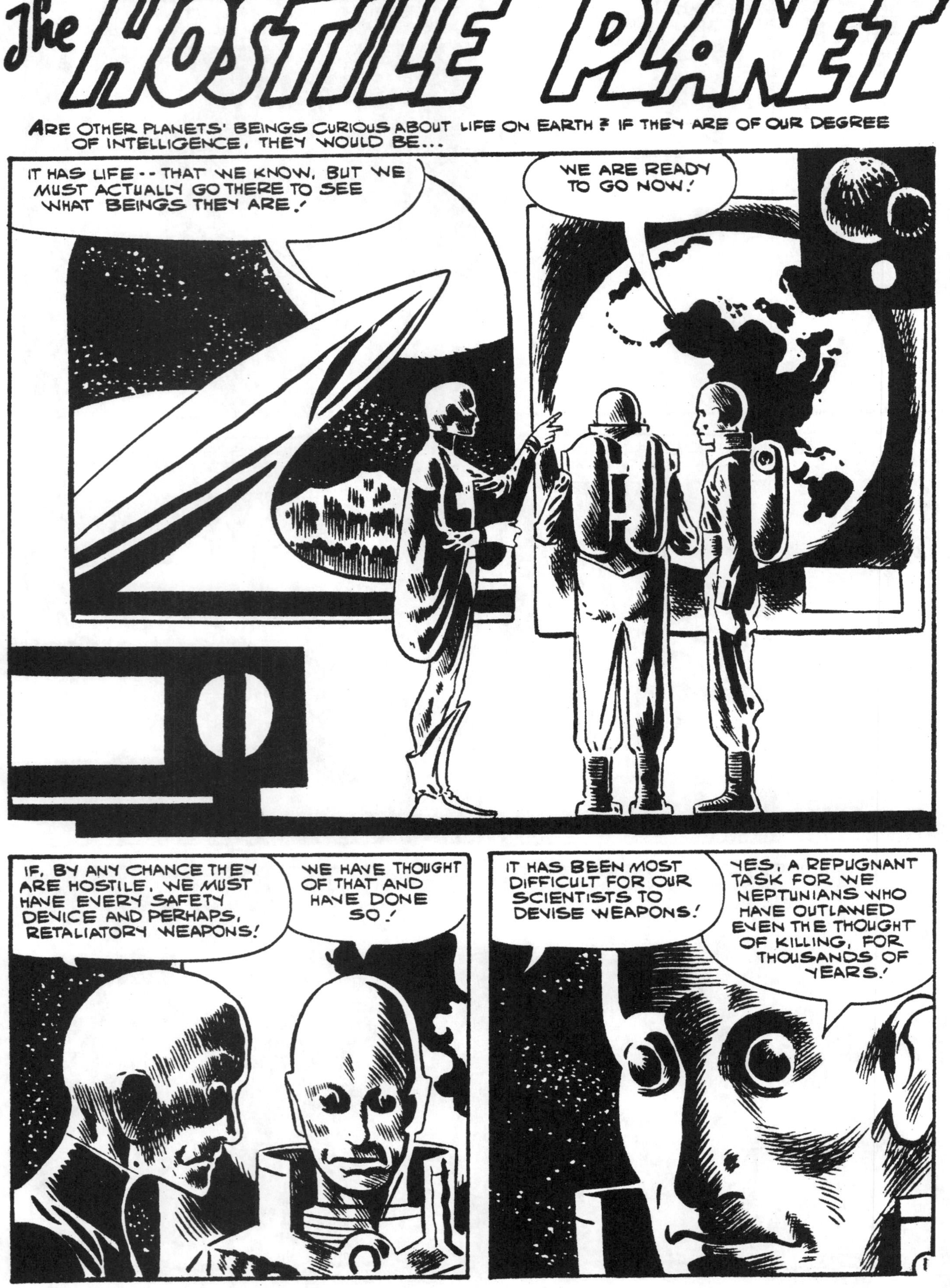
The HOSTILE PLANET
ARE OTHER PLANETS' BEINGS CURIOUS ABOUT LIFE ON EARTH? IF THEY ARE OF OUR DEGREE OF INTELLIGENCE, THEY WOULD BE...
IT HAS LIFE -- THAT WE KNOW, BUT WE MUST ACTUALLY GO THERE TO SEE WHAT BEINGS THEY ARE!
WE ARE READY TO GO NOW!
IF, BY ANY CHANCE THEY ARE HOSTILE, WE MUST HAVE EVERY SAFETY DEVICE AND PERHAPS, RETALIATORY WEAPONS!
WE HAVE THOUGHT OF THAT AND HAVE DONE SO!
IT HAS BEEN MOST DIFFICULT FOR OUR SCIENTISTS TO DEVISE WEAPONS!
YES, A REPUGNANT TASK FOR WE NEPTUNIANS WHO HAVE OUTLAWED EVEN THE THOUGHT OF KILLING, FOR THOUSANDS OF YEARS!

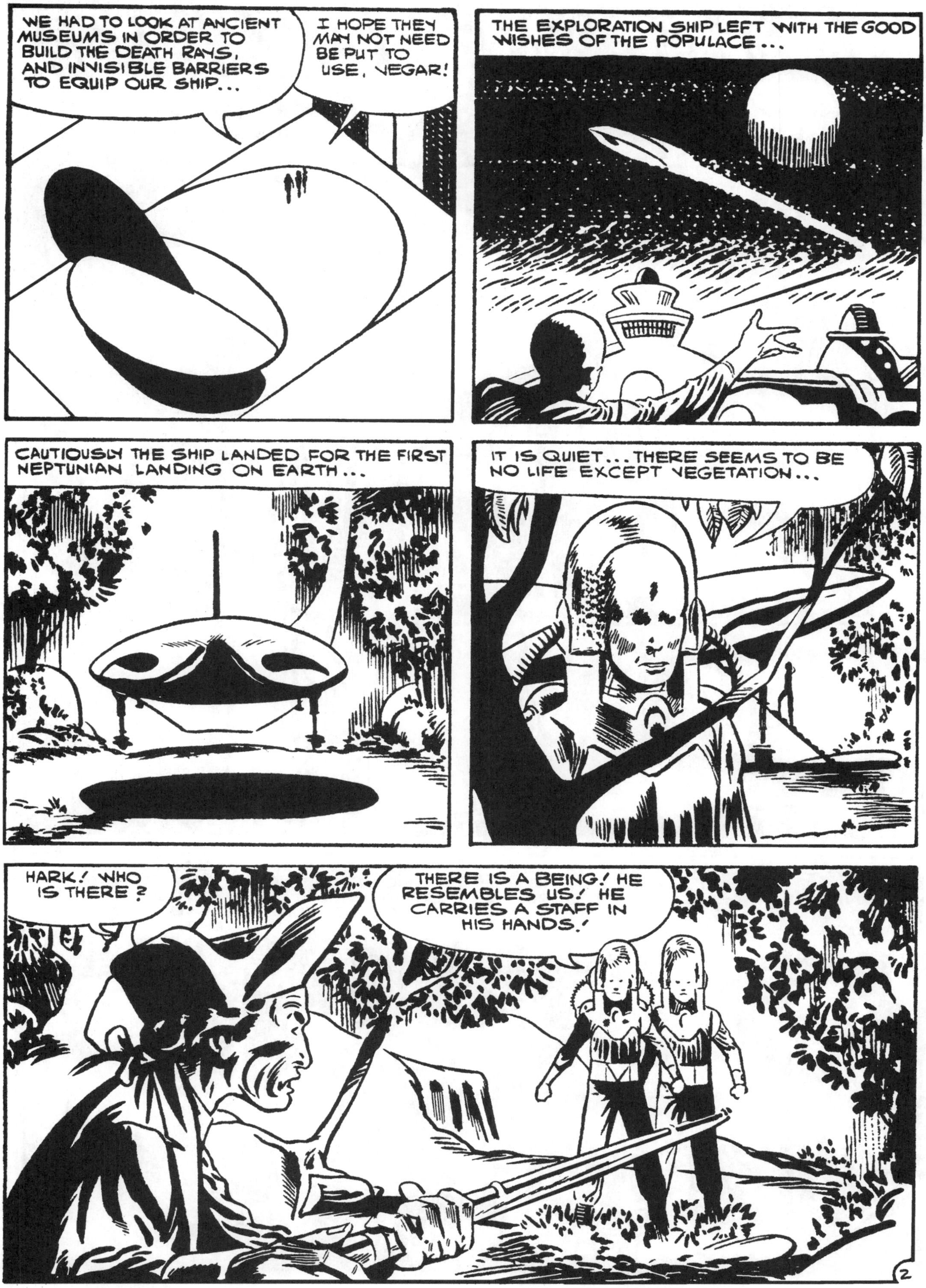
WE HAD TO LOOK AT ANCIENT MUSEUMS IN ORDER TO BUILD THE DEATH RAYS, AND INVISIBLE BARRIERS TO EQUIP OUR SHIP...
I HOPE THEY MAY NOT NEED BE PUT TO USE, VEGAR!
THE EXPLORATION SHIP LEFT WITH THE GOOD WISHES OF THE POPULACE...
CAUTIOUSLY THE SHIP LANDED FOR THE FIRST NEPTUNIAN LANDING ON EARTH...
IT IS QUIET... THERE SEEMS TO BE NO LIFE EXCEPT VEGETATION...
HARK! WHO IS THERE?
THERE IS A BEING! HE RESEMBLES US! HE CARRIES A STAFF IN HIS HANDS!
2

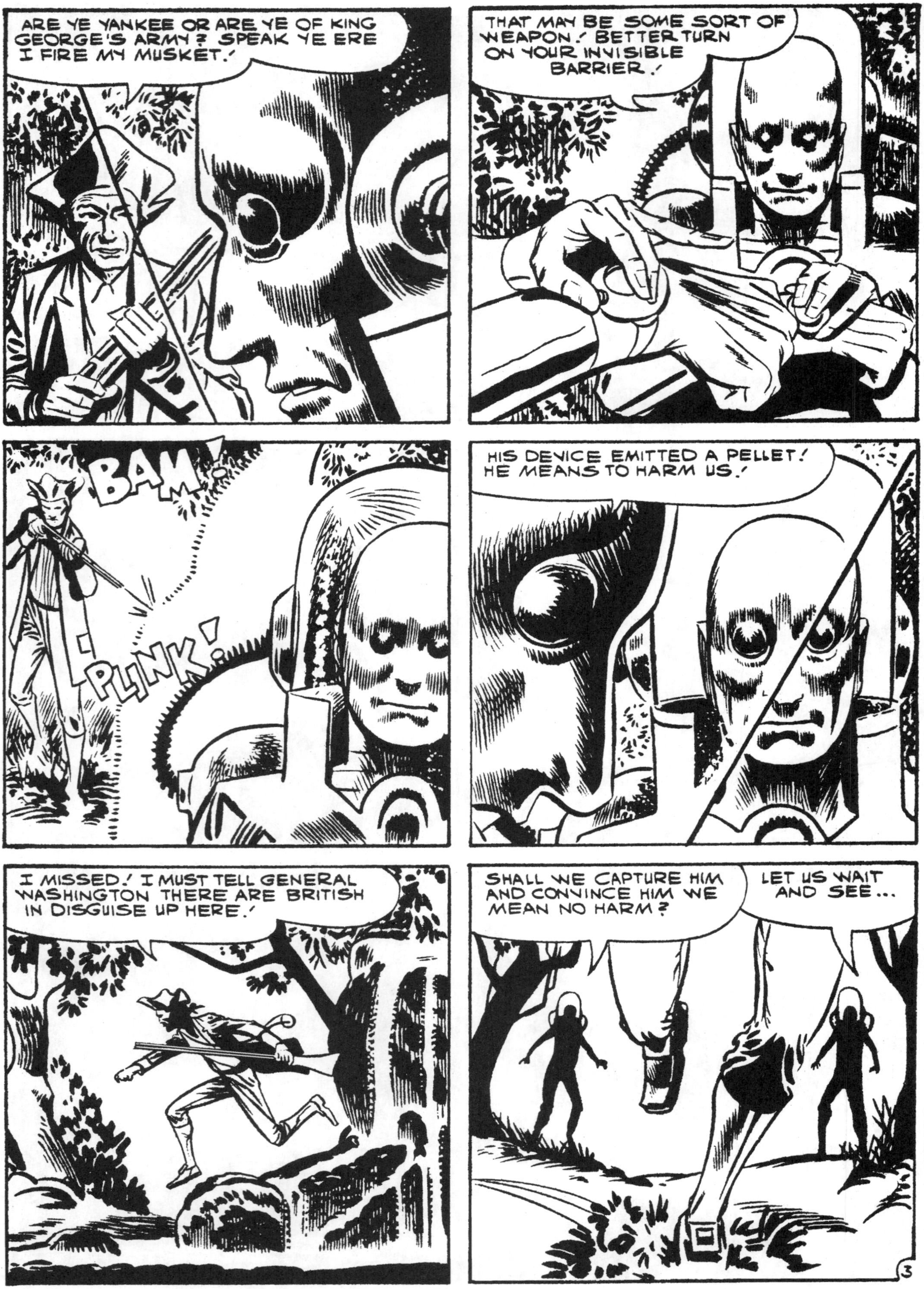

ARE YE YANKEE OR ARE YE OF KING GEORGE'S ARMY? SPEAK YE ERE I FIRE MY MUSKET!
THAT MAY BE SOME SORT OF WEAPON! BETTER TURN ON YOUR INVISIBLE BARRIER!
BAM!
PLINK!
HIS DEVICE EMITTED A PELLET! HE MEANS TO HARM US!
I MISSED! I MUST TELL GENERAL WASHINGTON THERE ARE BRITISH IN DISGUISE UP HERE!
SHALL WE CAPTURE HIM AND CONVINCE HIM WE MEAN NO HARM?
LET US WAIT AND SEE...
3

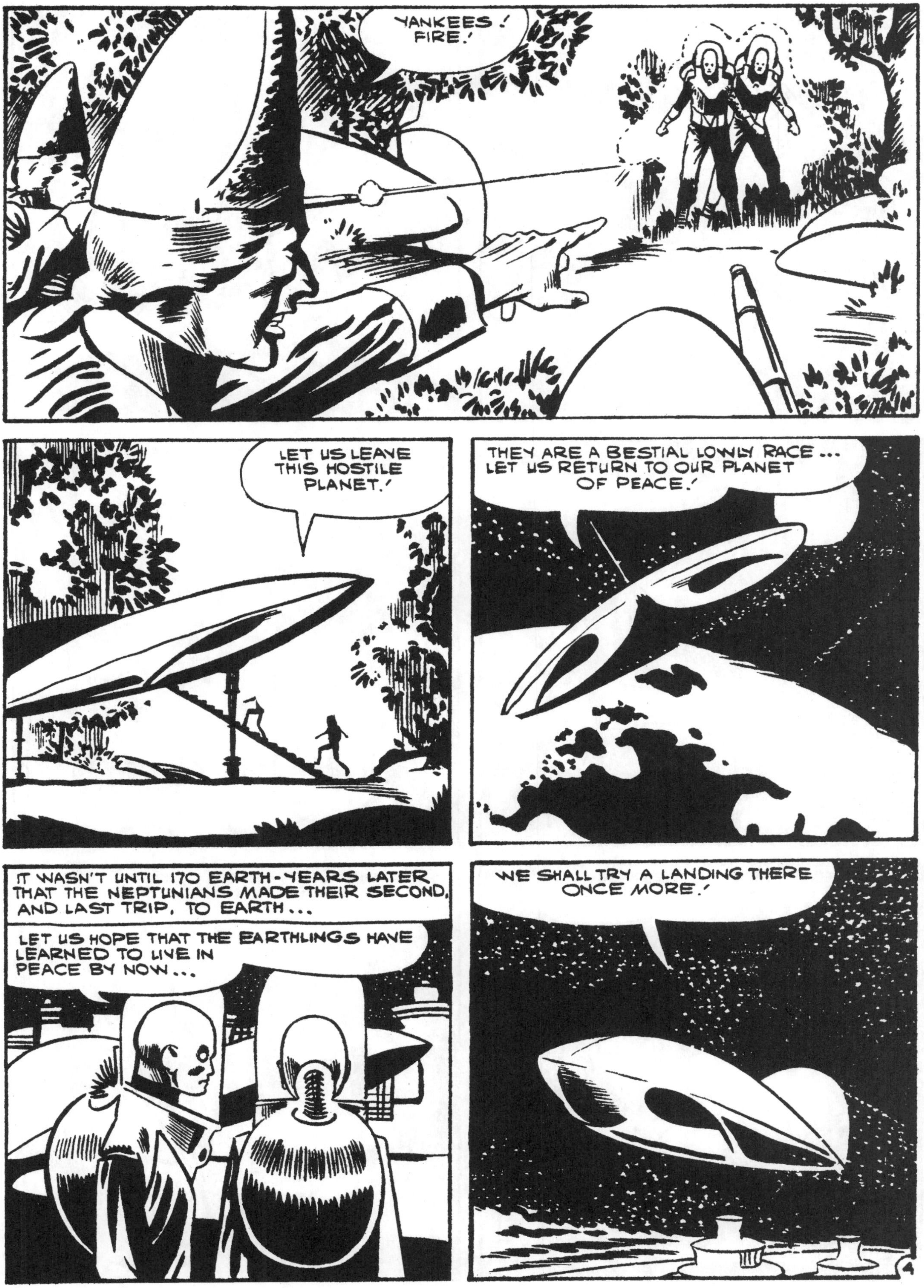
YANKEES! FIRE!
LET US LEAVE THIS HOSTILE PLANET!
THEY ARE A BESTIAL LOWLY RACE... LET US RETURN TO OUR PLANET OF PEACE!
IT WASN'T UNTIL 170 EARTH-YEARS LATER THAT THE NEPTUNIANS MADE THEIR SECOND, AND LAST TRIP, TO EARTH...
LET US HOPE THAT THE EARTHLINGS HAVE LEARNED TO LIVE IN PEACE BY NOW...
WE SHALL TRY A LANDING THERE ONCE MORE!

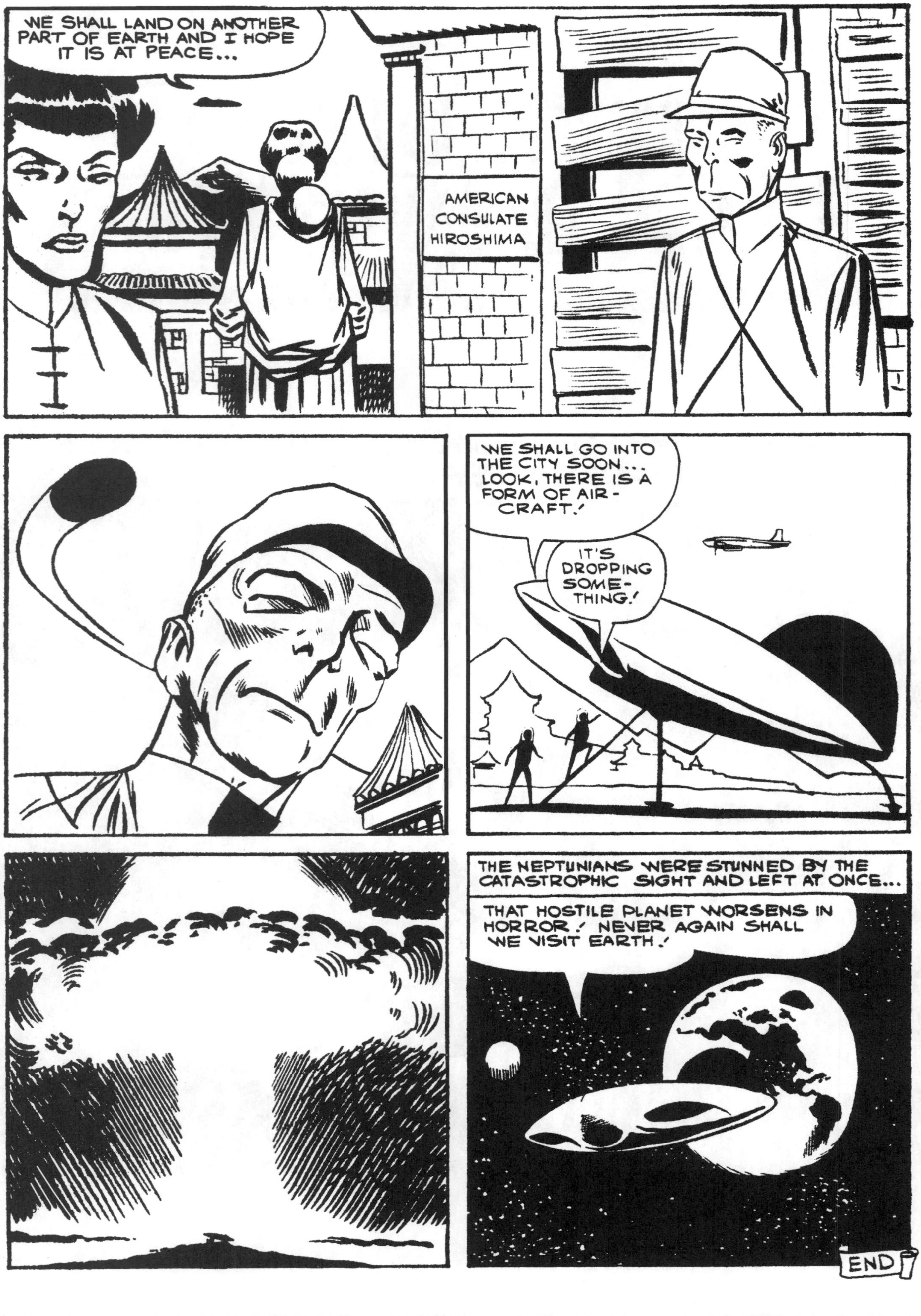
WE SHALL LAND ON ANOTHER PART OF EARTH AND I HOPE IT IS AT PEACE...
AMERICAN CONSULATE HIROSHIMA
WE SHALL GO INTO THE CITY SOON... LOOK, THERE IS A FORM OF AIR-CRAFT!
IT'S DROPPING SOME-THING!
THE NEPTUNIANS WERE STUNNED BY THE CATASTROPHIC SIGHT AND LEFT AT ONCE...
THAT HOSTILE PLANET WORSENS IN HORROR! NEVER AGAIN SHALL WE VISIT EARTH!
END

STEVE DITKO
SPACE WARS

DOWN THROUGH THE SKY THE SPACE SHIP PLUMMETED, DOWN, TOWARD THE SURFACE OF THE ASTEROID KLAXON...

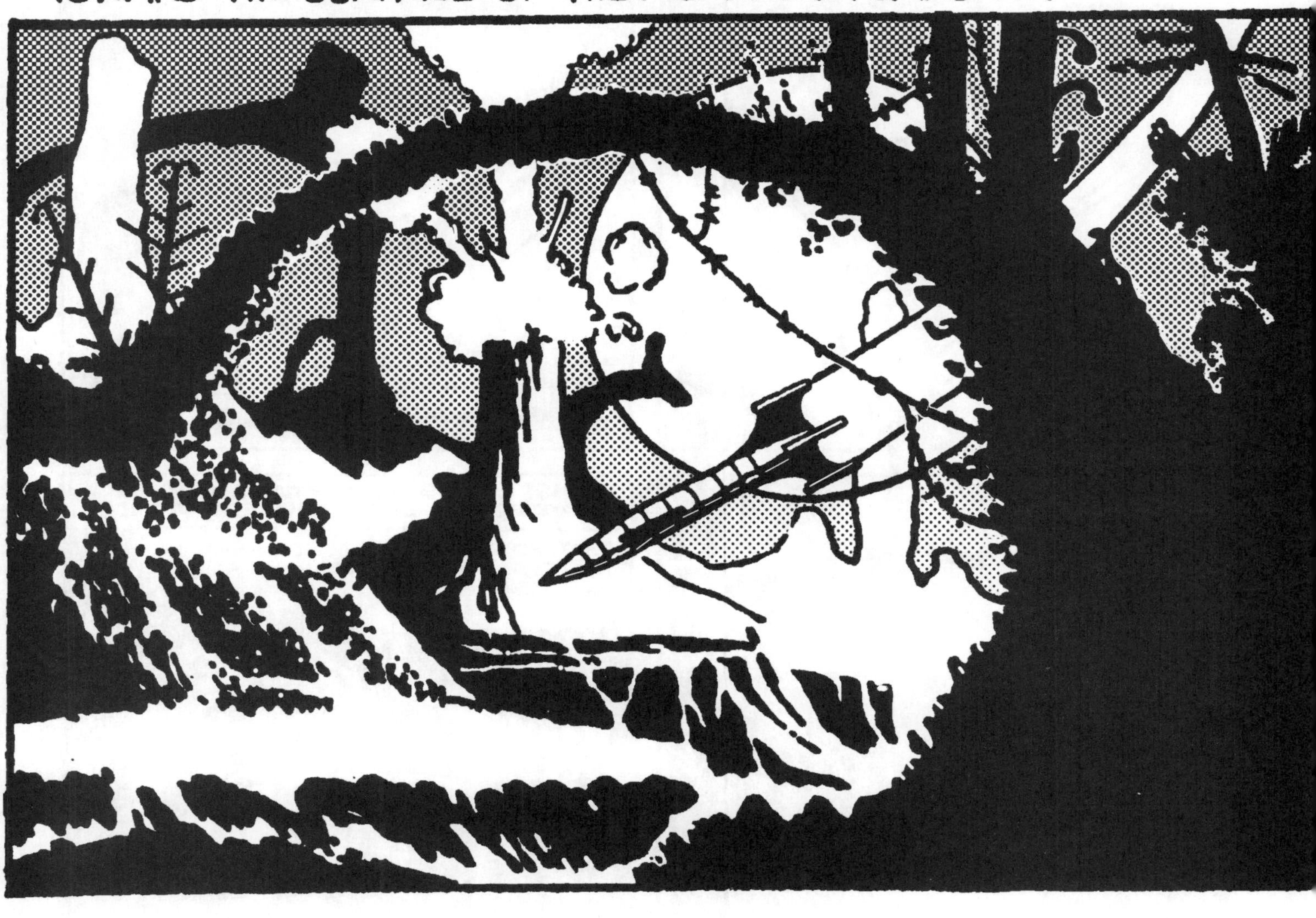

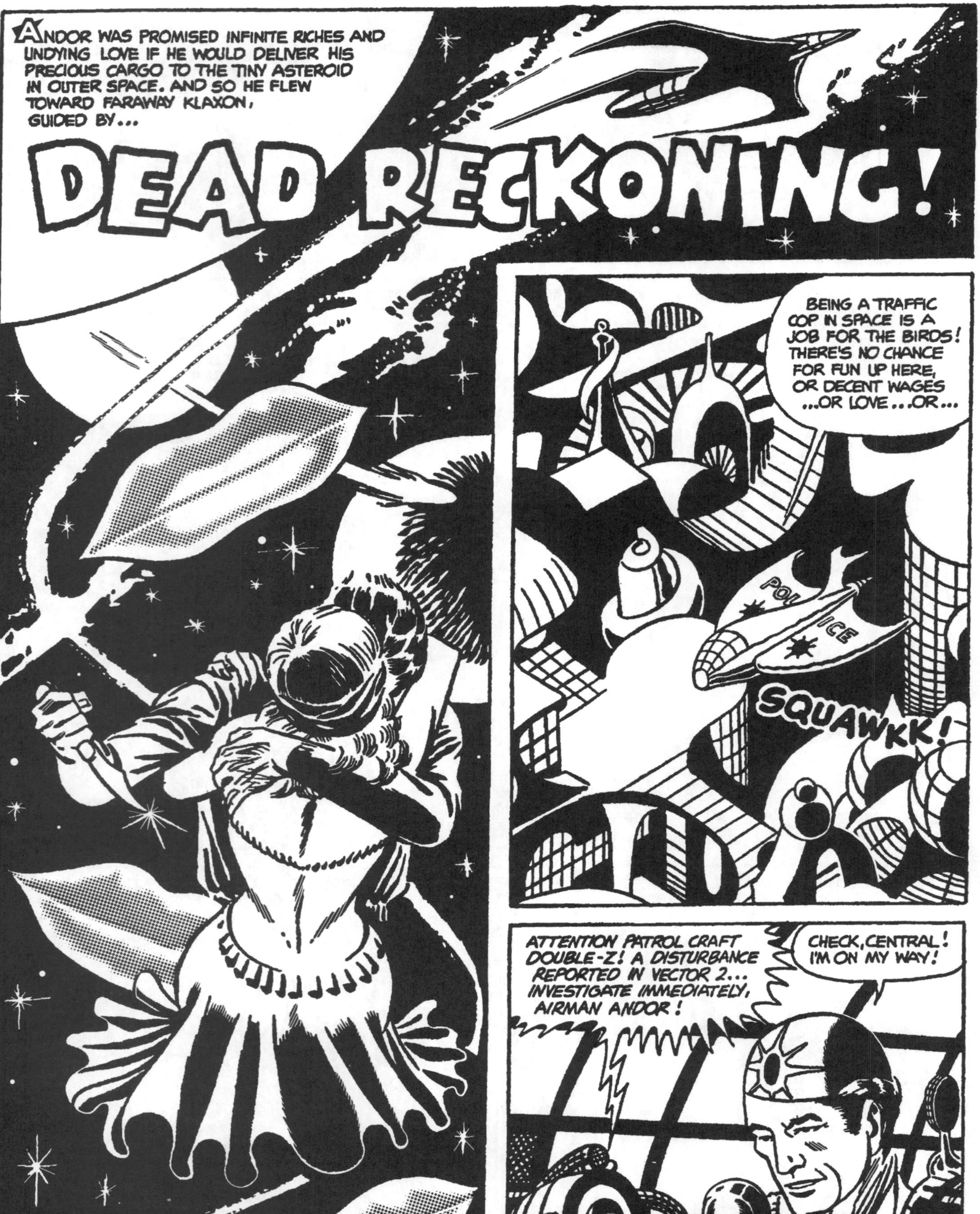

ANDOR WAS PROMISED INFINITE RICHES AND UNDYING LOVE IF HE WOULD DELIVER HIS PRECIOUS CARGO TO THE TINY ASTEROID IN OUTER SPACE. AND SO HE FLEW TOWARD FARAWAY KLAXON, GUIDED BY...
DEAD RECKONING!
Ditko
BEING A TRAFFIC COP IN SPACE IS A JOB FOR THE BIRDS! THERE'S NO CHANCE FOR FUN UP HERE, OR DECENT WAGES ...OR LOVE...OR...
POLICE
SQUAWKK!
ATTENTION PATROL CRAFT DOUBLE-Z! A DISTURBANCE REPORTED IN VECTOR 2... INVESTIGATE IMMEDIATELY, AIRMAN ANDOR!
CHECK, CENTRAL! I'M ON MY WAY!

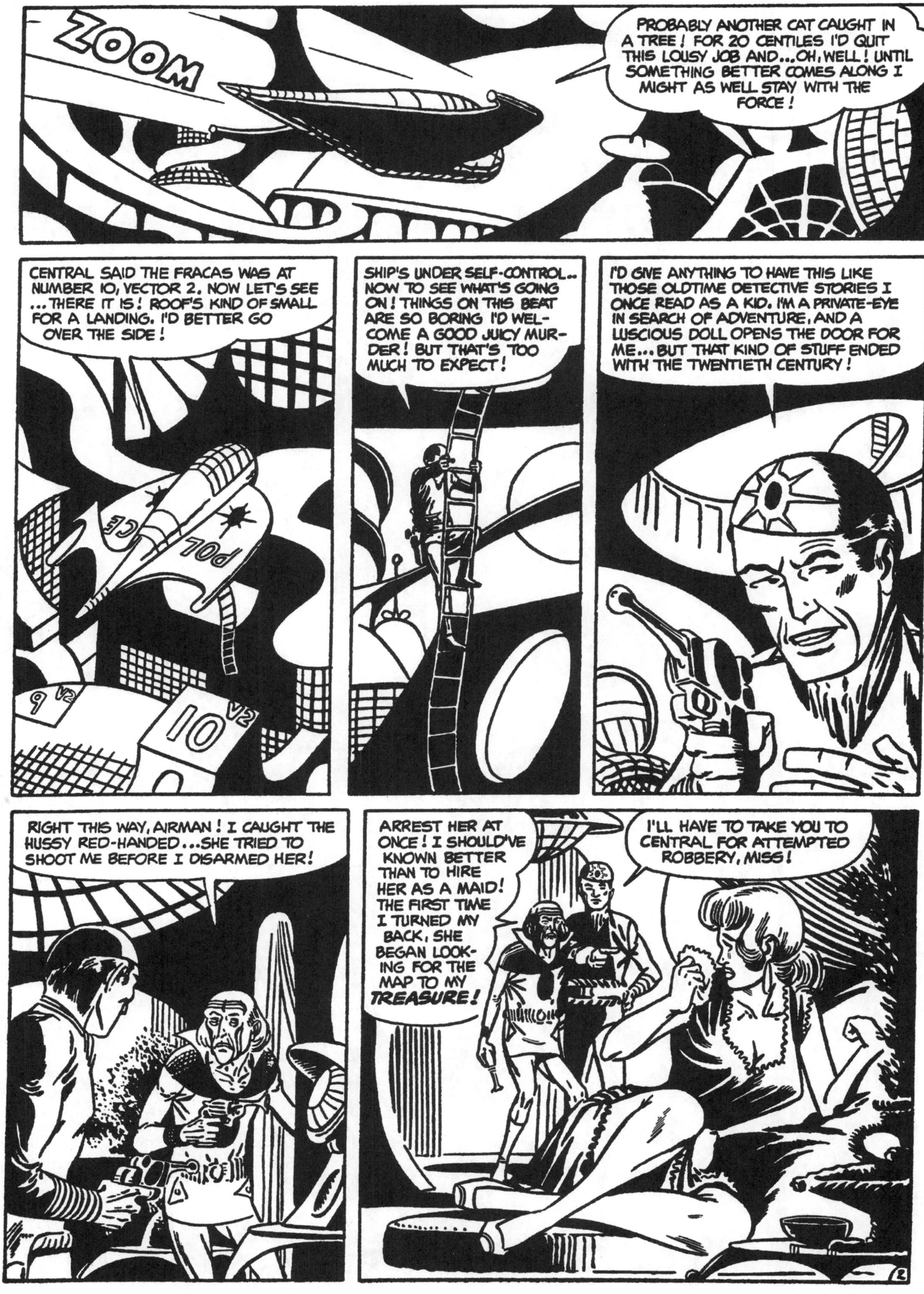
ZOOM
PROBABLY ANOTHER CAT CAUGHT IN A TREE! FOR 20 CENTILES I'D QUIT THIS LOUSY JOB AND...OH, WELL! UNTIL SOMETHING BETTER COMES ALONG I MIGHT AS WELL STAY WITH THE FORCE!
CENTRAL SAID THE FRACAS WAS AT NUMBER 10, VECTOR 2. NOW LET'S SEE ...THERE IT IS! ROOF'S KIND OF SMALL FOR A LANDING. I'D BETTER GO OVER THE SIDE!
POL CE
V2 9
V2 10
SHIP'S UNDER SELF-CONTROL.. NOW TO SEE WHAT'S GOING ON! THINGS ON THIS BEAT ARE SO BORING I'D WELCOME A GOOD JUICY MURDER! BUT THAT'S TOO MUCH TO EXPECT!
I'D GIVE ANYTHING TO HAVE THIS LIKE THOSE OLDTIME DETECTIVE STORIES I ONCE READ AS A KID. I'M A PRIVATE-EYE IN SEARCH OF ADVENTURE, AND A LUSCIOUS DOLL OPENS THE DOOR FOR ME...BUT THAT KIND OF STUFF ENDED WITH THE TWENTIETH CENTURY!
RIGHT THIS WAY, AIRMAN! I CAUGHT THE HUSSY RED-HANDED...SHE TRIED TO SHOOT ME BEFORE I DISARMED HER!
ARREST HER AT ONCE! I SHOULD'VE KNOWN BETTER THAN TO HIRE HER AS A MAID! THE FIRST TIME I TURNED MY BACK, SHE BEGAN LOOKING FOR THE MAP TO MY *TREASURE!*
I'LL HAVE TO TAKE YOU TO CENTRAL FOR ATTEMPTED ROBBERY, MISS!
2

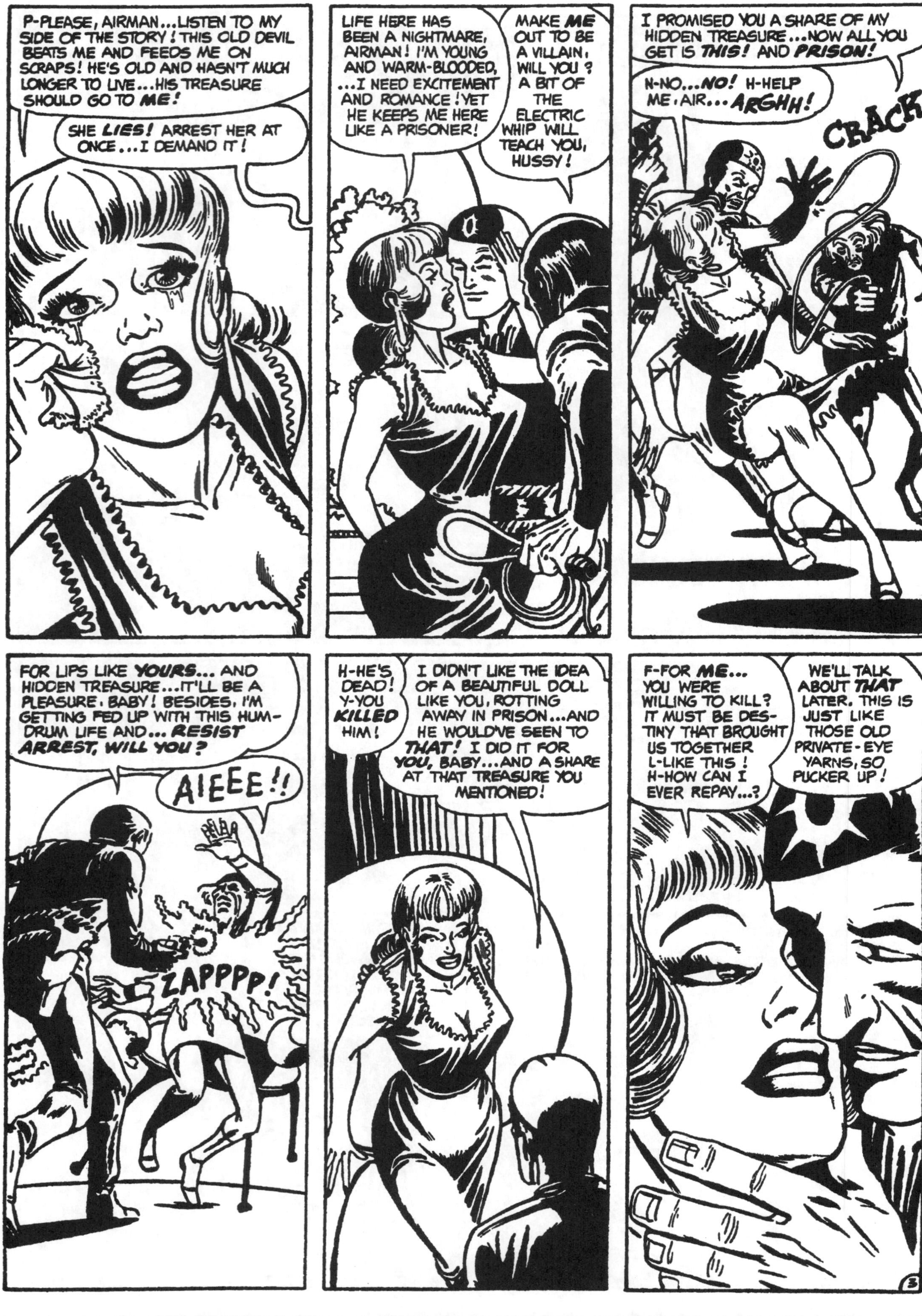
P-PLEASE, AIRMAN... LISTEN TO MY SIDE OF THE STORY! THIS OLD DEVIL BEATS ME AND FEEDS ME ON SCRAPS! HE'S OLD AND HASN'T MUCH LONGER TO LIVE... HIS TREASURE SHOULD GO TO ME!
SHE LIES! ARREST HER AT ONCE... I DEMAND IT!
LIFE HERE HAS BEEN A NIGHTMARE, AIRMAN! I'M YOUNG AND WARM-BLOODED, ...I NEED EXCITEMENT AND ROMANCE! YET HE KEEPS ME HERE LIKE A PRISONER!
MAKE ME OUT TO BE A VILLAIN, WILL YOU? A BIT OF THE ELECTRIC WHIP WILL TEACH YOU, HUSSY!
I PROMISED YOU A SHARE OF MY HIDDEN TREASURE... NOW ALL YOU GET IS THIS! AND PRISON!
N-NO... NO! H-HELP ME, AIR... ARGHH!
CRACK
FOR LIPS LIKE YOURS... AND HIDDEN TREASURE... IT'LL BE A PLEASURE, BABY! BESIDES, I'M GETTING FED UP WITH THIS HUM-DRUM LIFE AND... RESIST ARREST, WILL YOU?
AIEEE!!
ZAPPPP!
H-HE'S DEAD! Y-YOU KILLED HIM!
I DIDN'T LIKE THE IDEA OF A BEAUTIFUL DOLL LIKE YOU, ROTTING AWAY IN PRISON... AND HE WOULD'VE SEEN TO THAT! I DID IT FOR YOU, BABY... AND A SHARE AT THAT TREASURE YOU MENTIONED!
F-FOR ME... YOU WERE WILLING TO KILL? IT MUST BE DESTINY THAT BROUGHT US TOGETHER L-LIKE THIS! H-HOW CAN I EVER REPAY...?
WE'LL TALK ABOUT THAT LATER. THIS IS JUST LIKE THOSE OLD PRIVATE-EYE YARNS, SO PUCKER UP!

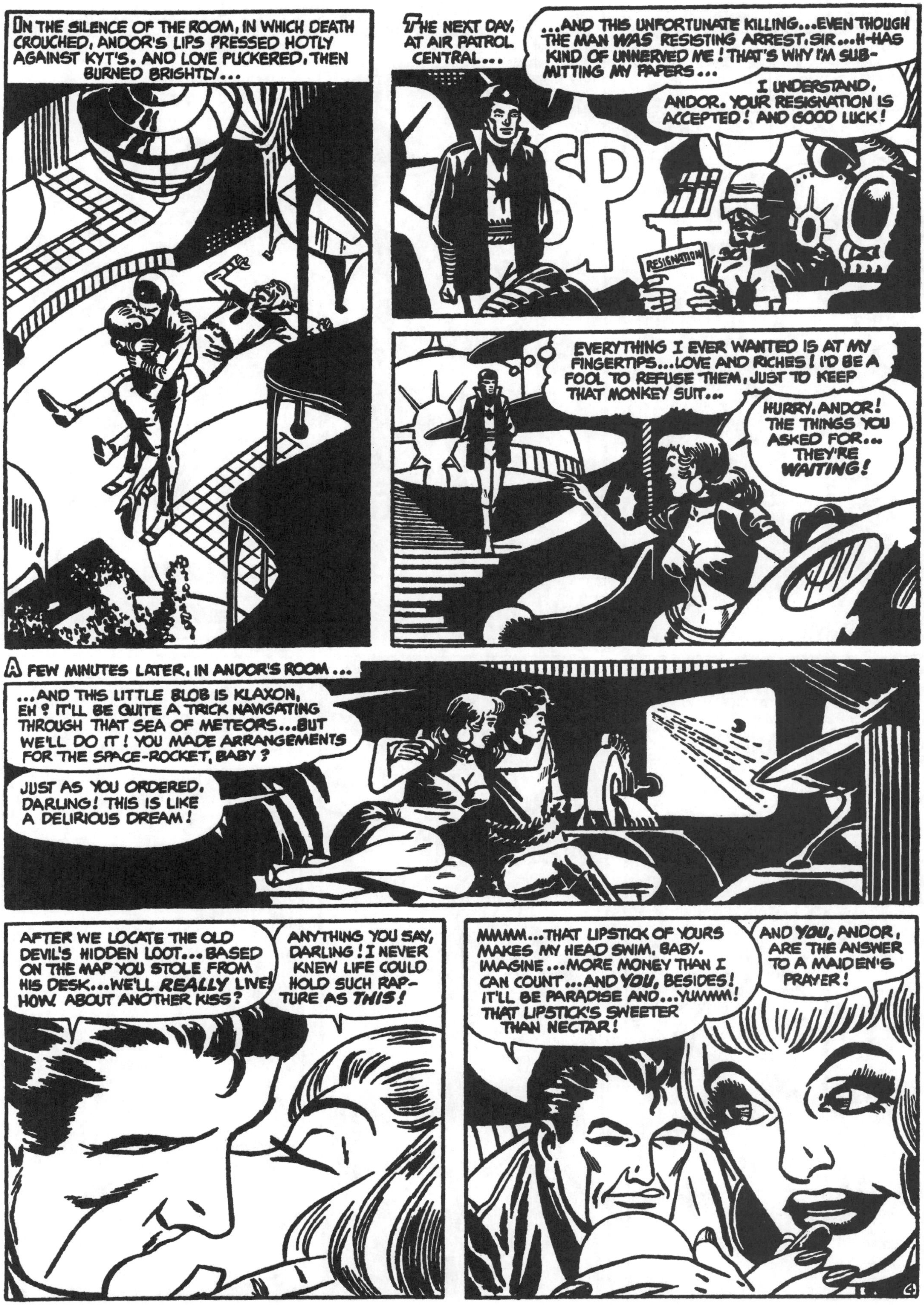
IN THE SILENCE OF THE ROOM, IN WHICH DEATH CROUCHED, ANDOR'S LIPS PRESSED HOTLY AGAINST KYT'S. AND LOVE PUCKERED, THEN BURNED BRIGHTLY...
THE NEXT DAY, AT AIR PATROL CENTRAL...
...AND THIS UNFORTUNATE KILLING...EVEN THOUGH THE MAN WAS RESISTING ARREST, SIR...H-HAS KIND OF UNNERVED ME! THAT'S WHY I'M SUBMITTING MY PAPERS...
I UNDERSTAND, ANDOR. YOUR RESIGNATION IS ACCEPTED! AND GOOD LUCK!
SP
RESIGNATION
EVERYTHING I EVER WANTED IS AT MY FINGERTIPS...LOVE AND RICHES! I'D BE A FOOL TO REFUSE THEM, JUST TO KEEP THAT MONKEY SUIT...
HURRY, ANDOR! THE THINGS YOU ASKED FOR... THEY'RE WAITING!
A FEW MINUTES LATER, IN ANDOR'S ROOM...
...AND THIS LITTLE BLOB IS KLAXON, EH? IT'LL BE QUITE A TRICK NAVIGATING THROUGH THAT SEA OF METEORS...BUT WE'LL DO IT! YOU MADE ARRANGEMENTS FOR THE SPACE-ROCKET, BABY?
JUST AS YOU ORDERED, DARLING! THIS IS LIKE A DELIRIOUS DREAM!
AFTER WE LOCATE THE OLD DEVIL'S HIDDEN LOOT...BASED ON THE MAP YOU STOLE FROM HIS DESK...WE'LL REALLY LIVE! HOW ABOUT ANOTHER KISS?
ANYTHING YOU SAY, DARLING! I NEVER KNEW LIFE COULD HOLD SUCH RAPTURE AS THIS!
MMMM...THAT LIPSTICK OF YOURS MAKES MY HEAD SWIM, BABY. IMAGINE...MORE MONEY THAN I CAN COUNT...AND YOU, BESIDES! IT'LL BE PARADISE AND...YUMMM! THAT LIPSTICK'S SWEETER THAN NECTAR!
AND YOU, ANDOR, ARE THE ANSWER TO A MAIDEN'S PRAYER!
4

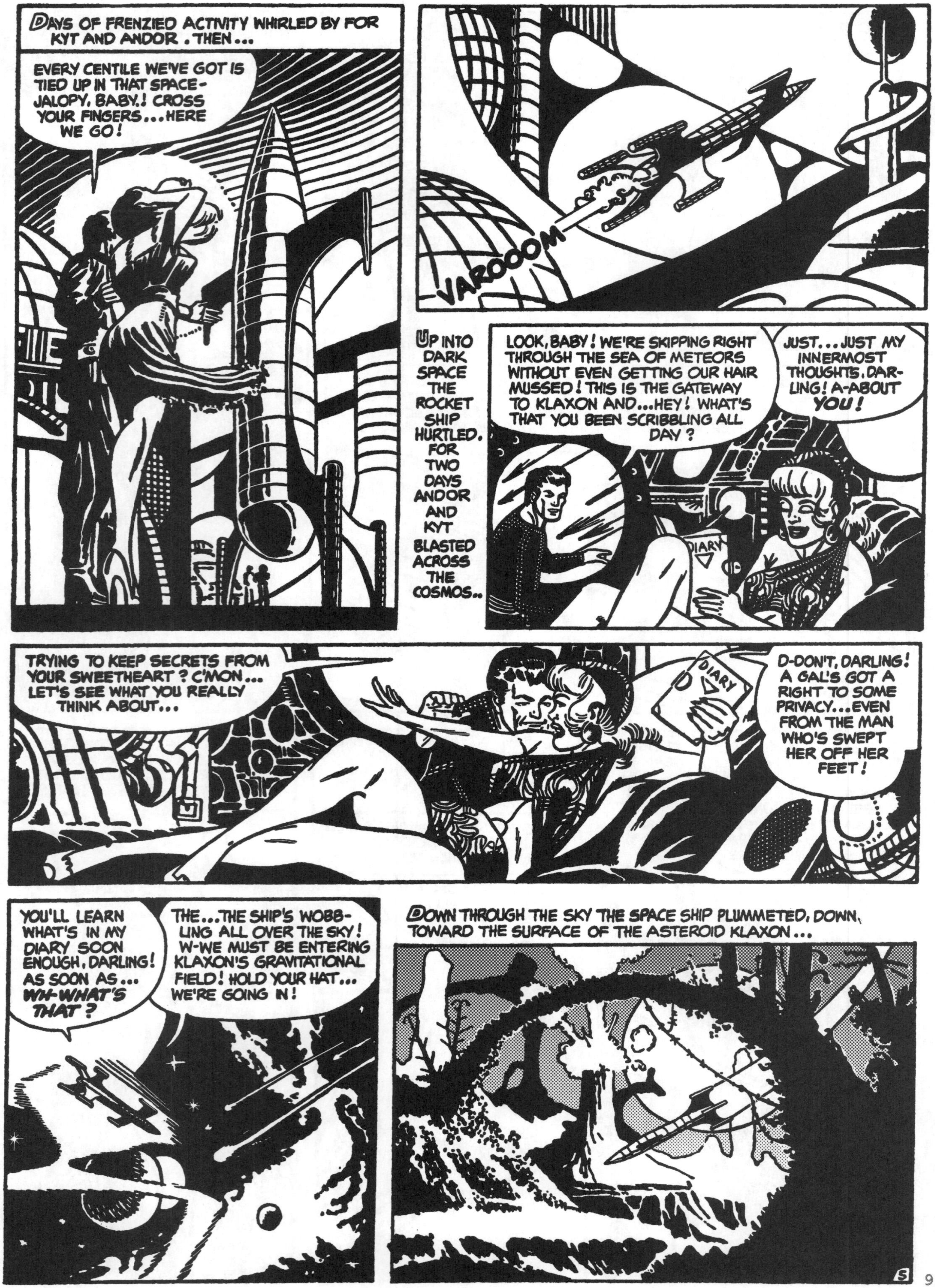
DAYS OF FRENZIED ACTIVITY WHIRLED BY FOR KYT AND ANDOR. THEN...
EVERY CENTILE WE'VE GOT IS TIED UP IN THAT SPACE-JALOPY, BABY.! CROSS YOUR FINGERS...HERE WE GO!
VAROOOM
UP INTO DARK SPACE THE ROCKET SHIP HURTLED. FOR TWO DAYS ANDOR AND KYT BLASTED ACROSS THE COSMOS..
LOOK, BABY! WE'RE SKIPPING RIGHT THROUGH THE SEA OF METEORS WITHOUT EVEN GETTING OUR HAIR MUSSED! THIS IS THE GATEWAY TO KLAXON AND...HEY! WHAT'S THAT YOU BEEN SCRIBBLING ALL DAY?
JUST...JUST MY INNERMOST THOUGHTS, DARLING! A-ABOUT YOU!
DIARY
TRYING TO KEEP SECRETS FROM YOUR SWEETHEART? C'MON... LET'S SEE WHAT YOU REALLY THINK ABOUT...
DIARY
D-DON'T, DARLING! A GAL'S GOT A RIGHT TO SOME PRIVACY...EVEN FROM THE MAN WHO'S SWEPT HER OFF HER FEET!
YOU'LL LEARN WHAT'S IN MY DIARY SOON ENOUGH, DARLING! AS SOON AS... WH-WHAT'S THAT?
THE...THE SHIP'S WOBBLING ALL OVER THE SKY! W-WE MUST BE ENTERING KLAXON'S GRAVITATIONAL FIELD! HOLD YOUR HAT... WE'RE GOING IN!
DOWN THROUGH THE SKY THE SPACE SHIP PLUMMETED, DOWN, TOWARD THE SURFACE OF THE ASTEROID KLAXON...
S

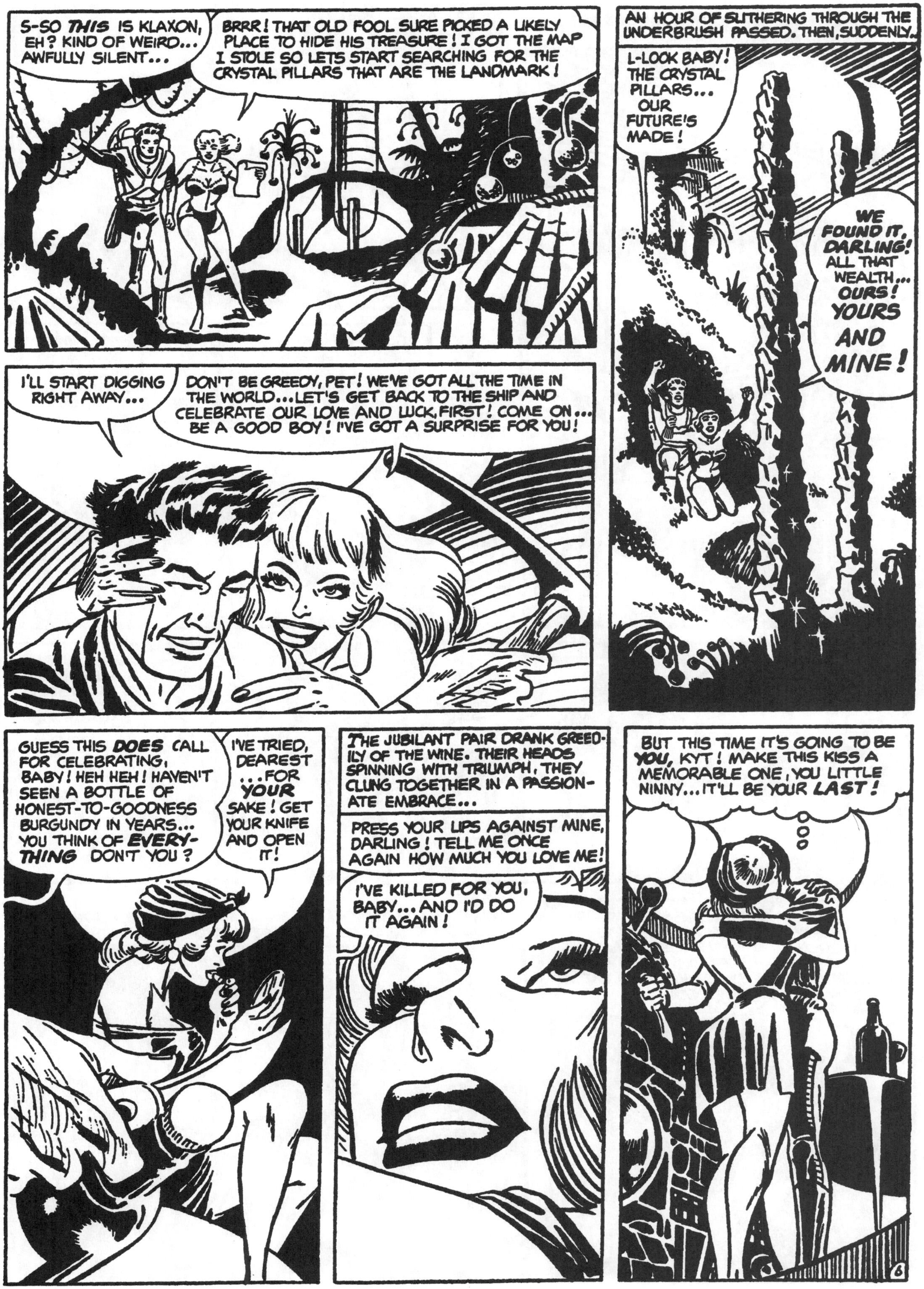

S-SO THIS IS KLAXON, EH? KIND OF WEIRD... AWFULLY SILENT...
BRRR! THAT OLD FOOL SURE PICKED A LIKELY PLACE TO HIDE HIS TREASURE! I GOT THE MAP I STOLE SO LETS START SEARCHING FOR THE CRYSTAL PILLARS THAT ARE THE LANDMARK!
I'LL START DIGGING RIGHT AWAY...
DON'T BE GREEDY, PET! WE'VE GOT ALL THE TIME IN THE WORLD... LET'S GET BACK TO THE SHIP AND CELEBRATE OUR LOVE AND LUCK, FIRST! COME ON... BE A GOOD BOY! I'VE GOT A SURPRISE FOR YOU!
AN HOUR OF SLITHERING THROUGH THE UNDERBRUSH PASSED. THEN, SUDDENLY...
L-LOOK BABY! THE CRYSTAL PILLARS... OUR FUTURE'S MADE!
WE FOUND IT, DARLING! ALL THAT WEALTH... OURS! YOURS AND MINE!
GUESS THIS DOES CALL FOR CELEBRATING, BABY! HEH HEH! HAVEN'T SEEN A BOTTLE OF HONEST-TO-GOODNESS BURGUNDY IN YEARS... YOU THINK OF EVERY-THING DON'T YOU?
I'VE TRIED, DEAREST ...FOR YOUR SAKE! GET YOUR KNIFE AND OPEN IT!
THE JUBILANT PAIR DRANK GREED-ILY OF THE WINE. THEIR HEADS SPINNING WITH TRIUMPH, THEY CLUNG TOGETHER IN A PASSION-ATE EMBRACE...
PRESS YOUR LIPS AGAINST MINE, DARLING! TELL ME ONCE AGAIN HOW MUCH YOU LOVE ME!
I'VE KILLED FOR YOU, BABY... AND I'D DO IT AGAIN!
BUT THIS TIME IT'S GOING TO BE YOU, KYT! MAKE THIS KISS A MEMORABLE ONE, YOU LITTLE NINNY... IT'LL BE YOUR LAST!

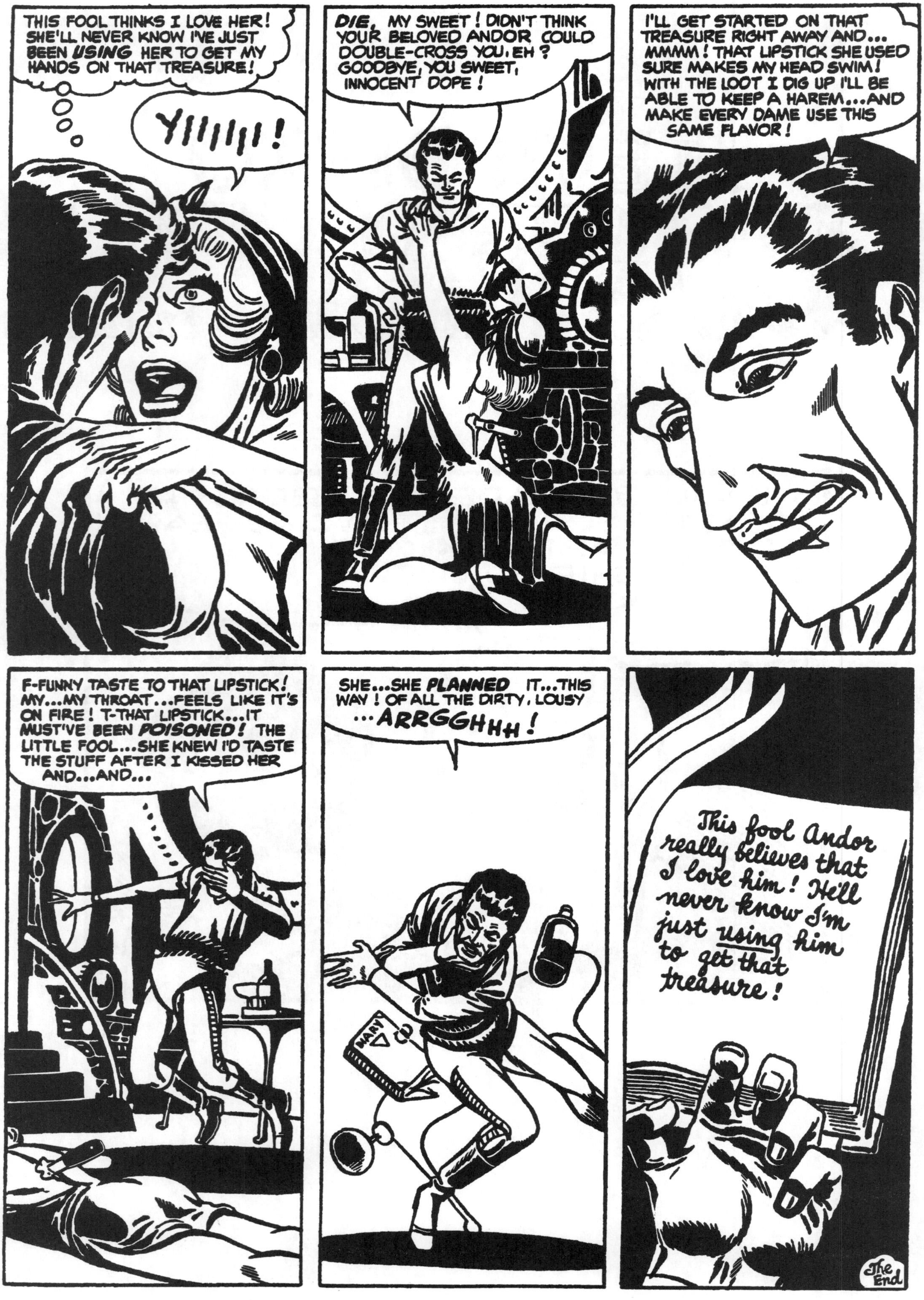
THIS FOOL THINKS I LOVE HER! SHE'LL NEVER KNOW I'VE JUST BEEN USING HER TO GET MY HANDS ON THAT TREASURE!
YIIIIII!
DIE, MY SWEET! DIDN'T THINK YOUR BELOVED ANDOR COULD DOUBLE-CROSS YOU, EH? GOODBYE, YOU SWEET, INNOCENT DOPE!
I'LL GET STARTED ON THAT TREASURE RIGHT AWAY AND... MMMM! THAT LIPSTICK SHE USED SURE MAKES MY HEAD SWIM! WITH THE LOOT I DIG UP I'LL BE ABLE TO KEEP A HAREM...AND MAKE EVERY DAME USE THIS SAME FLAVOR!
F-FUNNY TASTE TO THAT LIPSTICK! MY...MY THROAT...FEELS LIKE IT'S ON FIRE! T-THAT LIPSTICK...IT MUST'VE BEEN POISONED! THE LITTLE FOOL...SHE KNEW I'D TASTE THE STUFF AFTER I KISSED HER AND...AND...
SHE...SHE PLANNED IT...THIS WAY! OF ALL THE DIRTY, LOUSY ...ARRGGHHH!
MARY
This fool Andor really believes that I love him! He'll never know I'm just using him to get that treasure!
The End

STEVE DITKO SPACE WARS

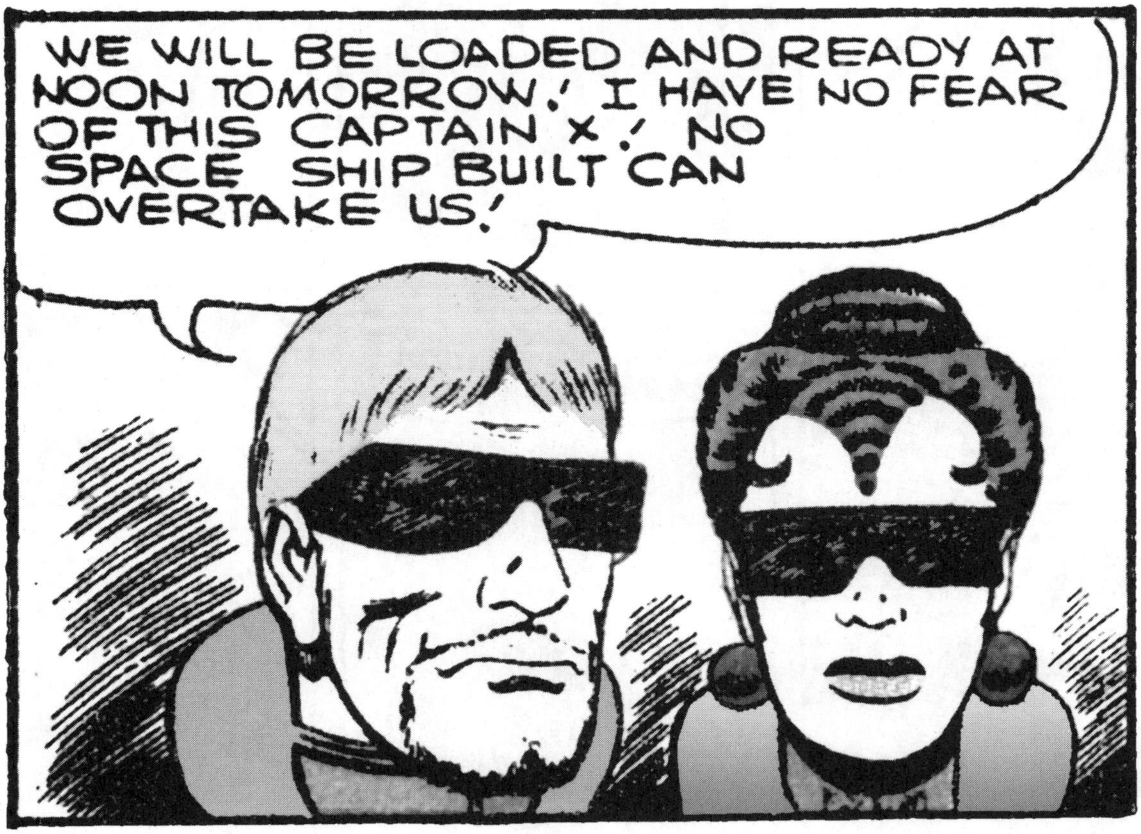
WE WILL BE LOADED AND READY AT NOON TOMORROW! I HAVE NO FEAR OF THIS CAPTAIN X! NO SPACE SHIP BUILT CAN OVERTAKE US!

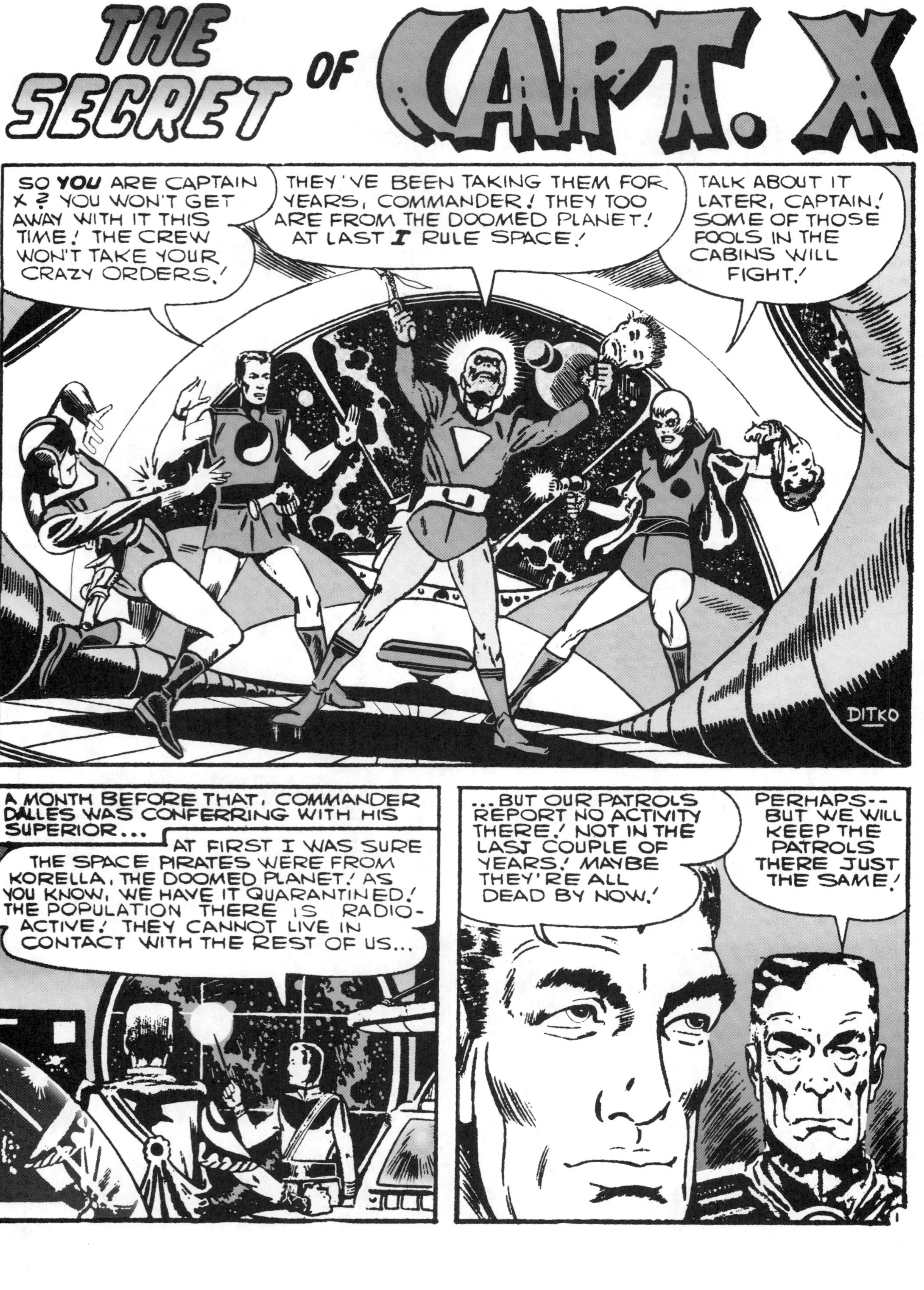
THE SECRET OF CAPT. X
SO YOU ARE CAPTAIN X ? YOU WON'T GET AWAY WITH IT THIS TIME! THE CREW WON'T TAKE YOUR CRAZY ORDERS!
THEY'VE BEEN TAKING THEM FOR YEARS, COMMANDER! THEY TOO ARE FROM THE DOOMED PLANET! AT LAST I RULE SPACE!
TALK ABOUT IT LATER, CAPTAIN! SOME OF THOSE FOOLS IN THE CABINS WILL FIGHT!
DITKO
A MONTH BEFORE THAT, COMMANDER DALLES WAS CONFERRING WITH HIS SUPERIOR...
AT FIRST I WAS SURE THE SPACE PIRATES WERE FROM KORELLA, THE DOOMED PLANET! AS YOU KNOW, WE HAVE IT QUARANTINED! THE POPULATION THERE IS RADIO-ACTIVE! THEY CANNOT LIVE IN CONTACT WITH THE REST OF US...
...BUT OUR PATROLS REPORT NO ACTIVITY THERE! NOT IN THE LAST COUPLE OF YEARS! MAYBE THEY'RE ALL DEAD BY NOW!
PERHAPS-- BUT WE WILL KEEP THE PATROLS THERE JUST THE SAME!

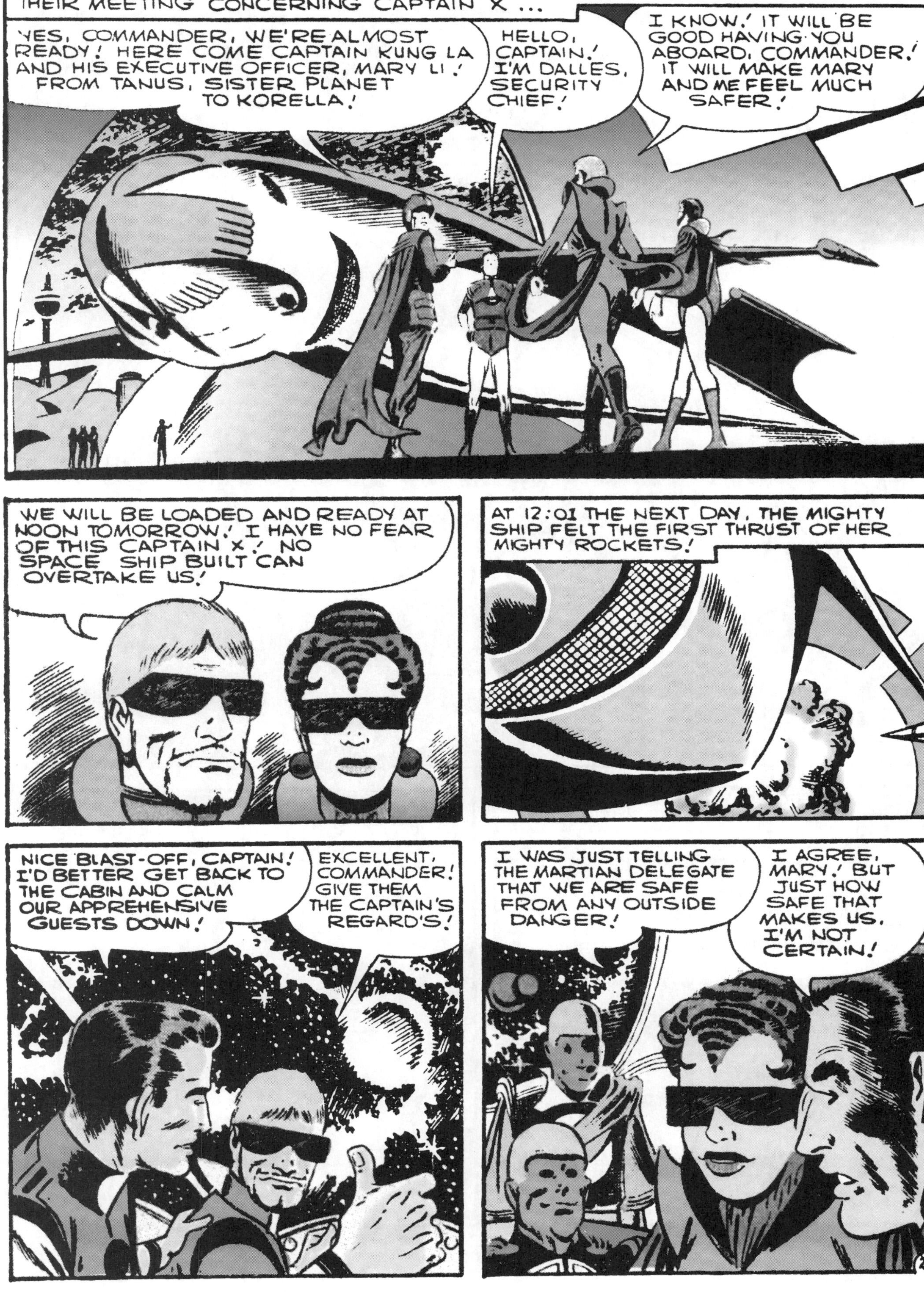
THE NEWEST, FASTEST SPACE SHIP EVER BUILT WAS NEARING COMPLETION! IT WAS ON THIS THAT THE LEADERS OF THE SOLAR SYSTEM WERE TO HOLD THEIR MEETING CONCERNING CAPTAIN X ...
YES, COMMANDER, WE'RE ALMOST READY! HERE COME CAPTAIN KUNG LA AND HIS EXECUTIVE OFFICER, MARY LI! FROM TANUS, SISTER PLANET TO KORELLA!
HELLO, CAPTAIN! I'M DALLES, SECURITY CHIEF!
I KNOW! IT WILL BE GOOD HAVING YOU ABOARD, COMMANDER! IT WILL MAKE MARY AND ME FEEL MUCH SAFER!
WE WILL BE LOADED AND READY AT NOON TOMORROW! I HAVE NO FEAR OF THIS CAPTAIN X! NO SPACE SHIP BUILT CAN OVERTAKE US!
AT 12:01 THE NEXT DAY, THE MIGHTY SHIP FELT THE FIRST THRUST OF HER MIGHTY ROCKETS!
NICE BLAST-OFF, CAPTAIN! I'D BETTER GET BACK TO THE CABIN AND CALM OUR APPREHENSIVE GUESTS DOWN!
EXCELLENT, COMMANDER! GIVE THEM THE CAPTAIN'S REGARD'S!
I WAS JUST TELLING THE MARTIAN DELEGATE THAT WE ARE SAFE FROM ANY OUTSIDE DANGER!
I AGREE, MARY! BUT JUST HOW SAFE THAT MAKES US, I'M NOT CERTAIN!

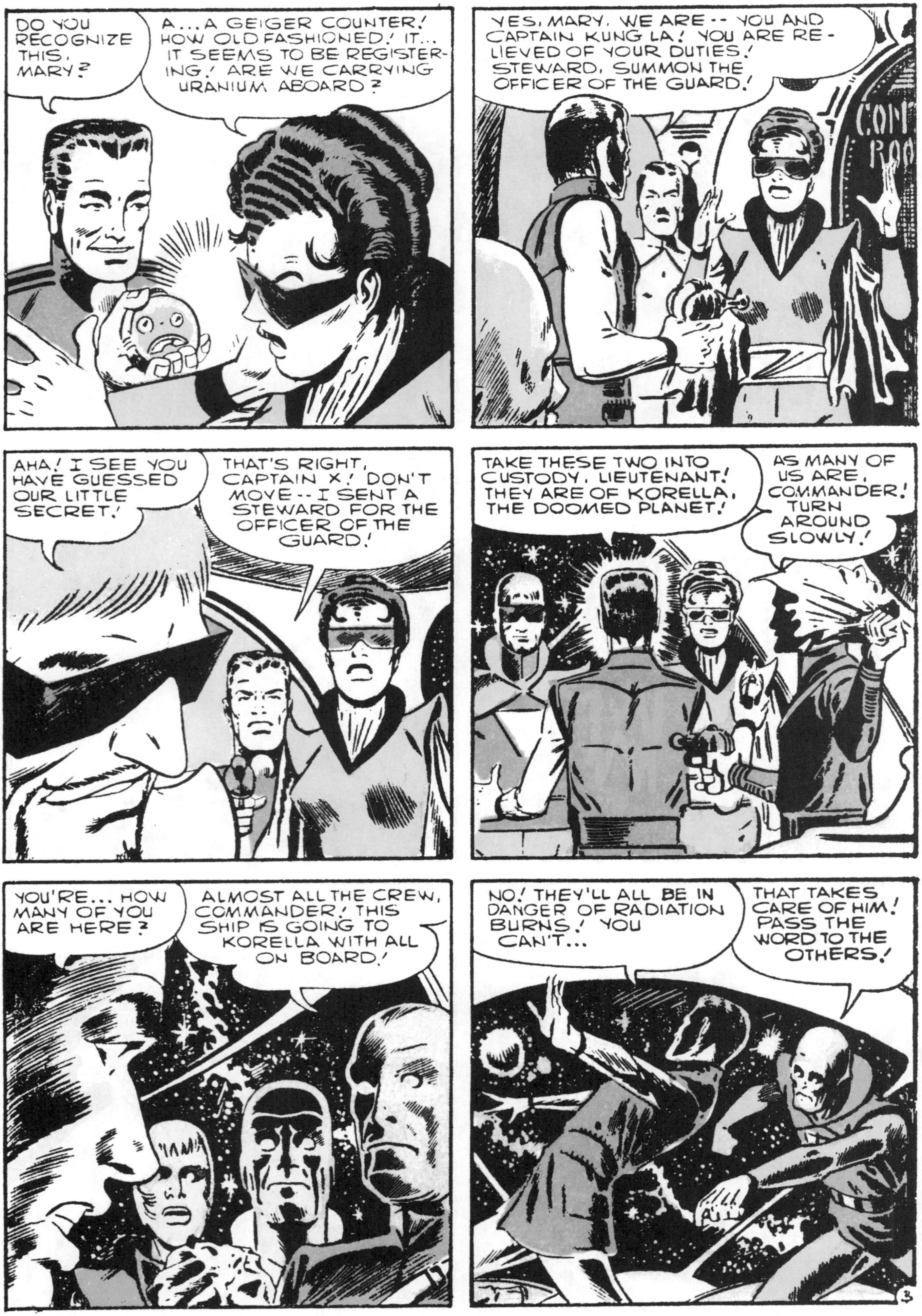
DO YOU RECOGNIZE THIS, MARY?
A... A GEIGER COUNTER! HOW OLD FASHIONED! IT... IT SEEMS TO BE REGISTERING! ARE WE CARRYING URANIUM ABOARD?
YES, MARY, WE ARE -- YOU AND CAPTAIN KUNG LA! YOU ARE RELIEVED OF YOUR DUTIES! STEWARD, SUMMON THE OFFICER OF THE GUARD!
AHA! I SEE YOU HAVE GUESSED OUR LITTLE SECRET!
THAT'S RIGHT, CAPTAIN X! DON'T MOVE -- I SENT A STEWARD FOR THE OFFICER OF THE GUARD!
TAKE THESE TWO INTO CUSTODY, LIEUTENANT! THEY ARE OF KORELLA, THE DOOMED PLANET!
AS MANY OF US ARE, COMMANDER! TURN AROUND SLOWLY!
YOU'RE... HOW MANY OF YOU ARE HERE?
ALMOST ALL THE CREW, COMMANDER! THIS SHIP IS GOING TO KORELLA WITH ALL ON BOARD!
NO! THEY'LL ALL BE IN DANGER OF RADIATION BURNS! YOU CAN'T...
THAT TAKES CARE OF HIM! PASS THE WORD TO THE OTHERS!

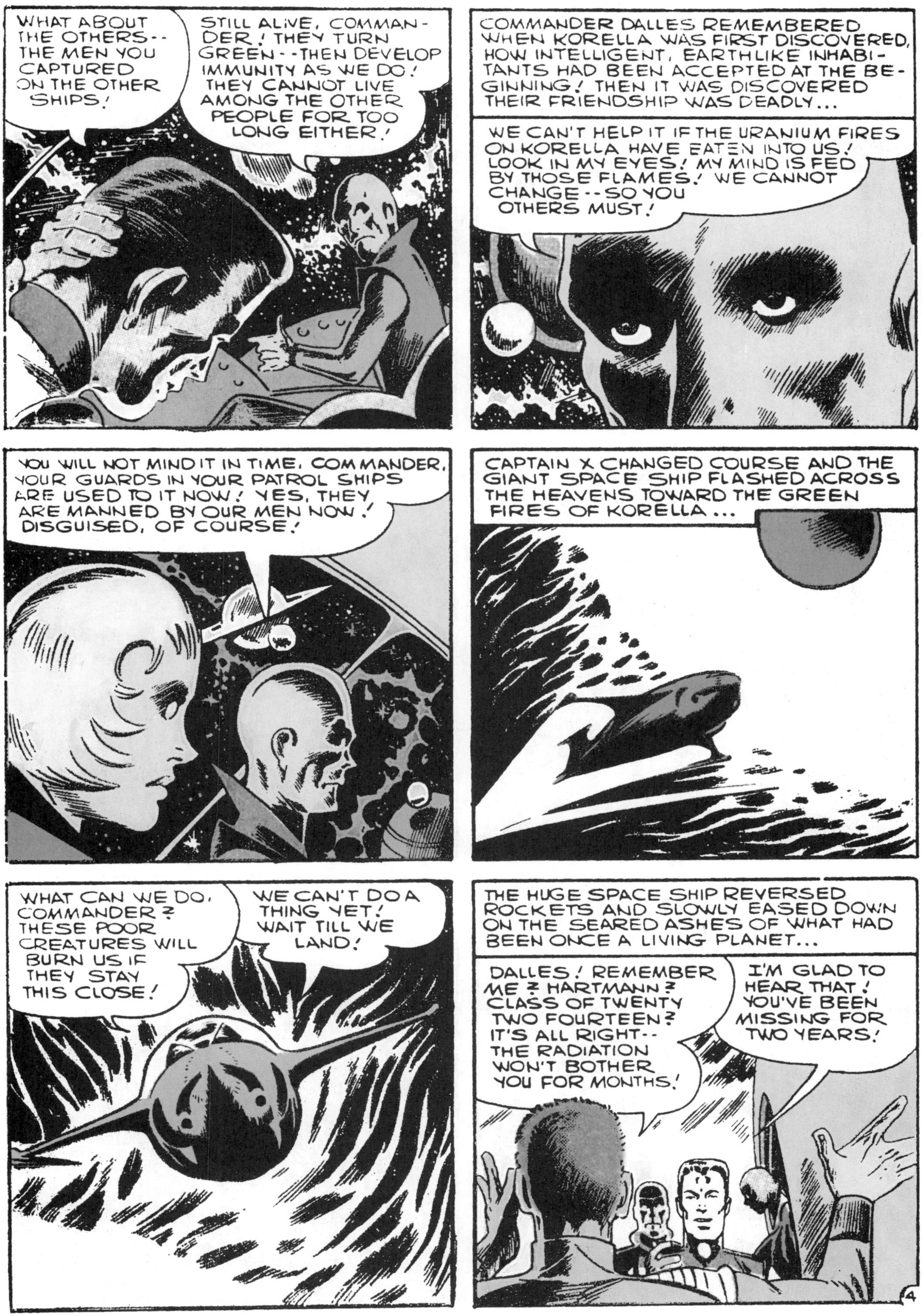
WHAT ABOUT THE OTHERS-- THE MEN YOU CAPTURED ON THE OTHER SHIPS!
STILL ALIVE, COMMANDER! THEY TURN GREEN--THEN DEVELOP IMMUNITY AS WE DO! THEY CANNOT LIVE AMONG THE OTHER PEOPLE FOR TOO LONG EITHER!
COMMANDER DALLES REMEMBERED WHEN KORELLA WAS FIRST DISCOVERED, HOW INTELLIGENT, EARTHLIKE INHABITANTS HAD BEEN ACCEPTED AT THE BEGINNING! THEN IT WAS DISCOVERED THEIR FRIENDSHIP WAS DEADLY...
WE CAN'T HELP IT IF THE URANIUM FIRES ON KORELLA HAVE EATEN INTO US! LOOK IN MY EYES! MY MIND IS FED BY THOSE FLAMES! WE CANNOT CHANGE--SO YOU OTHERS MUST!
YOU WILL NOT MIND IT IN TIME, COMMANDER, YOUR GUARDS IN YOUR PATROL SHIPS ARE USED TO IT NOW! YES, THEY ARE MANNED BY OUR MEN NOW! DISGUISED, OF COURSE!
CAPTAIN X CHANGED COURSE AND THE GIANT SPACE SHIP FLASHED ACROSS THE HEAVENS TOWARD THE GREEN FIRES OF KORELLA...
WHAT CAN WE DO, COMMANDER? THESE POOR CREATURES WILL BURN US IF THEY STAY THIS CLOSE!
WE CAN'T DO A THING YET! WAIT TILL WE LAND!
THE HUGE SPACE SHIP REVERSED ROCKETS AND SLOWLY EASED DOWN ON THE SEARED ASHES OF WHAT HAD BEEN ONCE A LIVING PLANET...
DALLES! REMEMBER ME? HARTMANN? CLASS OF TWENTY TWO FOURTEEN? IT'S ALL RIGHT-- THE RADIATION WON'T BOTHER YOU FOR MONTHS!
I'M GLAD TO HEAR THAT! YOU'VE BEEN MISSING FOR TWO YEARS!
4

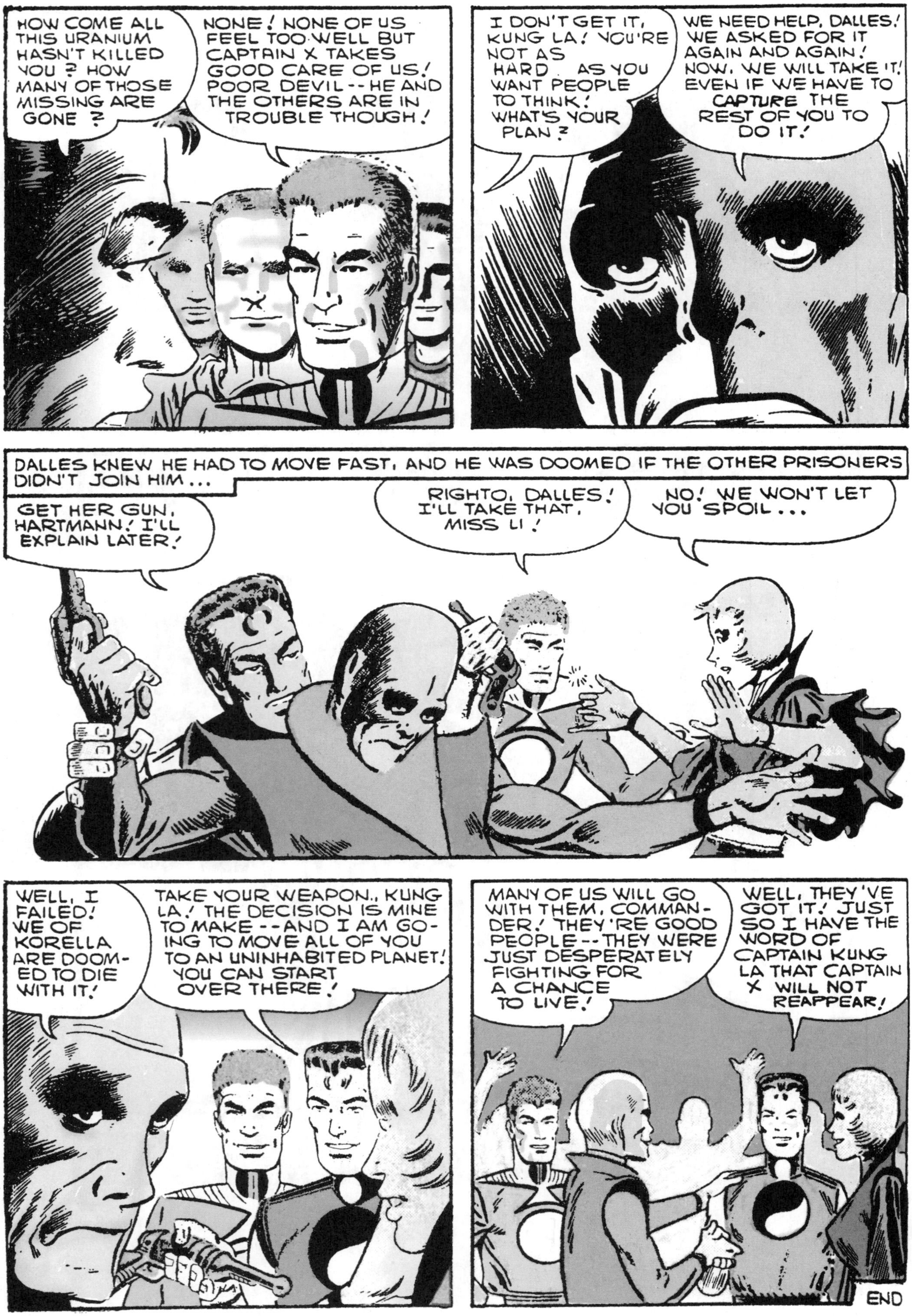
HOW COME ALL THIS URANIUM HASN'T KILLED YOU ? HOW MANY OF THOSE MISSING ARE GONE ?
NONE! NONE OF US FEEL TOO WELL BUT CAPTAIN X TAKES GOOD CARE OF US! POOR DEVIL -- HE AND THE OTHERS ARE IN TROUBLE THOUGH!
I DON'T GET IT, KUNG LA! YOU'RE NOT AS HARD AS YOU WANT PEOPLE TO THINK! WHAT'S YOUR PLAN ?
WE NEED HELP, DALLES! WE ASKED FOR IT AGAIN AND AGAIN! NOW, WE WILL TAKE IT! EVEN IF WE HAVE TO CAPTURE THE REST OF YOU TO DO IT!
DALLES KNEW HE HAD TO MOVE FAST, AND HE WAS DOOMED IF THE OTHER PRISONERS DIDN'T JOIN HIM...
GET HER GUN, HARTMANN! I'LL EXPLAIN LATER!
RIGHTO, DALLES! I'LL TAKE THAT, MISS LI!
NO! WE WON'T LET YOU SPOIL...
WELL, I FAILED! WE OF KORELLA ARE DOOMED TO DIE WITH IT!
TAKE YOUR WEAPON., KUNG LA! THE DECISION IS MINE TO MAKE -- AND I AM GOING TO MOVE ALL OF YOU TO AN UNINHABITED PLANET! YOU CAN START OVER THERE!
MANY OF US WILL GO WITH THEM, COMMANDER! THEY'RE GOOD PEOPLE -- THEY WERE JUST DESPERATELY FIGHTING FOR A CHANCE TO LIVE!
WELL, THEY'VE GOT IT! JUST SO I HAVE THE WORD OF CAPTAIN KUNG LA THAT CAPTAIN X WILL NOT REAPPEAR!
END

STEVE DITKO SPACE WARS

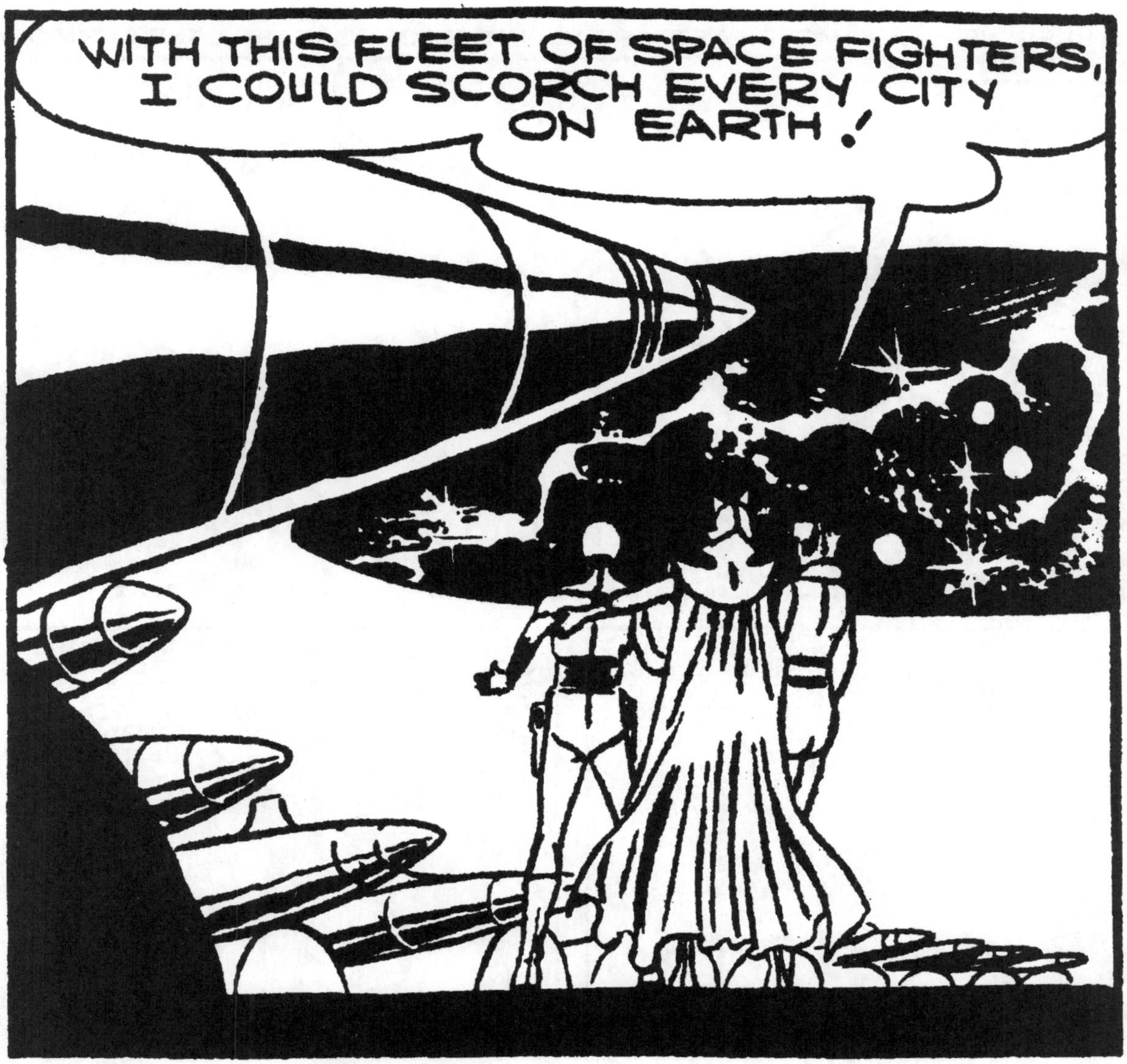
WITH THIS FLEET OF SPACE FIGHTERS, I COULD SCORCH EVERY CITY ON EARTH!

The Conquered Earth

The mighty ship--the deadliest ever seen in Earth's galaxy--hovered menacingly over us while the invader demanded complete surrender! Our military experts refused to attack ... said it would be useless! Noted men urged the nations to give up--and our space pilots stood by their ships awaiting orders--afraid to think of what could happen!

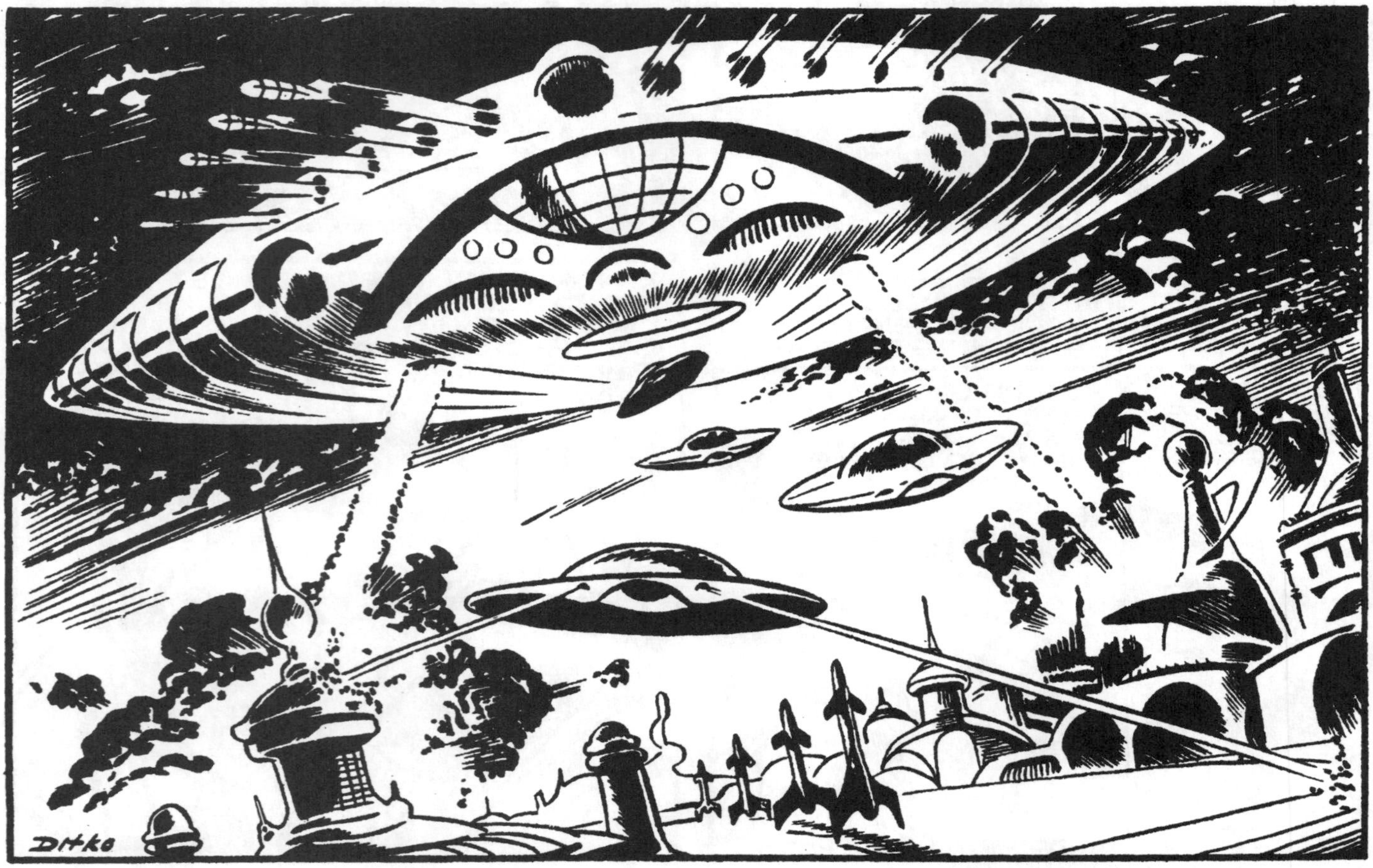
Ditko

WHEN FIRST REPORTED, THE HUGE MISSILE FROM EARTH II IN GALAXY XIV WAS APPROACHING SLOWLY! EVEN THEN OUR SCIENTISTS KNEW IT WAS HUGE...

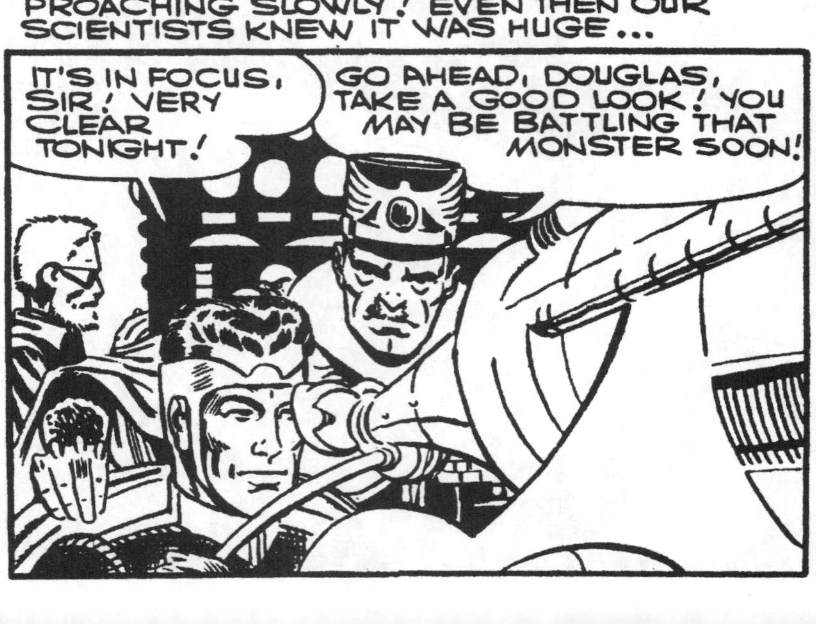
IT'S IN FOCUS, SIR! VERY CLEAR TONIGHT!
GO AHEAD, DOUGLAS, TAKE A GOOD LOOK! YOU MAY BE BATTLING THAT MONSTER SOON!

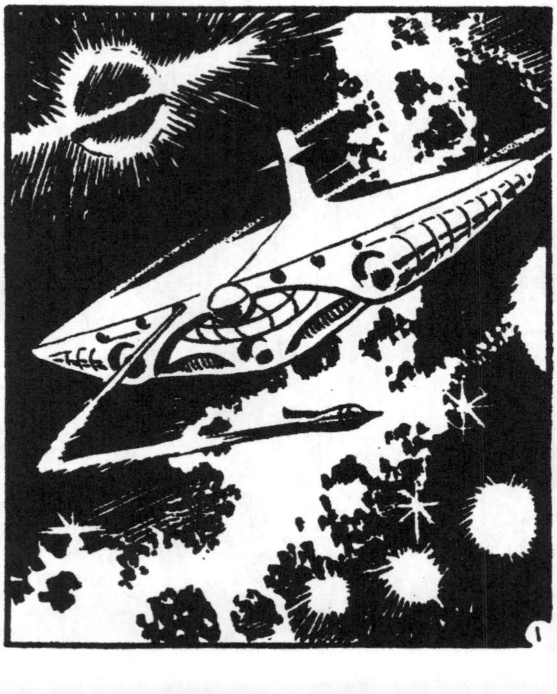

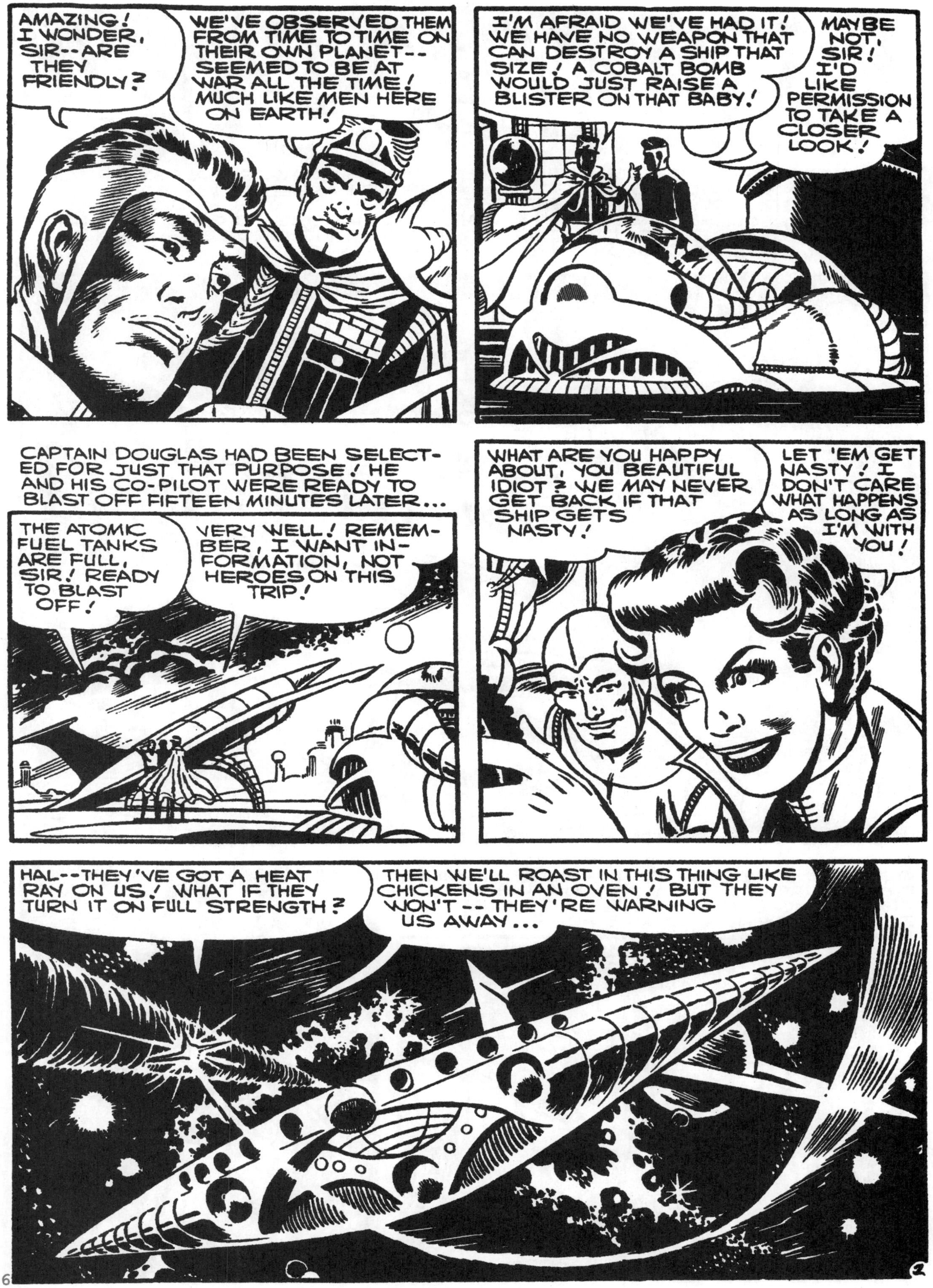
AMAZING! I WONDER, SIR--ARE THEY FRIENDLY?
WE'VE OBSERVED THEM FROM TIME TO TIME ON THEIR OWN PLANET--SEEMED TO BE AT WAR ALL THE TIME! MUCH LIKE MEN HERE ON EARTH!
I'M AFRAID WE'VE HAD IT! WE HAVE NO WEAPON THAT CAN DESTROY A SHIP THAT SIZE! A COBALT BOMB WOULD JUST RAISE A BLISTER ON THAT BABY!
MAYBE NOT, SIR! I'D LIKE PERMISSION TO TAKE A CLOSER LOOK!
CAPTAIN DOUGLAS HAD BEEN SELECTED FOR JUST THAT PURPOSE! HE AND HIS CO-PILOT WERE READY TO BLAST OFF FIFTEEN MINUTES LATER...
THE ATOMIC FUEL TANKS ARE FULL, SIR! READY TO BLAST OFF!
VERY WELL! REMEMBER, I WANT INFORMATION, NOT HEROES ON THIS TRIP!
WHAT ARE YOU HAPPY ABOUT, YOU BEAUTIFUL IDIOT? WE MAY NEVER GET BACK IF THAT SHIP GETS NASTY!
LET 'EM GET NASTY! I DON'T CARE WHAT HAPPENS AS LONG AS I'M WITH YOU!
HAL--THEY'VE GOT A HEAT RAY ON US! WHAT IF THEY TURN IT ON FULL STRENGTH?
THEN WE'LL ROAST IN THIS THING LIKE CHICKENS IN AN OVEN! BUT THEY WON'T -- THEY'RE WARNING US AWAY...
2

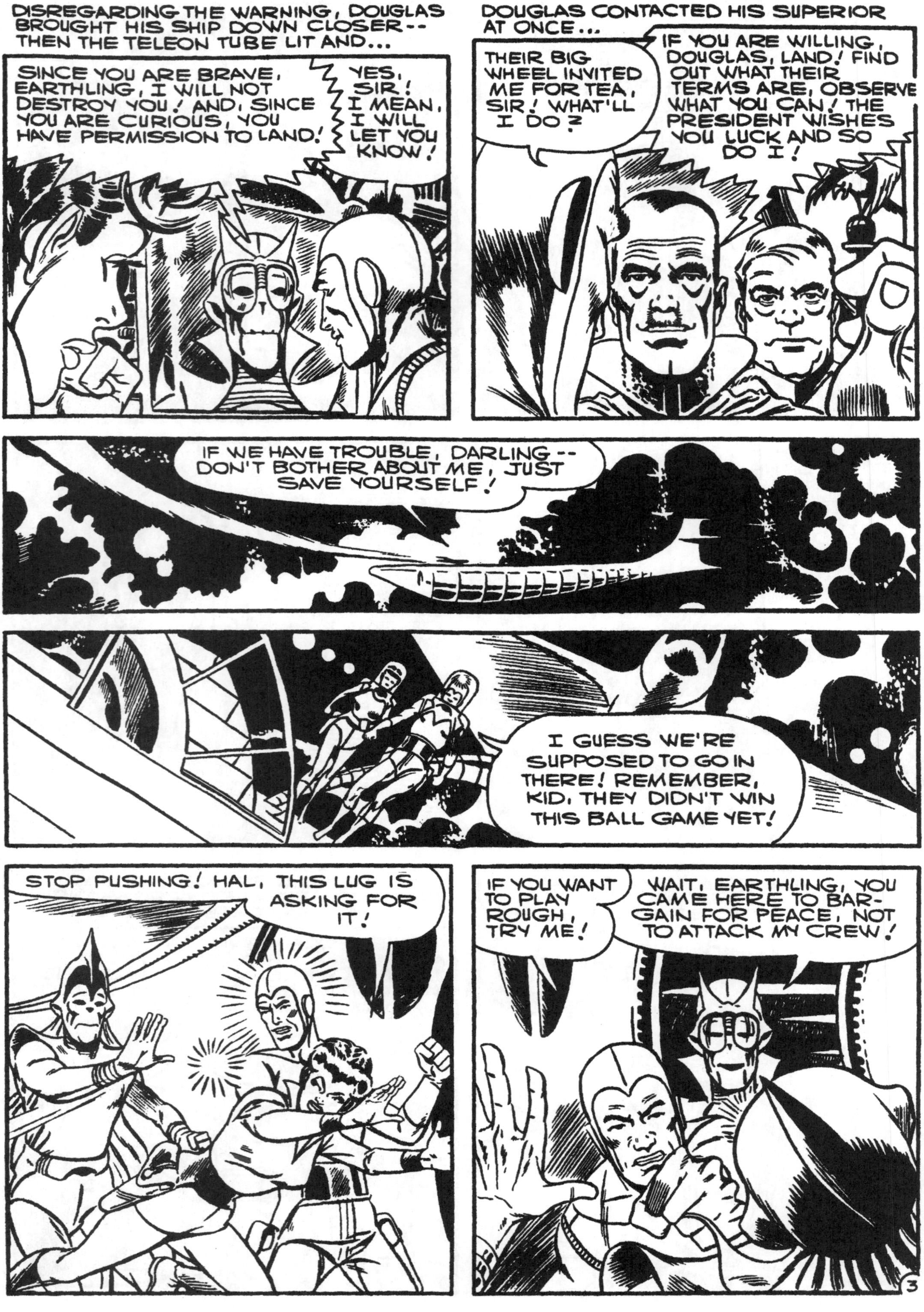
DISREGARDING THE WARNING, DOUGLAS BROUGHT HIS SHIP DOWN CLOSER-- THEN THE TELEON TUBE LIT AND...
SINCE YOU ARE BRAVE, EARTHLING, I WILL NOT DESTROY YOU! AND, SINCE YOU ARE CURIOUS, YOU HAVE PERMISSION TO LAND!
YES, SIR! I MEAN, I WILL LET YOU KNOW!
DOUGLAS CONTACTED HIS SUPERIOR AT ONCE...
THEIR BIG WHEEL INVITED ME FOR TEA, SIR! WHAT'LL I DO?
IF YOU ARE WILLING, DOUGLAS, LAND! FIND OUT WHAT THEIR TERMS ARE, OBSERVE WHAT YOU CAN! THE PRESIDENT WISHES YOU LUCK AND SO DO I!
IF WE HAVE TROUBLE, DARLING-- DON'T BOTHER ABOUT ME, JUST SAVE YOURSELF!
I GUESS WE'RE SUPPOSED TO GO IN THERE! REMEMBER, KID, THEY DIDN'T WIN THIS BALL GAME YET!
STOP PUSHING! HAL, THIS LUG IS ASKING FOR IT!
IF YOU WANT TO PLAY ROUGH, TRY ME!
WAIT, EARTHLING, YOU CAME HERE TO BARGAIN FOR PEACE, NOT TO ATTACK MY CREW!
3

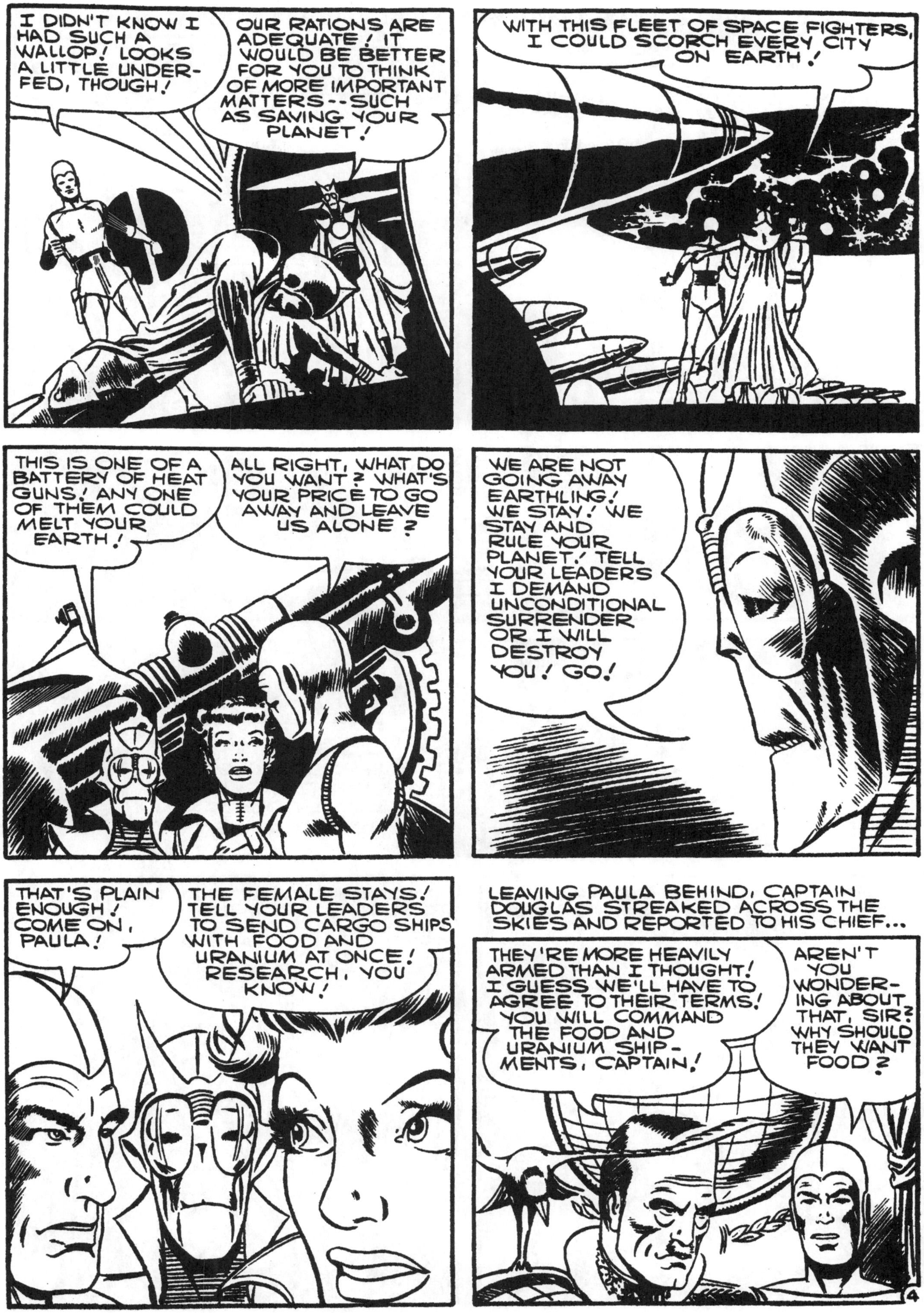
I DIDN'T KNOW I HAD SUCH A WALLOP! LOOKS A LITTLE UNDER-FED, THOUGH!
OUR RATIONS ARE ADEQUATE! IT WOULD BE BETTER FOR YOU TO THINK OF MORE IMPORTANT MATTERS--SUCH AS SAVING YOUR PLANET!
WITH THIS FLEET OF SPACE FIGHTERS, I COULD SCORCH EVERY CITY ON EARTH!
THIS IS ONE OF A BATTERY OF HEAT GUNS! ANY ONE OF THEM COULD MELT YOUR EARTH!
ALL RIGHT, WHAT DO YOU WANT? WHAT'S YOUR PRICE TO GO AWAY AND LEAVE US ALONE?
WE ARE NOT GOING AWAY EARTHLING! WE STAY! WE STAY AND RULE YOUR PLANET! TELL YOUR LEADERS I DEMAND UNCONDITIONAL SURRENDER OR I WILL DESTROY YOU! GO!
THAT'S PLAIN ENOUGH! COME ON, PAULA!
THE FEMALE STAYS! TELL YOUR LEADERS TO SEND CARGO SHIPS WITH FOOD AND URANIUM AT ONCE! RESEARCH, YOU KNOW!
LEAVING PAULA BEHIND, CAPTAIN DOUGLAS STREAKED ACROSS THE SKIES AND REPORTED TO HIS CHIEF...
THEY'RE MORE HEAVILY ARMED THAN I THOUGHT! I GUESS WE'LL HAVE TO AGREE TO THEIR TERMS! YOU WILL COMMAND THE FOOD AND URANIUM SHIP-MENTS, CAPTAIN!
AREN'T YOU WONDER-ING ABOUT THAT, SIR? WHY SHOULD THEY WANT FOOD?
4

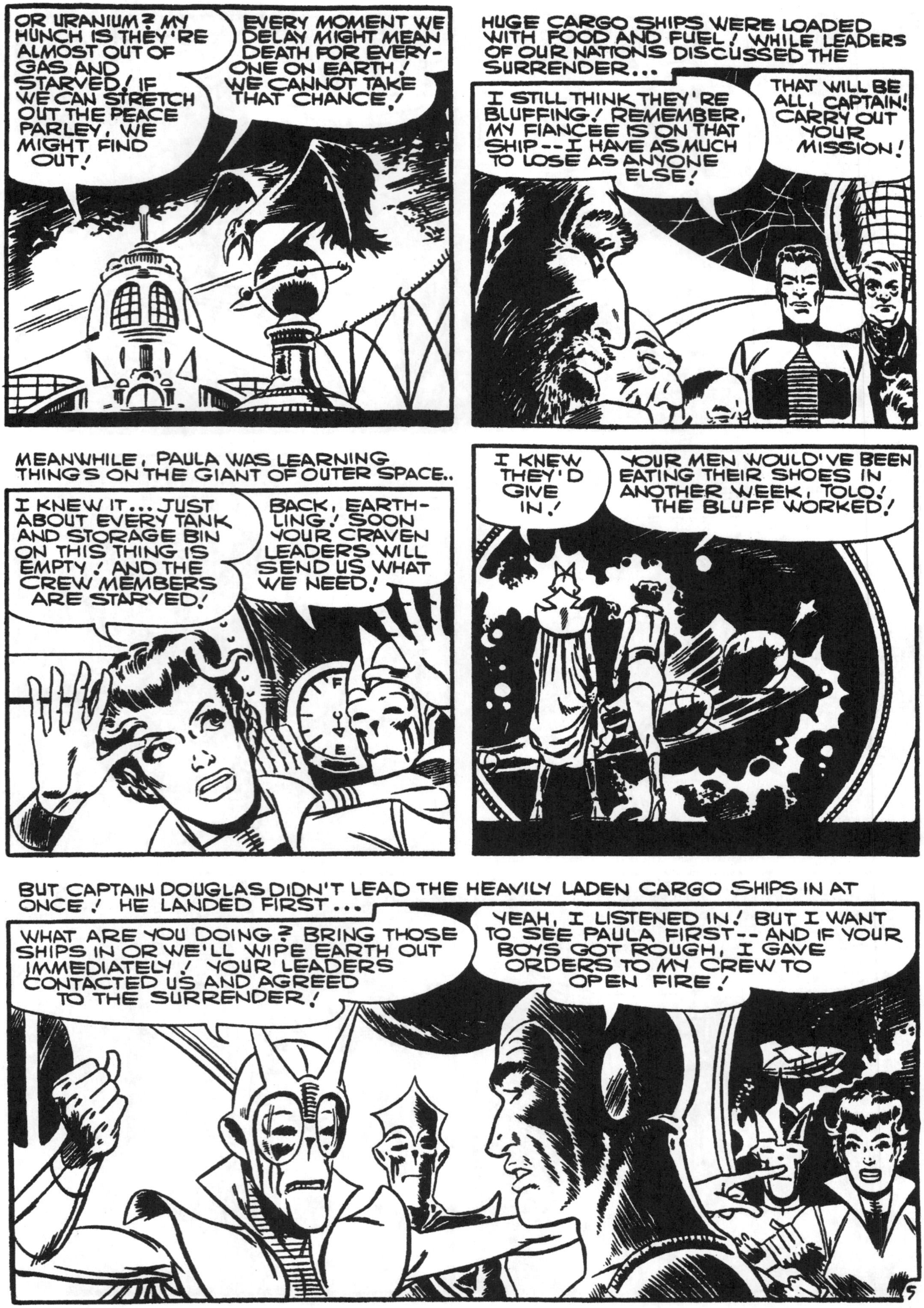
OR URANIUM? MY HUNCH IS THEY'RE ALMOST OUT OF GAS AND STARVED! IF WE CAN STRETCH OUT THE PEACE PARLEY, WE MIGHT FIND OUT!
EVERY MOMENT WE DELAY MIGHT MEAN DEATH FOR EVERY-ONE ON EARTH! WE CANNOT TAKE THAT CHANCE!
HUGE CARGO SHIPS WERE LOADED WITH FOOD AND FUEL! WHILE LEADERS OF OUR NATIONS DISCUSSED THE SURRENDER...
I STILL THINK THEY'RE BLUFFING! REMEMBER, MY FIANCEE IS ON THAT SHIP--I HAVE AS MUCH TO LOSE AS ANYONE ELSE!
THAT WILL BE ALL, CAPTAIN! CARRY OUT YOUR MISSION!
MEANWHILE, PAULA WAS LEARNING THINGS ON THE GIANT OF OUTER SPACE..
I KNEW IT... JUST ABOUT EVERY TANK AND STORAGE BIN ON THIS THING IS EMPTY! AND THE CREW MEMBERS ARE STARVED!
BACK, EARTH-LING! SOON YOUR CRAVEN LEADERS WILL SEND US WHAT WE NEED!
F
E
I KNEW THEY'D GIVE IN!
YOUR MEN WOULD'VE BEEN EATING THEIR SHOES IN ANOTHER WEEK, TOLO! THE BLUFF WORKED!
BUT CAPTAIN DOUGLAS DIDN'T LEAD THE HEAVILY LADEN CARGO SHIPS IN AT ONCE! HE LANDED FIRST...
WHAT ARE YOU DOING? BRING THOSE SHIPS IN OR WE'LL WIPE EARTH OUT IMMEDIATELY! YOUR LEADERS CONTACTED US AND AGREED TO THE SURRENDER!
YEAH, I LISTENED IN! BUT I WANT TO SEE PAULA FIRST-- AND IF YOUR BOYS GOT ROUGH, I GAVE ORDERS TO MY CREW TO OPEN FIRE!
5

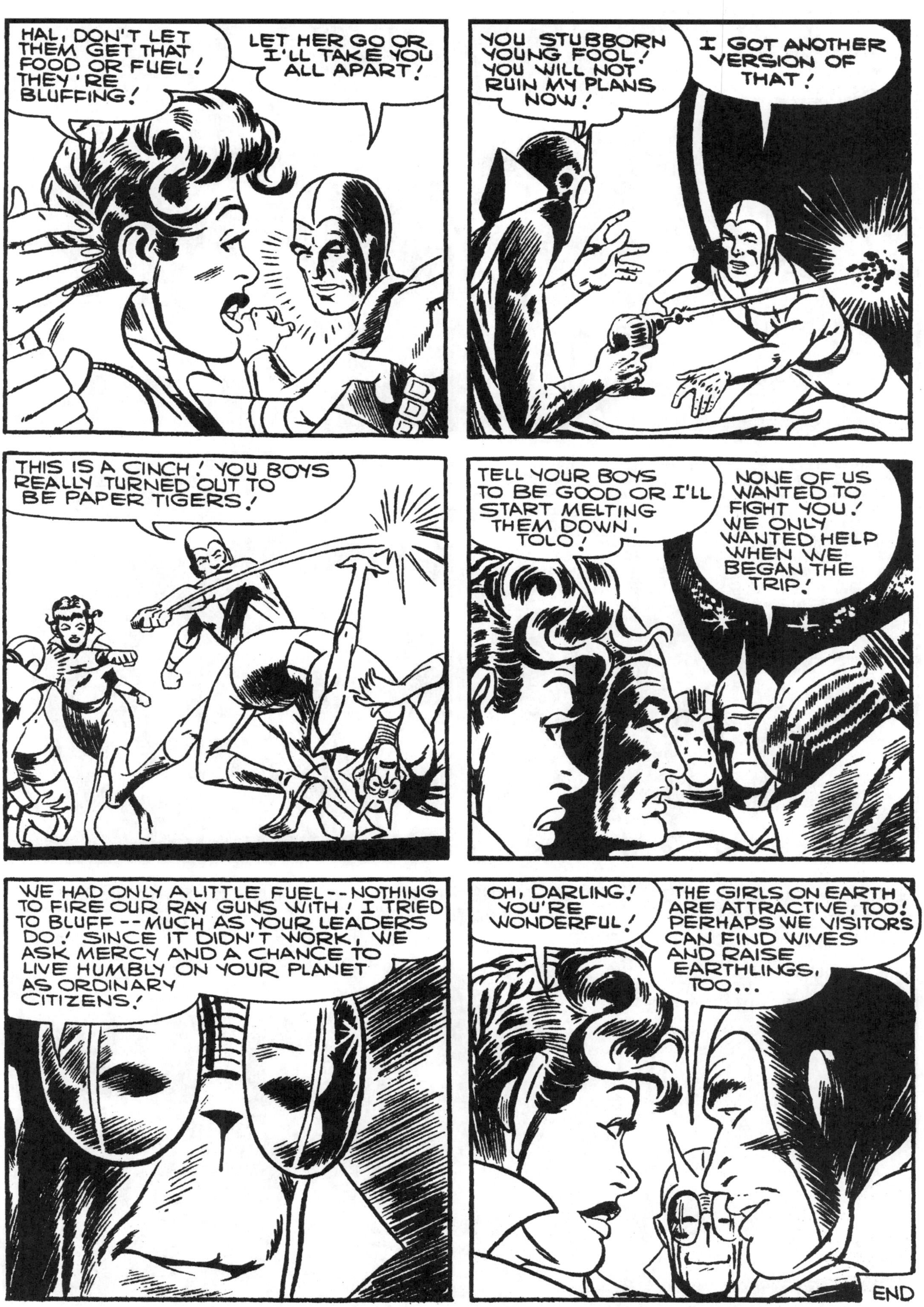
HAL, DON'T LET THEM GET THAT FOOD OR FUEL! THEY'RE BLUFFING!
LET HER GO OR I'LL TAKE YOU ALL APART!
YOU STUBBORN YOUNG FOOL! YOU WILL NOT RUIN MY PLANS NOW!
I GOT ANOTHER VERSION OF THAT!
THIS IS A CINCH! YOU BOYS REALLY TURNED OUT TO BE PAPER TIGERS!
TELL YOUR BOYS TO BE GOOD OR I'LL START MELTING THEM DOWN, TOLO!
NONE OF US WANTED TO FIGHT YOU! WE ONLY WANTED HELP WHEN WE BEGAN THE TRIP!
WE HAD ONLY A LITTLE FUEL--NOTHING TO FIRE OUR RAY GUNS WITH! I TRIED TO BLUFF--MUCH AS YOUR LEADERS DO! SINCE IT DIDN'T WORK, WE ASK MERCY AND A CHANCE TO LIVE HUMBLY ON YOUR PLANET AS ORDINARY CITIZENS!
OH, DARLING! YOU'RE WONDERFUL!
THE GIRLS ON EARTH ARE ATTRACTIVE, TOO! PERHAPS WE VISITORS CAN FIND WIVES AND RAISE EARTHLINGS, TOO...
END

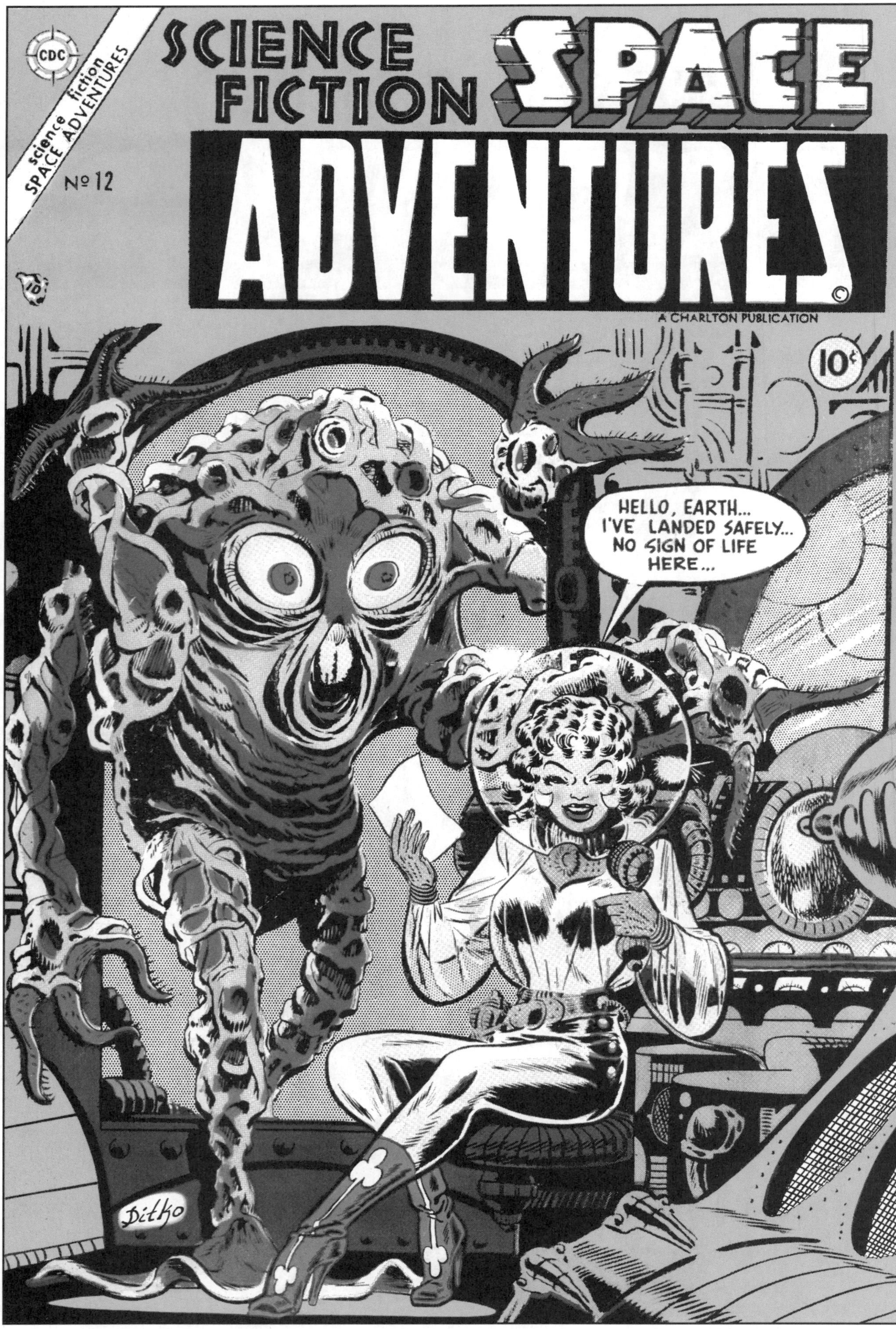
CDC
science fiction
SPACE ADVENTURES
SCIENCE FICTION SPACE
ADVENTURES
No 12
A CHARLTON PUBLICATION
10¢
HELLO, EARTH... I'VE LANDED SAFELY... NO SIGN OF LIFE HERE...
Ditko

STEVE DITKO SPACE WARS

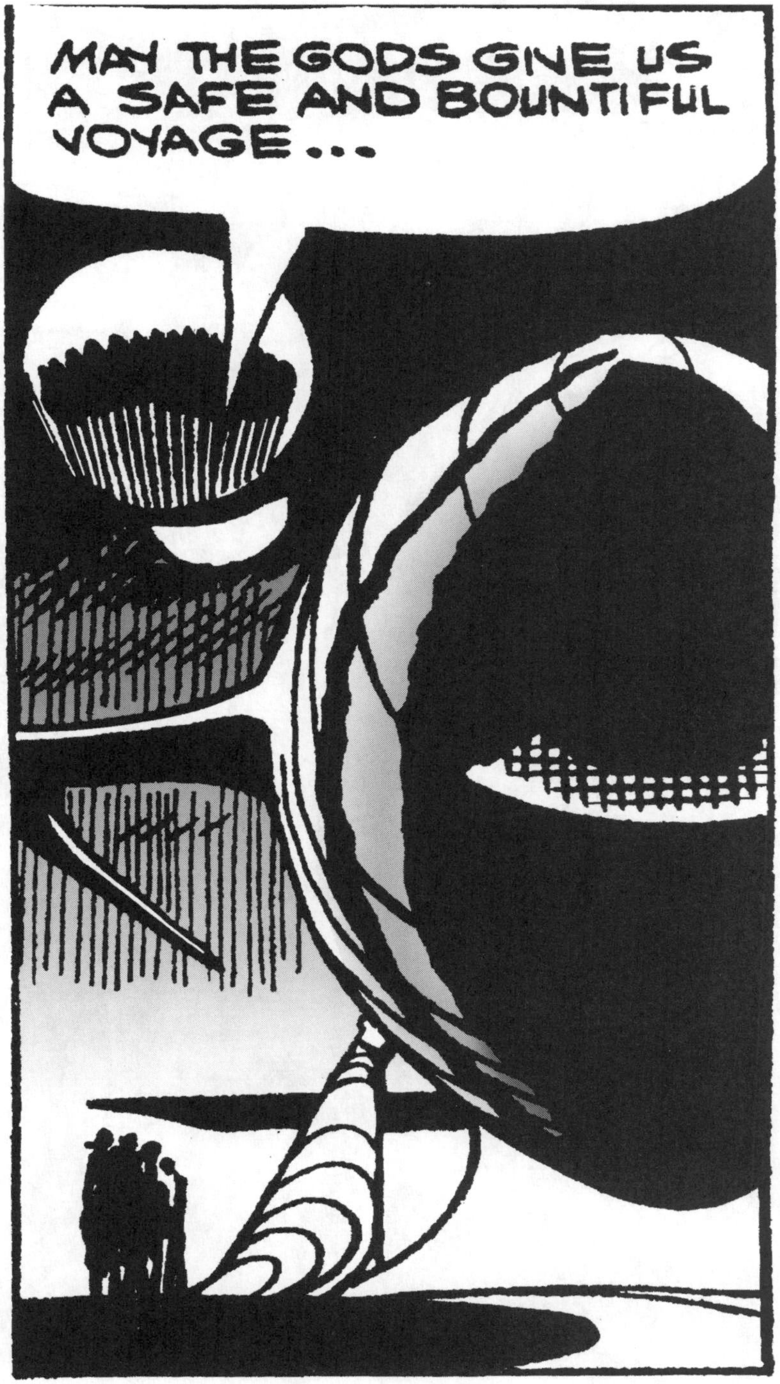
MAY THE GODS GIVE US A SAFE AND BOUNTIFUL VOYAGE...

THE GREATER JOVIANS

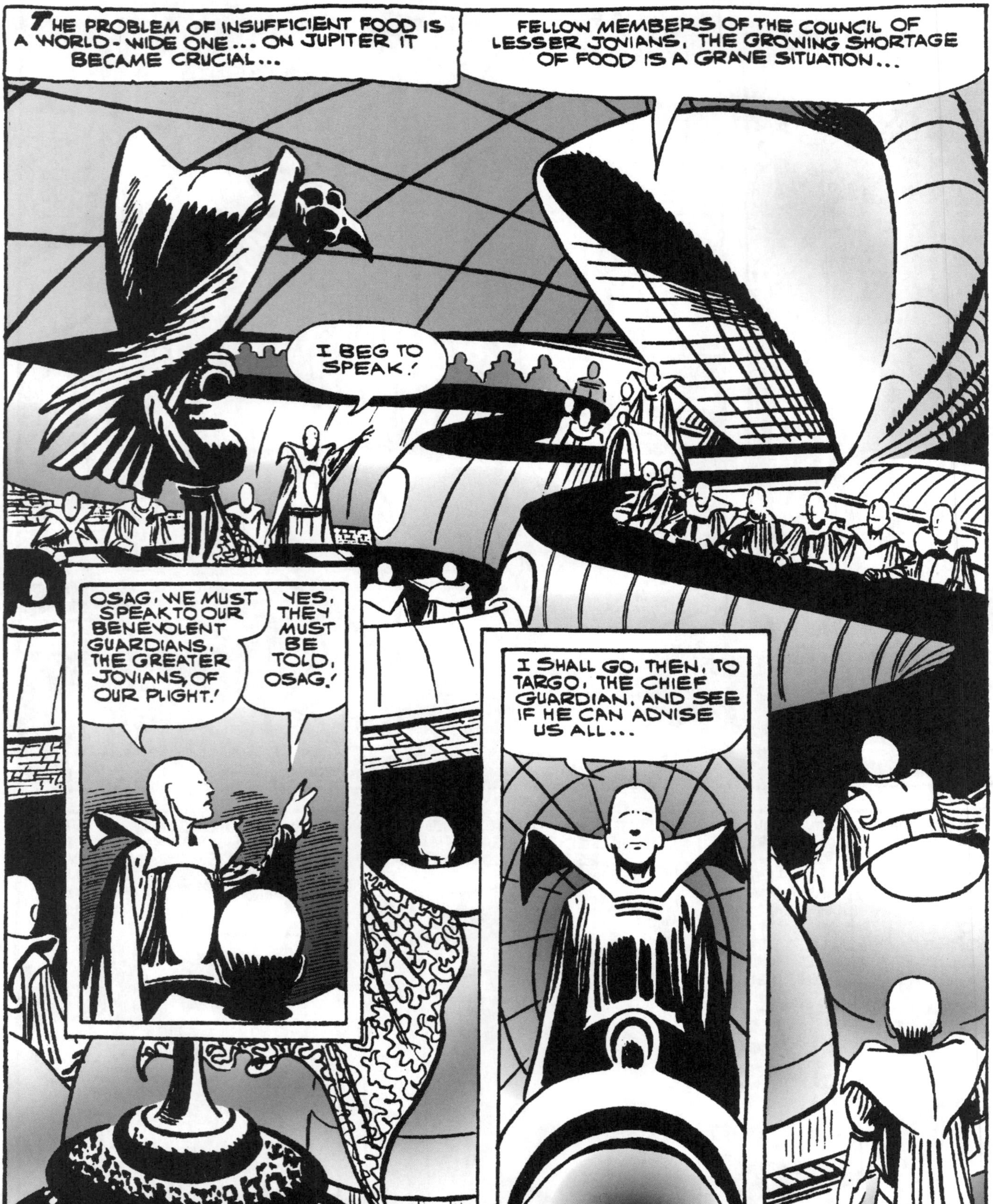

THE PROBLEM OF INSUFFICIENT FOOD IS A WORLD-WIDE ONE... ON JUPITER IT BECAME CRUCIAL...
FELLOW MEMBERS OF THE COUNCIL OF LESSER JOVIANS, THE GROWING SHORTAGE OF FOOD IS A GRAVE SITUATION...
I BEG TO SPEAK!
OSAG, WE MUST SPEAK TO OUR BENEVOLENT GUARDIANS, THE GREATER JOVIANS, OF OUR PLIGHT!
YES, THEY MUST BE TOLD, OSAG!
I SHALL GO, THEN, TO TARGO, THE CHIEF GUARDIAN, AND SEE IF HE CAN ADVISE US ALL...

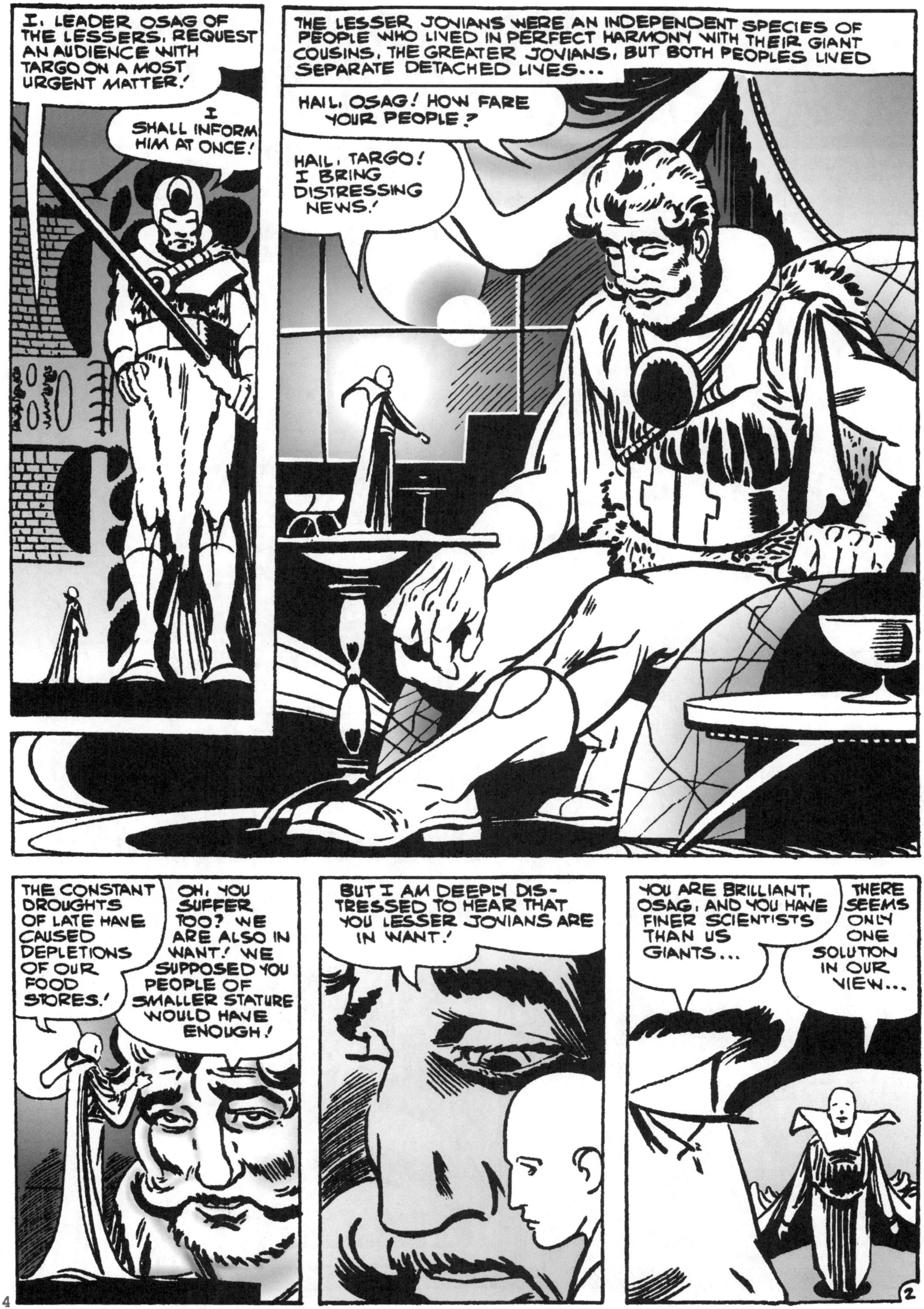
I, LEADER OSAG OF THE LESSERS, REQUEST AN AUDIENCE WITH TARGO ON A MOST URGENT MATTER!
I SHALL INFORM HIM AT ONCE!
THE LESSER JOVIANS WERE AN INDEPENDENT SPECIES OF PEOPLE WHO LIVED IN PERFECT HARMONY WITH THEIR GIANT COUSINS, THE GREATER JOVIANS, BUT BOTH PEOPLES LIVED SEPARATE DETACHED LIVES...
HAIL, OSAG! HOW FARE YOUR PEOPLE?
HAIL, TARGO! I BRING DISTRESSING NEWS!
THE CONSTANT DROUGHTS OF LATE HAVE CAUSED DEPLETIONS OF OUR FOOD STORES!
OH, YOU SUFFER TOO? WE ARE ALSO IN WANT! WE SUPPOSED YOU PEOPLE OF SMALLER STATURE WOULD HAVE ENOUGH!
BUT I AM DEEPLY DISTRESSED TO HEAR THAT YOU LESSER JOVIANS ARE IN WANT!
YOU ARE BRILLIANT, OSAG, AND YOU HAVE FINER SCIENTISTS THAN US GIANTS...
THERE SEEMS ONLY ONE SOLUTION IN OUR VIEW...
2

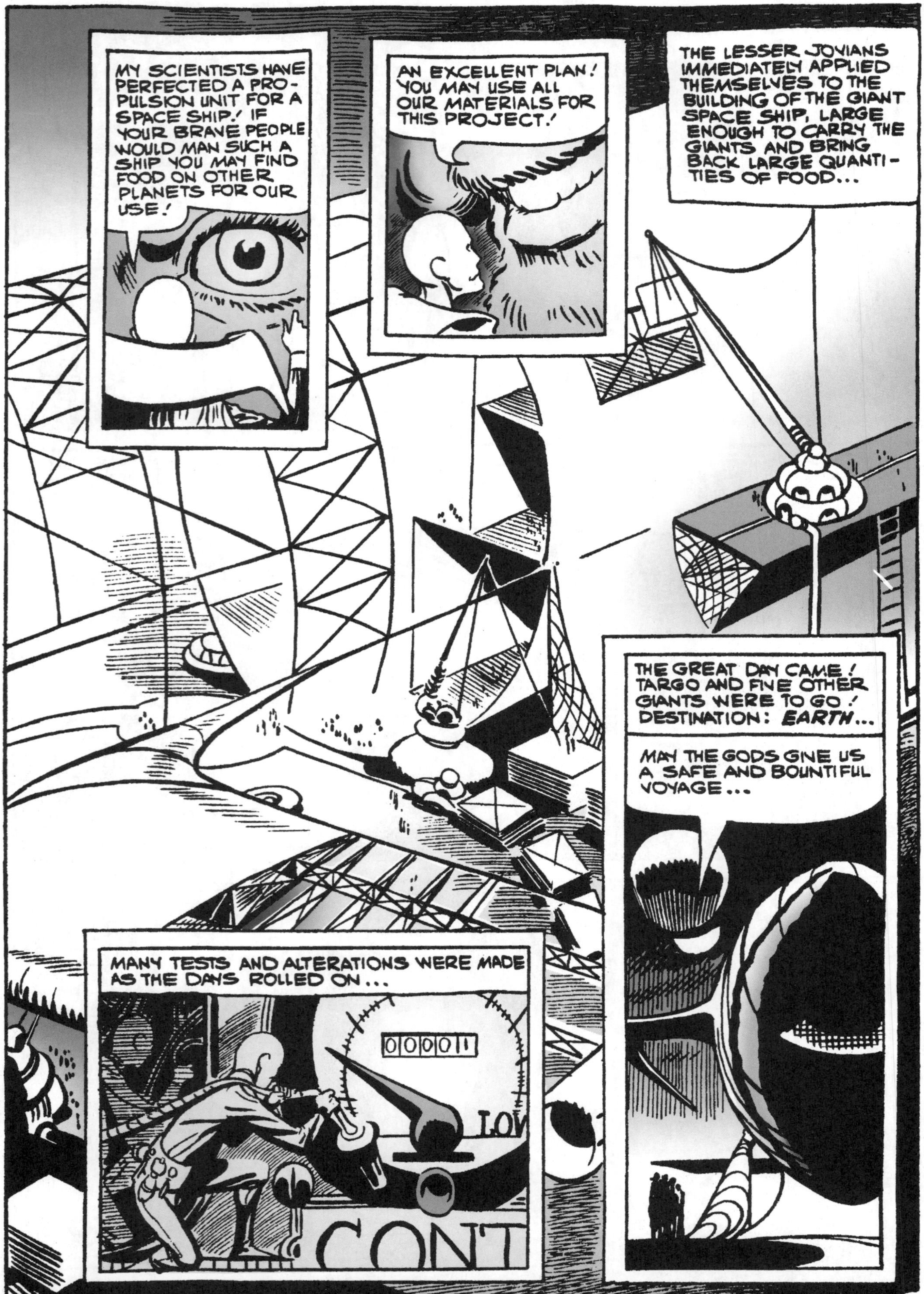
MY SCIENTISTS HAVE PERFECTED A PROPULSION UNIT FOR A SPACE SHIP! IF YOUR BRAVE PEOPLE WOULD MAN SUCH A SHIP YOU MAY FIND FOOD ON OTHER PLANETS FOR OUR USE!
AN EXCELLENT PLAN! YOU MAY USE ALL OUR MATERIALS FOR THIS PROJECT!
THE LESSER JOVIANS IMMEDIATELY APPLIED THEMSELVES TO THE BUILDING OF THE GIANT SPACE SHIP, LARGE ENOUGH TO CARRY THE GIANTS AND BRING BACK LARGE QUANTITIES OF FOOD...
THE GREAT DAY CAME! TARGO AND FIVE OTHER GIANTS WERE TO GO! DESTINATION: EARTH...
MAY THE GODS GIVE US A SAFE AND BOUNTIFUL VOYAGE...
MANY TESTS AND ALTERATIONS WERE MADE AS THE DAYS ROLLED ON...
000011
LOW
CONT
3

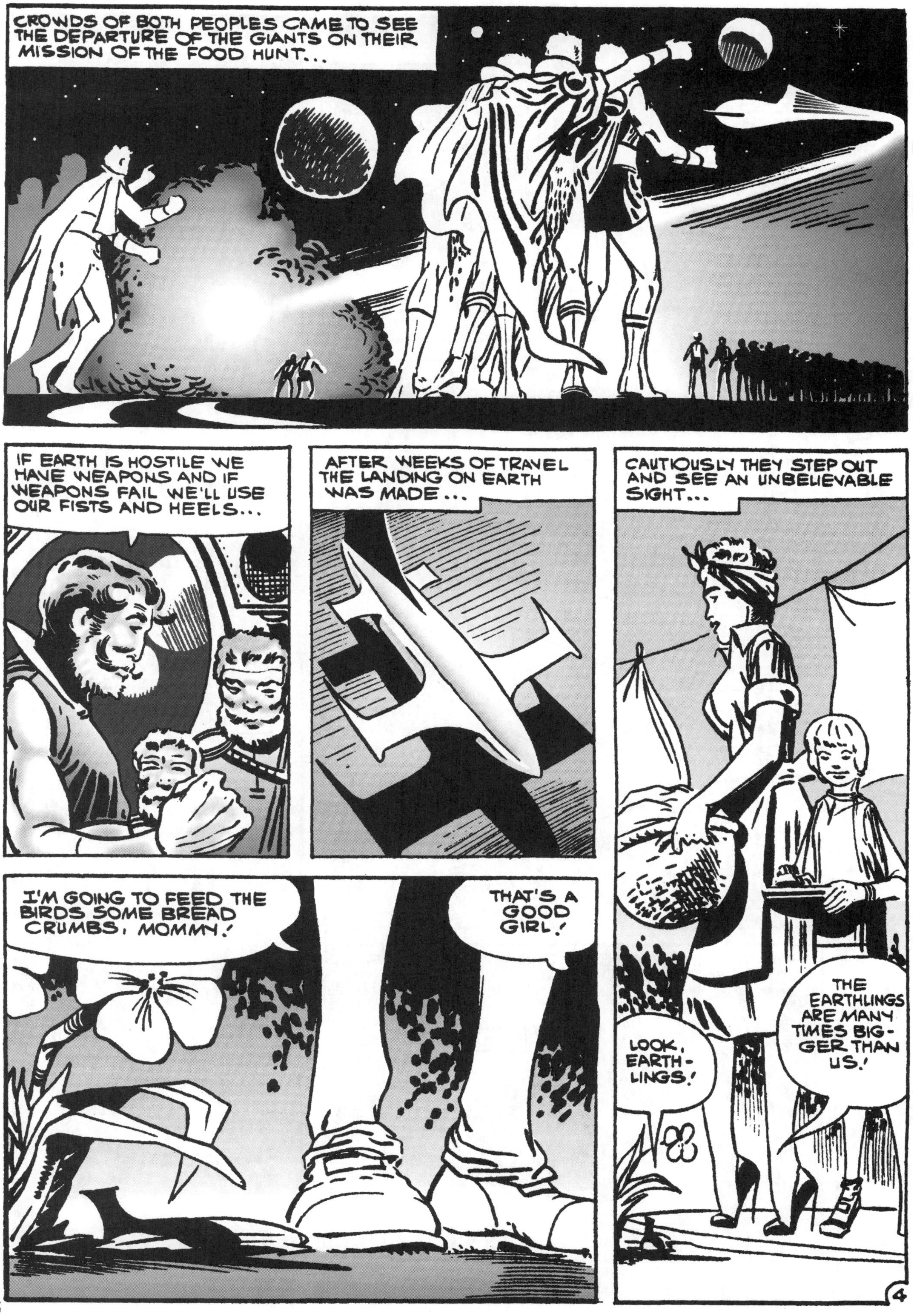
CROWDS OF BOTH PEOPLES CAME TO SEE THE DEPARTURE OF THE GIANTS ON THEIR MISSION OF THE FOOD HUNT...
IF EARTH IS HOSTILE WE HAVE WEAPONS AND IF WEAPONS FAIL WE'LL USE OUR FISTS AND HEELS...
AFTER WEEKS OF TRAVEL THE LANDING ON EARTH WAS MADE...
I'M GOING TO FEED THE BIRDS SOME BREAD CRUMBS, MOMMY!
THAT'S A GOOD GIRL!
CAUTIOUSLY THEY STEP OUT AND SEE AN UNBELIEVABLE SIGHT...
LOOK, EARTHLINGS!
THE EARTHLINGS ARE MANY TIMES BIGGER THAN US!
4

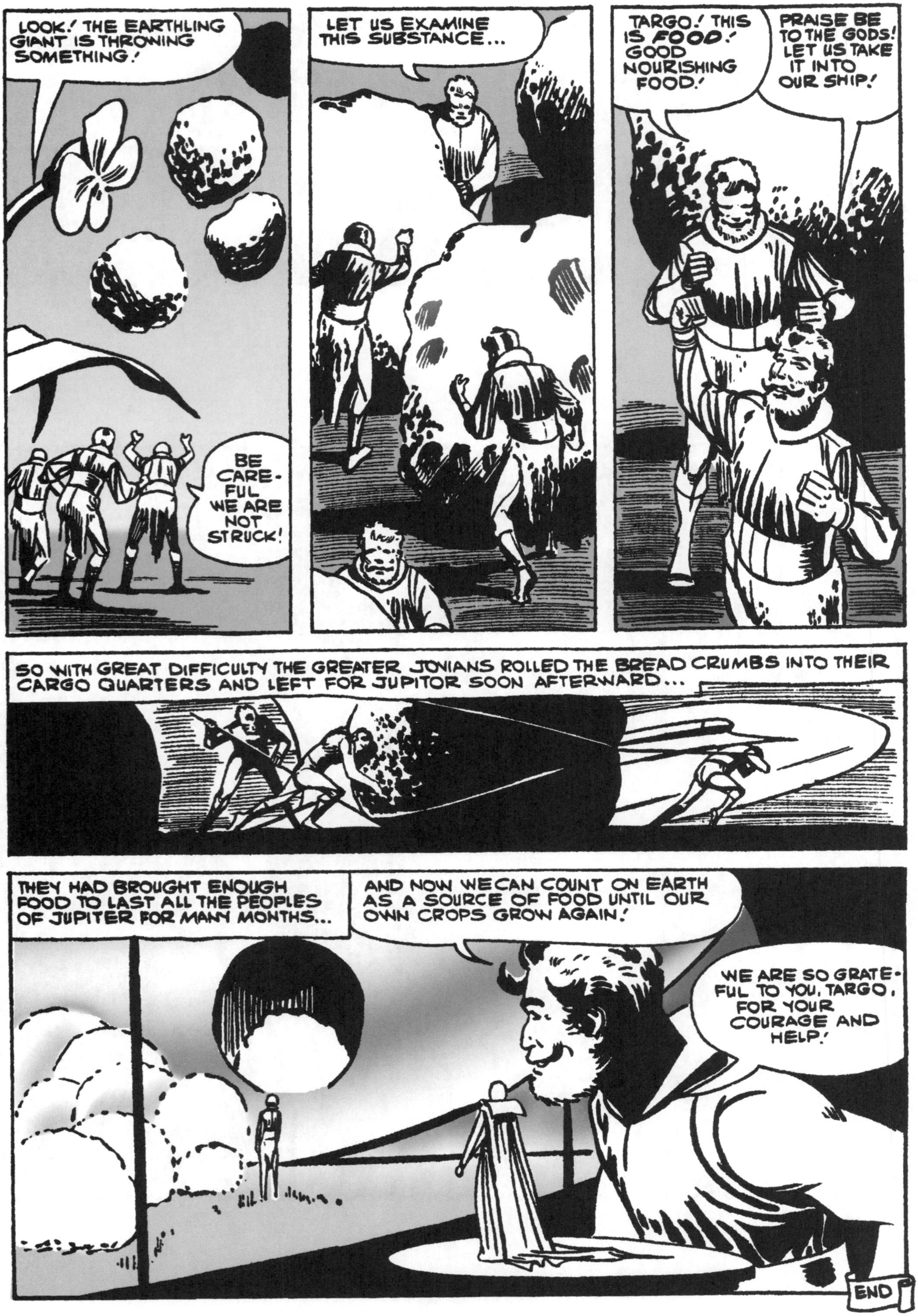
LOOK! THE EARTHLING GIANT IS THROWING SOMETHING!
BE CAREFUL WE ARE NOT STRUCK!
LET US EXAMINE THIS SUBSTANCE...
TARGO! THIS IS FOOD! GOOD NOURISHING FOOD!
PRAISE BE TO THE GODS! LET US TAKE IT INTO OUR SHIP!
SO WITH GREAT DIFFICULTY THE GREATER JONIANS ROLLED THE BREAD CRUMBS INTO THEIR CARGO QUARTERS AND LEFT FOR JUPITOR SOON AFTERWARD...
THEY HAD BROUGHT ENOUGH FOOD TO LAST ALL THE PEOPLES OF JUPITER FOR MANY MONTHS...
AND NOW WE CAN COUNT ON EARTH AS A SOURCE OF FOOD UNTIL OUR OWN CROPS GROW AGAIN!
WE ARE SO GRATEFUL TO YOU, TARGO, FOR YOUR COURAGE AND HELP!
END

STEVE DITKO SPACE WARS

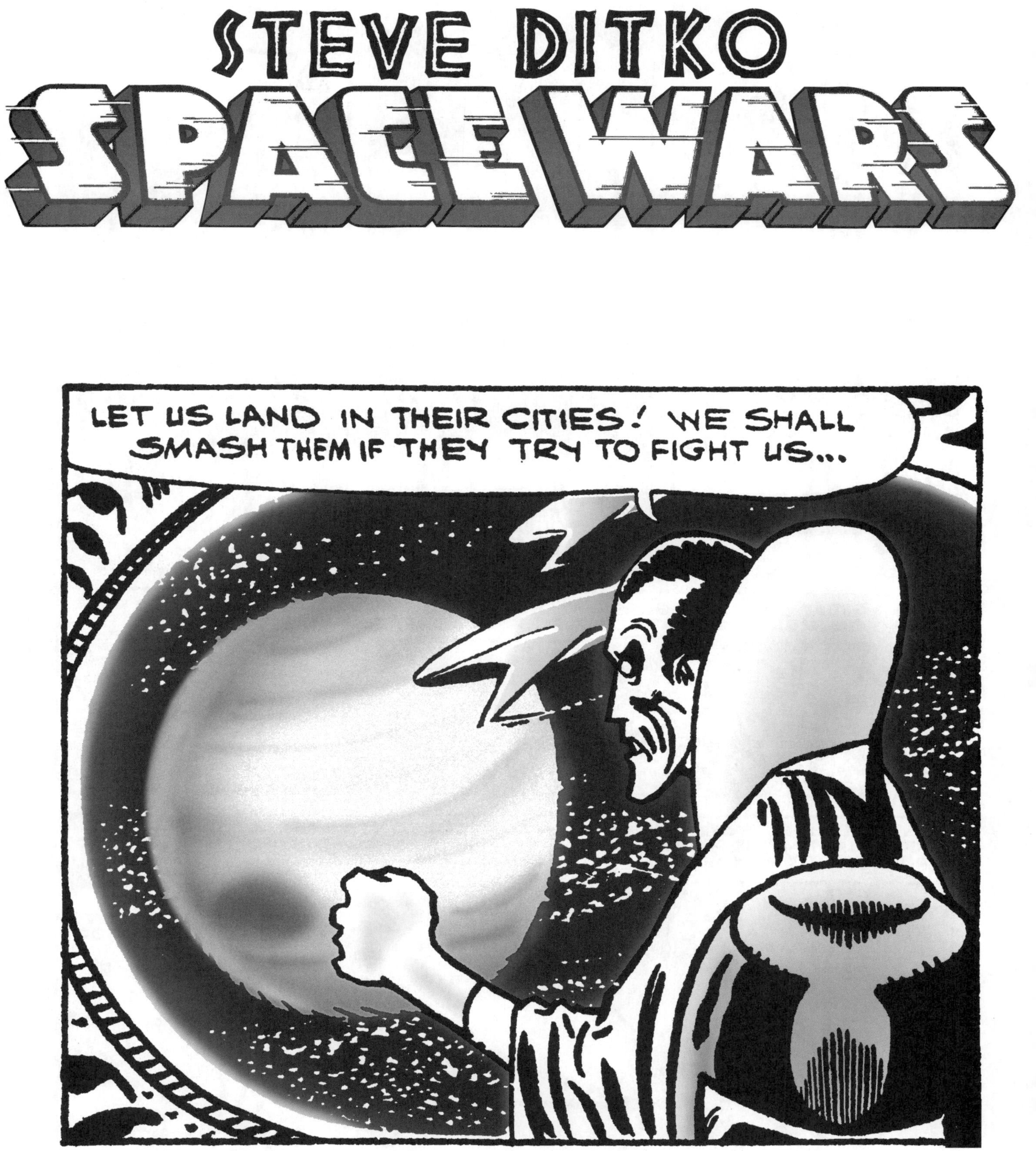

LET US LAND IN THEIR CITIES! WE SHALL SMASH THEM IF THEY TRY TO FIGHT US...

PLAGUE

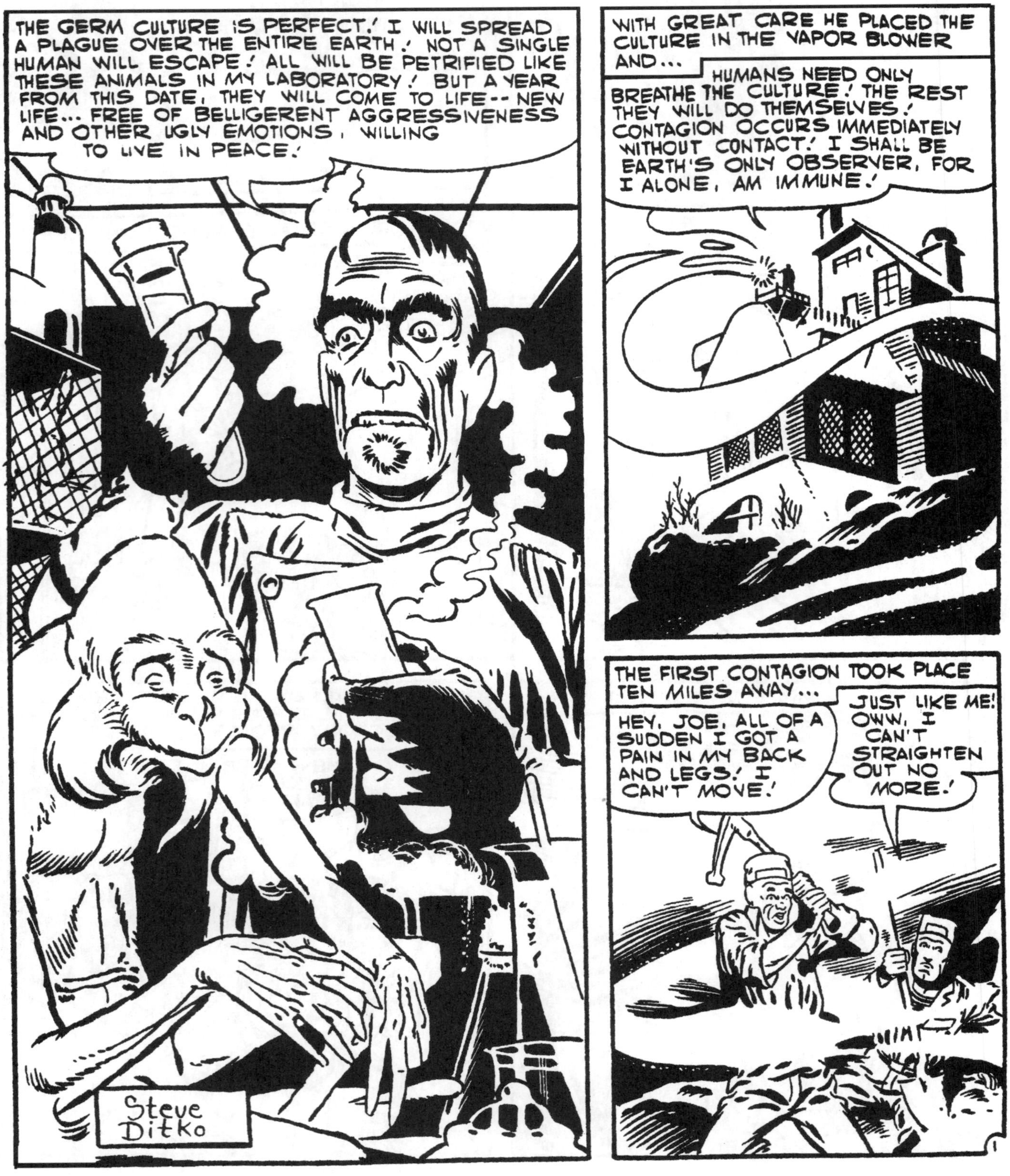

THE GERM CULTURE IS PERFECT! I WILL SPREAD A PLAGUE OVER THE ENTIRE EARTH! NOT A SINGLE HUMAN WILL ESCAPE! ALL WILL BE PETRIFIED LIKE THESE ANIMALS IN MY LABORATORY! BUT A YEAR FROM THIS DATE, THEY WILL COME TO LIFE-- NEW LIFE... FREE OF BELLIGERENT AGGRESSIVENESS AND OTHER UGLY EMOTIONS, WILLING TO LIVE IN PEACE!
Steve Ditko
WITH GREAT CARE HE PLACED THE CULTURE IN THE VAPOR BLOWER AND...
HUMANS NEED ONLY BREATHE THE CULTURE! THE REST THEY WILL DO THEMSELVES! CONTAGION OCCURS IMMEDIATELY WITHOUT CONTACT! I SHALL BE EARTH'S ONLY OBSERVER, FOR I ALONE, AM IMMUNE!
THE FIRST CONTAGION TOOK PLACE TEN MILES AWAY...
HEY, JOE, ALL OF A SUDDEN I GOT A PAIN IN MY BACK AND LEGS! I CAN'T MOVE!
JUST LIKE ME! OWW, I CAN'T STRAIGHTEN OUT NO MORE!

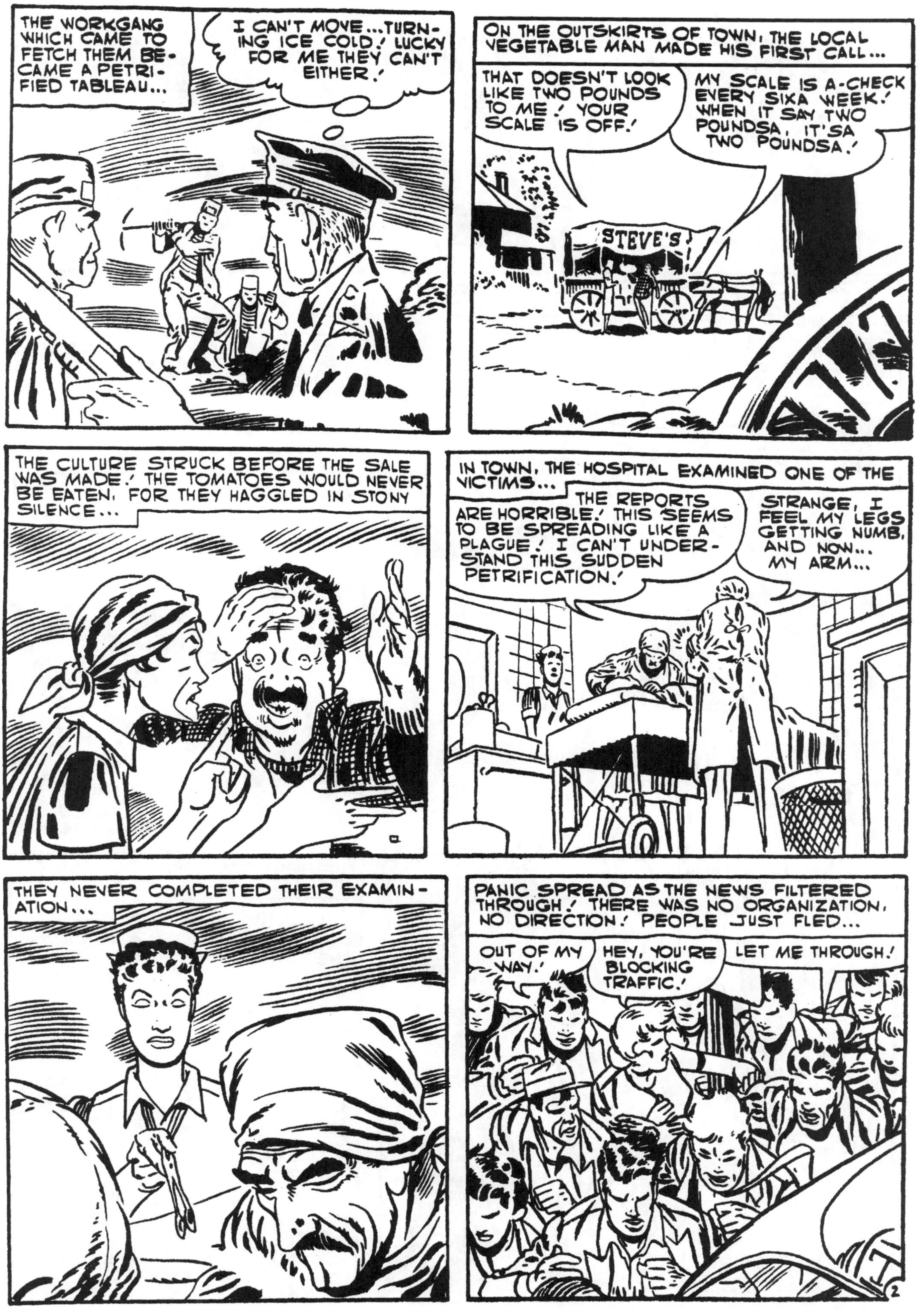
THE WORKGANG WHICH CAME TO FETCH THEM BECAME A PETRIFIED TABLEAU...
I CAN'T MOVE...TURNING ICE COLD! LUCKY FOR ME THEY CAN'T EITHER!
ON THE OUTSKIRTS OF TOWN, THE LOCAL VEGETABLE MAN MADE HIS FIRST CALL...
THAT DOESN'T LOOK LIKE TWO POUNDS TO ME! YOUR SCALE IS OFF!
MY SCALE IS A-CHECK EVERY SIXA WEEK! WHEN IT SAY TWO POUNDSA, IT'SA TWO POUNDSA!
STEVE'S
THE CULTURE STRUCK BEFORE THE SALE WAS MADE! THE TOMATOES WOULD NEVER BE EATEN, FOR THEY HAGGLED IN STONY SILENCE...
IN TOWN, THE HOSPITAL EXAMINED ONE OF THE VICTIMS...
THE REPORTS ARE HORRIBLE! THIS SEEMS TO BE SPREADING LIKE A PLAGUE! I CAN'T UNDERSTAND THIS SUDDEN PETRIFICATION!
STRANGE, I FEEL MY LEGS GETTING NUMB, AND NOW... MY ARM...
THEY NEVER COMPLETED THEIR EXAMINATION...
PANIC SPREAD AS THE NEWS FILTERED THROUGH! THERE WAS NO ORGANIZATION, NO DIRECTION! PEOPLE JUST FLED...
OUT OF MY WAY!
HEY, YOU'RE BLOCKING TRAFFIC!
LET ME THROUGH!
2

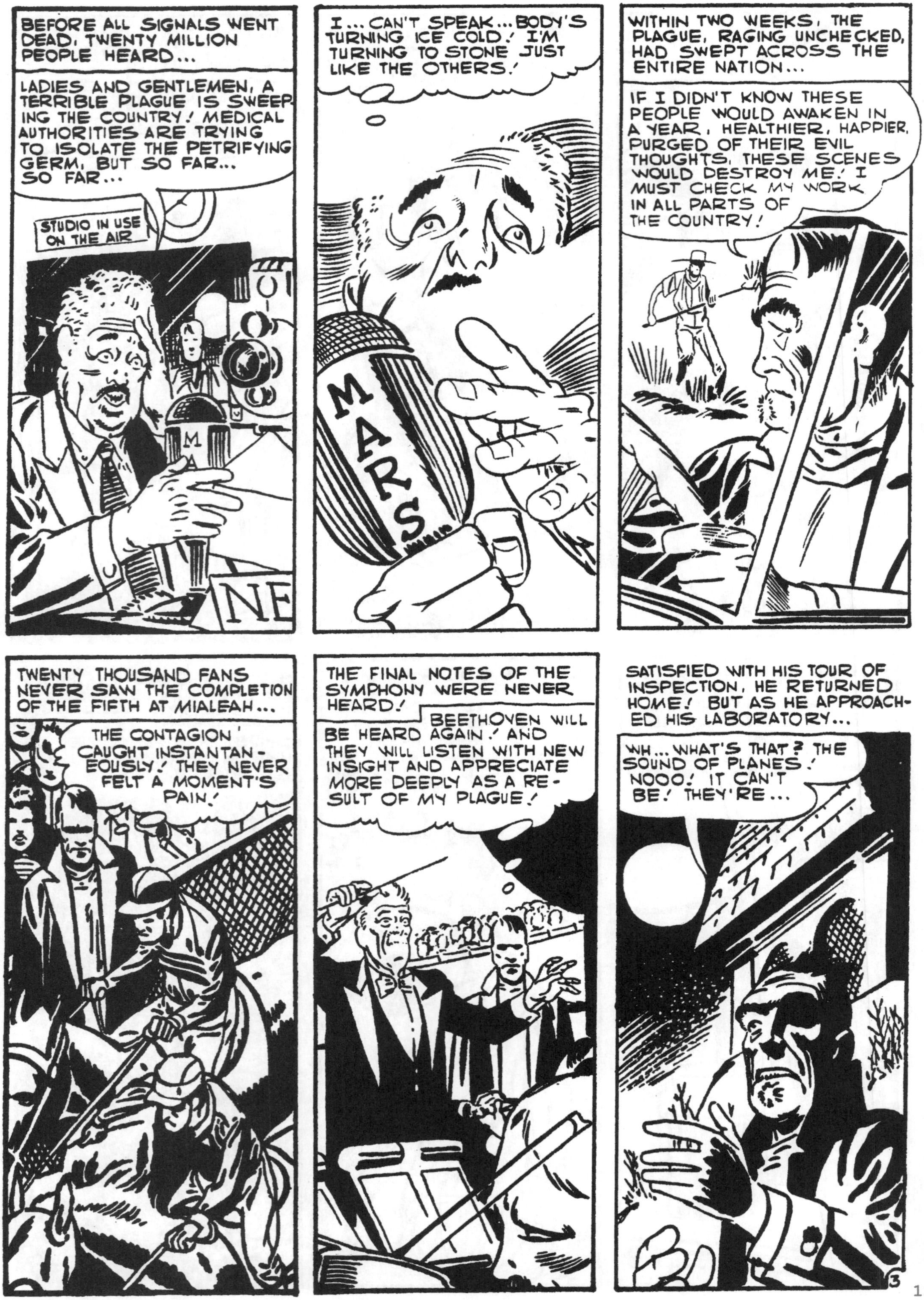
BEFORE ALL SIGNALS WENT DEAD, TWENTY MILLION PEOPLE HEARD...
LADIES AND GENTLEMEN, A TERRIBLE PLAGUE IS SWEEPING THE COUNTRY! MEDICAL AUTHORITIES ARE TRYING TO ISOLATE THE PETRIFYING GERM, BUT SO FAR... SO FAR...
STUDIO IN USE ON THE AIR
NE
I... CAN'T SPEAK... BODY'S TURNING ICE COLD! I'M TURNING TO STONE JUST LIKE THE OTHERS!
MARS
WITHIN TWO WEEKS, THE PLAGUE, RAGING UNCHECKED, HAD SWEPT ACROSS THE ENTIRE NATION...
IF I DIDN'T KNOW THESE PEOPLE WOULD AWAKEN IN A YEAR, HEALTHIER, HAPPIER, PURGED OF THEIR EVIL THOUGHTS, THESE SCENES WOULD DESTROY ME! I MUST CHECK MY WORK IN ALL PARTS OF THE COUNTRY!
TWENTY THOUSAND FANS NEVER SAW THE COMPLETION OF THE FIFTH AT MIALEAH...
THE CONTAGION CAUGHT INSTANTANEOUSLY! THEY NEVER FELT A MOMENT'S PAIN!
THE FINAL NOTES OF THE SYMPHONY WERE NEVER HEARD!
BEETHOVEN WILL BE HEARD AGAIN! AND THEY WILL LISTEN WITH NEW INSIGHT AND APPRECIATE MORE DEEPLY AS A RESULT OF MY PLAGUE!
SATISFIED WITH HIS TOUR OF INSPECTION, HE RETURNED HOME! BUT AS HE APPROACHED HIS LABORATORY...
WH... WHAT'S THAT? THE SOUND OF PLANES! NOOO! IT CAN'T BE! THEY'RE...
3

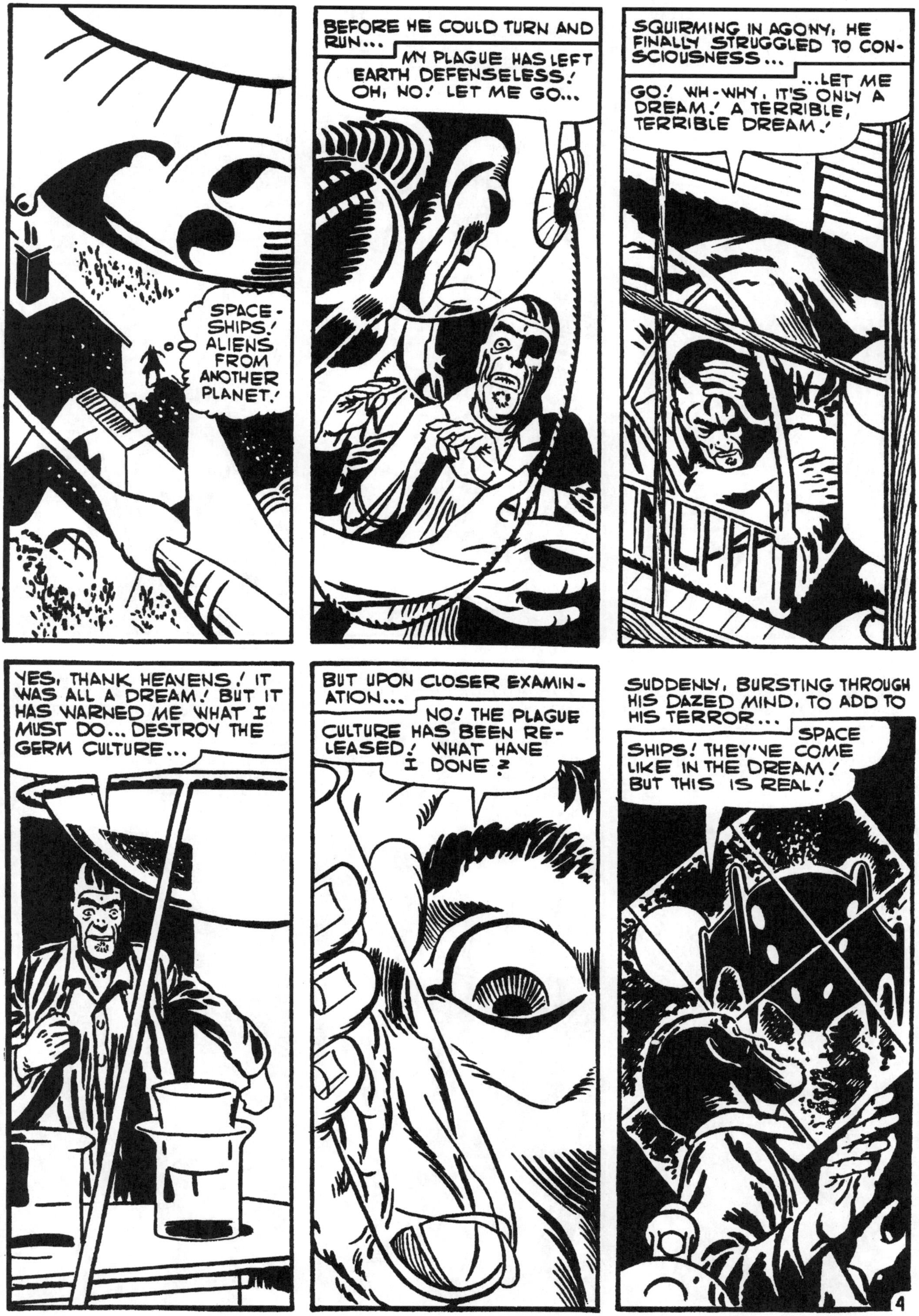
SPACE-SHIPS! ALIENS FROM ANOTHER PLANET!
BEFORE HE COULD TURN AND RUN...
MY PLAGUE HAS LEFT EARTH DEFENSELESS! OH, NO! LET ME GO...
SQUIRMING IN AGONY, HE FINALLY STRUGGLED TO CONSCIOUSNESS...
...LET ME GO! WH-WHY, IT'S ONLY A DREAM! A TERRIBLE, TERRIBLE DREAM!
YES, THANK HEAVENS! IT WAS ALL A DREAM! BUT IT HAS WARNED ME WHAT I MUST DO... DESTROY THE GERM CULTURE...
BUT UPON CLOSER EXAMINATION...
NO! THE PLAGUE CULTURE HAS BEEN RELEASED! WHAT HAVE I DONE?
SUDDENLY, BURSTING THROUGH HIS DAZED MIND, TO ADD TO HIS TERROR...
SPACE SHIPS! THEY'VE COME LIKE IN THE DREAM! BUT THIS IS REAL!
4

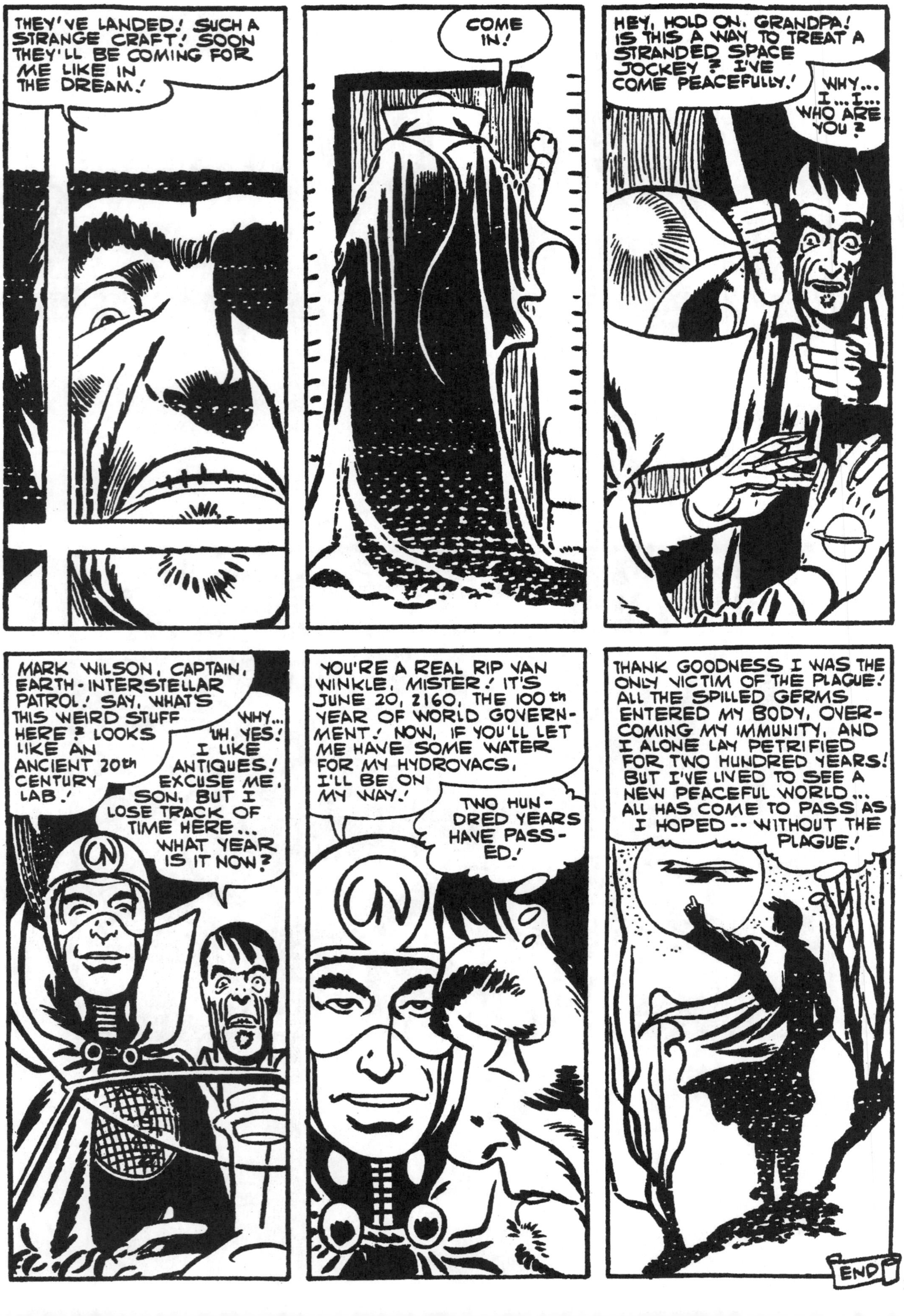

THEY'VE LANDED! SUCH A STRANGE CRAFT! SOON THEY'LL BE COMING FOR ME LIKE IN THE DREAM!
COME IN!
HEY, HOLD ON, GRANDPA! IS THIS A WAY TO TREAT A STRANDED SPACE JOCKEY? I'VE COME PEACEFULLY!
WHY... I...I... WHO ARE YOU?
MARK WILSON, CAPTAIN, EARTH-INTERSTELLAR PATROL! SAY, WHAT'S THIS WEIRD STUFF HERE? LOOKS LIKE AN ANCIENT 20th CENTURY LAB!
WHY... UH, YES! I LIKE ANTIQUES! EXCUSE ME, SON, BUT I LOSE TRACK OF TIME HERE... WHAT YEAR IS IT NOW?
YOU'RE A REAL RIP VAN WINKLE, MISTER! IT'S JUNE 20, 2160, THE 100th YEAR OF WORLD GOVERNMENT! NOW, IF YOU'LL LET ME HAVE SOME WATER FOR MY HYDROVACS, I'LL BE ON MY WAY!
TWO HUNDRED YEARS HAVE PASSED!
THANK GOODNESS I WAS THE ONLY VICTIM OF THE PLAGUE! ALL THE SPILLED GERMS ENTERED MY BODY, OVERCOMING MY IMMUNITY, AND I ALONE LAY PETRIFIED FOR TWO HUNDRED YEARS! BUT I'VE LIVED TO SEE A NEW PEACEFUL WORLD... ALL HAS COME TO PASS AS I HOPED -- WITHOUT THE PLAGUE!
END

STEVE DITKO
SPACE WARS

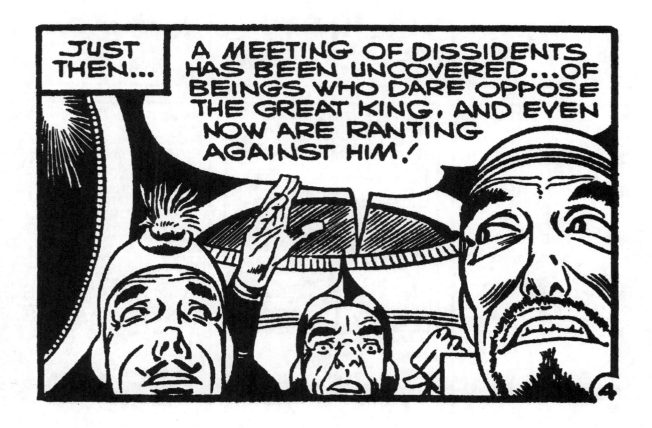

THE KING OF PLANETOID X

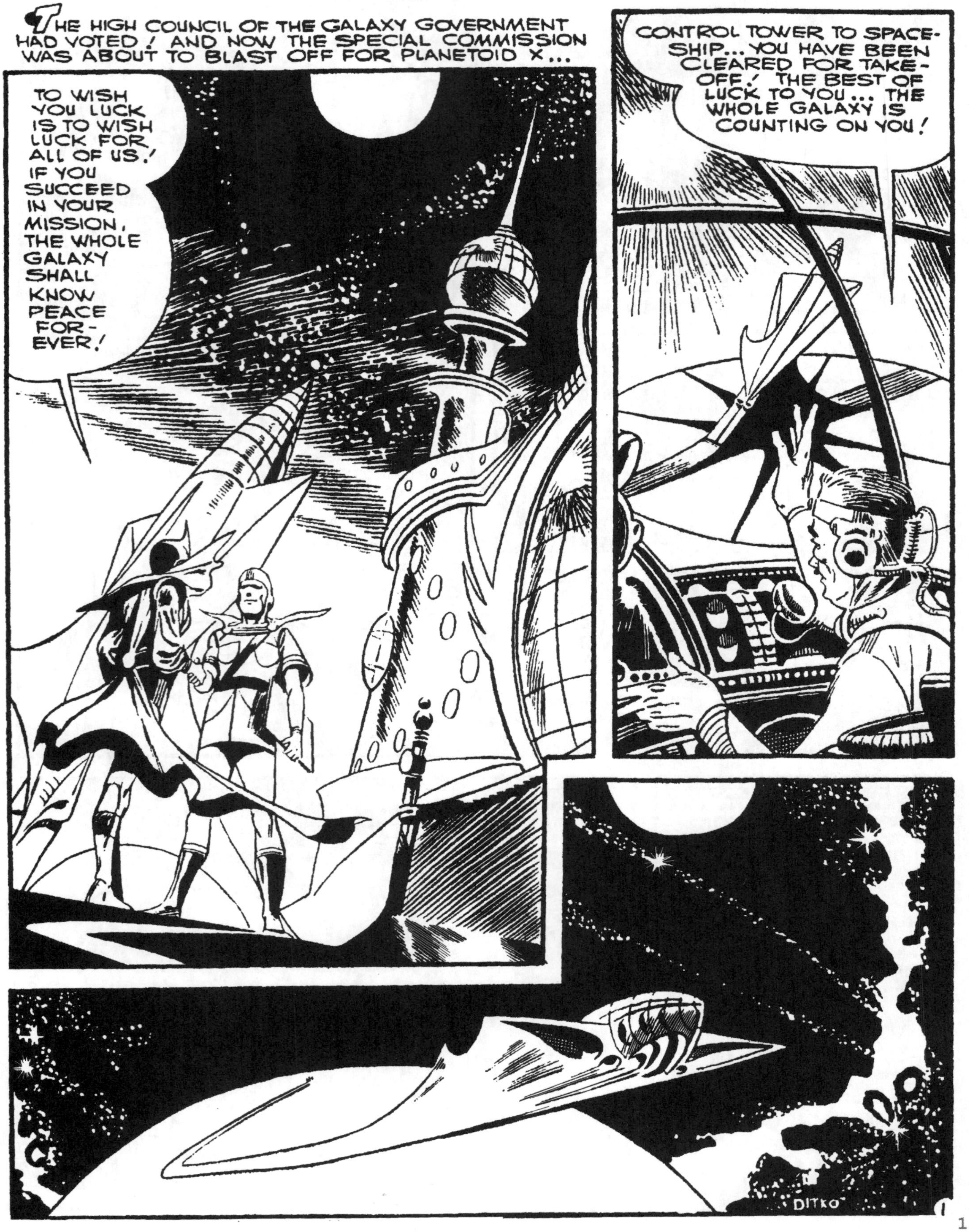

THE HIGH COUNCIL OF THE GALAXY GOVERNMENT HAD VOTED! AND NOW THE SPECIAL COMMISSION WAS ABOUT TO BLAST OFF FOR PLANETOID X...
TO WISH YOU LUCK IS TO WISH LUCK FOR ALL OF US! IF YOU SUCCEED IN YOUR MISSION, THE WHOLE GALAXY SHALL KNOW PEACE FOR-EVER!
CONTROL TOWER TO SPACE-SHIP... YOU HAVE BEEN CLEARED FOR TAKE-OFF! THE BEST OF LUCK TO YOU... THE WHOLE GALAXY IS COUNTING ON YOU!
DITKO
1

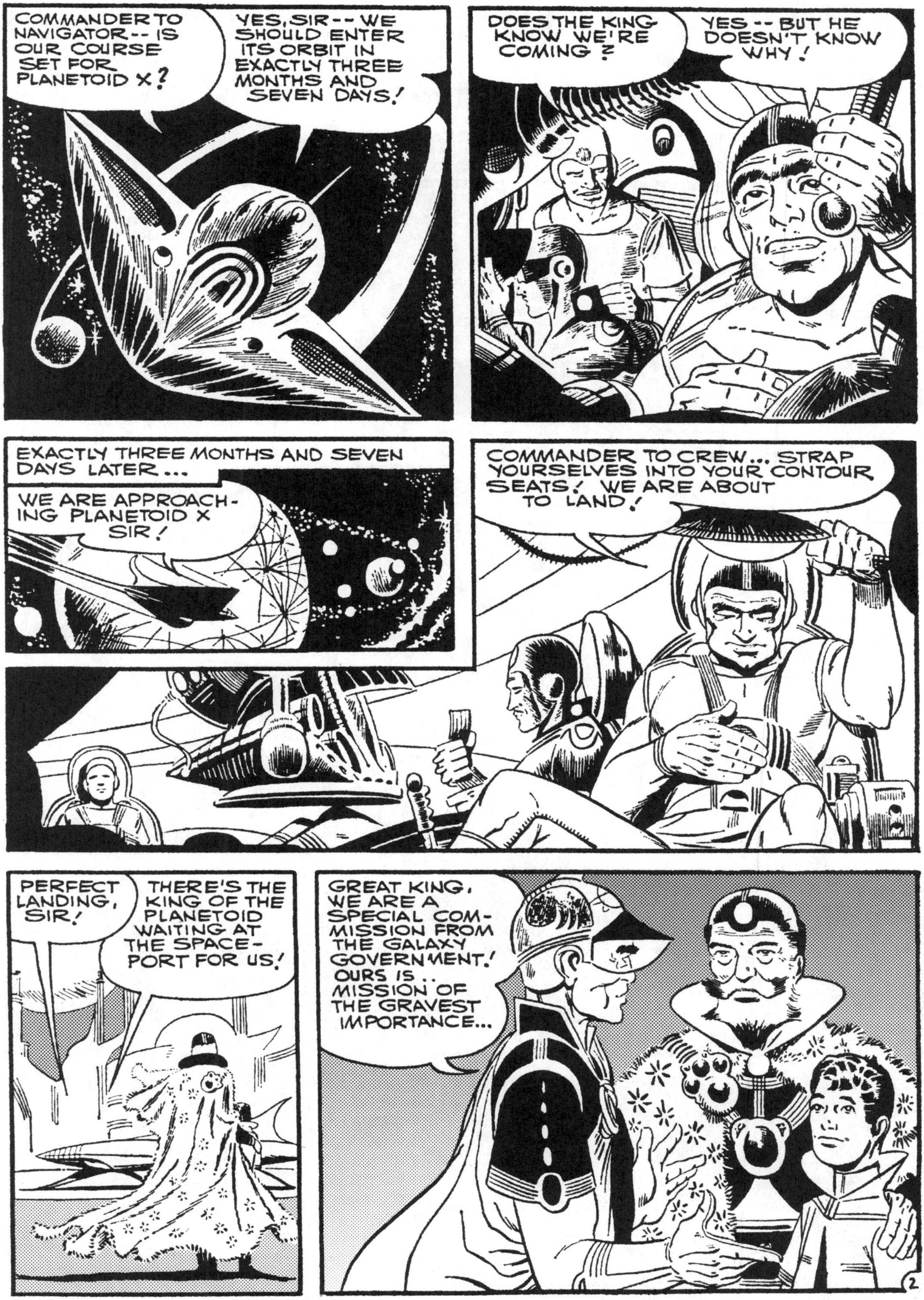
COMMANDER TO NAVIGATOR-- IS OUR COURSE SET FOR PLANETOID X?
YES, SIR-- WE SHOULD ENTER ITS ORBIT IN EXACTLY THREE MONTHS AND SEVEN DAYS!
DOES THE KING KNOW WE'RE COMING?
YES -- BUT HE DOESN'T KNOW WHY!
EXACTLY THREE MONTHS AND SEVEN DAYS LATER...
WE ARE APPROACH-ING PLANETOID X SIR!
COMMANDER TO CREW... STRAP YOURSELVES INTO YOUR CONTOUR SEATS! WE ARE ABOUT TO LAND!
PERFECT LANDING, SIR!
THERE'S THE KING OF THE PLANETOID WAITING AT THE SPACE-PORT FOR US!
GREAT KING, WE ARE A SPECIAL COM-MISSION FROM THE GALAXY GOVERNMENT! OURS IS.. MISSION OF THE GRAVEST IMPORTANCE...
2

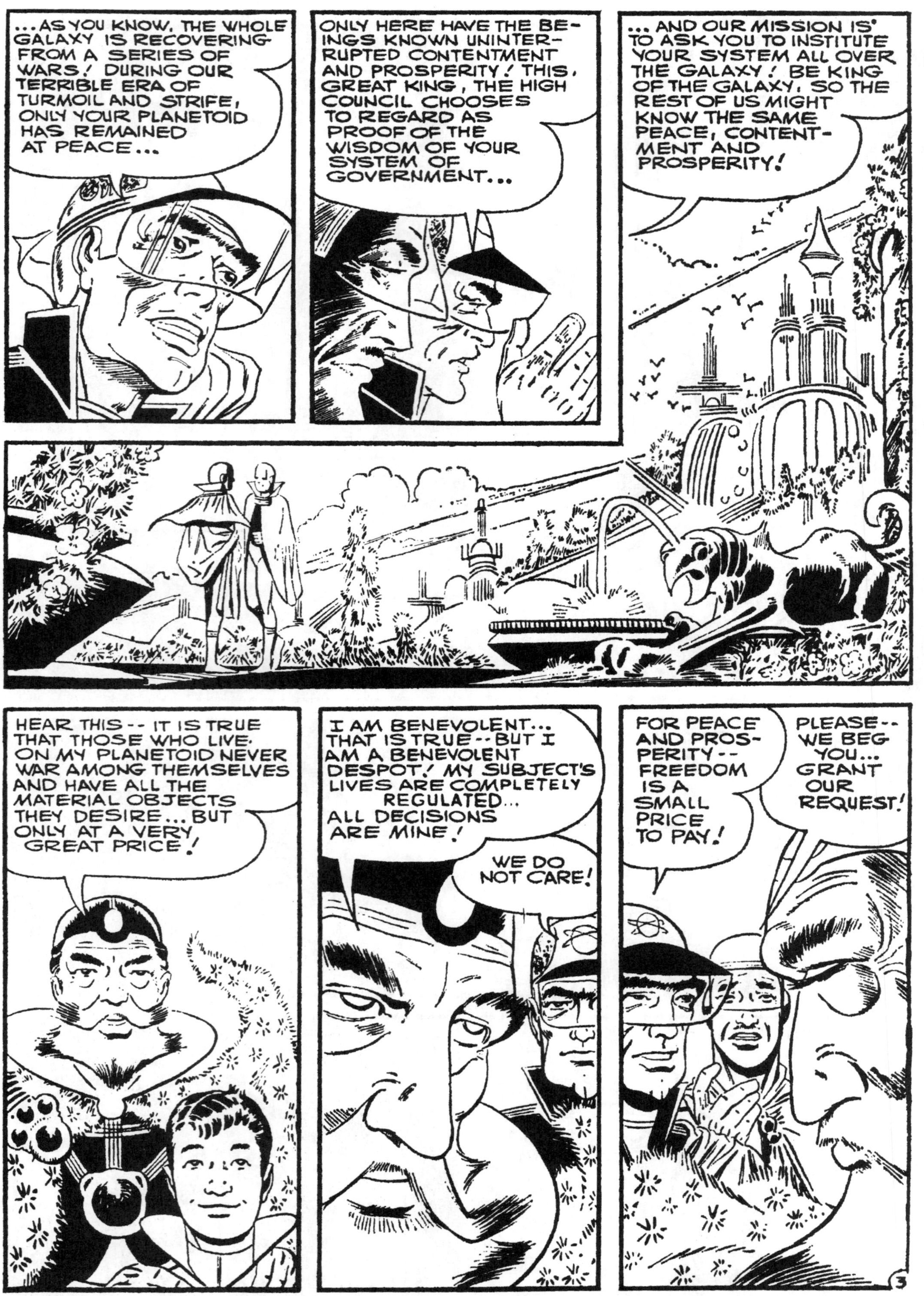
...AS YOU KNOW, THE WHOLE GALAXY IS RECOVERING FROM A SERIES OF WARS! DURING OUR TERRIBLE ERA OF TURMOIL AND STRIFE, ONLY YOUR PLANETOID HAS REMAINED AT PEACE...
ONLY HERE HAVE THE BEINGS KNOWN UNINTERRUPTED CONTENTMENT AND PROSPERITY! THIS, GREAT KING, THE HIGH COUNCIL CHOOSES TO REGARD AS PROOF OF THE WISDOM OF YOUR SYSTEM OF GOVERNMENT...
...AND OUR MISSION IS TO ASK YOU TO INSTITUTE YOUR SYSTEM ALL OVER THE GALAXY! BE KING OF THE GALAXY, SO THE REST OF US MIGHT KNOW THE SAME PEACE, CONTENTMENT AND PROSPERITY!
HEAR THIS -- IT IS TRUE THAT THOSE WHO LIVE ON MY PLANETOID NEVER WAR AMONG THEMSELVES AND HAVE ALL THE MATERIAL OBJECTS THEY DESIRE... BUT ONLY AT A VERY GREAT PRICE!
I AM BENEVOLENT... THAT IS TRUE -- BUT I AM A BENEVOLENT DESPOT! MY SUBJECT'S LIVES ARE COMPLETELY REGULATED... ALL DECISIONS ARE MINE!
WE DO NOT CARE!
FOR PEACE AND PROSPERITY -- FREEDOM IS A SMALL PRICE TO PAY!
PLEASE -- WE BEG YOU... GRANT OUR REQUEST!
3

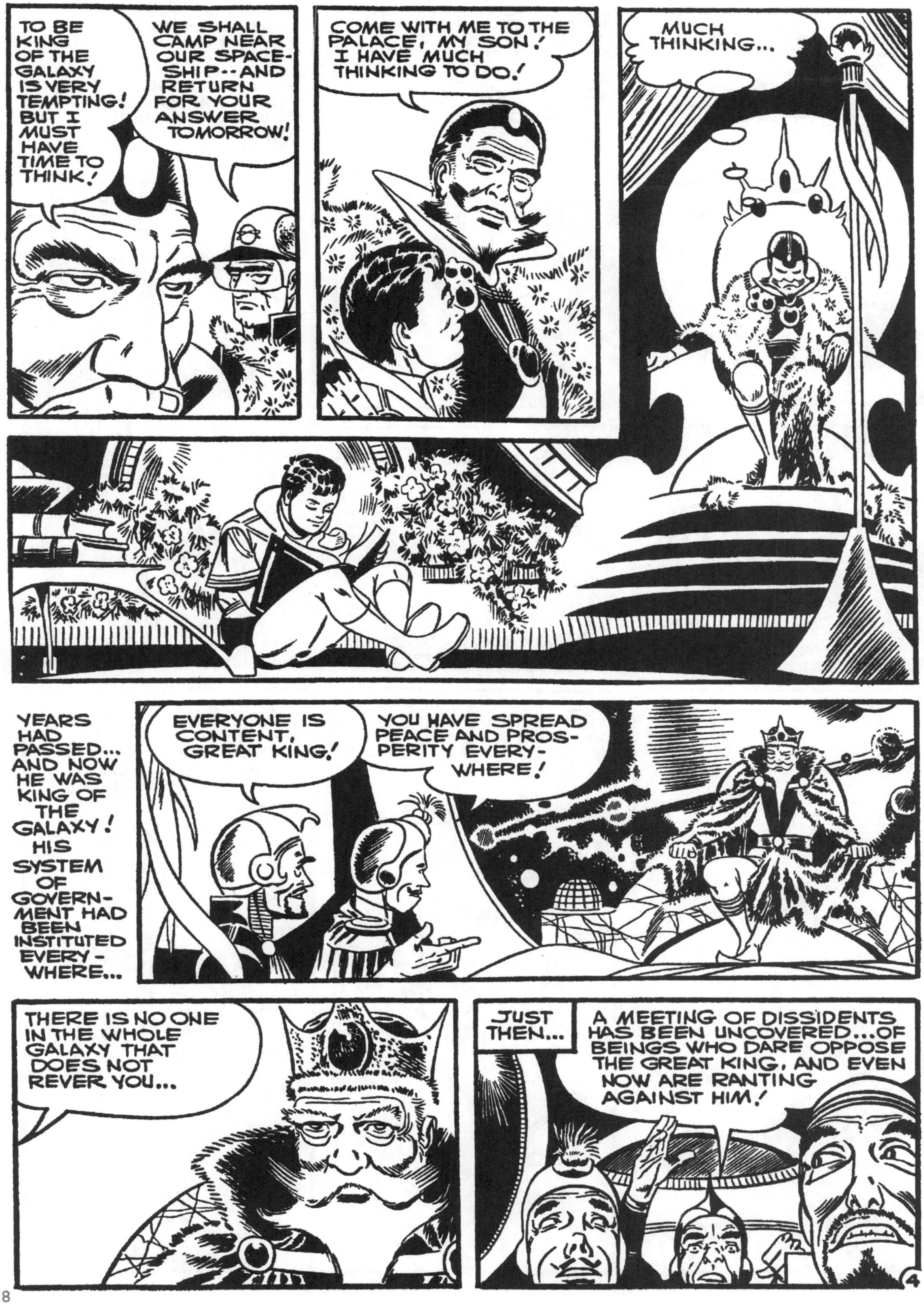
TO BE KING OF THE GALAXY IS VERY TEMPTING! BUT I MUST HAVE TIME TO THINK!
WE SHALL CAMP NEAR OUR SPACE-SHIP--AND RETURN FOR YOUR ANSWER TOMORROW!
COME WITH ME TO THE PALACE, MY SON! I HAVE MUCH THINKING TO DO!
MUCH THINKING...
YEARS HAD PASSED... AND NOW HE WAS KING OF THE GALAXY! HIS SYSTEM OF GOVERNMENT HAD BEEN INSTITUTED EVERY-WHERE...
EVERYONE IS CONTENT, GREAT KING!
YOU HAVE SPREAD PEACE AND PROS-PERITY EVERY-WHERE!
THERE IS NO ONE IN THE WHOLE GALAXY THAT DOES NOT REVER YOU...
JUST THEN...
A MEETING OF DISSIDENTS HAS BEEN UNCOVERED...OF BEINGS WHO DARE OPPOSE THE GREAT KING, AND EVEN NOW ARE RANTING AGAINST HIM!
4

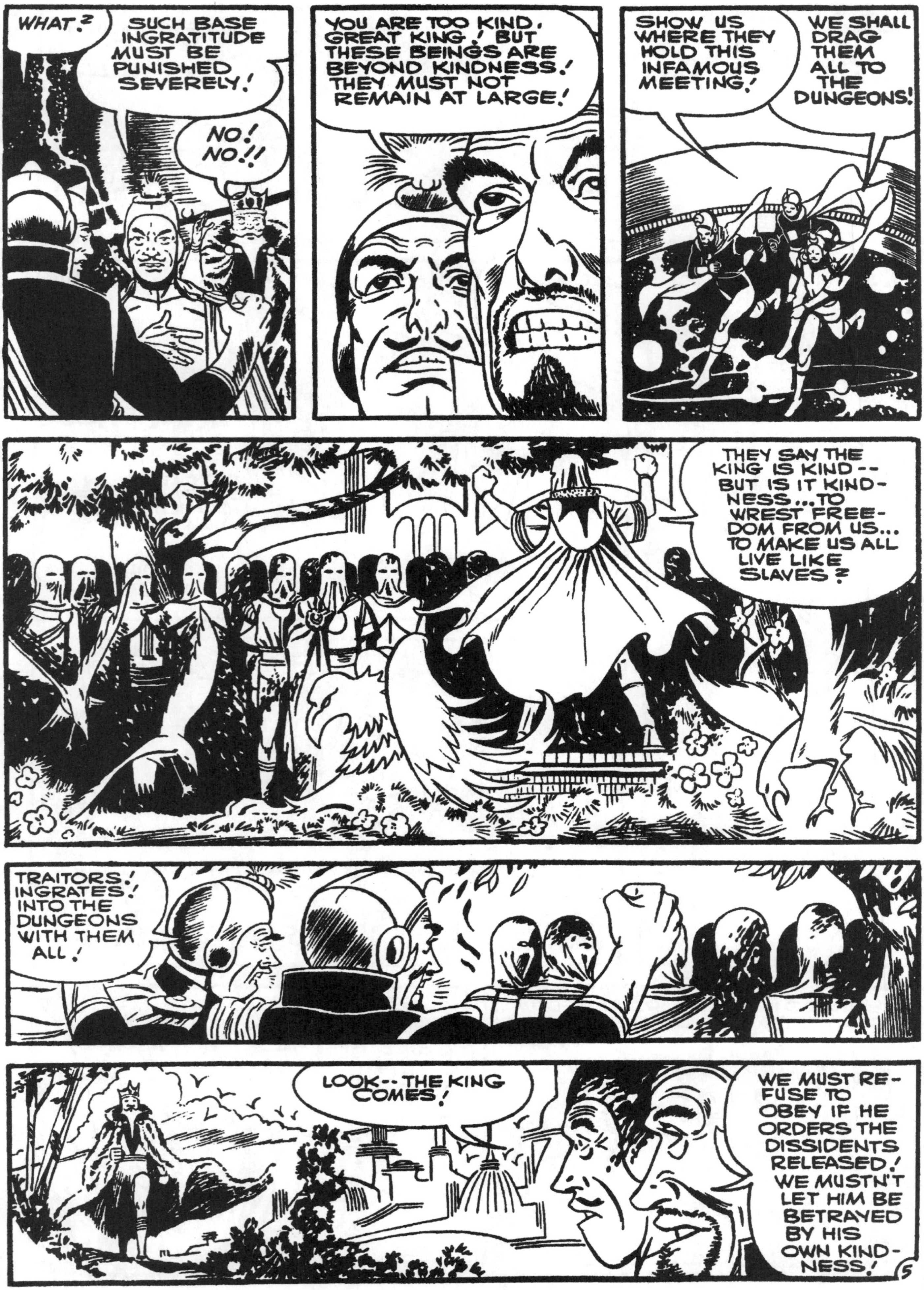
WHAT?
SUCH BASE INGRATITUDE MUST BE PUNISHED SEVERELY!
NO! NO!!
YOU ARE TOO KIND, GREAT KING! BUT THESE BEINGS ARE BEYOND KINDNESS! THEY MUST NOT REMAIN AT LARGE!
SHOW US WHERE THEY HOLD THIS INFAMOUS MEETING!
WE SHALL DRAG THEM ALL TO THE DUNGEONS!
THEY SAY THE KING IS KIND-- BUT IS IT KINDNESS...TO WREST FREEDOM FROM US... TO MAKE US ALL LIVE LIKE SLAVES?
TRAITORS! INGRATES! INTO THE DUNGEONS WITH THEM ALL!
LOOK--THE KING COMES!
WE MUST REFUSE TO OBEY IF HE ORDERS THE DISSIDENTS RELEASED! WE MUSTN'T LET HIM BE BETRAYED BY HIS OWN KINDNESS!
5

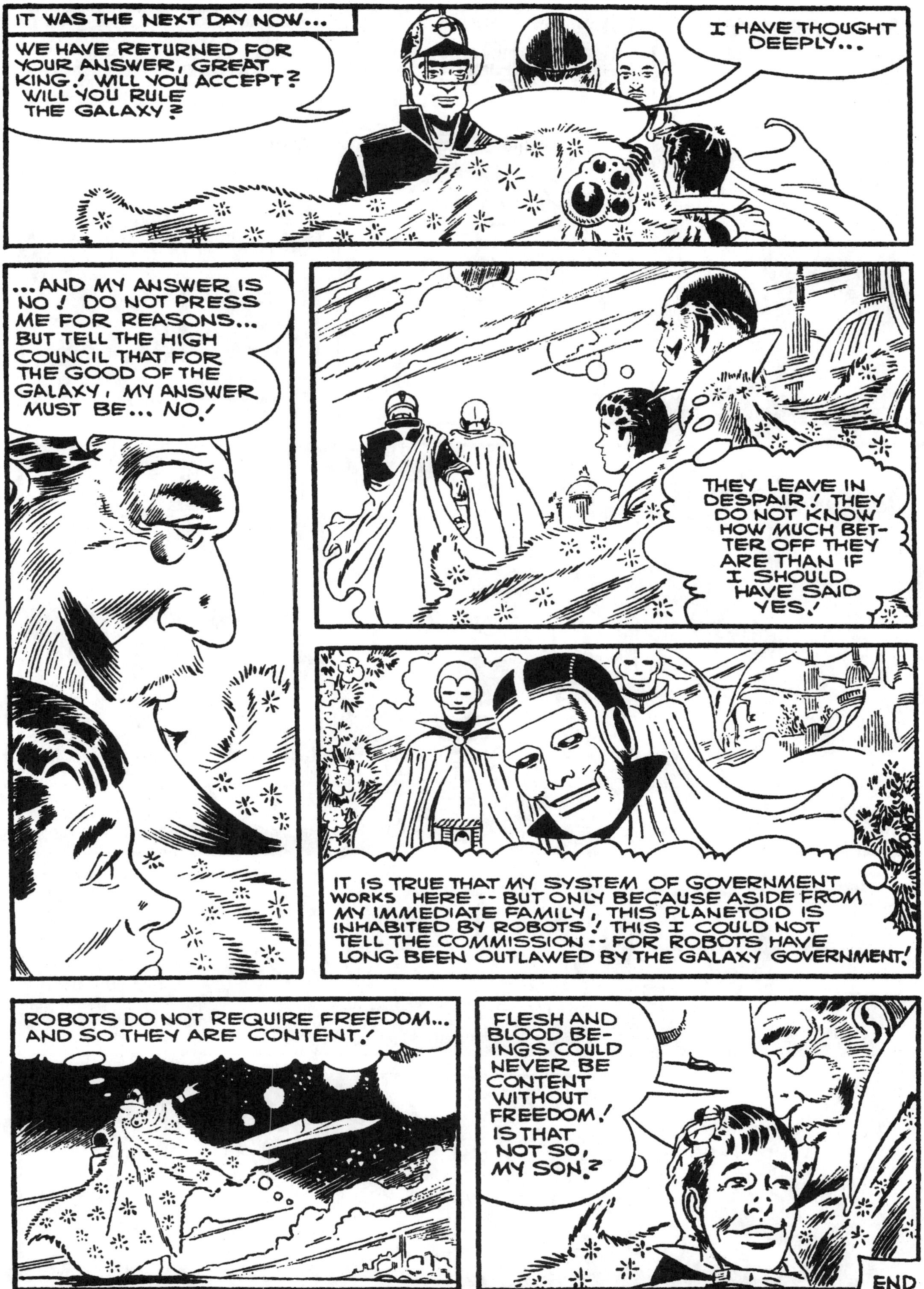
IT WAS THE NEXT DAY NOW...
WE HAVE RETURNED FOR YOUR ANSWER, GREAT KING! WILL YOU ACCEPT? WILL YOU RULE THE GALAXY?
I HAVE THOUGHT DEEPLY...
...AND MY ANSWER IS NO! DO NOT PRESS ME FOR REASONS... BUT TELL THE HIGH COUNCIL THAT FOR THE GOOD OF THE GALAXY, MY ANSWER MUST BE... NO!
THEY LEAVE IN DESPAIR! THEY DO NOT KNOW HOW MUCH BETTER OFF THEY ARE THAN IF I SHOULD HAVE SAID YES!
IT IS TRUE THAT MY SYSTEM OF GOVERNMENT WORKS HERE -- BUT ONLY BECAUSE ASIDE FROM MY IMMEDIATE FAMILY, THIS PLANETOID IS INHABITED BY ROBOTS! THIS I COULD NOT TELL THE COMMISSION -- FOR ROBOTS HAVE LONG BEEN OUTLAWED BY THE GALAXY GOVERNMENT!
ROBOTS DO NOT REQUIRE FREEDOM... AND SO THEY ARE CONTENT!
FLESH AND BLOOD BEINGS COULD NEVER BE CONTENT WITHOUT FREEDOM! IS THAT NOT SO, MY SON?
END

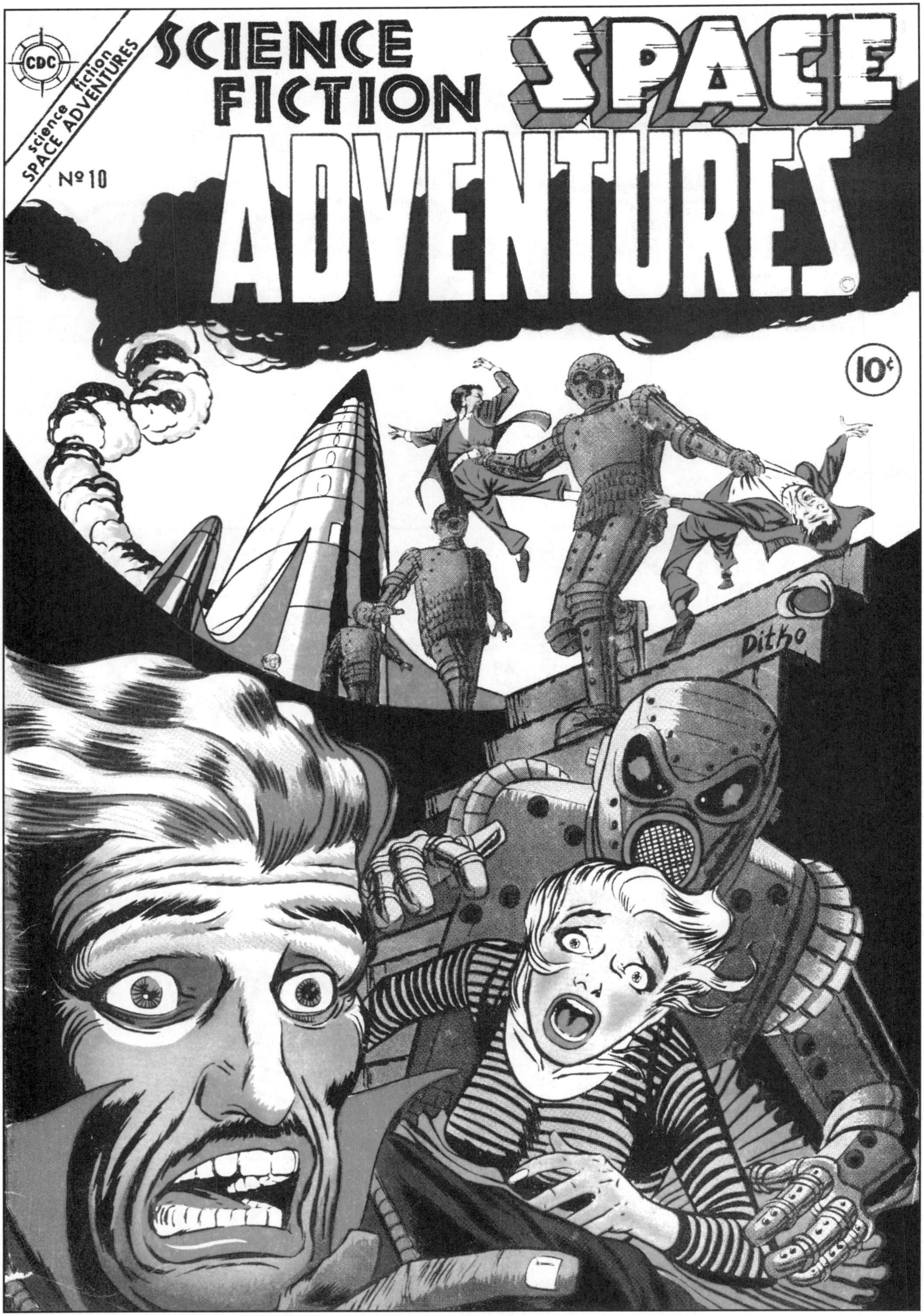
CDC
science fiction
SPACE ADVENTURES
SCIENCE FICTION
SPACE ADVENTURES
№10
10¢
Ditko

STEVE DITKO SPACE WARS

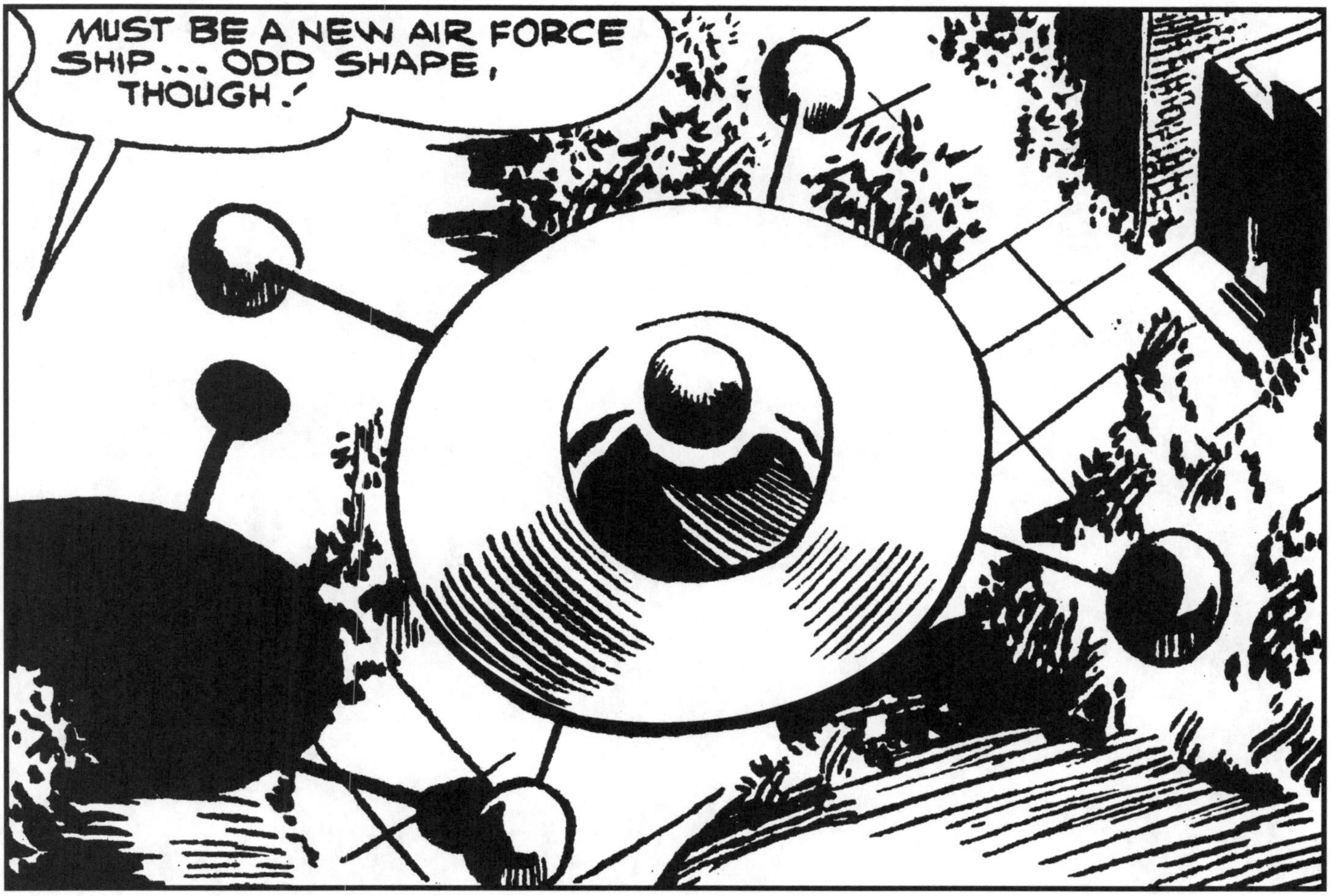
MUST BE A NEW AIR FORCE SHIP... ODD SHAPE, THOUGH.!

They must be like us

ARE THERE LIVING BEINGS LIKE EARTH HUMANS ON OTHER PLANETS? PROFESSOR VAN BRUCK BELIEVED THERE WERE AND TOLD HIS COLLEGE CLASSES SO...

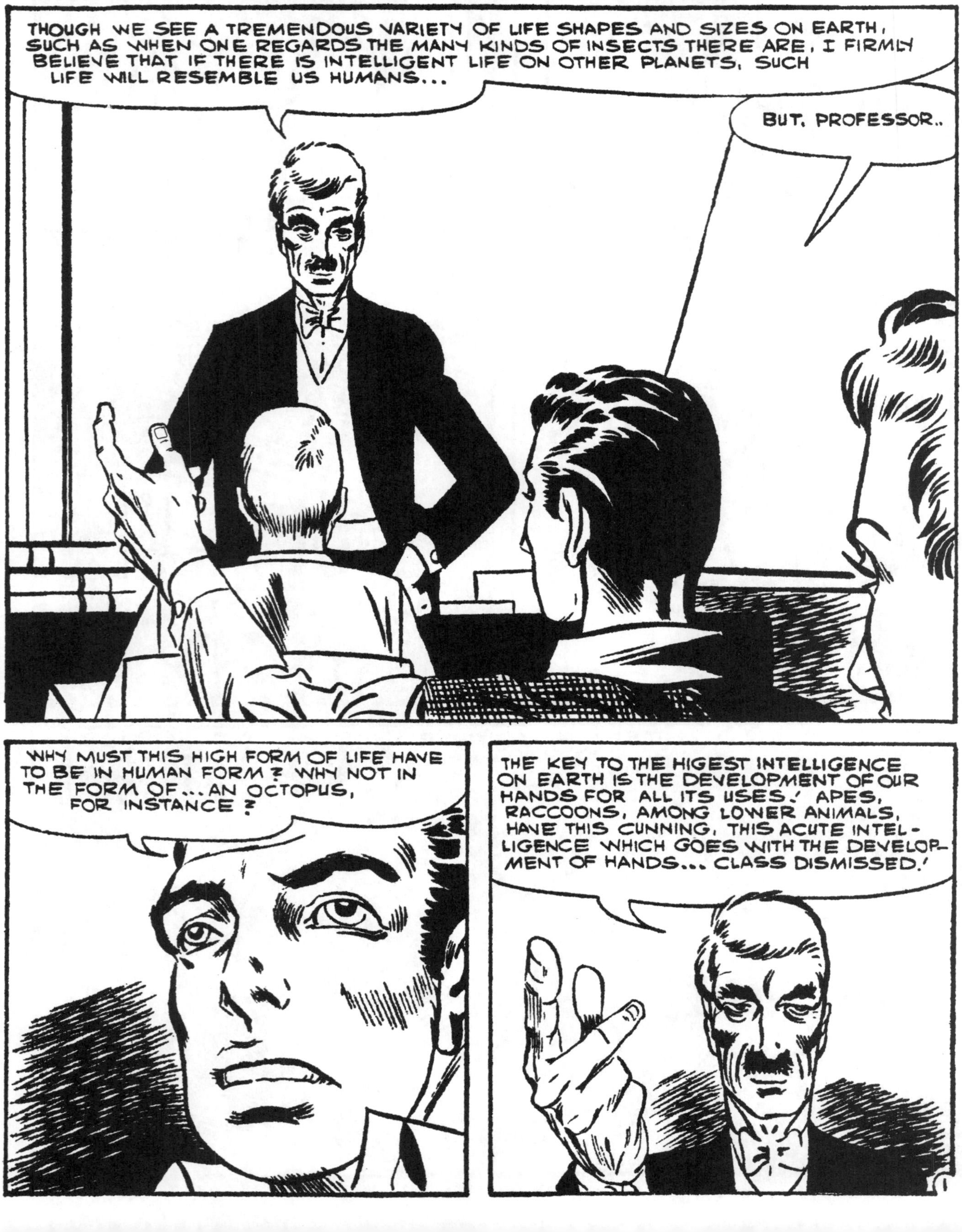

THOUGH WE SEE A TREMENDOUS VARIETY OF LIFE SHAPES AND SIZES ON EARTH, SUCH AS WHEN ONE REGARDS THE MANY KINDS OF INSECTS THERE ARE, I FIRMLY BELIEVE THAT IF THERE IS INTELLIGENT LIFE ON OTHER PLANETS, SUCH LIFE WILL RESEMBLE US HUMANS...
BUT, PROFESSOR..
WHY MUST THIS HIGH FORM OF LIFE HAVE TO BE IN HUMAN FORM? WHY NOT IN THE FORM OF... AN OCTOPUS, FOR INSTANCE?
THE KEY TO THE HIGEST INTELLIGENCE ON EARTH IS THE DEVELOPMENT OF OUR HANDS FOR ALL ITS USES! APES, RACCOONS, AMONG LOWER ANIMALS, HAVE THIS CUNNING, THIS ACUTE INTELLIGENCE WHICH GOES WITH THE DEVELOPMENT OF HANDS... CLASS DISMISSED!
1

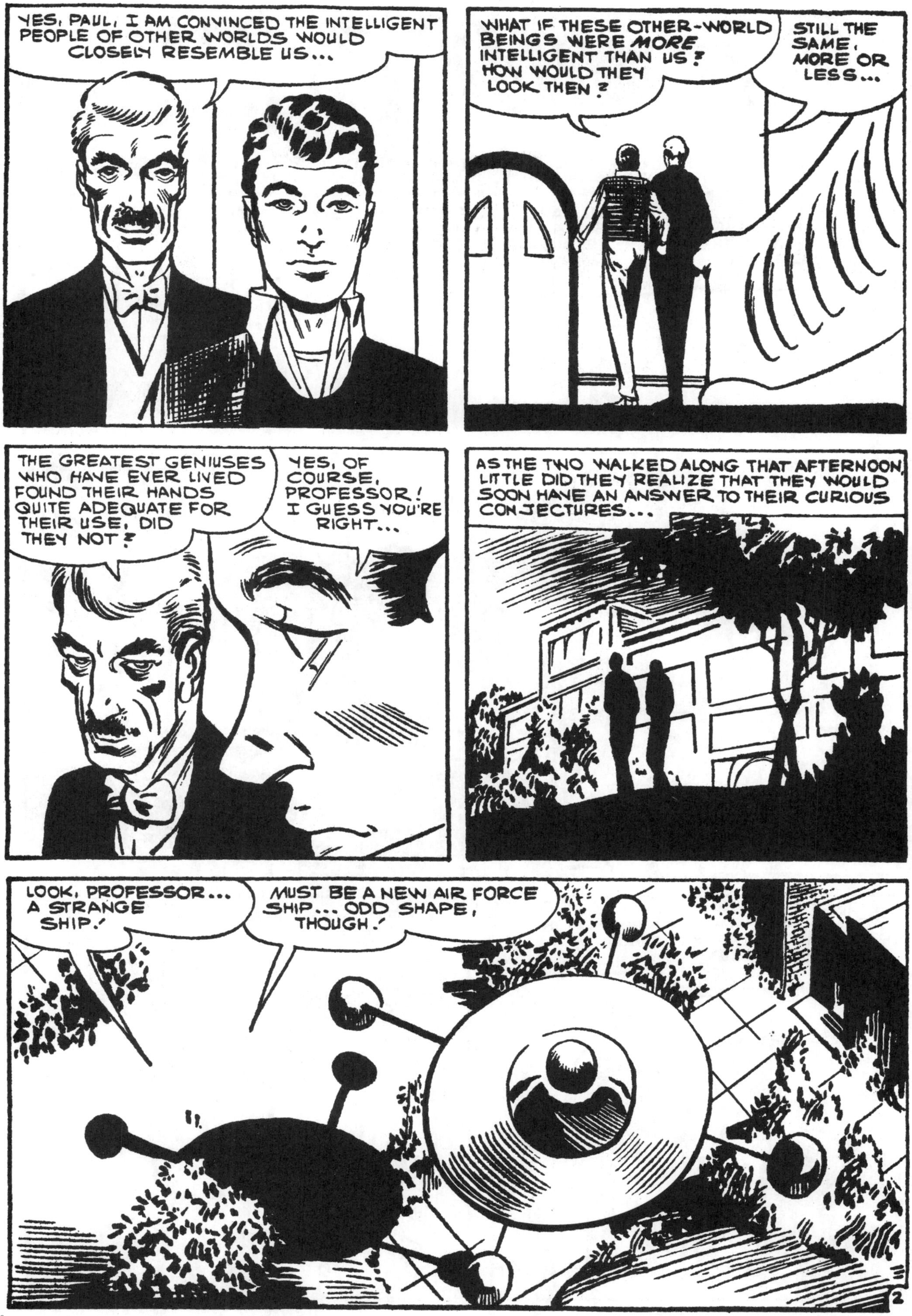
YES, PAUL, I AM CONVINCED THE INTELLIGENT PEOPLE OF OTHER WORLDS WOULD CLOSELY RESEMBLE US...
WHAT IF THESE OTHER-WORLD BEINGS WERE MORE INTELLIGENT THAN US? HOW WOULD THEY LOOK THEN?
STILL THE SAME, MORE OR LESS...
THE GREATEST GENIUSES WHO HAVE EVER LIVED FOUND THEIR HANDS QUITE ADEQUATE FOR THEIR USE, DID THEY NOT?
YES, OF COURSE, PROFESSOR! I GUESS YOU'RE RIGHT...
AS THE TWO WALKED ALONG THAT AFTERNOON, LITTLE DID THEY REALIZE THAT THEY WOULD SOON HAVE AN ANSWER TO THEIR CURIOUS CONJECTURES...
LOOK, PROFESSOR... A STRANGE SHIP!
MUST BE A NEW AIR FORCE SHIP... ODD SHAPE, THOUGH!
2

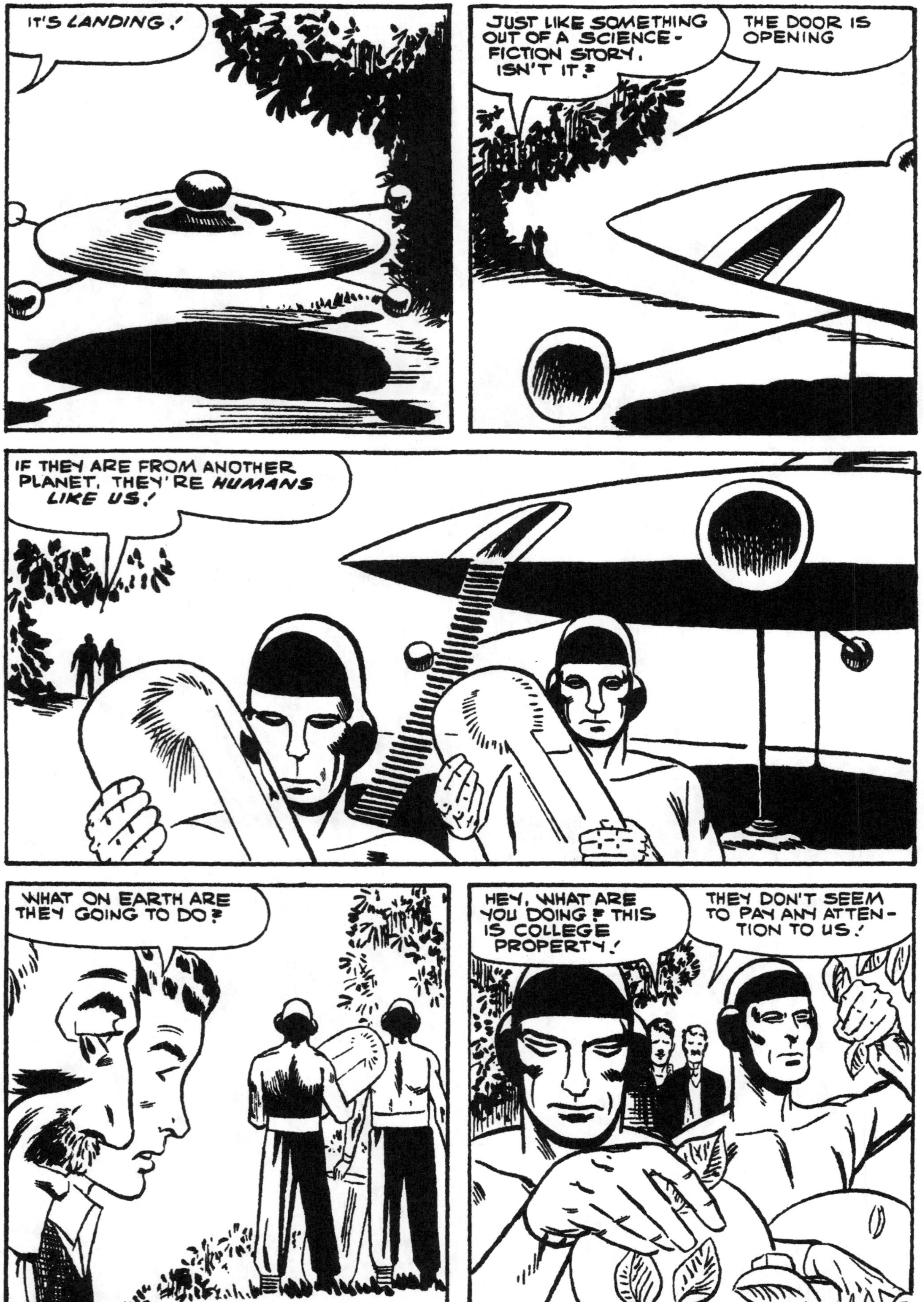
IT'S LANDING!
JUST LIKE SOMETHING OUT OF A SCIENCE-FICTION STORY, ISN'T IT?
THE DOOR IS OPENING
IF THEY ARE FROM ANOTHER PLANET, THEY'RE HUMANS LIKE US!
WHAT ON EARTH ARE THEY GOING TO DO?
HEY, WHAT ARE YOU DOING? THIS IS COLLEGE PROPERTY!
THEY DON'T SEEM TO PAY ANY ATTENTION TO US!
3

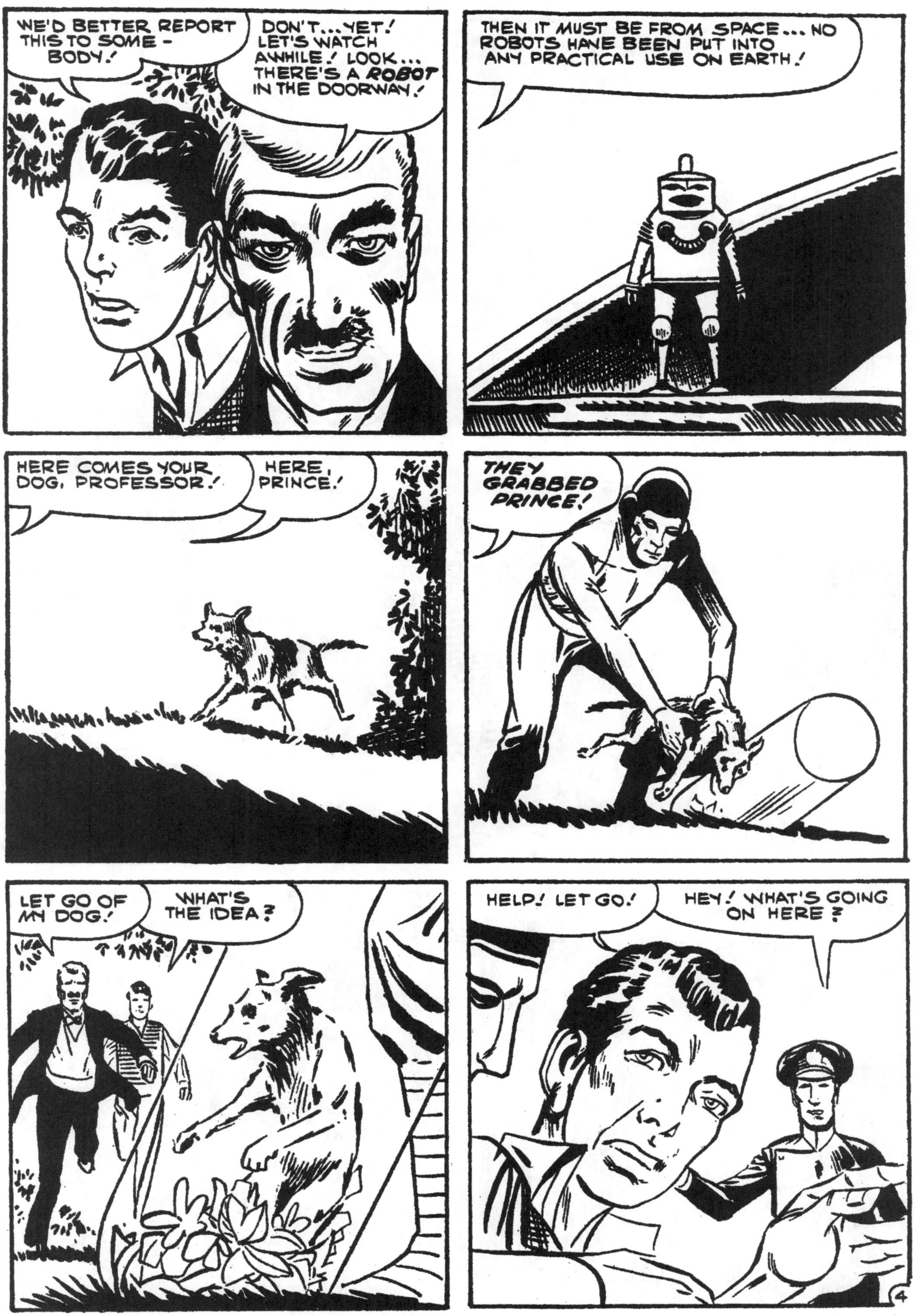
WE'D BETTER REPORT THIS TO SOME-BODY!
DON'T...YET! LET'S WATCH AWHILE! LOOK... THERE'S A ROBOT IN THE DOORWAY!
THEN IT MUST BE FROM SPACE... NO ROBOTS HAVE BEEN PUT INTO ANY PRACTICAL USE ON EARTH!
HERE COMES YOUR DOG, PROFESSOR!
HERE, PRINCE!
THEY GRABBED PRINCE!
LET GO OF MY DOG!
WHAT'S THE IDEA?
HELP! LET GO!
HEY! WHAT'S GOING ON HERE?
4

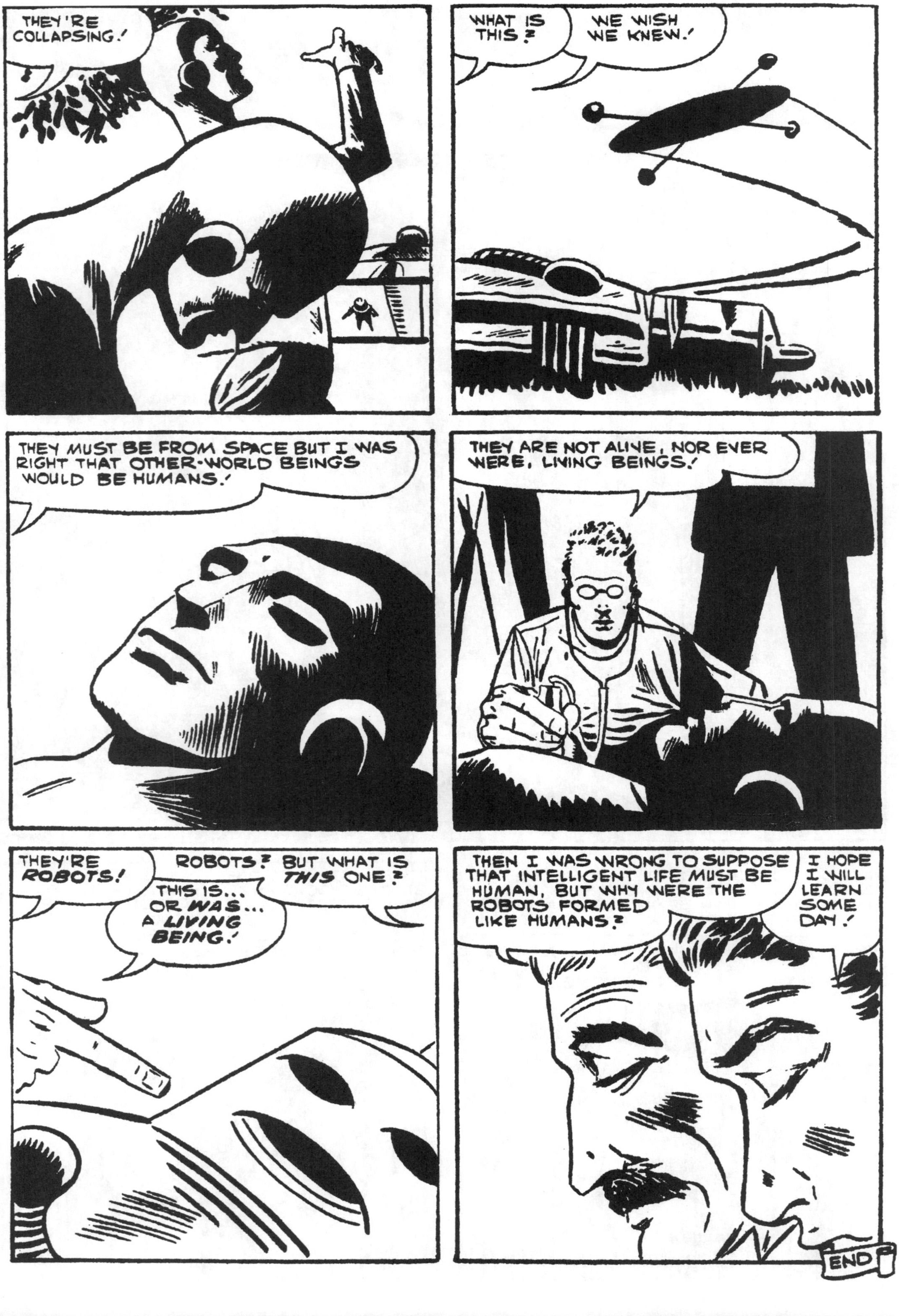
THEY'RE COLLAPSING!
WHAT IS THIS?
WE WISH WE KNEW!
THEY MUST BE FROM SPACE BUT I WAS RIGHT THAT OTHER-WORLD BEINGS WOULD BE HUMANS!
THEY ARE NOT ALIVE, NOR EVER WERE, LIVING BEINGS!
THEY'RE *ROBOTS!*
ROBOTS? BUT WHAT IS *THIS* ONE?
THIS IS... OR *WAS*... A *LIVING BEING!*
THEN I WAS WRONG TO SUPPOSE THAT INTELLIGENT LIFE MUST BE HUMAN, BUT WHY WERE THE ROBOTS FORMED LIKE HUMANS?
I HOPE I WILL LEARN SOME DAY!
END

The ENCHANTED PLANET

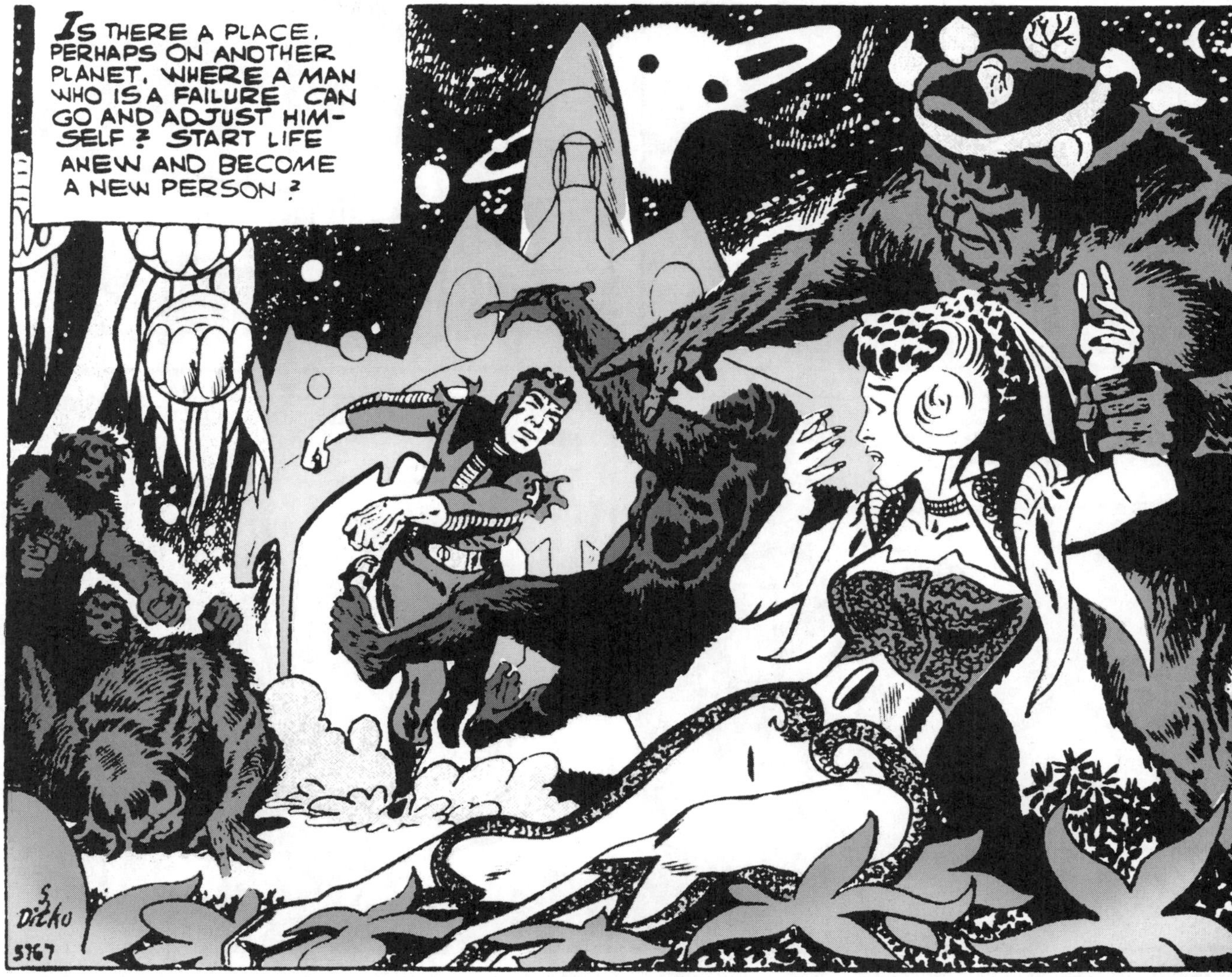
IS THERE A PLACE, PERHAPS ON ANOTHER PLANET, WHERE A MAN WHO IS A FAILURE CAN GO AND ADJUST HIMSELF? START LIFE ANEW AND BECOME A NEW PERSON?
S. DITKO
5767

BRUCE COLSTON, ONLY SON OF RICH JACOB COLSTON, HAD EVERYTHING, BUT HE WAS A FAILURE AS A HUMAN BEING... ONLY A SHORT TIME BEFORE, HIS FATHER HAD SCOLDED HIM...

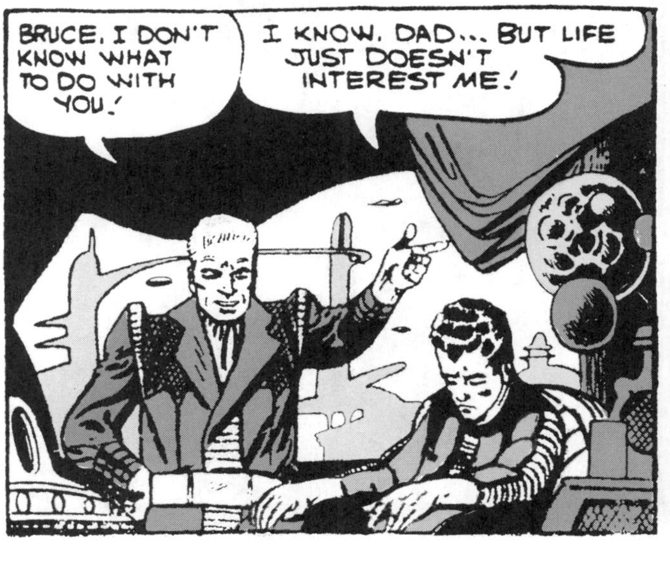
BRUCE, I DON'T KNOW WHAT TO DO WITH YOU!
I KNOW, DAD... BUT LIFE JUST DOESN'T INTEREST ME!

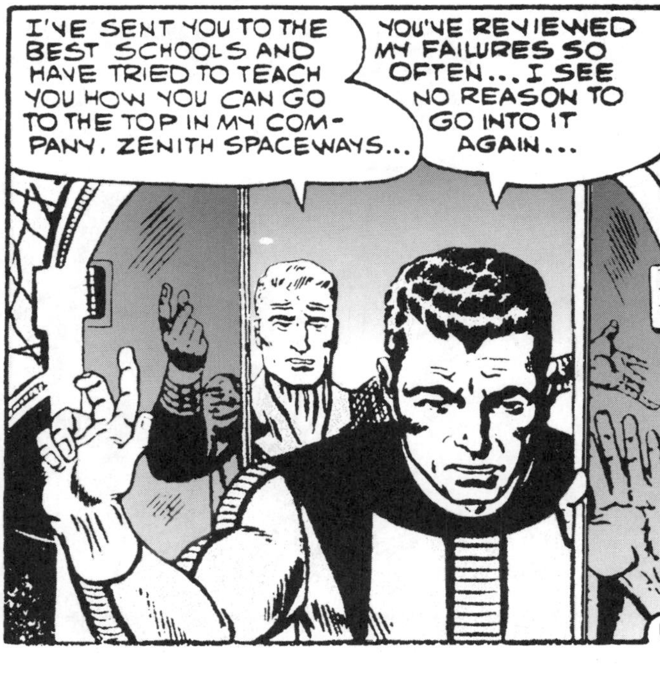
I'VE SENT YOU TO THE BEST SCHOOLS AND HAVE TRIED TO TEACH YOU HOW YOU CAN GO TO THE TOP IN MY COMPANY, ZENITH SPACEWAYS...
YOU'VE REVIEWED MY FAILURES SO OFTEN... I SEE NO REASON TO GO INTO IT AGAIN...

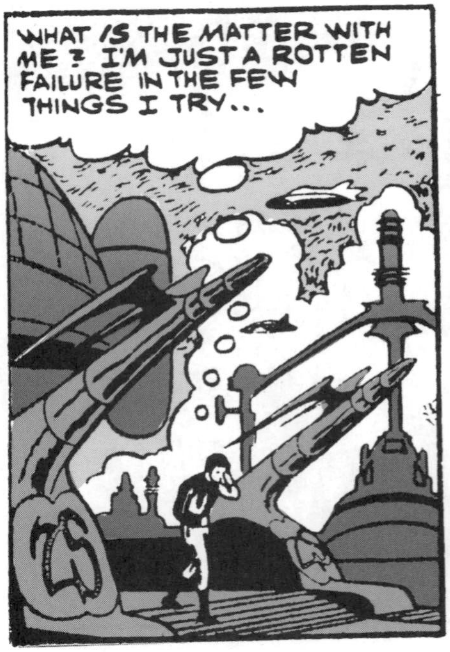
WHAT IS THE MATTER WITH ME? I'M JUST A ROTTEN FAILURE IN THE FEW THINGS I TRY...

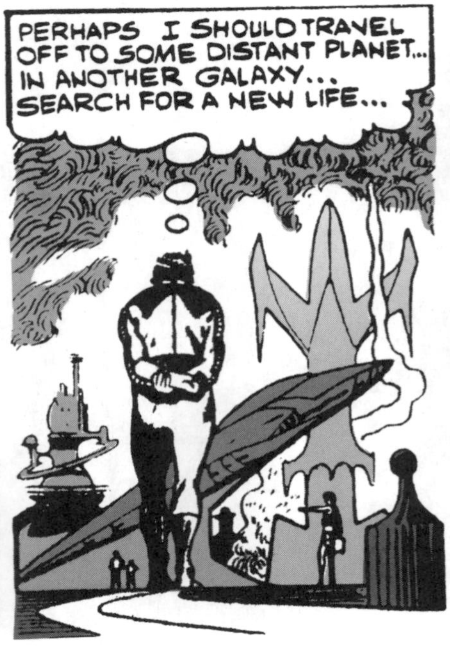
PERHAPS I SHOULD TRAVEL OFF TO SOME DISTANT PLANET... IN ANOTHER GALAXY... SEARCH FOR A NEW LIFE...

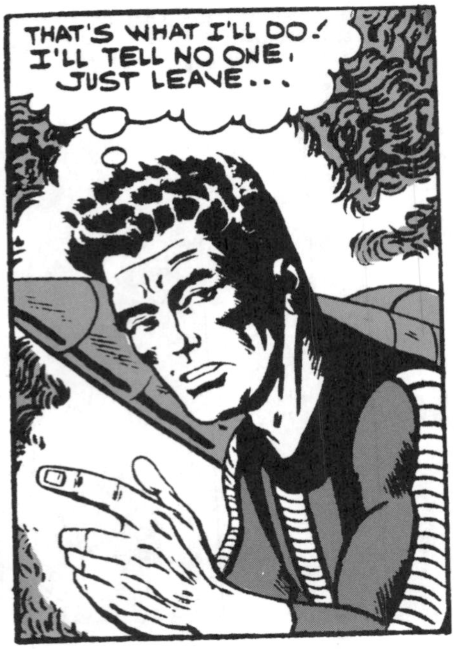
THAT'S WHAT I'LL DO! I'LL TELL NO ONE. JUST LEAVE...

THE COSMIC-RAY POWERED CRAFT, A BIRTHDAY PRESENT FROM HIS FATHER, LIFTED BRUCE FROM THE EARTH AT AN AMAZING SPEED UP, UP INTO THE UNCHARTED REGIONS STILL UNEXPLORED IN THIS SPACE AGE OF THE 26th CENTURY...

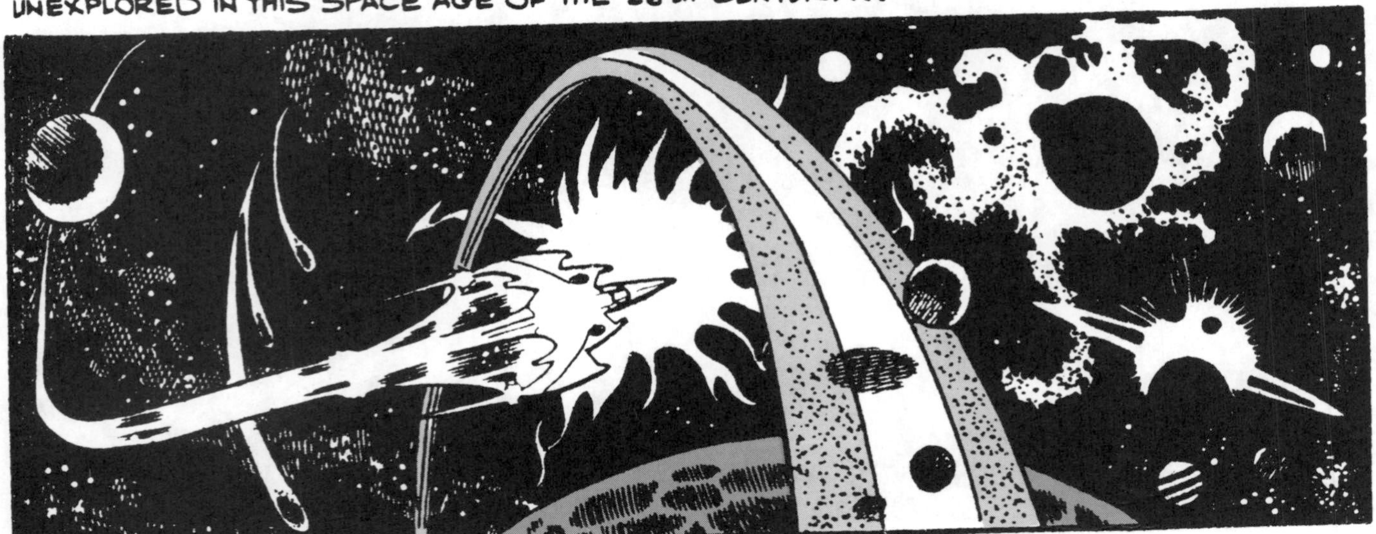

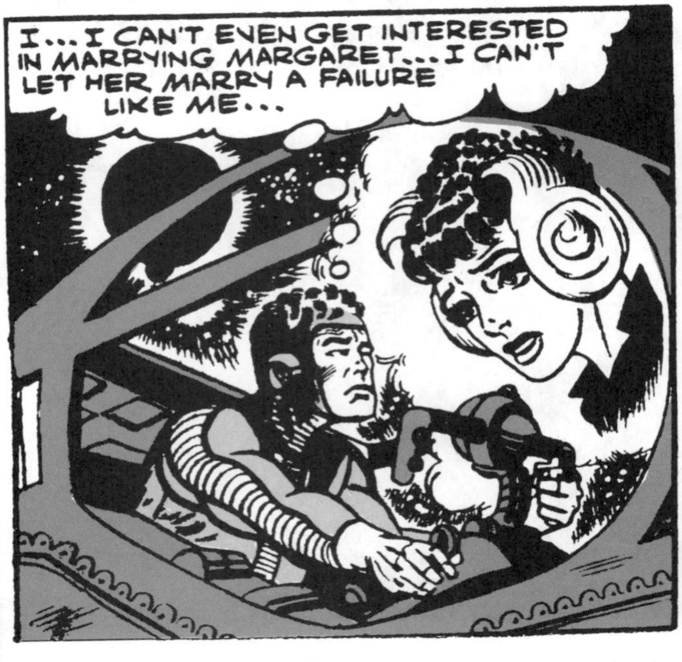
I... I CAN'T EVEN GET INTERESTED IN MARRYING MARGARET... I CAN'T LET HER MARRY A FAILURE LIKE ME...

WEARY FROM HIS TROUBLES, BRUCE SET THE AUTOMATIC CONTROLS, AND FELL ASLEEP...

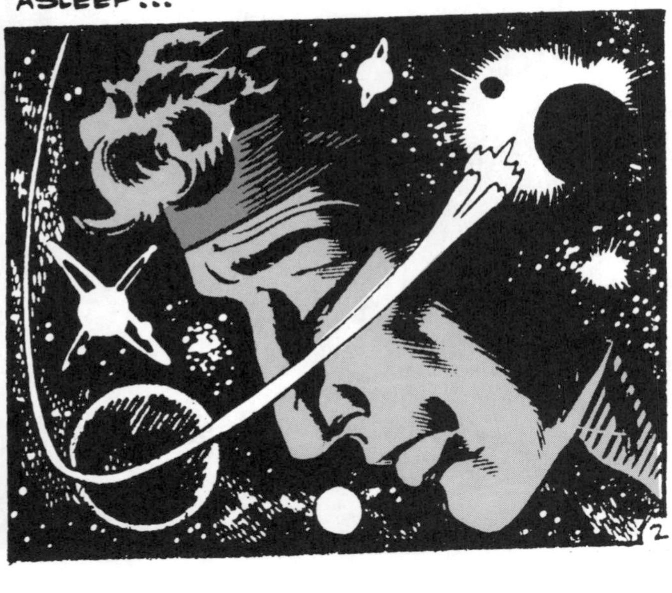
2

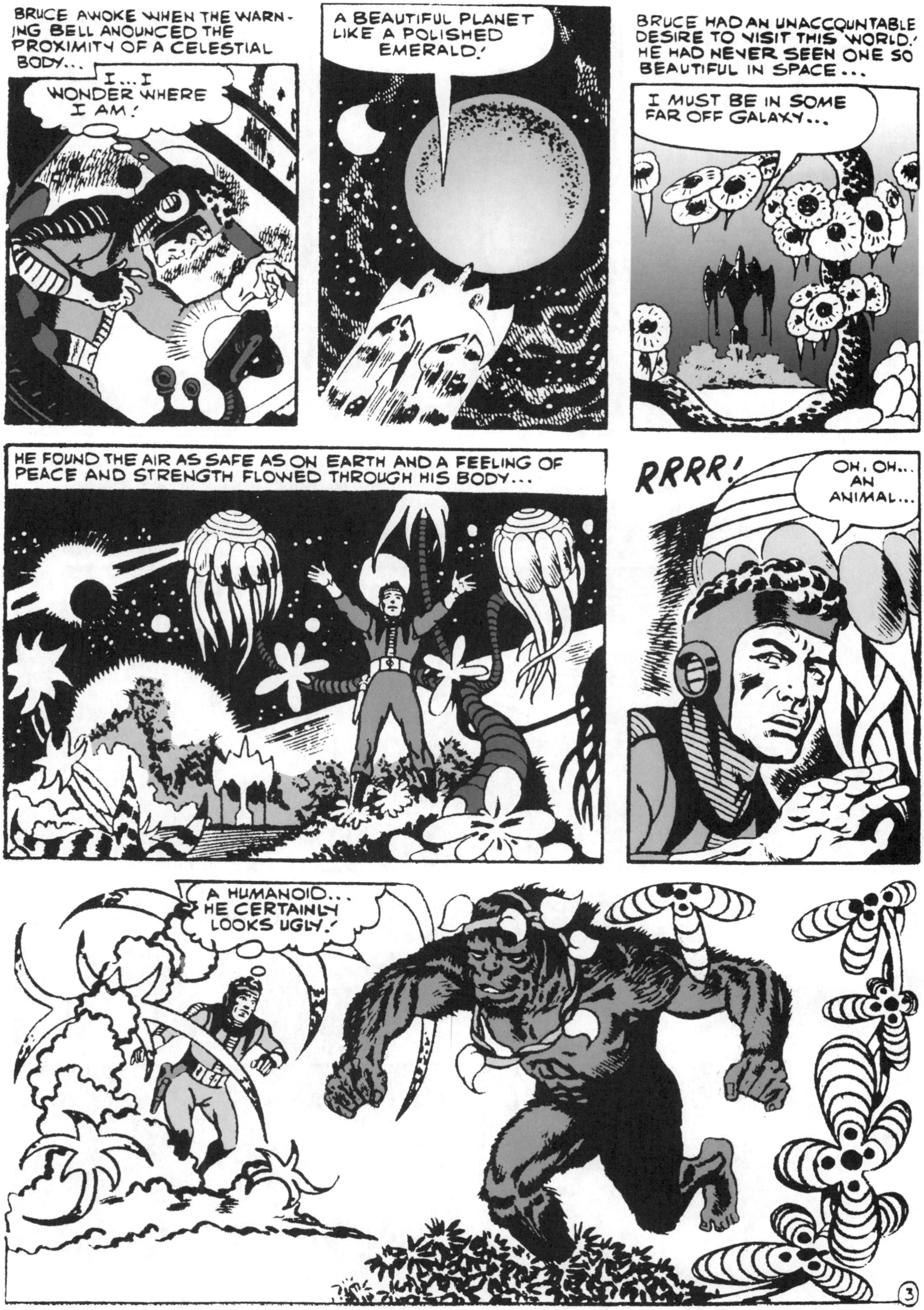
BRUCE AWOKE WHEN THE WARNING BELL ANOUNCED THE PROXIMITY OF A CELESTIAL BODY...
I... I WONDER WHERE I AM!
A BEAUTIFUL PLANET LIKE A POLISHED EMERALD!
BRUCE HAD AN UNACCOUNTABLE DESIRE TO VISIT THIS WORLD! HE HAD NEVER SEEN ONE SO BEAUTIFUL IN SPACE...
I MUST BE IN SOME FAR OFF GALAXY...
HE FOUND THE AIR AS SAFE AS ON EARTH AND A FEELING OF PEACE AND STRENGTH FLOWED THROUGH HIS BODY...
RRRR!
OH, OH... AN ANIMAL...
A HUMANOID... HE CERTAINLY LOOKS UGLY!
3

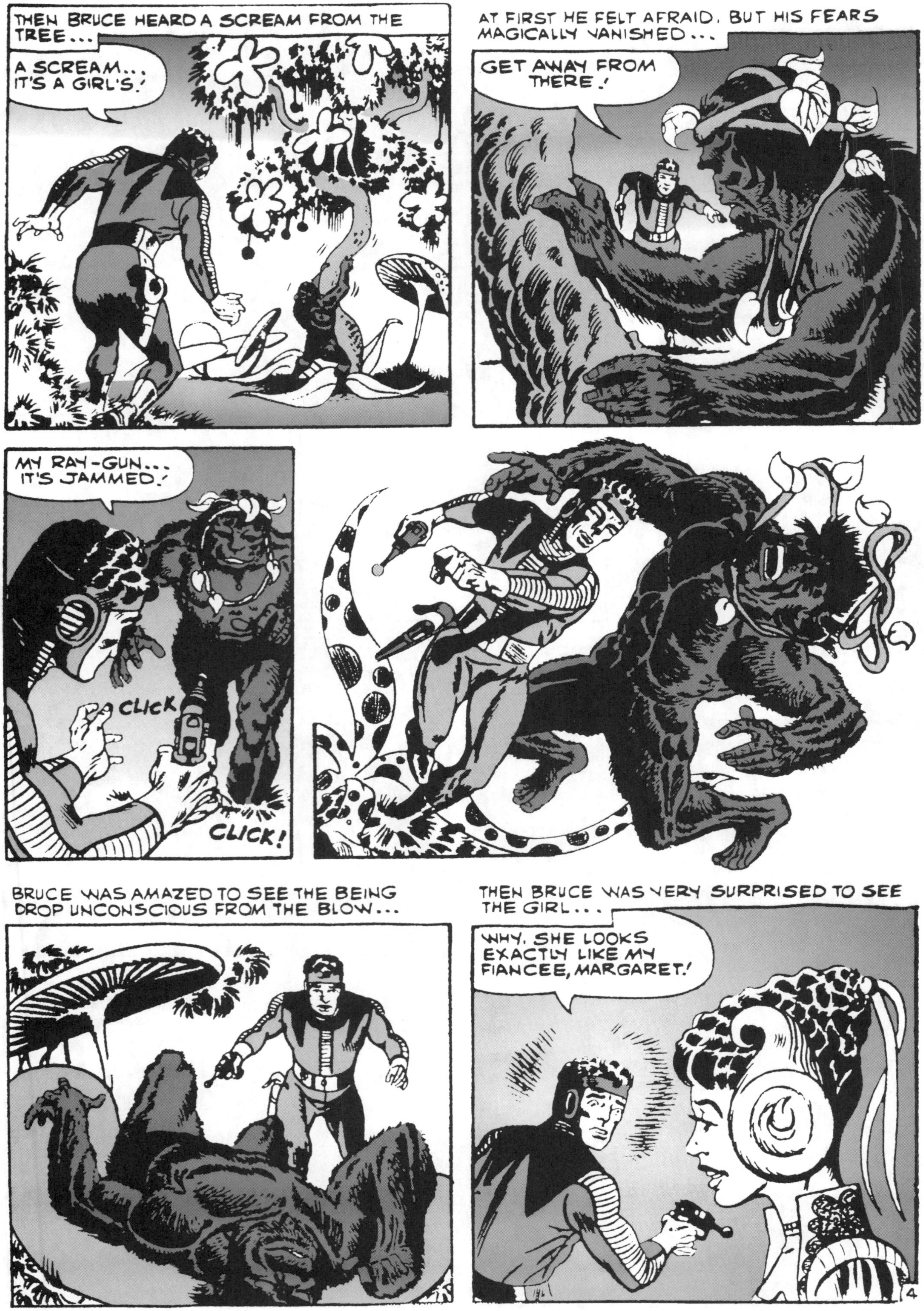
THEN BRUCE HEARD A SCREAM FROM THE TREE...
A SCREAM... IT'S A GIRL'S!
AT FIRST HE FELT AFRAID, BUT HIS FEARS MAGICALLY VANISHED...
GET AWAY FROM THERE!
MY RAY-GUN... IT'S JAMMED!
CLICK
CLICK!
BRUCE WAS AMAZED TO SEE THE BEING DROP UNCONSCIOUS FROM THE BLOW...
THEN BRUCE WAS VERY SURPRISED TO SEE THE GIRL...
WHY, SHE LOOKS EXACTLY LIKE MY FIANCEE, MARGARET!
4

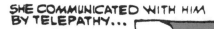

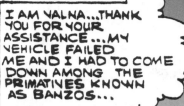
SHE COMMUNICATED WITH HIM BY TELEPATHY...

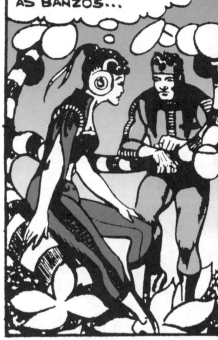
I AM VALNA...THANK YOU FOR YOUR ASSISTANCE...MY VEHICLE FAILED ME AND I HAD TO COME DOWN AMONG THE PRIMATIVES KNOWN AS BANZOS...

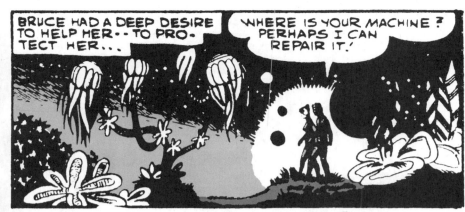
BRUCE HAD A DEEP DESIRE TO HELP HER--TO PROTECT HER...

WHERE IS YOUR MACHINE? PERHAPS I CAN REPAIR IT!

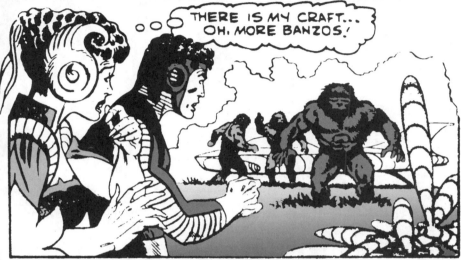
THERE IS MY CRAFT... OH, MORE BANZOS!

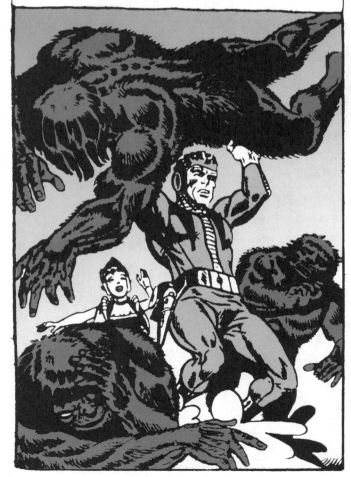
AGAIN BRUCE FOUND HIMSELF STRONGER THAN THESE HOSTILE BEASTS...

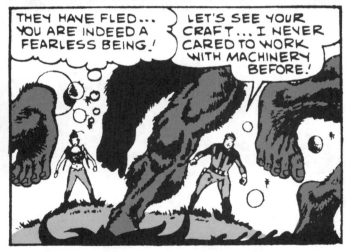
THEY HAVE FLED... YOU ARE INDEED A FEARLESS BEING!

LET'S SEE YOUR CRAFT... I NEVER CARED TO WORK WITH MACHINERY BEFORE!

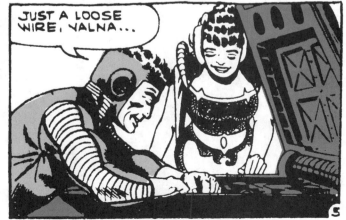
BUT NOW BRUCE FEARED NO OBSTACLE! HE WANTED TO DO THINGS FOR OTHERS...

JUST A LOOSE WIRE, VALNA...

5

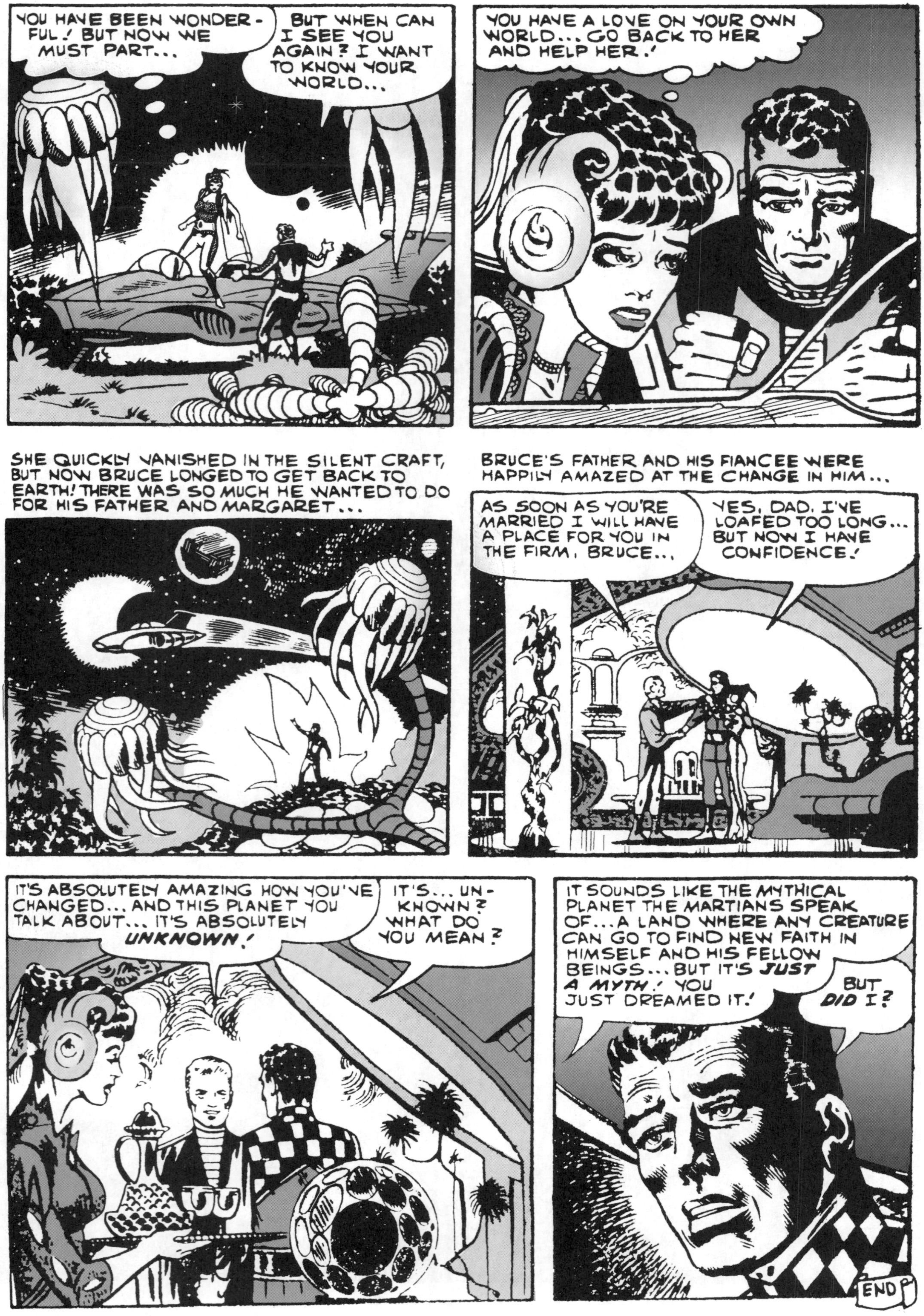
YOU HAVE BEEN WONDER-FUL! BUT NOW WE MUST PART...
BUT WHEN CAN I SEE YOU AGAIN? I WANT TO KNOW YOUR WORLD...
YOU HAVE A LOVE ON YOUR OWN WORLD... GO BACK TO HER AND HELP HER!
SHE QUICKLY VANISHED IN THE SILENT CRAFT, BUT NOW BRUCE LONGED TO GET BACK TO EARTH! THERE WAS SO MUCH HE WANTED TO DO FOR HIS FATHER AND MARGARET...
BRUCE'S FATHER AND HIS FIANCEE WERE HAPPILY AMAZED AT THE CHANGE IN HIM...
AS SOON AS YOU'RE MARRIED I WILL HAVE A PLACE FOR YOU IN THE FIRM, BRUCE...
YES, DAD. I'VE LOAFED TOO LONG... BUT NOW I HAVE CONFIDENCE!
IT'S ABSOLUTELY AMAZING HOW YOU'VE CHANGED... AND THIS PLANET YOU TALK ABOUT... IT'S ABSOLUTELY ***UNKNOWN!***
IT'S... UN-KNOWN? WHAT DO YOU MEAN?
IT SOUNDS LIKE THE MYTHICAL PLANET THE MARTIANS SPEAK OF... A LAND WHERE ANY CREATURE CAN GO TO FIND NEW FAITH IN HIMSELF AND HIS FELLOW BEINGS... BUT IT'S ***JUST A MYTH!*** YOU JUST DREAMED IT!
BUT ***DID*** I?
END

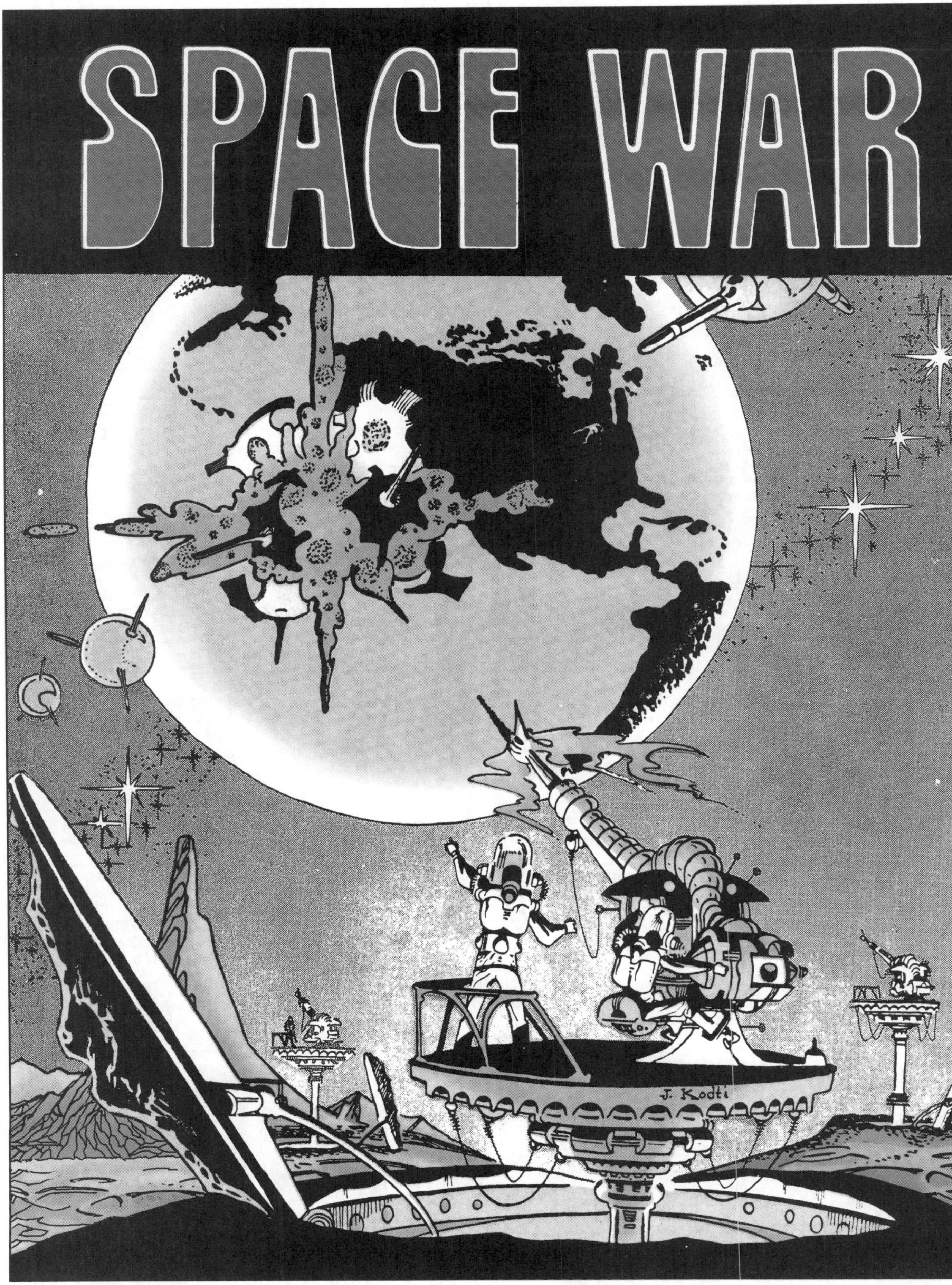
SPACE WAR
J. Kodti

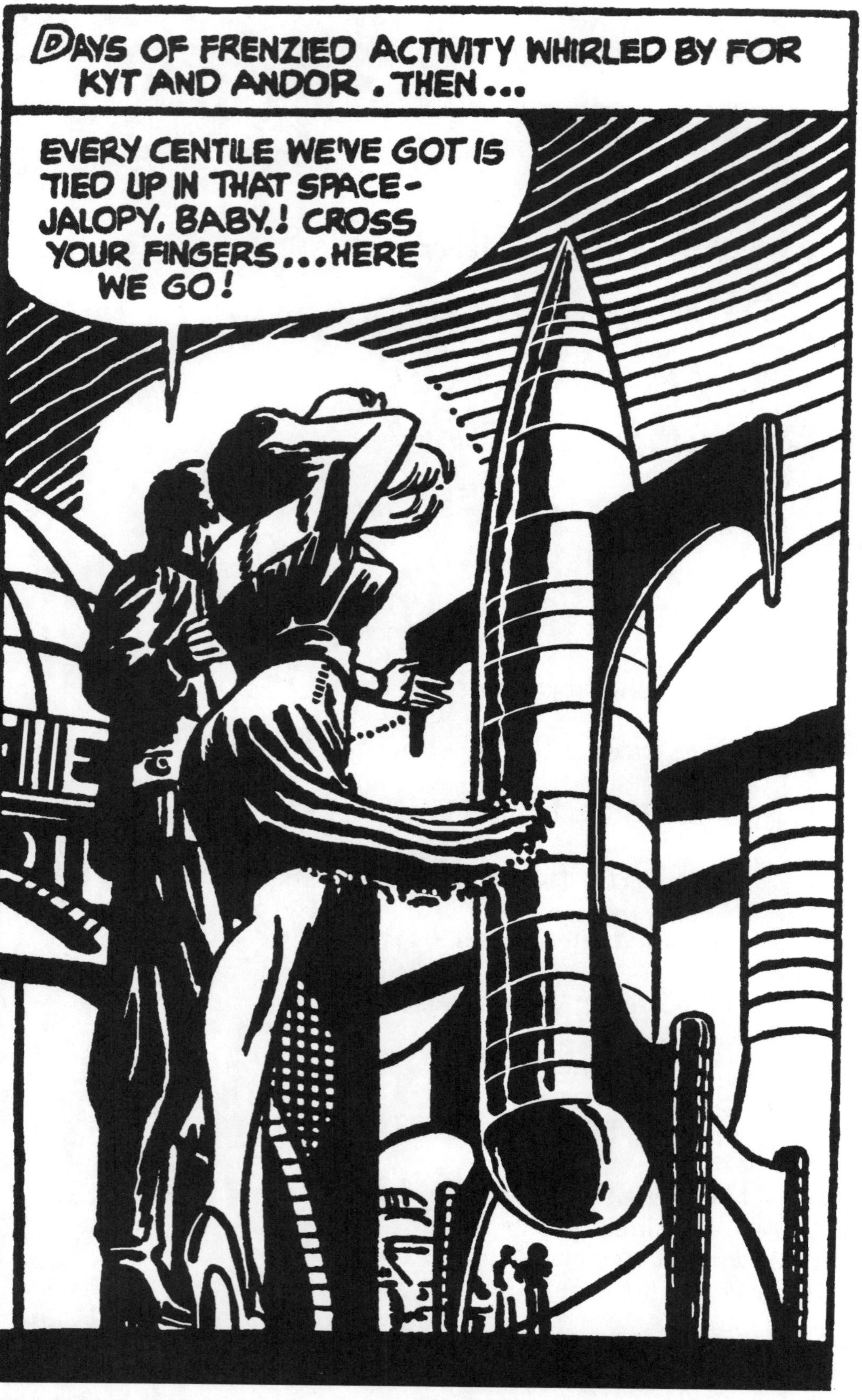
DAYS OF FRENZIED ACTIVITY WHIRLED BY FOR KYT AND ANDOR . THEN...
EVERY CENTILE WE'VE GOT IS TIED UP IN THAT SPACE-JALOPY, BABY.! CROSS YOUR FINGERS...HERE WE GO!